From Dad

To Tiff, With
Love

it's a most Brook

martin
quinn

Anthony Lee

wm

WILLIAM MORROW

An Imprint of HarperCollins*Publishers*

This book is a work of fiction. The characters, incidents, and dialogue
are drawn from the author's imagination and are not to be
construed as real. Any resemblance to actual events or persons, living or dead,
is entirely coincidental.

HarperCollins books may be purchased for educational, business, or sales promotional
use. For information please write: Special Markets Department, HarperCollins Publishers Inc.,
10 East 53rd Street, New York, NY 10022.

FIRST EDITION

Printed on acid-free paper

Library of Congress Cataloging-in-Publication Data
Lee, Anthony, 1970–
Martin Quinn / Anthony Lee.— 1st ed.
p. cm.
ISBN 0-06-009042-1
1. Gangsters—Fiction. 2. Young men—Fiction.
3. New York (N.Y.)—Fiction. I. Title.
PS3612.E3425 M37 2003
813'.6—dc21   2002031537

03   04   05   06   07   WB/QW   10   9   8   7   6   5   4   3   2   1

Helia's

acknowledgments

The author thanks John Vernon,
the Thayer Fellowship in the Arts,
and Nat Sobel.

one

Felix

He thought, again, You're not going to kill him. It was an awakening, the idea. It was like emerging from the woods into a dusk-lit clearing in your head. It was peace coming down.

Felix caught him smiling, did a double take. "What are you grinning at? You're like 'Kool-Aid' Quinn over there with that grin."

Martin smiled harder, kept his eyes in the grass. Not going to kill him anymore and him never even knowing the end had been coming. Felix Pasko's enchanted life continues.

They crossed toward the shed.

He was innocent, Felix. Loyal. Brutal and naive. He hadn't changed at all, in thirteen years.

Fee switching hands now with the rifle, patting his pockets for keys. Martin Quinn slowed, hung back, beside him. Don't ever underestimate him again, told himself.

Fee said, "What about dinner?"

"What's in the house?"

"I meant eat on the road—" found the keys—"or wait till the city. There's nothing inside."

"In town, then."

"You have an appetite."

"I could eat."

"Yeah, me, too"—walking slower, Fee. Flipping the keys for the one to the padlock. Stopped, then. Turned. Stared him in the face. Martin stopped, stared him back. Thought their shoes were making a racket, like the grass got louder as the night came. Fee said, "You know what I'm thinking, right?"—his face like something hurt him. Pained somewhere, but just a bit. The whitewashed shed glowing softly behind him, the sky, beyond that, going purple with the sun gone. Martin took it all in, a moment. Looked back at him. Saw his reflection in Fee's lenses. "Do you know what I'm thinking, Q, or no?"

"We won't hang out enough anymore, after the deal is done. You been saying it for weeks."

Fee turned his face away. Went quiet. Intensifying. Like an angry cartoon.

"Speak, Felix. Your glasses'll steam up."

"My fucking worry is that the deal's going to ramify. Some bizarre circumstance that we didn't foresee, then our lives are different from anything we ever expected. Unforeseen circumstances, I'm talking about. Unimagined."

"Like us not hanging out."

He looked down fast, Fee—keeping composed. Worked through the keys. "It's not . . ."—getting beside himself. "I'm not really kidding here, you fucker."

"I am?"

But, when Fee looked at him, he looked away.

Because the idea suddenly got to him, too.

He saw the strangeness in that—things so moment-to-moment sometimes they were nearly impossible to figure. A few minutes ago, he'd been picking the instant to sneak a pistol behind Fee's ear, for Christ's sake; now that madness was past. Life was back, and normal. Business as fucking usual.

"What assholes we are," he said. Half to himself, half to the dusk.

"What'd you say?"

He didn't turn. "I said, 'No, I'm not kidding.' But you do know what *I'm* thinking."

"Yeah, and I don't give a shit. He's a dangerous fucking man, my father; I can sweat him all I want. You should finally learn to start."

"Big gangster you are. Made your bones but still sweating your old man . . ." waited.

But got no response. Turned.

And saw that Fee just wasn't up to it.

The old man too close in his thoughts, scaring the fight out of him. Even with all he'd been up to lately, Felix. All he'd done. "Fee, he isn't going to care."

"He might."

"Man, what the fuck did we come up here for, Felix?" *I* did to kill you, he thought. So long ago. Minutes like weeks, now, falling away. "We're supposed to be relaxing. It's your country house. We're in the fucking Catskills, for Christ's sake. We take a break for a day. *Your* fucking idea. How much more shit you going to lay on me? I'm all tensed up again."

"Do I care?"

" 'Do I care?' Do I duh-duh-duh? Even if he cuts you off without a fucking kopeck, man, you won't need a thing from your father when the deal is over. Ever. You can't get your head around that? You truck with him on your own terms from then on. You're equals."

Fee glassy-eyed.

But paying attention.

Would come around, eventually—would cool out.

So ease off him, Martin thought. Go lightly here. We been through enough shit already today. "You just got to get past this, Fee—"

Fee saying "It's not that simple" though—waving it off. "Didn't you ever betray your father? Not once while he was alive?"

"Betray him how? I was *nine* when he died."

"I'm saying you feel it on some primitive, elementary level. Way back in the mind. It makes your nuts seize up and hide. Does *that* make sense to you?"

"Yeah, but it's for shit—it's irrelevant. You're not betraying the man, technically. And second—"

"Technically. What the fuck does—"

"It means you took a little initiative. Decided he didn't need to know every fucking step you take as you fast approach your fucking *thir*ties, boy-ass. That's first off. Second, if you want to fucking worry about something, take stock of your situation here. You're in narcotics now. You worry about your business associates—your fucking KAs." He held up his thumb, his index, his second finger—enumerating—"Worry about Monya, worry about Bunny, worry about Terry fucking Hughes, man. Keep your eye on *those* motherfuckers. Every second you can. Do it." Aimed the finger gun at him and fired—a little bursting "pop" noise with his lips. "Worry about them." Fee saying—

"You motherfucker, man, you're serious here? You said things were cool before we came up. I asked you specifically—"

"And I told you what was what. And that things were moving how they should. That means, with heroin, watch them close. But with this other shit? Forget your father for five fucking minutes. Realize how good things are going to be. Monya and Bunny and Terror are covered. We covered them. *I* did, anyway. I'm not really sure *what* you've been up to lately—" paused. To see if his point was made. Fee's eyes off in the woods, though. Looking for the comfort in what he'd heard. "Of course, Penny's still pissed at you. But she's your wife; it's expected."

Fee's eyes slid back. And he smiled. Reluctantly—let his lips pull tight. Turned away, breathed deep. "Yeah, if the old man doesn't kill me, the old ball and chain will."

Martin shrugged, palms up—*What can you do?* Figured to himself she'd probably called ten times while they were out in the woods. Probably a bit frantic by now. Or plain crazed.

"I'll bet she called ten times," Fee said.

Martin smiled.

"Found our retreat up here too inopportune to be honored at *all,*" Fee said, and looked at him. Looked him over. Head to toe. Then back into his face. Openly regarding.

Martin quit smiling, regarded him back. Something wordless between them here, he understood. Fee still holding the keys and the Remington, he with his hands in the pockets of his jacket. One in a ball, the other on the Glock.

Still needed a moment to himself so he could clear it. When Fee had stepped into the shed, he'd been figuring.

"It's not perfect, the marriage" Fee saying, "but, shit, whose is, you know?" Shook his head. Looked off, again. At the tree line, the twilight.

Martin nodded. Didn't want to get into this again—Fee all grave about it now. Plus, *you're* the one brought it up, he thought. What did you think was going to happen? "Fee, you hear about that new pirate movie?"—change the mood here. Fee narrowed his eyes, looked at him. "It's rated *arrrr.*"

Fee smiled. Closed his eyes, and stopped. "What, you've been saving that one?"—looked at him. "You're fucking retarded, Q."

"Retarded, but you smiled."

"I smiled. So what? That what you think we are—pirates? We're not stealing from anybody—"

"Man, what are you, fucking crazy, Felix? It's official now. Your mind is so . . . locked, I can't even crack a joke—"

"A wide-open market, heroin. You said it yourself, a thousand times—"

"You're fucking nuts"—raised his free hand—in submission—walked away. Turned, went back. "You're never going to get it, Fee. That's it. You'll never appreciate what you have in this world. The enchanted life you live. You'll never appreciate it."

"Yeah, you mentioned"—walking to the shed. Popped the lock, opened the door. "Tells me a joke"—went inside.

Martin listened. Heard him setting the thirty-aught back on its rack. Then shifting other things, banging around. Wouldn't be out for a while, till he cooled.

He took out the Glock, and listened, another few seconds. Put it away, again—wasn't satisfied here. "Fee, be cool. Don't be mad, for Christ's sake. Felix. Hey."

"Yeah. No. I'm not mad."

Speaking in normal tones, both of them—apology offered and accepted. And Fee stopping the banging. Turning on a faucet, it sounded like. Filling something. Yelled over the water—"He's going near fully legitimate, my father. Finally. We're going back to basics. Starting at street level. It throws me off; that's all. The imbalance."

"He'll be *proud*"—loudly, he said it. Pictured Fee in there, at the sink, probably shaking his head, still uncertain. Whatever he was filling probably overflowing now but Fee only seeing the old man furious.

The faucet stopping. Fee came out. Carrying a watering can. Hot pink plastic. Walked past.

"You hear me, Felix Pasko?"

"Perfectly, as always"—crossing the yard.

Martin watched him. Said, "He'd be *damned* proud to see you doing yard work," and Fee ignored him. Circled the small, sorry-looking rose patch out in the clearing, picked a place to stop. Stared down at it, stupidly.

"I told my mother I'd check on them for her. There's like nothing here, though." He tipped the can up, tried it out. A little here, there. Engrossed immediately. Such a little kid, still. Martin smiled, turned his back and took out the Glock, worked fast but nonchalant. Loosened the mag, a fraction. Unchambered the round against his stomach to muffle the sound and dropped it in the other pocket to put back later, pressed the clip in again. Eyed sideways down into the barrel and closed the chamber and thought, Made it safe, Drill Sergeant, and shook his head at the persistence of memory. Checked the safety again. Looked at the gun—so conformed to his hand. He sighted at a point down in the grass before his feet and let his eyes blur. Peace coming down, he thought. Men of grace don't sneak up close and shoot you; they tell you truth right to your face and let you figure for yourself if blood's your recourse.

And, if you loved your best friend's wife and she loved you, you told the man.

He put it away. Zipped the jacket up, an inch, then down again, absently. Remembered he'd had a hint of something like this before, in the woods, when he'd known he wouldn't shoot him. A feeling that something still had to change. Had already begun to, even.

So just tell the man, he thought. He'll talk through anything to the end.

He put his hands back in his pockets. Didn't know where else to put them now. He took a breath and pressed his eyes shut tight and opened them full. Thought, You were going to kill him over Penelope? Over a woman? and turned and looked at him. Fee moving dainty around the rose patch—still so young, really. And too muscular. Out of his league against a harmless mound of nature. Been nothing but straight with you since you were nervous little high school freshmen. Thirteen years. Be straight—return the favor.

And then a part of his mind said, Yes. Penelope. So keep your gun in your hand. She's well worth killing for.

"Fee."

"I'm here"—still pondering the bushes—the spiny growths. Dribbled water around.

"Fee"—all he could get out yet.

"What?"—looking up. "What's on your mind?"

"I do. What you said before. Before we went in the woods."

Fee shrugged. "You what? What were we talking about, food?"

"I lied. I still love her."

Fee straightened.

Almost past his full height, somehow.

Like his sensibilities were getting shocked—slowly, steadily.

But he's refined, even now.

"She's still my wife."

"I know."

"You slept with her?"

Dozens of times—shit yeah.

His instinct was to lighten things up.

But loving her once was all that would matter, he knew. Knowing her that way. The one true trespass. The same way that Fee's ever screwing her in the first place was the thing that had brought all this on.

Was the only real reason you came back in their lives, he realized suddenly. To break them up—"Does it matter?"

"That means yes. I should fucking kill you."

"With a watering can? I was going to kill you in the woods before, but I didn't. I don't want either of us—"

"That's fucked-up, man"—took a step forward. "What do you mean you were going to kill me?"—took another—through the rose patch—

oblivious, wide-eyed. Pointed up, back into his face. "Do you know what this is, this look? Affronted . . . fucking . . . disbelief. What do you mean you were going to kill me?"

"The gun's still in my pocket, bro—you saw it before. It's still in my hand. Just stay there"—didn't close his fingers on it, though. Kept it rested, beneath his palm. "You're scaring me, Fee. No shit. You're going to force something here. This isn't what I expected."

Fee paused. Was quiet, a second. Then—"What you expected? You're . . . fucking . . . with *Pen*ny, man. Now you say you'd fucking kill me? What—"

"I've loved her longer. I loved her *first,* man. I figured I'd say my piece and let you deal with it. I didn't think you love her like I do." He pointed at the ground—in earnest—Down-By-Law—"I *still* don't. I'll tell you right here. I don't think you would have stopped coming on, just now, otherwise."

"Fuck you."

"It's true, man. *And* it's my turn. From here out. I've loved her longer." He thought, Sink in. "The three of us are starting over—this time she marries me. I joined the army and I was working, going to school, and I got that fucking invitation to your fucking wedding and I came back thinking I hated you. But I let her go in the first place. I knew that. And, I'll tell you right now I never hated you—we both know that. But don't make me say some queer shit here, man." Sink in. "I love her. You're closer to me than my own brother is, but it's my turn. I'm not losing her again." Or you.

"Your turn."

"From now on. I get her till death do us part. I deserve that. You can fucking come over, weekends, for dinner. Or every night, for all I care, but . . . Say something."

Considering, Fee.

Much to think about.

"Take your hands out of your pockets" saying.

Martin judged it. At least twenty feet between them. If Fee wanted to rush him, there'd be a good two seconds to dig in and then *smash* his ass. He took them out. Raised them half-high. Moody-felon-like.

"How can you say you'd kill me?"

"Why'd you fucking marry her?"

"How could you say it?"

"Am I under arrest, or what?"

Fee raised the watering can, eye-level. Aimed it. Martin raised his hands higher. Fee looked at the house. Squinted to see better, like he'd seen something move. Martin turned, saw their reflections in the dark windows, saw Terry. Knew him, but didn't get what he was doing there, out of place and coming fast from the side of the house aiming a gun saying "On your knees. Both of you"—and all at once thought, My god, he's here to shoot us; Bunny sent him here to shoot us—execute us—and stuffed his hand in for the Glock before the thought was even complete, Terry saying something louder—yelling—"Keep your hands . . . No"—and Martin had the Glock out, squeezed the trigger before aiming, even, but it was frozen. The gun was safe. Terry was sighting. Martin heard the shot, saw the flash, felt his head spin. Saw his blood spray onto the shed and felt he was falling.

He blacked out. He came around. He saw Terry Hughes walking over, aiming sideways down the yard at Fee, eyeing back and forth between them. Martin peered. Saw the Glock out of reach—he'd fucking *dropped* it—saw Terry bend and pick it up. Knew it wouldn't take him long to find the safety—he'd handled the piece before, Terry. Terry turning now and squaring off with Felix across the yard, racked the slide. Martin closed his eyes, quit breathing—it hurt too much to. Terry said, "Don't fucking move, dickhead," his voice receding, and Martin looked, saw him crossing the yard toward Felix, aiming—Felix poised to bolt. Or petrified, maybe. His face like Shit, I hardly know you, man. The watering can at his feet, glugging into the grass. Terry said, "Don't. Don't make me chase—" but Fee was gone—headed toward the woods. Terry paused and fired. Felix spinning, three-sixty—a doofy ballet—kept going. But slower. An injured run. Still determined, though. Tee fired again, and Fee lurched and stumbled, sprawled, Terry keeping after him. Fee got to his knees. But that was all. Slowing up. Dropped down to his hands and crawled. Toward the woods. Then stopped. Flopped to his side and moaned—hard. Turned onto his back. Terry got up close and stood over him. Said something low, harsh. Said something. Fired.

Martin looked away. He looked at his blood on the shed. He looked at the sky. He closed his eyes. Felt the slosh of the pool of blood beneath his head and heard his heartbeat and the whip of the grass on Terry's shoes as he crossed the yard coming back. Fear flooded his chest, scalding things inside him, the blood in his head blaring up in silence. You'll choke on fear, he thought. Terry over him—his shape absorbing sound—then leaning closer, squatting, knees cracking. Laid something in Martin's hand and closed his fingers on the thing—a gun, Martin could feel. Terry stood. Was walking away.

Martin opened his eyes. Saw it was the Glock and saw Terry's back— wide, solid. The death-still fear disappeared. He clenched soundly, aimed supine, fired, and moved to stand, Terry staggering, turning around, facing him. Martin fired again and hit him high, throwing him back and down. Stood up full and walked the dozen-odd feet to him, stopped, and stood over him. Aimed the gun down at his face. And waited. Too scared of him, even now, beyond the gun barrel and the killing pose, to know what to do.

Terry sneered. Blood was in his teeth. "You're Billy the fucking Kid now, Quinn? You *draw* on me? *Jesus*"—turned his head, looked around at things weird—his eyes big, then narrow. "You fucking . . ." then moaned— bad pain. Martin realized he hadn't ever thought Terry might *feel* pain. "You fucking . . . *Jesus* . . ." Tee saying, talking softer now. To himself, almost. Or to the pain. *But he's talking to you*, Martin knew. *Let him finish. Listen to him. Must be some sin to ignore a guy dying*—Tee saying "You're always in my way. You fuck up everything. Can't just be the pussy you are and stay away"—looked up at him, straight. Groaned again. *Amazing to think he could feel it. Amazing to think it would show*—Saying "Fuck, you pussy, what're you waiting for?—you're fucking *this* up. *Do* it."

Martin squeezed. Held the trigger two rounds, on accident—the first jamming Terror's face away, the second one missing. Chunked the dirt. Sent a small plume of dust up.

He looked back. And around. Across the yard. Fee still moving, he saw. Bandy-legged little jerks. Like to get some purchase in the grass. But a dying movement.

He started toward him. Whipped his own feet through the grass.

Wondered what the sound would mean in Feel's head. Would it soothe him, maybe. Or would it bug him out completely. Bring a whole new fear on him.

Kept approaching. Feel's legs stopping. Looked down at him—at his eyes. Saw a consciousness, but just dumb and scared now—with a bullet in the folds of his brain somewhere, the small hole over his eye burping blood. Glasses cockeyed. Head lolling—back, forth. Primitive, animal resistance.

A car—up into the yard, behind. Been hearing it, a while, he realized—coming the long length of the driveway. He watched Fee die. Car doors opening and voices shouting his name, commanding him to put it down. Cops. From nowhere. No surprise, somehow. He glanced and saw two, in suits and ties, wide-stanced and barking. Mission men.

He laid the Glock by Feel's head, careful of the path of spreading fluid. Fee's eyes flat, finally. His breathing done, fear snuffed.

Your hands up and walk toward them, motherfucker, get on your knees, your face. Hands behind the head and lace the fingers. The pain unreal. His ear was gone, he guessed.

He lay his other cheek in the grass and heard the sound of soil beneath, and above, blood filling the hole where his ear had been. It pooled and ran over his face and down his neck. The cops were coming, cautious, like bad hungry dogs.

He felt himself disappearing. Heard the deep, slow whip of shoes coming on through the grass.

I *n the ambulance he cries. He discovers it thinking of other things, but has no recollection of beginning to. Feels a sadness in him welling, and a pain from that, like his heart has collapsed, and a pain down his arms and over his back that's an ache from fear, he knows, because fear fucking hurts, but it will pass because the fear has passed, but there's no pain where he's been shot with Terry's Sig Sauer—nothing where his ear ought to be but the pressure from the bandage the medics applied—one of them still beside him—and, down the ambulance, on a fold-out stool, one of the feds, the figure elbows-on-knees. Not with compassion, though, with impatience. Ready to work, to get in his face. And his face was vulnerable now. Blown open on the side from Terry's Sig. But, no reason to cry.*

He looked at the paramedic—the teenage boy—beside him— "I got no pain," told him. Realized, then, what he thought it meant—that he was dying.

The cop said, "What? What he say?" An older voice. There'd been two cops. One young, one not.

"He said his pain's gone . . . It's your body doing it, sir. Compensating, like shock."

Making me cry? he thought. Just run with tears? "It's normal?"

"It's shock."

"You didn't give me something?" He wanted to know, suddenly. Had to; it was important. Details were.

"They'll prescribe morphine at General, I'm sure. For a GSW, hell. I can't administer, though."

"Of course not," and nodded at him—just a boy—to say, I understand, and, I forgive you—and looked away, back at the ceiling. Steel diamond plate.

The ambulance screamed and swung wide, came back. Soon the rocking subsided. His tears adjusted to their new tracks, slid over the blood dried to his face and released its metal smell again—like a penny on the tongue, still warm from your hand. Kids always putting money in their mouths, he thought. Then don't anymore, one day— realize for themselves that it's dirty.

Was there a general age they stopped? he wondered. Saw it for themselves? And had he just watched Felix die?

He'd thought through all he could, made all the initial considerations. That it was Bunny, yes—there was no doubt in his mind, and that was fine; Terry was Bunny's right hand, and if Easter Bunny Pasquale wanted to send old Terror to cut a few partners from the deal, that was the choice he'd made. Maybe I should have seen it coming and I didn't, but, whatever the reason, fuck it. Fuck Pasquale Bunny Lamentia; he'd made things easier, was all. The feds could have him. He'd gambled everything and lost, and the feds would much rather have a hood like him to lock up than you. Than Martin Quinn. Kool-Aid Martin.

Which was the number two thing he'd considered. That, provided the feds had Bunny instead, they'd most likely cut *him* a deal, like protective custody. Or, cut him loose entirely. Bunny was the real fucking menace. The kind of drug-dealing, counterfeiting, murdering racketeer, still shy of his twenty-eighth birthday, that the government loved to announce it had pulled from the population.

And, if not—if there were no deals to be made, no real differences to be seen between him and Bunny as defendants?—better to do it in a federal lockup for some pleaded-down version of conspiracy to traffic narcotics than even a weekend in the state prison system.

That was the third thing he'd considered. In all the thinking he'd done. The bargain for minimum security. The hardest consideration to make.

So, nothing to do now anyway but wait to see what the feds would want from him. What punishment for a diffused, first adult offense narcotics beef with no physical evidence but coded phone calls.

His feds. His mission men. With their orders and their dark suits, and their hair too short to mistake them for anything else but what they were. The older one practically neighborhood issue he was so Italian, the young one from somewhere west of the Hudson—anywhere west—just not New York. It rested with them.

So, rest, yourself, he thought. All the initial considerations are made.

Two other things lingered, though, every time he thought he was done with his thinking. Months ago Penny saying you shouldn't sell heroin if your father'd been a junkie, being the first thing. And though he'd dismissed it even then as just superstition, he'd once told *her* something himself that fit even better here. You were responsible for the rippling-out of everything you did, he'd told her. Even the shit you couldn't ever foresee coming. Good and bad.

A tough philosophy, he knew, but straight-up honest.

And, plus, fuck every last bit of it anyway. If Bunny wanted to negotiate by opening fire, the responsibility for anyone dead or missing an ear would fall on him, no? So? Fuck him.

Was one thought that lingered.

Led to the other one.

Maybe Bunny'd reacted to something you did yourself. A fuckup all your own. Two days ago, switching the storage unit locker they'd been stashing the deal money in. A final precaution, kept to himself. In the event he had to heist the whole stake alone and bolt, if things went any other way than in his favor. So, maybe Bunny checked the unit—because he couldn't sleep or maybe went to do a little skimming himself—and found it empty. Called up Terry and that was that. All this mayhem, and the money just a few lockers down.

In case you had to steal it, he thought.

Nice job, you fuck.

But he knew it was just guilt talking. Because he survived. Survivor's syndrome they'd called it in the army. Trying to convince a platoon of kids that it was a condition worse than death, So always be the first one out of the foxhole, boys. Those assholes.

If Bunny *had* just called Terry and that *had* been that, it meant he'd sent Terry following them in the first place. So, fuck his suspicious ass.

And if Bunny found the money *gone,* the last thing he'd do was kill the ones who took it, before he got it back. *That* was the central point. The fact that Terry didn't question them about the cash meant Easter Bunny didn't know the dough was elsewhere—Tee coming out from behind the house to execute them, *"Get on your knees,"* no one holding a gun but him. Wanted his risk-free shot, the pussy. Easter Bunny was no hothead; he was famous for his chill since grammar school. He'd have killed them only if he thought he was certain he knew where the money was. Plain. Simple. Sent Terror to do murder and murder was done. It was how he did business. And fine, the feds could have him.

They just had to ask.

He opened his eyes, looked up, out of focus, across the room at the mirror he was sure was two-way and was sure they were standing just beyond. The kind in every cops-and-robbers movie he'd ever seen and on every door to every manager's booth in every supermarket he'd ever shopped in. The reflection just slightly darker than the reality it showed you back.

Which, here, wasn't much. This room was spare, clean. Returned every sound it heard without discretion. Every shift in your chair, every sniff of your nose. Reverberated your words, a while, and sent them murmuring along the ceiling till they knocked into the mirrorglass mumbled-up and self-conscious-sounding. It amplified solitude, the mirror. Like being aware of yourself in a crowd.

He looked away—his image finally coming into focus. He wasn't ready for that shit again. New man with a new future, and bandaged up. Swaddled man. Not man. Fully conscious now, for hours. More than a day, they'd had him. First the hospital, then here, so they could get down to taking care of business.

What the fuck are they waiting for?

"Martin?"—Frito's voice. Warm-sounding through the gauze. Through the thin bit across his good ear that anchored the wad they'd piled on the missing one. "Martin? You still there?"—warm-sounding, and far. Through the long hundred miles of phone line back to Manhattan. Saying Martin. "Martin"—again.

"I'm here, little brother."

"The silences are killing me. They're not easy on this end."

He apologized. Said he guessed he was still pretty out of it.

Though his head was clearer than in the ambulance, definitely.

Plus, he was numb from the chest up now. Morphine not a bad ride, as far as that went. Though it was wearing off again, he was pretty sure—the metal taste coming back. Like a spoon left in a teacup—sugar and steel-plating. "I'm just gone, Frito. I'm sorry." He leaned his head on the wall beside him, gently. Closed his eyes again.

Frito said, "I mean, take your time. I need to process everything, too. And it's your dime, right?"—laughed, a little. "I can't believe Felix is gone, though. Out of the world, and all, you know? But, you said there was a *lot* to tell me; I'm assuming there's more."

It was true; there *was* a lot. He nodded. Realized Frito couldn't see it. Said, "Yeah, there is," and nodded again. Liked the feeling—the rubbing—just that little bit, along the wall. Soft pressure on the skull.

"Martin."

"Yes."

"They're giving you something strong, hunh?—for the pain?"

Martin smiled. Thought, Considerate Frito, being patient. Patronizing, sometimes, these days, but couldn't ever be ugly, or cruel. Simply didn't have it in him.

And it *was* goofy to call him in still such a daze and then not hardly talk.

But it was reassurance, was all, just to hear him. To know, for a minute, the kid was there. Frito could wait while he enjoyed that privilege, no?

"*Roxinol*, Frito," he said. And left it at that.

Though it was liquid morphine, full story be told. And was the hair of the God-damned dog, he'd decided. If your heroin deal partner decided to shoot you, and at the hospital they gave you morphine for the pain, you got the hair of the God-damned dog that came back to bite you in the ass, was what you got. Morphine sulfate for the many woes of diacetylmorphine. Sister for Scag. Morpheus for Horse. Dope.

And it fucking worked. There was no joke there. Made even the reason to need it in the first place feel not so bad—So I'm disfigured, you say. Is that so? You'd think it would hurt more.

"Martin, come on, now—please."

The metal taste coming back. Definitely. Head clearer and clearer. Talk to Frito, though. Let him in. "Did I tell you it was a federal pinch? I did, right?"

"Yes."

"Well, that's the upside."

"You can't go to jail for it, you mean?"

"I can."

"How's that an upside?—you can go to jail."

"There are worse things in life."

"Like what? It's prison, for God's sake."

"No shit, kid," he said, and the pain pulsing up—like a knot in the flesh migrating fast up his head. Then it burst in his eyes. Left them aching. "No shit."

"I'm sorry."

Waited. For it to pass—"Don't apologize. I didn't shelter you all those years to have you apologize for it"—kept his lids low. Then it was past. He breathed in. With purpose. Thought of the act of it—lungs filling up somewhere inside him. "And I'm sorry I called you 'kid.' I don't even think that. My mouth just . . . I mean, you're married, for Christ's sake."

"I was *acting* like a kid—it's fine."

"That's all right, though. I'm just saying your priorities change. They readjust with shit like this. Like the schedule boards at Grand Central, you know? They flip. Flipflipflip, then there's your new plans for you. Your new fate."

Frito said, "Okay."

Lungs filled up with carbon dioxide, and turned it into oxygen somehow.

In school no one had ever been able to explain that to him. How flesh transformed chemicals.

Or the moment of conception, either. Sperm hits egg. A being begins. It didn't seem possible that could happen with no flash of light, no sanctified glow. "And don't just agree, Frito; you can stand your ground. I can tell you're more pissed at me than worried, but, it's about time you looked out for yourself. It means you're thinking like the rest of the family, so maybe it runs in the blood, then. I was afraid you'd be a saint all your life."

"You make it tough."

He smiled. Knew the kid meant him to. "And you're right anyway—it's prison, for Christ's sake. It's not like I'd go back in willingly."

Frito said, "Jesus Christ"—but soft.

"You forgot. I know. There are stretches where *I* even do."

"I'm not sure I even actually re*mem*ber it; I think I only remember being *told* you were in jail. The rest I imagined."

"I was inside a week. Mom didn't tell you till you were older. But it was the *state* system—that's where I'm coming from on this. If this has to end with me doing a hitch, better I'm in federal custody doing time-served, a while. Then, if they lock me up?—for the remainder of the jolt?—shit, even general population in the pen is better than any kind of state time. Fucking *Attica*? *Sing* Sing? The feds know you as an individual. In the Greater New York prison system, you end up . . . fucking . . . lost in the fucking *sea* of convicts—" He thought, Open *sew*er of them, and reached back, above him, felt for the coin slot in the box and pressed a dime in from his handful. Heard it fall through the phone. Felt it. Every plunk and rattle. He kept his eyes closed.

"You're on a public phone?" Frito said.

He ignored him. The kind of question said you didn't know how to respond to what someone was telling you. Federal custody was definitely the key, though, he knew, now. Absolutely. Saying it aloud had made him sure. He would bide his time and appear against Bunny, grab Penny, and be gone. Maybe even score the deal money back from the new storage unit if the feds never figured where to find it. If they even knew about it. The money just sitting there.

Penny has to pay the monthly storage fee, he thought—he'd have to get that message to her. They had a good three weeks on it still, but. "Things are over, now, Frito, that's all. Part of me's even relieved. Worst possible sce-nario where you're concerned, I'll ask you to sell the car Felix bought you, to post bond. Even though I don't think this is going to be a standard jail-and-bail. I have that feeling pretty clear. Only thing for you to do is be aware of Bunny Lamentia. Don't *avoid* him, or anything; just tell him you don't know anything if he tries to talk to you. And he'll believe you; he knows you're a citizen—straight-up, kept in the dark—all of that. Okay? Frito?"

"Uh-hunh."

"Okay." He would just have to wait, now, Bunny, was all. Wouldn't be able to make a move for a good few months. Thinking every sedan on the street was prowling him and every van packed full of surveillance. Wouldn't even be able to make a dash for the wrong, old locker unit for a while, assuming he hadn't done it on that first night. And if he had, he was probably pulling his hair out, right this second, wondering where the fuck the money was. His blow-dried-perfect, *cusin* hair.

Frito breathed—a sigh, like. Then regular again. Martin listened. His oldest memory of the kid. Just a baby. Home from the hospital in the old man's arms, and into the crib. Martin swearing if he could just watch him sleep he wouldn't make a sound. Frito lying there motionless. Pink, and wrinkled. His chest taking momentous little heaves.

"Frito, man, I'm sorry. That this is happening again. My life . . . spilling into yours."

Drew another breath in, Frito—long. And held it. Said nothing. But he was there.

Just nothing else to say.

The morphine was definitely wearing off, though.

He reached up, back, fed a dime.

Feeling an inch off the ground all the time was starting to get sickening.

Frito said, "We've been on that long?"

"No. I guess not." Looked in his palm. Metal silver-gray cluster. "The local sheriff gave me a shitload of change, though, you know? I figure why not go mad?"

Frito quiet.

"I guess you'd have to be here, Free, but I always thought an upstate police station would look like Mayberry, you know? Otis in the drunk tank, cops with their feet up. But it's state of the art. It's bright, clean. Someone's tax dollars at work."

Still quiet.

"I told you I'm going to be okay, Frito."

"I don't think you know that."

"Oh, no? Well, I *do* know—"

"And *maybe* . . . maybe," Frito said, "that's fucked-up for me to say right now, but I'm scared. For you, me, Juliet, Mom."

"I understand." Thought, Can't beg a younger brother's trust; you either earn it or you don't—

"I'm scared for *all* of us, Martin. I really don't like it."

You could dazzle him, impress him. Make the years between you count. Even when he was looking right into you. "Frito, you want to know something bizarre? You asked before, I said they gave me Roxinol for the pain. It's liquid morphine. I'm doped up. Like the old man. What do you think of that?"

"Well, how's it feel to you?"—with no pause.

"To be honest, not half bad." He whispered—"Cook it up with acetic anhydride, you've got the old man's poison. And it ain't half bad."

"I know."

"Wearing off kind of feels like shit, even not being hooked, but—" he stopped. "What do you mean you know?"

"I remember."

"You re*mem*ber?"

What was he *talk*ing about?

"I remember."

Then he got it—remembered, himself. The IV, and Frito whacked-out cold, completely. For days. Far worse than *your* hurts, he thought.

He lowered his voice. From contrition. Said, "Of course you do."—the pain pulsing again—across his mind—but he kept talking through it—"I'm so sorry. I didn't really pay attention to shit like that when you were shot, buddy—the details of your treatment. They told me you'd be all right. That was what I heard."

"It's okay, Martin."

"And I'm *still* sorry. You know that. I'm always going to be, if that makes any sense."

"I'm sure I'll fuck up badly, one day, and be hoping everyone—"

"I doubt it."

"I don't."

"There are certain kinds of things people are ready to forgive a person for. That's the kind of shit *you* do wrong. You don't do the kind of shit people have to move mountains to forgive. I guess I share that with the old man. You got the musical gifts; I got the compulsion to push things to the hilt."

Frito quiet again.

Good. If there's going to be anyone talking, I only want to hear myself.

"Martin, what's going to happen to you?" Frito saying, though.

God knows. Let's just have silence.

"Martin, tell me. What."

"I'm going to be fine. When everything's over. I'm going to fucking miss Felix, but I don't want to talk about that ever, and otherwise . . ." God knows.

"Are you scared?"

"I'm stoned."

"Are you scared?"

Yes, he thought. Jesus, yeah. Maybe the fed from New York—the Italian one—might tell his enforcer, "Break his head" or "Break his ribs" or "Break his hands." Or maybe they'll just lock me up. Tell me, "Thank you for your help with Bunny Lamentia, enjoy your ten years in the jay."

Though the chances they had anything at all besides tapped phone conversations was practically nothing, he knew—he had to remind himself of that. They'd burst in on a situation they'd probably never expected—Terry stepping in, shooting teammates. Plus, the heroin wasn't even in the country, and wouldn't ever be without a final call to Sicily from all major players—Bunny, Fee, *and* him. Chances were, the feds'd be happy for whatever case they could make. He'd just have to play ignorant, let them come to him, ask for his cooperation.

And brutality? The worst he'd gotten so far was the Italian's sarcasm—

par for the background—and the young one's sour squint—which was the requisite military posturing. Which he *also* knew well. In some ways, he felt he already knew them, he guessed. They were nothing like anything he'd have expected. None of *any* of this was like a fucking movie.

Then what the fuck are you scared of, man?

He opened his eyes. Straightened. "I'm alone in an interrogation room. No handcuffs, a public phone, and a pile of change. They asked me if I wanted coffee or something to eat, then they left me alone to make my calls and do a little thinking. I've done both."

"You called a lawyer?"

"Public defender can handle what I need. Just some questions answered. The rest is formalities."

"You're sure."

"I'm sure."

Frito quiet. Then—"Okay. I guess."

"Okay."

Then nothing more.

Which meant that was it—nothing else to say.

He saw himself in focus now, down the room. The glint of the phone box and the round white circle glow of the bandage, and his face in there, bound-up inside it, young-man-older-brother-secret-boyfriend thinking This is who you are now, a young, organized-crimer who survived a hit attempt. Which happened all the time—there were always stories. The Federal Bureau of Investigation caught you doing wrong, and they're right behind me here, other side of this glass. Look right, you'll see their ghosty outlines. The suit-jacket shoulders, the close-cropped hair.

But, he only saw himself. Thought even when you didn't know who the fuck you were anymore, you still recognized your own inner voice.

"I guess we should hang up then?"—Frito.

Every consequence your own fucking doing, he'd told her. Standing on a railroad platform. In lower Westchester. Her town. Hidden suburb. So sophisticated. He'd told her his philosophy. A tough one to bear the weight of, but straight-up honest, and he could bear it. Yes, he could. The legal heat for what he'd done. But not the guilt. Not over Felix. He wouldn't permit it, because it was Bunny's. And I'll turn him over for it. Get back to Penny, in time, get the money, start over.

"Martin?"

"Yeah. Yes," he said, "we should go." This new life, other side of the glass. Hang up and the feds come in, help you detail the future.

"Okay," his little brother said.

"Okay."

He reached up, back behind him, put another dime in and listened to it fall. In the amplified solitude. Listened to his brother keeping quiet. Keeping still. Just breathing.

So many things you can't tell him, he thought. Things you only ever would have told Felix. Such simple things, too.

His little brother was quiet.

He listened to him breathe.

O
h, no no no. Hell no.

His legs seized up, his groin, his chest—constricting from fear. He *saw* it now, what they intended. He *realized*. And fast as he understood, it was too late for going back.

The older agent—the Italian—Corso—looking surprised and opening his hands where they rested on the table, fingers spreading like a bouquet. A gesture of honesty. "If that wasn't clear from the very start here, I apologize."

No no no. Fuck no. Fuck you, Martin thought; this is a narcotics case—

"We're pursuing P and D here. Premeditated and deliberated murder. We caught you fat. You murdered two people."

Martin Quinn said, "Terry. I only killed Terry. I had no choice. I told you that. That's self-defense."

"You told us a lot, and that may help you, come the time. Until that time, we'll think about it. What we know at this moment is that you killed two of your associates, and we can prove that, given all we have so far— what the sheriff here has, I should say, *will* have, as we've elected not to take jurisdiction. He has our cooperation, our reports, our files. Our preliminary ballistics are on their way—we're expecting that call anytime—and, to be honest, I don't think we'll need much more. Or the sheriff won't, rather. When we turn it all over to him. Which is soon. A couple of hours, maybe. Maybe tomorrow. That's bureaucratic monkeying around, though. Not important for you. Not relevant to your concerns."

"I . . ."

"What. You what"—right on him, the agent. But not impatient, really.

"I . . ."—he started again.

But that word, alone, seemed most important. A reminder to himself and to the world that he wasn't gone, wiped away so fast by errors, lies. "You can't say . . . bullshit," he said. "You can't say . . . You can't fucking just *charge* somebody with something they didn't do"—though they could, of course; he knew that, but it wasn't the point. The truth was the only thing keeping his mind clear, clearing out the way up ahead—"I mean, you can, of course—you can say anything. But this is my *life.* The facts are that someone shot *me,* and fucking . . . killed somebody else, man. Then goes around switching guns so he's out of the picture altogether. He removes himself from the history of what went down. It was . . ." Clever. More than he'd ever considered Terry capable of—waiting around the side of the house and planning it, waiting for his hand to be the only one near a trigger.

Plus, now, this new detail that hadn't been clear back in the yard—a Sig Sauer that the feds found under Feel's back. He'd been trying to kick himself off of it, Felix, God help him. The last thing he'd felt was something sticking in his back. He'd dropped it and fallen on it, the feds had concluded. Naturally. Which had to be exactly what Terry'd been going for. Terry'd probably wiped it, dropped it, and kicked it under him. *Jammed* it in good.

Poor Felix.

The agent saying now "I don't believe you—A—we'll keep that much up front. And B, I have no reason to, and I'll tell you why. What I saw was straightforward—"

Martin Quinn looked around—for corroboration—to break eye contact—anything. What the agent *saw,* he already knew; just getting the *truth* into him for good, though, was all that would matter now. They were just guys with jobs who wanted to do well, after all; they had no interest in being made fools of down the line. Not with the truth so obvious once you saw it. The younger fed, Dolan, right behind, not quite leaning on the wall, hands out of sight, at ease—*much* younger fed. And the local sheriff in the corner. Arms crossed low, middle-aged and trim, sheriff's hat at an angle. Little cowboy hat. His eyes and the younger agent's both saying Bullshit us all you want; our satisfaction comes when the bullshit runs out ". . . and you the only man standing. Last man standing, so to speak" this agent, Corso, still talking . . . talking.

Martin looked back at him, met his eyes. Direct eyes trying to keep him put. Keep him right-here-right-now. Martin took a good breath. Told himself, Stay honest. Speak clear—"Those are the details of my life where you walked in on it. Me saving my life and going to my friend. And that's not even your business, in a way. But I'll tell you as many times as you need to hear it. Till you know it like *I* do. I didn't do anything. I took nothing into my own hands. You can't punish me for self-defense."

The agent, Corso, standing up then. Not fast. More like he'd made up his mind to before. Just waited till I was finished, Martin Quinn guessed.

Pushed his chair in, the agent. "We're at a deadlock, then. You want to leave it at that."

Martin said, "If you plan to try to punish me for nothing, get me a lawyer before anything else," and had the impulse to stand, himself. A strange thing to feel, he thought. He and the agent just saying their parts, though, now, he understood. Stacking up walls of words.

The agent stopping, though—on his way to the door. Looked down at the floor. Up again. Eyes hard but honest. Nothing personal-seeming. "You want to do it this way, you can. It's your life, like you said. But include this in your thinking. If you plead not guilty, assuming the self-defense tack stands up past the grand jury, and they *still* prove you killed them? It's life inside." The eyes lingering. Right-here-right-now. Then away. He leaned sideways, rapped on the door. It opened, a slit. He spoke through it, soft. Listened to what was said back to him . . . Nodded . . . Nodded . . .

Reached and took what they handed him. A paper cup. And pills into the other hand—Martin heard the soft click of them. The door closed again. Corso slid the cup over, held the pills out—pinched in three fingers and a thumb, ready for dropping. Martin put his hand underneath, accepted them.

"Apparently you're on pills now. A weaker strength. Tomorrow, it's Demerol. They'll take the shunt out of your hand later. You in pain?"

Martin didn't answer him . . .

"You let someone know if you're in pain."

. . . popped the pills and drank the water. Prayed they worked as well as the injections—the pain coming on like a fever now—an inkling at first, then more there steadily. He'd be screaming soon, if he wasn't careful.

Corso took the cup again. Being helpful, at least. Then looked at the ceiling. Kept looking at it.

Wants me to look up, too.

I won't.

"One round fired from the Sig," Corso said—"slug unaccounted for, seven fired from your Glock. Three of them in Felix Pasko. One in the left kidney, one in the spine, and one in the head, close range. Three in Terrible Terry. Belly, right lung through the back, and forehead, close range. One in the dirt, by his face." He looked across the room. At the other agent. "Not bad, no?"

Martin said, "He touched that gun all over, God damn it—I saw him pick it up by the barrel. It's not like he had some fucking *poli*shing cloth with him—he didn't know you were going to show up. He did it fast. Fucking idiot thought it would look like we shot each other, and you, you fucking *fall* for it? I don't believe this. Do your job, man; find his fucking prints. Jesus *Christ*."

"Excuse me?"—the agent's eyes changing. Getting dark. Something in the comment stinging him bad.

Do your job.

He'd botched his job.

"You can't charge me for . . . fucking . . . reacting," Martin said. Take a breath, told himself.

The agent looked away. Took one himself. Put his hands on his hips and let it out. Like a kid thinking hard. The little paper cup crushed in his fingers, forgotten. Like there's no one in the room but us, Martin thought.

"Your lawyer's here, Quinn, but I'll tell you right now what he'll tell you, so you'll know where you stand, where I do. Where the local police here do, whatever. Cop to it, you can haggle. Fight it, get life. You understand? If you plead not guilty with what we have, you'll go away. They'll arraign you first thing, then it's the grand jury, and then, basically, you're through. If you come clean on both bodies, you have a chance. *That's* the facts. Your life from now on? This is as good as it gets, sitting here with us."

Martin opened his mouth, to talk. His chest sucked air—involuntarily. He knew if he spoke his voice would tremble. His whole body might shake. But he had to say—"You bust in on something not your business"— trembling—"Two dead people and me"—his thoughts storming around now, tossing his words, something inside going Pain killer—"I do nothing but shoot a killer. You owe me decent respect for that"—Pain killer—"You owe me the decency of saying 'So, what happened to you, Mr. Quinn?' You don't tell me what I did or I didn't."

"They're going to indict you. You won't even be there. They'll arraign you tomorrow and you'll come back here and wait in your cell with some guy they caught banging a cow and they'll bring what we give them to the grand jury. In a week, you'll be up in Attica reminiscing with half your neighborhood. After that, it's a circumstantial case, we both know that; it's no secret. But the evidence will bury you. So, to be honest, all we really have to do is pin down a motive, and when we do, you're done. And I'll figure it; believe me. Before I step out of this case. Maybe something as simple as you had a thing for someone's wife. Something stupid as that. I'm not kidding. We'll figure it. I promise—"

Martin said it again—"You don't tell me what I did, what I didn't"— the words shaky. A shaky wall, wavering in his head. This agent knew too fucking *much*.

"Martin, let me ask you something, and *think* about it. Even if there's some kind of miracle—the sky opens up and God tells your jurors you're telling the truth—where are you going to go? The way I don't believe you now is the way, according to you, whoever sent Terry Hughes isn't *ever* going to believe you. *And,* listen to me here, it's the way Felix Pasko's old man, Lexi, isn't going to believe you. Do you understand what I'm saying? And don't answer me right away; *think.* Do you understand . . . what I'm saying."

He didn't say anything.

He brought a hand back into his lap from the table, folded his fingers, and looked at his nails. Something he'd never done before in his life, he realized. It was something he'd seen somewhere. Picked up years ago from a wiseguy in the neighborhood, maybe, or from some movie when he was a kid. It looked unnatural, the move, and he knew they could see it did, but he couldn't pull his eyes up or drop his hand. He'd done it to hide his eyes in the first place.

This Corso knew *that* much, too, he was sure.

Still, though—nothing to say.

Corso saying "You think things through, get your story straight. I'm sure you can figure a way out of this for yourself," and looked at the other agent. "Ready?" Got some kind of silent response. Looked at the sheriff. "We'll leave him to you?" and gave a smile. Rapped on the door and watched it open. Seemed to be letting in the station house buzz, himself. Allowing it to enter, like. As though he'd controlled every detail in this production.

Martin got it.

Said, "Jesus Christ."

Said it to himself, but said it for this Corso, too, though he wasn't sure why, yet. Feared the moment he did.

Corso closed the door.

Martin looked around, felt he needed new bearings. Like the earth had skewed, a bit, with his figuring-out.

The sheriff hadn't moved. The other agent—the young-ass—had started toward the door but was stepping back toward his spot on the wall, behind, out of sight, again. Corso waited.

Martin said, "I need a minute. To myself. Before the lawyer comes. Let these pills kick in."

Corso said, "You can have a minute, an hour, whatever."

Martin nodded.

Corso nodded. "That it?"

Martin thought, You know it isn't. Said to him, "Do you even fucking care, man?"

Corso's eyes going flat. Not the response he'd wanted. Waiting, though, for more.

"You even care I didn't do it, you fucking cocksucker?"—and heard the sound of the young agent coming off the wall, behind him, and tightened, braced for the blow, prayed it wasn't in the missing ear.

This Corso putting a stop to it, though. With a hand up. Just like that. A palm out, quick but Jesus-like.

Then stillness again.

The air in the room different now, though. Humming. Like it was keeping everything from flying apart.

An informer, he thought. Aninformeraninformeraninformeraninformer, till it had no meaning but sound. They led him, from the interrogation room to meet his lawyer—Corso and Dolan walking behind, and the sheriff beside, with a guiding hand, crook of the elbow. Cuffed again. Feet threatening stumbles. His cops let him shuffle. Morphine in little red pills still definitely potent. The station house a dull, fluorescent, slow-passing blur to be ignored because his head was in the future now, waiting for this new reality to join him there when it could. He took in the floor tiles up ahead and the shambling, rhythmic darting-in of his feet at the base of his vision, carrying him on.

He'd had his minute to himself, back in the room. An informer left alone to start to recollect who he could offer. The feds had taken from him the right to fork over Bunny in a him-or-me switch, and that was too bad. Bunny had made his loyalties clear, so *he* could have made his own moves against Bunny. No one on the street would have ever, in their hearts, truly faulted him for it. *"Bunny tried to kill you for nothing?"* they'd have said—

"Fuck him. Tell him you'll see him in Hell when you pass him on your way out the courthouse," but the feds had taken that small bit of vengeance away. Were probably thinking, themselves, now *"Quinn? He works for us. He's a source. A witness. Our best boy. Our bitch."* The informer with his minute to himself. Had known it wasn't about him anymore. Knew who they wanted now, if they could get him. Who they'd be willing to let it all go for, for just a crack at. Just a look at his books. Just a whisper from someone inside about what he might truly be guilty of. *"Felix Pasko's old man, Lexi,"* the agent had said, *"isn't going to believe you. Do you understand what I'm saying to you? Figure a way out of this for yourself."*

They wanted Lexi. Though he wasn't involved here, did nothing at all here.

They figure I can deliver him.

They figured right.

He knew enough about dozens of men to help start solid cases, but with Lexi, he knew secrets. Simple truths. In his minute to himself he'd calculated fast what they might be worth and it had tired him out and made him sad, and he'd said to the mirror, then—sideways—not really looking at it— "Where's that defender?" because he knew someone would always be there behind the glass now. They had come in, cuffed him. Explained that the lawyer was in a soundproof room down the hall, other side of the building. He let himself be led.

Your fate shifts around, he'd told Frito. Your plans rearrange.

So many times now in the last few weeks and days and hours, it had begun to feel like a way of being, in itself. A destiny of its own. A fucking miserable thought, that—No rest, ever. Nothing in his world, this moment, was what he'd ever dreamed.

The sheriff led him gently past a trash can. He'd been headed for it.

He'd never dreamed he'd be shambling like a junkie. Or walking from an interrogation with a kind of shame on him. He'd always imagined he could stick out a questioning, in fact—would be watching some guy in a movie getting grilled, and think, Shit, I wouldn't even open my mouth; I'd just smile at those saps. But the saps were leading him now, patient and business-like. A real bop to their movements. Down a hall to a lawyer he wasn't sure anymore what to say to. This was his life. His reality. Stoned but not dreaming. Sudden, it was—brand new—but not unreal. Not a bit of it. And, when he came out the other side, if he was lucky, what had been real before this would still be there, in part—Penny and stolen cash so hot he might never be able to retrieve it. A hell of a start, if she'd still want him.

Christ, he thought—for the love of *God,* you got to *hope,* no?

He remembered, again, three words of hers he'd thought of while he was being cuffed. He'd been lying with her, two weeks ago, staring at the ceiling, after making love, the heroin shipment nearly packed to come transatlantic, he unable to think of anything else, and she had tapped him on his temple and said, "Hey, Mastermind, how clearly these days do I fit into all that planning I hear clanking around in there?" and he looked at her there on her pillow. The room in long, thin shadows. She smiling. He said, "When you're taught all your life *ad majorum gloriam Dei,* how big does God figure? Assuming you're not handing out daisies in Washington Square, telling the winos God loves them." "So it's *all* for me? For the greater glory of me?" "In the end," he said, "yeah." "In the meantime I have to be patient, though. While you ignore me and cover your angles." *"Ad majorum gloriam Penelopum,"* he said. *"Penelopeum,"* she corrected—satisfied—and looked back at the ceiling. To think about it, he'd guessed. And had gone back to his thinking, knowing his answer had been as vague as the Great Church Mysteries. That maybe it wasn't *really* all for her. It was *all* for her if she was *all* for him, but that this wasn't the time to be sweating those things. And, staring at her part of the ceiling, leaving him in peace, she'd said softly, like a kid—to herself, almost—"I can wait."

Two weeks ago, and in another world. With sunlight and long stretching shadows. *"I can wait."* But, if he emerged from Witness Protection with a year or two time-served and a rat jacket, earned or not, would she even want him?

He didn't know. He just had his plans.

Which had holes in them big enough for a man to fall through and never stop falling.

There was nothing else to work with, though. Not yet. He would just follow through now, till he could set something else up.

Christ, it weakened him, the not knowing. He'd never walked into trouble so unprepared in all his life.

They stopped. At a door like the dozen they'd passed. The sheriff backed him up, Corso leaned and opened it, stepped aside. Martin walked in thinking Lexi Pasko was hard and cold and had never treated him like a son though he'd practically watched him grow into a man. Lexi had granted him, instead, a kind of unspoken respect because Felix had. And had *loved* Felix. Powerfully. His only living son. Only child. Hardened gangster, loving father.

The cuffs were off.

He looked at his hands, looked at the sheriff. Who showed him a seat, then left. Tight-lipped old cowboy. Closed the door behind him.

He stayed where he was. On his feet. Took in the lawyer sitting there, writing. Glasses and short sleeves. Papers around him. Like some nervous new teacher, first day of school—neat piles, but too many of them. Said, "One moment? Mr. Quinn?" like it was a question, the hand still scrawling. Getting the facts straight maybe, or preparing strategy, but knowing how important his role here was. That was obvious.

Eager, the guy. A pleasant, genuine air to him.

Martin didn't like it.

He wanted a shark. Some arrogant bastard with balls enough for the both of them. Because at some point soon, he knew, he'd have nothing left.

He sat.

"My name is Jason Davis, Mr. Quinn"—still writing, finishing up. "I'm your court-appointed counsel and I'll represent you at your arraignment tomorrow morning, and, should you choose"—jabbed the pencil down—*pop*—for a period—"at any further"—looked up. Stopped.

Not expecting the bandages, maybe.

"I know your role here, counselor. Your responsibilities. It's fine. We'll proceed."

"Okay."

"Am I still bleeding?"

"No." Shook it off, the lawyer. Jason Davis. Rattled his head. "I'm sorry.

I knew you were shot. I was caught up in the case. There's a good deal to know already. I'm sorry."

"Not a problem."

A young, intelligent guy. Polite. Thirty pounds overweight, maybe—half of it in his face. Honest eyes pressed back into flesh behind his lenses. Hair curly like Fee's. Not puffed half as high, though. "Are you in pain?" saying. "They say your pain should be less by now. And that your prescription will be weakened every day. Have they been giving you your painkillers?"

Martin nodded. Said to him, "Yes." Figured, Help him along. Even with the polite, pointless stuff.

"And did they beat you? Rough you up? They didn't, did they?"

Do I look that bad? "No."

"Good. You look as though you've been through enough"—a smile. Looked at his notes again. Crossed something off.

Martin said, "I'm feeling no pain, and they didn't beat me. Can we . . . ?"—made a motion to move on, rolled his hand forward.

"Of course"—and looked around at things, the guy. To get focused, maybe. Stretched a hand onto a pile down the table, like he had the truth right there and he'd get to it. "The first thing—"

"Look, I got to ask you," Martin said—the guy was coming off weak with this earnestness shit—"can you give me something here? I mean, who are you? What are your qualifications? Your education. Because when they first brought me in, I thought I had things figured, but they twisted me around, a minute ago. They turned me on my head. And . . ." Now *I'm* sounding weak, he thought. Jesus Christ.

"I studied law at Georgetown," the guy said. "I was top of my class. I understand—that you didn't think you'd really need a lawyer. It's okay."

"See, I don't have any money—" he stopped. And took a breath. The phrase burned him. No money I can *get* to, he wanted to say—but I'm fucking loaded; believe me. "I'm broke right now, counselor."

"I think you'll find I do a good job"—looking like he knew this was difficult, the guy. Another bad sign. "A superlative one. And I'm from New Jersey, originally. If that matters to you."

Martin shrugged. Didn't get him.

"It's just that I'm not from Ohio, or anything."

"I'm from New York."

"Yes, I know"—squinting, the guy. Looked down at his notes again.

"They turned me on my head," Martin said, "but I'm right-side-up again. And I have a plan, is what I want to tell you. We should talk about it."

"Good. The first thing, then, that I need from you is the truth. The officers have already given me a great deal to think about and look over—not really by the book, the way they work, but that's okay for now—but what I need from *you,* at the moment, is the facts. We need to start by you telling me what happened at Felix Pasko's country house, and, as I need to, I'll ask you questions as you tell me, okay? Mr. Quinn?"

Martin looked away—the bile starting to crawl up his throat the second he'd heard Fee's name. Dead two days and left in the past. Stuck there. Life moving on. Just a body in a court case, now.

"Before you ask me, man, I didn't kill Felix. I don't want you to ever ask me that. Terry shot us both."

The guy nodded. Martin saw it peripherally. Didn't look.

"Why did Terry Hughes shoot you, Mr. Quinn?"

Because he was an animal. *"Don't make me chase you . . ."*

"The agents," Davis said, "mentioned that Felix was Lexi Pasko's son? Did that have something to do with it?"

Martin smiled.

And knew now. Had his answer and plan. "They mentioned that to you, hunh?"

All Felix's life meant to them was Lexi.

And *yours?* he thought. Mr. Quinn? What does your life mean? "What else they say, counselor?"

"We should get to that. And we will—"

"Did they mention what they were doing here, the feds?"

"No, they didn't. I didn't ask yet. I intend to, of course."

"I know; it's scary talking to them—they're the government; you figure they must have more than you do. But I'll tell you right now what they have and what they don't. I'll give you my educated guess. You ready? They were following Felix and me for narcotics, building a case, and they found themselves racing into a shootout." He looked off, a second. Saw the images. Buried them. Looked back. "And the case they had was slim-to-nothing, I think, so when Terry opened fire, it fell through to shit. Now they want to save face by using the shootings as leverage for a new investigation."

Davis raised an eyebrow—reluctantly, but sending the message clear—*Well, yes; there* are *dead bodies.*

Martin looked away, tried to ignore it. Said, "They know a round was fired from Terry's automatic. Do a residue test on him and Felix; that issue's resolved. All the slugs from my gun are accounted for. It stands to reason he shot me with that bullet. And, maybe, left a print or two on my gun—I saw him pick it up by the barrel. I assume he wiped it off when he was coming back from Felix before he put it in my hand, but, still, things were turning over fast out there."

Davis put his pencil down, nodded.

"They want me for something else," Martin said.

"Okay."

"I've known Lexi Pasko since I'm fourteen. Except for some time in the army and a few years after, I've seen him practically every day for ten years."

"Okay."

"You know why they told you that Fee was his son?"

"They think he's involved with the narcotics issue, perhaps? Is he?"

"No. He doesn't even know about it. Even if they thought he was, they already told me to my face they're pursuing murder charges. Like they were just driving the back roads of the Catskills and heard some shots. They're playing dumb on the narcotics because if they pretend that they want me to take a murder bounce, they can push me to testify. The murder jacket's just a threat. We're talking about Lexi fucking Pasko, man. Who's never even been in custody. Do you know how embarrassing that is for them?"—Davis's eyes straight-fixed now, on his, though there were other things popping behind them—"If it's only drug charges I'm hit with in the end, I'll get time-served, I figure, or maybe a year. Sound right? But, even *if* it's murder, maybe three years in the federal pen and *out* of general pop. Protective custody. Plus, I didn't fucking murder anybody, except in self-defense, so, it's got to be easier to prove *that*—the *truth*—than what they have in mind. Which is *your* job, of course"—smiled at the guy, polite as he could. Took a breath. Said, "That's it. That's how I see everything now. If it makes sense to you, we should probably talk about a next step. If I'm right about the kind of time I would do if I testified. More than three years and I'll fucking smash through that wall, run off down the highway." He smiled again. Forced it.

"There could have been other reasons they mentioned Pasko," the guy said. Was thinking something else, same time—his eyes somewhere else in his thoughts.

"He's not involved here," Martin said, "on any level"—and dismissed it—waved it off. "He didn't even want us *dealing* heroin. He didn't even know."

"Might that be a reason for *him* to have shot you?"

"To have *what*?"

"Some kind of pride over being betrayed. He has a reputation for ruthlessness."

"He's not involved here," Martin said. Thought, Please don't make me think you're an asshole. *Please.* And closed his eyes.

"But they could be assuming he is," the guy said. "The police have been aware of him since the day he came here from Odessa. The rumors of his career go back to when he was a boy."

He'd read the article, Martin realized—*New York* magazine—"RED GOD-FATHER? *How could a man never even arrested be the country's most feared new criminal? Blah, blah.*"

Martin set his teeth, told himself, Patience here. Raised his eyebrows, looked at the guy. "If I'm right about the kind of time I would do, man, we should talk, right now, about a next step. Yes?"

"If you're right, about the sentencing—and you probably are—"

"I could finish college while I was inside, too, and get veteran's benefits. Reduce my bid that much more—"

"Yes, but we still start with the facts."

Martin stared at him.

"Why were you three at Pasko's country house? Why did Terry Hughes shoot you? Both of you."

Martin clasped his hands—gently—leaned forward on the table. Disappointment was crawling all through him. "I'm running out of gas here, Mr. Davis, so . . ."—but the guy wasn't here anymore, was distracted completely, it looked like—"I need to be sure—okay?—that one way or a fucking nother—either they come to *you* or you go to them—we have to make a deal. Are you listening, chief?"

"Of course."

"Are you?"

"Mr. Quinn—"

Martin said, "If they want me to testify against the old man, I will. Do you hear what I'm saying to you? Look in my eyes. I've known him since I'm fourteen. I've seen everything. I can fucking put Lexi Pasko away"— and smiled.

Tried to stop, but couldn't. Took his head in his hands and stared down at the table and forced himself to, but knew, for certain now, that he would never turn Lexi in. He hadn't really been convinced of it till saying the opposite aloud.

Lexi'd treated him with respect, always. Never like a son, but like Felix's guardian. Like a man. Even when they were boys.

"I'll put Alexi Pasko away, counselor. I know every detail." He laid his hands down. His senses back in place, the smiling forgotten. He'd given the lie. He would ride it out until his time was served or they forced him to take it back, somehow. Or until things changed again. Because things always changed.

But the lie was there.

It was the front he'd move behind.

He wished he had a mirror to see himself. Fake self. A twister now. He'd survive.

This lawyer, Davis, staring. Then looked away. Shy-like.

Overwhelmed? "Are you starstruck, counselor? I know you read that article."

"Perhaps a little"—nodded, didn't look up. "A side of me would like to see this with some distance. History would be made. You'd be the first eyewitness against any Russian Mafia, as far as I know. I'd wonder how you'd feel."

"How I'd *feel*? You worried about my conscience? What, my soul? What about my best interests? Get me the fucking *deal,* chief—" Davis's eyes on the floor now. His voice low—

"I apologize. You're right. I'm sorry."

"My soul or my self-respect?" Martin said.

"Just . . ."—wanted to get past this—"your role in it all."

"And *yours.*"

He looked up. "You can petition to change counsel at any time if you feel—"

"I don't want to fall out with you over this, man; I want to know if we can *do* it."

They sat there.

Davis said, "Before the arraignment tomorrow we must explore our other options. But in keeping with your ideas, I'll need to know everything, regardless of—"

"Just tell me if you—"

"Mr. Quinn, please. Hear me out. All right? Please?"

Martin stared at him, a second. Nodded. Looked down at the table. "Okay."

"Any negotiations would begin after the arraignment. Because the sheriff . . . well, the agents, need to hold you. No matter what you're arraigned for, it will have something to do with those two men's deaths. We'll just enter our plea—not guilty, obviously—explain it was self-defense, that they have the wrong man and the right one's dead, and so on, and try for bail. Though it's extremely unlikely."

"Impossible, I figured."

"Nothing's impossible in the legal system. It's like science fiction, sometimes. But it's unlikely. We could reduce the bond, perhaps, if something surreal did occur."

"But no remand to the system. They'd send me back here to start talking to them. Keep me in federal custody."

"If the government really wants you, yes—I think they'd keep you very close."

Martin breathed in, and held it, a moment. Let it out. His mind easing—this guy's simple cooperation, simple agreement, bringing some peace. The guy becoming a kind of partner. Saying to him now "Okay?"

He nodded. And sat back. Said to him, "I was arrested for assault, as a kid. Aggravated, but my first offense."

Davis wrote it down and nodded. Martin said, "You don't have to write this. I just want to tell you something."

Davis put the pen down, looked at him. Was listening.

"My first offense, so they said I'd be sent to a group home till my arraignment. I was arrested on a Friday, though."

"Arraigned on a Monday."

He nodded. "Supposed to be. Only I didn't go to the group home. I ended up on a bus to Spofford. When my mother called the home, they'd never heard of me. You know about Spofford? The Hunts Point Juvenile Detention Center, AKA?"

Davis nodded.

"Three hundred kids and two hundred beds?" Martin said. "Roaches in the food, and the guards giving out beat-downs when the tougher kids weren't? And the fucking *noise*? You can't imagine." Like Hell would sound, he'd always thought. "It took her a week to find me. I couldn't call out because none of the phones worked. There was a row of like ten of them with a sign above it that said, 'These phones are recorded,' and someone crossed out 'recorded' and wrote, 'broke.' It took her a week." During which time he'd slept an hour. Maybe. He'd fought and waited. Fought and waited. "So just make sure it's federal, all right? I had to scrap every minute I was in the state system; believe me. I'm tired now just thinking about it."

"Yes. I'll do what I can."

"I didn't do anything, counselor—you should keep that in mind. A guy I've had problems with for twenty years shot me in the head and then killed my best friend. Then I shot him in self-defense. I didn't know what he planned to do next. That's it. Charging me with murder? It's not right. It's incorrect." Unjust, he thought. And wanted to talk it through once more, before he lost it. "Just find a way to tell them. But, you know, don't show our hand. Make them come to us. Then, tell them I'll cooperate. They'll put me in protection. From protection I can plan my life again. I can think." He looked off, a second, to feel it if he could—the new chance. Looked back at him. "I can't tell you how loud prison is, man, Davis."

He thought, When you lose your freedom, those are your choices—your own voice inside you, merciless, or the constant shriek of the whole fucking crazy system.

Davis was scribbling.

He thought, I guess I like this guy. I'm pleased he's here. "You want some coffee or something, counselor?" said to him.

Davis nodded, scribbling. "Sure."

He sat back, said, "I'll wait for you to get up and knock," and he nodded, Davis, not listening. Looked up soon enough, though. Was ready. Had forgotten about coffee, though. Too set to get things going *his* way. And . . . fucking . . . *let* him be set; I'm tired. Tell him everything I need to and let *him* work.

He tipped his head, stretched his legs out full. Crossed his ankles, and laced his fingers. He could talk to this guy now. Young Jason Davis. His counsel. A guy his age or a few years older. Top of his class. They'd get their coffees later; there was plenty of time. Because the gangster life was over now; it was time to get on to the next one. To safety, and peace, and lying beside Penny, staring at the ceiling.

He waited. For his lawyer's first question.

"So exactly what happened? At Felix Pasko's country house. Why did Terrence Hughes shoot you?"

He thought, Over money—what else? Me and Penny will be lying in a bed of it, one day.

"Mr. Quinn? Martin?"

He jerked his chin up, asking what.

"Why did he shoot you?"

He thought about it. And realized for a moment he didn't really have any idea.

The nurse worked carefully, mercifully, her face right in close above his and her eyes on her work. Cutting the dressing off. Her forearms crisscrossing his vision. Her uniform hugging tight across her breasts.

She was clean and he was dirty. He could smell himself. It made him uncomfortable. A bit ashamed. Clear skin she had, too. No scent to her at all that he could perceive beneath the choke of the hospital pine and his own bacteria.

He'd been as clean as she was everyday since he was a kid, just into his teens. When the running around the neighborhood had begun to make him stink. Coming home after dark, and the older girls in Thompson Park beginning to look at him, hard, with their hard eyes, seeing him for the first time. He bought deodorant, a hairbrush. Dressed well and stayed that way. He'd known even then that he was decent-looking. This nurse couldn't see any of that though.

She was young. Twenty-two or -three, probably. Working so carefully. Confidently. He respected that.

"I'm sorry about the smell," he said—tried to look up at her, not moving his head.

"Sorry?"

"They haven't let me take a shower."

She smiled, over her forearm. "I didn't notice. It's okay." Looked behind him. Over his head. At Corso. Paused. Kept working.

No one spoke. Corso and Dolan behind him and a doctor down the end of the table.

After a minute, she stopped again. "This may hurt." Peeled off the last square of gauze and laid it aside in the tray and stepped back, her eyes on the side of his head. Then she took him in—his face, his eyes. Trying to fit the wound with what she saw.

He tried a smile.

Something crossed her face.

Fear? Doubt? A kid's face she was making.

The doctor stepped in, between them, looking only at the side of his head. Raised a hand slow to touch him and he eyed the hand, and the doctor leaning in, close, behind it. Said, "Wait," and heard something in his voice he didn't like. Felt the cuffs holding his hands back tight, saw the doctor's close face, and felt his earhole now, suddenly, exposed.

The doctor moved, again.

"Wait!"

He thought he'd kick him.

The doctor looked past him, at Corso. Had a dead-looking face. Nothing bad or good in it, but nothing kind. "My hands," Martin said. "Undo my hands—the cuffs."

"What's the matter with you?" Corso said. Came around the table, looked him over.

"Just take off the cuffs, Corso. Do me a favor."

"For what?"

His ear was burning, and cold. Some breeze blowing off it he couldn't feel anywhere else. "This isn't right—it's like torture."

"No one even touched you. What are you talking about?"

Martin looked past him. The doctor dead-looking. Like the dead come back to touch him. But the nurse got it, he saw. By her eyes. "Tell him," he said to her.

She frowned. Looked at Corso when he turned to look at her. But she didn't say anything.

Corso turned back.

"Just take the cuffs off, Corso, all right? Please. You know what I'm talking about."

"Uhn-uhn. They stay tight as a wedding ring."

He said, "Then let her clean it," because he guessed he could handle that. Her softness. Her youth. He just admired her somehow.

"Can't," Corso said. "Doc?" and stepped aside. The doctor came forward.

Martin lurched.

Corso caught him. By the shirtfront first, then shot his hand up, around his throat, righted him on the table. And someone holding his arms—was cranking him up, by the cuffs. The young one—Dolan. The nurse said, "No!"—muffled—had her hands on her mouth. "No!"

Corso yelled, "Get out!" choking him now. The sheriff and a kid deputy in the door then, coming fast, the kid's hand on his gun.

Martin couldn't breathe. There was Corso's face and his eyes, determined, then only the pain, pulsing, spreading. He couldn't yell. There was pain, and blackness.

He'd been out. It was the same room, same pitch of light, same shade on the walls, but he was different. Was on his back. Time had passed. Not much, but it had. Someone holding his head up, a hand behind his neck, small and strong. He glanced. Saw a new nurse. Older. A little thicker. Who was paying him no attention. The doctor there, just past her, wrapping his head for him. Corso there, beyond them. The fury only in his face now—his body at ease.

The pain was gone. Maybe that was why he'd woken, he thought. He wondered if they'd injected Demerol or gone back to morphine.

The doctor finished. Moved off. The new nurse laid his head back. Straightened a few things, moved off. Corso told him to sit up; they'd be late.

No one spoke in the car. Five of them in there, but no one spoke. They turned the corner at the courthouse and he saw the crowd. Maybe fifty of them. Local-looking. Flannel shirts. Boots. Baseball hats. Some women. In denim shirts. He scanned them all, men and women, best he could. Looked carefully. "Slow down, sheriff, would you?"—all of them turning now. Knew he was coming. He'd recognize what he was looking for, if he saw it. Some cold, calm set to the eyes that could never be masked, or, someone who wouldn't look up at all knowing that they couldn't hide it. Every one of them looking straight on, though. Sheriff saying "We're here," and pulling the cruiser up at the curb in front of them and killing the engine. Tired, country faces. Indignance the worst thing he saw. Things looking safe, so far. Dolan took him under the elbow and he looked around at Corso. "We're getting *out* here, man?"

"Uh-hunh."

"You're taking me through the street? Through this crowd?" They'd left for the hospital through the station house garage.

"There's no perp's walk here. This is rural America."

"Don't give me that shit. Are you wearing a vest?"

"No."

"I can see it"—it had risen up, under his shirt collar, when he'd shifted his ass to move.

"You got delusions, Quinn? These are farmers. You going to cry again?"

He looked quick out the window, once more—looked them over again while he could. Sheriff out of the car now and clearing a path to the steps.

Dolan opening the door, stepping down, then ducked out, stood up. Corso leaning with his shoulder, pushing him to go. Dolan smoothed himself— jacket, tie—and turned back, helped him onto the sidewalk.

They moved fast, steady.

Martin kept his head down, side-to-side looking, checking every face he could. Saw quiet hate, quiet fear, quiet wonder.

Going up the stairs. And, then, they were up. Dolan opened the door and Martin looked back, down at the street. The crowd still split in half and looking up at him. Keeping their distance till he was inside. He turned, went in. Davis came into step with them, had been just inside the door, asked how he was. The lobby tall and open, polished wood and marble. Dolan steering him through it by the arm, toward the tall twin doors. "Martin?" Davis looking at him, keeping up with him. Martin smiled.

"I'm all right. How about you? You look nervous." Dolan stopped, yanked the door open hard. Warm hush from the room. Took Martin more firmly by the arm and turned him sideways. Martin tugged back. "Would you relax?"

Dolan ignored him, continued pulling him on.

The courtroom nearly full, too. Bright. Every single head turning to watch him, no exceptions. The sunlight through the windows in broad, dusty beams. He looked casually at the rows of faces, like he might find a seat. Got here early, this bunch, he thought.

Past the rail, Dolan stopped him, turned him toward a seat behind a table and pressed him toward it. He sat. Davis sat beside him, saying something again. Dolan walking away. Martin didn't watch him. Behind, in the rows of seats, people talking again. He looked over the judge's box, the witness stand, the flags. Said, "Trial of the fucking century."

"Why are you late, I said."

"Little incident at the hospital on the way here."

"What does that mean? How do you mean that?"

"Why you so nervous, Davis?"

"What happened at the hospital?"

"I bugged. They wanted to clean up my head and they kept me cuffed.

It was like being tortured"—he laughed—to himself—embarrassed. "I fucking passed out."

"Are you all right? Can you do this?"

"I'm fine. I can breathe again."

They were starting to come in now, back at the door. He listened to them coming. Finding seats, whispering. He watched the windows. Blue sky out there, unaware of all this. The room starting to stir now. He said, "You believe all these people? They think it's the arraignment of the century."

"Few murders up here," Davis said, reviewing his notes.

"Yeah, hunting accidents these people have. I was in the army with guys like this."

He'd given thought to killing Felix with the thirty-aught and saying it was an accident. Then just brought the Glock. Thinking ending a life would be easy and the devil in the details of cleaning up.

Davis said, "That's what they tell the cops. 'Thought he was a bear, sheriff.'"

Martin looked at him, saw him smiling, a second. Nudged him, still cuffed. "Yeah, you see? It's not so bad," said to him. "Change of scene. No more of that fucking room. No more of that Corso. This shit I can take."

"Where is Corso?"

"Don't know, don't care. He was in the car. Hey, you think you should tell them it was a hunting accident?"

Davis looked at his pad. "We'll stick with what we have. Just plead how we rehearsed. We'll go from there."

"Rehearsed," Martin said. "Four freaking words. Gee, I hope I don't blow it. You think I will?"—Davis working hard to ignore him now, though. Martin ran his eyes over the bench. Latin in the front panel. Davis turned a page. Clouds passed outside the windows. Someone reading his own pad of notes at the table on their right. "That the ADA?"

"Blue suit?"

"Yeah."

Davis nodded.

Martin looked over. Good suit. Good haircut. In his forties.

He looked back at the window. Said, "This is agony." Felt Davis look at him. Heard him say, after a moment—

"It's the first step in the process. As we discussed. You take what they give you, we go off, decide how to use it, make it ours as best we can."

Martin nodded. Tried to appreciate the vagueness. A solid approach it had seemed, last night.

A door opened beside the bench. Corso came through it. "*He's* thinking the same thing," Martin said. "He's waiting to make things *his.*"

"Who?" Davis said, looked up. "God damn it, that's chambers"—and began to stand.

"He's telling him who I am. He's giving them a little background."

"They know who you are"—he sat, Davis. Watched Corso pass, not looking at them. Davis cursed, wrote something on his pad.

The judge came in. Looked at the crowd and shook his head, raised the hem of his robe, stepped up behind the bench. Big bald head. No glasses. Martin thought he'd have glasses. The room stood up at the bailiff's command. Martin said, "Don't sweat it, counselor," and looked over at Corso, and at the crowd behind him—all faces on the judge. He turned back. The judge looked all right, he guessed. Impartial.

He said the word in his mind. No part. No side.

They sat again. Were quiet. Then the judge told him to come forward. Davis came with him. The ADA met them, stood beside Davis where they all stopped, the bailiff with a hand out stomach-level for Martin, then stepping away. "Can you hear me well enough, Mr. Quinn?" the judge saying. He motioned toward Martin's head. The bandage.

"This ear still works." He raised his shoulder at the good one.

Davis made a sound. Like something in his throat.

"You've been accused of murdering two people, Mr. Quinn. Do you understand that? The charges against you?"

"I do."

"*Don't say, 'Yes,'*" Davis had said, talking to him like he was a child; "*say, 'I do.' Then, when it's your turn again, 'Not guilty, Your Honor.'*"

"And how do you plead, Mr. Quinn, to the charges?"

"Not guilty, Your Honor."

The judge looked at him, a second or two longer. Then at Davis. "Mr. Davis?"

"Your Honor, it was an act of self-defense. My client has maintained this from the moment the agents arrived. He was defending his life against a known violent felon and repeat offender, a man whose criminal history he was fully aware of and who shot my client *first,* hitting him in the head, then shot the other victim in this case, Felix Pasko. When the agents arrived, Mr. Quinn went with them without any resistance, believing he had done nothing wrong, and hadn't. And has maintained his innocence throughout all of the agents' and the sheriff's questioning, Your Honor—I must repeat that. He's a veteran of the armed forces. Has only a juvenile record—"

"He was incarcerated for assault."

"He was awaiting arraignment, Your Honor, then released with time-served. You know the system."

The judge smiling—"Yes, I do. You've established he was a convicted violent juvenile offender. Go on."

"He was a boy. And that record is immaterial in this court. I simply didn't want to pretend it didn't exist."

"Fair enough"—waved a hand easy, the judge, like to clear the air. Accepted the argument. "Mr. Carling? Your recommendation?"

Martin looked over at him—Carling—then at Davis again. Next to him, Davis looked like a guy who caught the bus here. "For bail?" the ADA said—"none. He should be held without it. This is a heinous crime, Your Honor, not self-defense—a double murder. All the ballistic evidence points to it. He's also under investigation for narcotics—"

I fucking knew it, Martin thought—they were bringing out everything. Which meant they had nothing. "He hasn't been charged with anything," Davis saying.

The judge raised it again—the calm hand—to quiet him.

The ADA—"His known associates are a who's who of gangsters in New York, both Italian and Russian—"

"And?" Davis said. "Your Honor, please."

The hand again. And a finger leveled.

"The accused has a prior record, is clearly a budding, if not established, mobster, despite his age, who has simply skirted capture until now. He has no job, no traceable income, no home or family, no ties to the community at all, and is an obvious flight risk. He tried to escape this morning from the hospital."

"*What?*" Davis said.

Holy shit, Martin thought. He turned to find Corso.

Front row. Face all respectful, flat, eyes up past them on the judge.

"Your Honor, I was told nothing about this," Davis saying. "My client was taken to the hospital to be treated for his wound—"

"Where he tried to flee, Mr. Davis."

"According to whom? This is *absurd.*"

"According to all those present in the hospital room, counselor. I suggest you ask your client about it when—"

"I have to speak with him now."

Martin thought, The nurse, with her hands to her mouth. And *his* hands jacked up, Corso cutting his air. He said, "It never happened, Your Honor," was losing feeling below his knees. He knew what was coming.

"Be quiet, please, Mr. Quinn. Mr. Davis, I suggest that at the end of these proceedings you get to work on this. But, for the moment, it's my opinion that both you and Mr. Carling have made your recommendations . . ."

They wanted to crush him.

". . . and that he be remanded to the state department of corrections . . ."

He'd made them lose face, then had told them, "Do your job." They were going to lock him up in the system, make him sorry. And he was already sorry. He was sorry right now. "*You can't believe how loud prison is,*" he'd told his lawyer. Davis. The guy yelling now beside him. ". . . the right to certain information!"

"Counselor, you mind your tone and your role in this court."

"My role has been compromised, been undermined . . ."

Freedom was leaving, Martin knew. Something was trembling in his chest. He had to sit.

"Mr. Davis, you may have your big client now, and may even get your chance to try the patience of other members of the bench, but we will follow procedure here—"

"I have to sit," Martin said, began to turn. The bailiff caught him, by the arm.

"Mr. Quinn?"

"Have to sit . . ."

"Bailiff—"

"Fuck," Martin said—his legs were going. He leaned in the direction of the table, didn't know if he'd make it.

"Sit him down, bailiff."

"I'll get him," his lawyer, Davis, saying, taking him around the waist. "I'll take him, bailiff."

"Counselor, step back here, please."

"I must be with my client, Your Honor"—tugging Martin by the hips, the bailiff still trying to bring him by the arm, take him himself. They were headed for the table, though. Martin bumped against it and leaned, stopped.

"Counselor!"

Davis in his face, his eyes asking something behind the lenses. "Did you?" he said.

Martin found the tabletop, behind him, with his hand, lowered his weight to it.

"Did you try to run?"

"No."

"Counselor!"

"I must be with my client."

"Bailiff, bring Mr. Davis here."

The bailiff took him.

Martin looked away, looked behind him for the chair around the table, began to move to it, slid along the table's edge. It was outrageous, Davis was saying. *". . . being treated like a criminal." ". . . treated as you should be, counselor . . ."* the crowd all watching it—the faces all fixed but two—two pale, steady ovals that Martin Quinn saw, peripherally, were watching him. corso and the sheriff. He kept his eyes on them thinking nothing, slid along on the table edge, saw them shift their eyes past him—at something beyond him. Squinting, like animals. Then starting up, both of them, their bodies emerging full. He turned. Saw a young man coming at him, something in his fist.

Fuck, he thought—no. Tried to put his hands up. Locked behind him. A frightened shrug he gave, something piercing him under the arm and tearing him, and such pain. The kid shanked again and caught him, shanked again, caught him. Puncturing. Again. Saying something. Hissing. Martin back against the table, going down, the kid coming over the rail and raising the thing up beside him, by his hip, to come in sideways. Then was tackled.

There was a blur of dark suits, and bodies grappling, tipping, falling. People stepping over, falling flat. He shimmied under the table, a drag mark of his blood stretching away. He thought to curl his hand around it and draw it back to him, shore it in, along the floorboards. Someone stepped on his ankle. He pulled his legs in. People shouting. The pain becoming everything for an instant, all throughout him, then gone. One voice yelling over and over in sounds he knew. In Russian. A word he knew in the yelling. The kid yelling *"Suki . . . Suki . . ."*

The old man had sent a killer. To put out all fires. Close all mouths.

Or to take some revenge and ease his pain.

Oh, fuuuck, Martin thought, deep in his mind. Heard himself whimper. I'm so sorry.

Things were slowing down—his thoughts, his senses. The pain was coming back. Was intolerable.

"Bitch," Felix said. "Traitor. Scab. It means a lot of things. There's really not a lot of bad curses in Russian, so you take what you can get."

They were young, fourteen. Felix teaching him the language. Martin said, "It sounds like a Chinese girl. Suki. Come here, Suki, my love."

"It's bad; believe me. You don't ever say it in front of my father."

"Of course not."

He'd only met the old man a few times but had heard Felix's stories. One look at the old man and you knew they were true. "I won't."

"You ever do it with a Chinese girl?" Felix said.

Funny, in a way. Being conscious again of being alive. Because the mind had to know it from the beginning, he guessed. It never doubted it. All it ever knew was you were living, you're alive, you're living . . . and then you're not, and it doesn't even realize.

He thought, Why ever fear *any*thing then?

This room was quiet. And dark. There was a low steel rail beside him, a hospital curtain beyond it, drawn back. A window with the blinds down, and a black television on the wall, up high. And someone next to him. Sleeping, by the sound of them, or staring hard. He didn't care. He turned his head full, slowly, to take them in.

A nun. Old, and bony. And napping in the dim light, sitting up. An IV pole between her and the bed, nearly too high up for him to see, but the tube cascading down into him somewhere, under the blanket. Too tight blanket. He didn't wrestle, though. He just closed his eyes again. Thought of a series of paintings down the Paskos' hallway in their place on Lafayette Street. Some heretical Jewish school, Fee's mother had told him. Almost two years ago. At the beginning of all this. Pictures of prophets. Running from God. Who never showed Himself formally. Was always a cloud, or a wind, or a tree reaching out with a long, wicked branch to grab the poor bastards as they booked away. All of them giving a glance over their shoulder to see if they really had a chance. White beards flowing back behind them.

People always looked back at the thing that was chasing them, he thought. Not like animals, who got away *then* looked. People never quit believing something would actually chase them. Especially God.

Why not just give them the lightning bolt, though? he thought.

Though it made some sense. What would you learn with a lightning bolt? If He were going to plague you, He'd plague you. Hound you down? You'd be hounded. And, sometimes, if His point was to really give you time to think, He'd shoot you, stab you, fill you with morphine, tuck you in too tight, and leave you with a bride of Christ, like you were back in kindergarten. Everything could be a joke to Him. Though the point didn't really seem to be to ever get you to laugh.

He sighed. Pain simmered in his chest. His body already healing and not caring what his mind understood. That there'd been a kind of death inside him even though he was living. A death inside a life. His body'd just heal.

He closed his eyes. Was nothing but awake, though.

How, he wondered, could he slip back again into unconsciousness.

He tried.

two

Years later, when he and Felix had the club, he would understand that the beach house in Puerto Rico was as much about business as pleasure, like most things in the old man's life. He would learn that dozens of Mafiosi, large and small, had places there, and that the old man had bought one of the best, decorated it with opulence, threw a dinner party or two, and then had called a meeting with the Italians, over gasoline, to decide who would be a partner forever and who would be out, from that day on. A summit meeting that would begin to make him one of the richer men in the world. His children, for generations to come, like royalty. At the time, though—high school—all Martin really gave two shits about was how Fee was back and forth to San Juan constantly, and *he* was never invited. Junior year, Felix coming home from spring recess saying he met two girls down there from Westchester who needed dates for their junior prom. "Two sisters. Good-looking," he said, "so don't sweat that"—Martin looking him over, half listening—his tan, his salt-air calm, a bit of a burn on the nose—*that* would teach him. Down there three times in the last two months. "It's that they're too good-looking" Fee saying. "Their father's a Sicilian who runs Westchester and half of the Bronx, so no one will even talk to them, forget ask them out. Can you believe that? They're too freaking scared. I have their picture. They're freaking fine." He dropped his bag, unzipped a pocket. "Their old man loved me. He knew who my father was. My father says the guy's a joke, though. Talks about having Frank Sinatra over to dinner once, in the fifties. Here." He handed the photograph up. Three girls at the beach. Holding on to each other, and laughing, arms around shoulders and waists—*"We're inseparable."* Healthy, thin, young bodies. All tan. All three in bikinis with flowers. The sisters were brunettes, the other one blond.

Martin said, "They're in the same class? They're twins?"

"No . . . wouldn't that be awesome? No. There's like two years between them. But the older one's dumb and the younger one skipped a grade. I'm taking the older one. I already freaking *got* her when we were down there. Her sister was in the next bed. She kept going, 'What are you doing, Gina? Are you awake?' And Gina was *blow*ing me; she couldn't answer."

Martin studied the picture. "So I get the whiny one."

"She's *fine. Tot*ally. Look at the picture."

"Who's this one?" he said. "The blonde."

"Penelope. She's all right. She was down there with them. She'll be at the prom, but she's got a date. Their freaking brother. Can you believe that? He's an animal. He kept asking me what I bench. Like three times he asked me. 'I keep forgetting,' he goes. A fucking *id*iot."

"She's good-looking," Martin said.

"Yeah, she's all right. That's a rare moment, though, her smiling. She's kind of a bitch."

"She's with their brother for real, or it's just a date?"

Fee said no—"He's like twenty-two, he wants to go to a prom. 'I never been to one,' he says. Because he dropped out of high school. You won't believe this guy. He'll run Westchester one day."

Martin smiled.

Said only that he'd come.

And knew that the next time everyone was off to P.R.?—they'd say he *had* to go.

As for the brother, he kept his take on the guy to himself. He knew a dozen hoods like him in the neighborhood. Felix was just used to a whole different kind of gangster.

B y the dressing rooms at the tuxedo place, back, a bit, off the show-room floor, they waited for the tailor to come back with Felix's pants, Martin's outfit already bagged and hanging beside the three-way mirror because his measurements had been easy to accommodate, but Felix's waist and legs were thin and his chest and shoulders were growing by the week since his father had bought him the home gym and set it up in the connecting apartment he'd also just given him. He'd also gotten glasses, Fee. Was finally starting to look like a young man, and act like one now. Full time. Was finally catching up, Martin saw. Himself, he'd always felt a bit too old for his age, a bit too cool in general. But Fee was getting to be just right.

Something dangerous about that, he thought. In some way.

Fee checked himself, up close, in the mirrors, wore a T-shirt, boxer shorts, black calf-high socks, velvet rental loafers. Martin looked him over, smiled. In the mirror saw a guy come in the shop and pass behind them. And something about the guy held his attention. "Legs are shot from the car crash" Feel saying . . . "Shoulders are separating at the cuffs from lifting . . . Now my eyes. From jerking off. The rabbi was right."

"You'd be freaking blind," Martin said; "believe me—filthy like you are"—the guy at the counter now, waiting. Was Irish-looking, early forties, mustache. A suit jacket over a shirt, opened up at the collar. An impatience in him. Which was what Martin recognized. Impatient and resigned a long time ago to wait for the rest of the world while they worked hard. The thumbreakers in the neighborhood had that look whenever they went north of Houston Street. He said to Fee quietly, "Hit man. Look."

Fee stepped sideways in the mirror, saw him.

"I need a tuxedo," the guy said to the clerk. "For somebody else. Fifty-two regular."

"Oh, shit," Martin said, "definitely."

Felix said, "Yeah. Bodyguard. Driver."

"What, bodyguard? He's a hitter."

"Whatever, a hitter, a *byk*. Somebody's bull."

The clerk went into the back. The hit man browsed the displays. Kept his hands in his pockets. Martin followed him with his eyes. "There's a difference, Fee."

"Whatever"—Felix back in the mirror, by his voice. Nothing distracting him too much anymore—had other things on his mind. It was part of his transformation.

"Your father has *body*guards? That's what he calls them? *Byki?*"

"Why, you going to whack him? Steal the maid? The big-screen TV?"

"What does he have?"

"Nothing."

"He's got no one?" he said. Though he realized he'd never seen the old man with anyone but family. Lexi drove for himself. Traveled alone. They had dropped him off once, at Kennedy, for a late-night flight he was catching for business back in Russia, and he'd gone alone. Smiling. Felix asking him if he had everything.

Later, they'd come back doing eighty on the expressway in the Lincoln, he remembered. Felix only had his permit. Martin seeing in his eyes for the first time the crash that had killed the older brother and put Fee in the hospital for three months just before starting high school. Just before they met. The brother who'd always kept a picture of Sean Connery with him, Fee'd once told him. Hardly knowing Martin at the time, but opening up. Even cried, a bit. The brother used to put the picture in the edge of every mirror he'd be spending any time with. Wore blazers and cashmere turtlenecks. Had a European sportscar.

Martin looked at Fee in the half-ring of mirrors. You're older now than your brother in that crack-up, he thought.

"It's different," Fee said. "My father's just used to working alone. In Russia, you made your way up on your own. With the Italians, everyone's got to have a piece. A job. A button. A thousand people coming around, and you send them to do this and that while you sit there like the pope. It's stupid. Do things yourself. If you can't, hire out. It's the way of the West. The guys over in Russia still, have a brotherhood. An old-fashioned kind of thing. My father was a virtuoso in the black market, though. The first, and still the best. Forget brotherhood. Hands to hold. Mouths to feed."

Exactly how the neighborhood was, Martin thought. Rocco on top, Joe Moon and Peter, Charlie Mirra, Marzolino, below him, then everybody else just scratching by. Hanging out for scraps off the table. Fee was right about that. Though he'd never had to deal with them himself. Had met them, he'd said, once or twice with the old man, but that was it. *"This is my son, Felix."*

It was a definite difference between Fee and him. Fee with no interest in the charade, just the power. Let other people play games. Fee saying now "They were hustlers. There was no tradition anymore. After World War Two everything stopped over there. My father didn't go to kindergarten till he was fourteen."

"You told me. Ten times."

"I'm just saying, the *vori*—the old-time guys—were in jail. *All* of them. The government locked them up for good, with no trials or anything. The new guys had to take over everything. Dodging hits the old-timers put out from jail. He did everything alone."

" 'Dodging hits,' " Martin said. "Don't talk like a toughguy, Fee, please. The velvet shoes ruin it."

"I'm just saying."

"I'm just saying he should get a bodyguard. He's up there with the guineas now. The capos."

" 'The *ca*pos,' why? Someone pulls a gun, he'll push my uncle, Monya, in front of it. He's gotten this far with no one on the payroll. Maybe a little for Monya so he doesn't embarrass himself, but there's no one hanging around. No *famiglia*." He ran his fingerbacks out from under his chin. Then smiled, looked around for the hit man. Like a nervous little kid. "Keep my voice down," he said. The hit man walking back from the other side of the store. Fee said, "Over here, there's no need for strict organizing. Part of all *zapodlo* is sent up to him—"

"Crime money," Martin said.

"Very good. He mediates disputes and gives counsel. And he's cleared for takeoff on absolutely everything by the Italians because they take their shitty little risk-free eight percent. But he never goes down into the street. I mean, he lives in Manhattan, yes, but if he has to meet someone in Brooklyn, he does it in his car. Everyone knows you never make a move for somebody in their car. They always have the advantage. If they meet you in their car it's like, 'I'm prepared to kill you, but, please, feel free to come in.' "

Martin shrugged—*Okay*—but still wanted to make his point—"He should look out more; that's all I'm saying. Guys are always dying in my neighborhood. He should be a little nervous. And . . . fucking . . . he *is*. Don't give me that."

"What are you talking about?"

"You said he took a gun to *syn*agogue."

"Just the holster, I told you. That was three years ago."

"It's a synagogue, for Christ's sake."

"He took it there one time. The first time he'd been, in like thirty years, and the last time for another thirty. One time. When my mother's tests came back negative. He gave a little thanks."

"You think the guineas bring their *pistolas* to mass, Christmas Eve, when their mother-in-laws drag them out of the house?"

"The Italians are chumps now, my father says. They fight mock battles with each other to make themselves feel like they're doing something. Little territory wars, with guys just a bit older than us shooting each other in discos. The old ones go to jail for contempt of court for refusing to testify in cases that are ten years old. They come out talking about how they read Machiavelli the whole time. Six months to read a fifty-page book you read in a night. It's like a fad with them now. And they actually take it seriously."

"You took it seriously when we read it for class. You were all 'This is the blueprint. The how-to manual for absolute power.' You think you *are* the prince."

"I *am* a prince. But I'm not Italian. And what Machiavelli teaches is how to suppress your weaknesses. Then shows what logically follows when you do. He taught by example. 'Cunning in exile,' remember?" He shrugged, Fee. Like it wasn't his fault that the truth was true. "They're chumps." The kind of thing he'd been saying a lot of lately.

There was more to it than his trying out toughguy talk, though. He spoke like the old man would be taking over soon without the guineas even knowing it. Like Lexi'd be smiling politely the whole time.

Fee took off his glasses, cleaned them with his T-shirt. Went over to the suit bag where it was hanging and read the store logo on it up close. "This place is the best. We're going to look good. Yours looked good on you." Put the glasses back on. Looked himself over. Bent and brushed at the shoes with his fingers. "This guy is getting really bad headaches," he said, "so he goes to the doctor. Doctor examines him and says, 'I've got mixed news. I can get rid of your headaches for you but there'll be some surgery. Have to take your genitals off.' 'My genitals?' the guy says. Doctor says, 'Yup. The whole package.' But these headaches," Fee said—"you can't imagine, so he gets the surgery." He stood up, kept studying the shoes. "And the headaches *are* gone, it's true. And the guy gets out of the hospital and says, 'You know, my package wasn't everything; life goes on. And should be celebrated. In style. I'm going to get myself a new suit of clothes.' So he goes to the tailor, first thing, and says, 'I need a suit. The best you have.' The tailor looks him over, nods, says, 'Excellent. You're a thirty-eight regular?' The guy says, 'Yeah. How'd you know?' Tailor says, 'Am I a professional? It's my business. Fifty years. You want a shirt?—thirty-four, sixteen?' Guy says, 'Yeah'— impressed. 'You want the whole outfit?' tailor says—'socks? Underwear?' 'Yeah. Why not? And the underwear . . . ?' the guy says—'What size?'— trying to catch him. The tailor says, 'Thirty-six.' Guy says, 'Aw . . . Not quite. But close, I'll give you that. I'm a thirty-four.' Tailor says, 'No, thirty-four's too tight; they'll press your nuts against your spine; you'll get headaches.' "

They laughed.

Looked at each other and laughed again. Martin saw the hit man glance their way and backed out of view to laugh harder. Stopped and asked the thing that the guy'd reminded him of in the first place—"So your uncle does them?" Took a good breath.

"Does what? Monya doesn't do anything. He drinks."

"The hits."

"What hits?"

"Who does them, asshole? You say this Severed Nazi—"

"Shevard*nadze*—"

"No shit, man, I'm kidding. You say he kicked you out of Russia and it cost your father so much you came here with nothing. That's nine years ago. Your father's a janitor in a hotel at first, and two years later he's running Brooklyn?"

"Shrewd businessman."

"Just . . . who does them?"

"Well, think about it; I just freaking told you no one works for him but Monya and Monya's a waste. Put it together."

"Tell me *one* example. Why's everything got to be a freaking mystery?" Fee went back in the mirrors.

Was thinking of *some*thing, but wouldn't come out and say it.

The idea of it shimmered in the air, though. Difficult to see beside familiar reality. Lexi an all-business shooter, whenever necessary.

"How many, you think, Feel?" Martin said. "Come on."

Felix didn't say anything.

The image crowded in in flashes—the look on the old man's face walking up, taking the Walther from the holster, and *bang*. Someone who'd been in the way. Or someone who'd crossed him. Or was just a disappointment, maybe. Martin had *seen* that look. When Fee took a bottle of Chivas from the credenza, brought it to a party, and returned it near empty. The old man going to make a drink one afternoon and, smiling while Felix was telling him about some girl he'd met, lifted the bottle and turned. Wondrous paternal love drying up, disappearing. Disgust coming into his eyes. Felix froze, stammered. "I drank it, Mr. Pasko," Martin had said. Said now, "You should tell me, Feel. At least something."

Felix looked in the mirrors—left, right. More deciding than looking, really, put his hands on his hips. "Before Puerto Rico this time, he killed his former boss and partner. A guy who happened to get here first because he was kicked out of *Rus*sia first because he came from Schevardnadze's home district."

They stared at each other through the mirror. Fee's eyes were locked. He was serious.

Whoa.

But there was something wrong in the story, Martin realized. Came up closer to him—"You said Lexi *was* the boss. You just *said* that, man."

"Now he is. It was just details. Matter of time. This guy worked in the street. He was basically just an extortionist with a cattleprod, but my father was earning. He thought of all the gas scams, started them alone, cut the Italians in. He got tired, finally, of this guy saying he wanted some. It was time to be lonely at the top. And the police still haven't even found the *body*." Fee shrugged, eyebrows up.

Martin couldn't look away from him. Thought how Fee was born from that man. Had his blood.

Fee said, "Happy I told you?" weird-cheerful-like.

"Actually no. You talk too much for a Mafia kid. You're chatty."

"Because I know you'd never tell anyone. As long as we live, we'll never know anyone as well as we know each other. It's fate."

"It's that you're gay, I think."

"Extremely possible. Here's this guy, finally"—motioning with his head. The tailor coming back, with his pants. "I thought maybe he didn't even work here. Measured my inseam and left."

"Fee, how fucking many?" Martin said. He just wanted a number. Thought *then* he'd have some idea what it took to be a man who feared no one. Which was simply *being* a man—there was no other way to be one.

Fee shrugged.

"Come *on*," Martin said. The tailor came up between them, turned toward Fee, saw they were talking, and hesitated. Martin ignored him, said, "They say Capone killed over a hundred guys on his way up. By himself."

Fee said, "Great businessman."

"He died in jail."

"The person we're talking about pays his taxes."

The tailor looked from Felix's face to Martin's, and back again. Smiled. Was a little confused. Looked stalled-out-like. Glanced down at the pants and then held them out, remembering what he was there for, and, now, not wanting to be. A small old man.

Felix took the pants by the waist and stepped in. He'd been getting off recently saying suggestive little things in front of people about who he might know, or be. Liked to make them wonder, these people who didn't matter. Had a growing confidence now that could sometimes turn a tailor, or anyone like that, into a nervous servant. *"Lift your arms, please, sir . . . We can finish this up at the counter, if you like"* and not another word. Probably slipping in back for a nervous cigarette when this teenage heir apparent was gone.

Martin studied himself, over Fee's shoulder, in the mirror. Wondered could he ever pull a trigger when the opportunity came. He'd certainly looked at his reflection a hundred times, Travis Bickle–style, and tried it, seeing his eyes as *they* would see them—the neighborhood guys who fucked around too much, the black kids on the subway who stared for a second too long before turning away, dismissive, not knowing who he was, where he'd been. He'd say to them, in the bathroom mirror, *"You think you know me? You don't know me."*

Felix caught his look, recoiled. Said, "This mirror ain't big enough for the both of us. I better get my pants and mosey."

Martin smiled. Got red. Said, "Much obliged," and stepped back, out of everyone's view.

When the Irish hit man left, a while later, with his boss's tux slung over his shoulder in the same steel-gray garment bag as Martin's, Fee turned his head and watched him go. The hit man glancing at the three of them there and opening the door and going out. Not a fraction of interest crossing his face. Fee turned back again, his arms still out beside him. A muscular teenage scarecrow. "Freaking gofer," he said, and looked down at the tailor and smiled—the tailor pulling the tape around him timidly, respectfully.

Eminence, Martin had thought, certain it was the right use of the word. And felt his take on Feel beginning to change again, just a little, right there—his having money, having a father. It could make you confident in front of anybody, he realized. And make you look like a bit of a fool if you weren't careful.

A bit of one.

Felix said to the tailor, not smiling suddenly, "Sir, let me ask you a question. I've been getting these terrible headaches—" and laughed.

The tailor jerked back a little, then smiled. Kept working. "I think I know that one."

Fee laughed again. "You do?" Looked around at Martin. "Q, he knows that one—" Martin already nodding.

"I heard, Feel," he said.

▪   ▪   ▪

T he one who was his, Connie Duomo, was kind of weepy. In the beach picture, she'd been smiling, but in person, the money, the cars, and the world of Westchester all around like an embrace was wasted on her. Something else had a hold of her. Made her look like she'd cry, any second. He didn't care what that other thing was; there was too much to take in tonight.

The older sister, Gina Duomo, Felix's date, was a dink, but nice enough.

And the brother, Marco, was what the neighborhood would call a retard. Not truly handicapped above the neck, but the kind of guy who fucked up everything, from your good mood to the whole neighborhood's reputation, because he just didn't give a shit and knew you knew that there was nothing to stop him short of killing him. Which sometimes happened, but not too often. This retard, though, was so connected, you couldn't even get in his face without permission—his father a don. And, plus, he was twenty-two—was a man. So, he was simply to be avoided, shut out completely.

Which was the thing to do with *all* the dumb Duomo siblings, Martin decided.

He sat watching the evening in Westchester pass outside the window of the limo, the banquet hall coming into view as they mounted a hill into a long, circular drive, the building glowing in the darkness, all white, with columns and terraces—a luxury hotel rising up out of nothing, like—like a mirage, but real—and he stepped out of the car and gave his hand for this Connie to hold, and didn't take his eyes off of the place. He accompanied her inside, all the way to the table, and didn't say a word for a while. What he felt was that this hall had been waiting here over the hill like a proof of something God would do. Like it had been waiting for him since the day he was born. This night, just starting, would end, he knew, and he'd be back to high school and muling smack for Peter and Joe, throwing the loft parties with Fee, and running stupid errands for Rocco. But, a ballroom with chandeliers and centerpieces? Escorting good-looking Italian girls out of limousines in a tuxedo? This was going to stay with him. He was going to have to find a way to simply make *this* be, from now on. He'd sit here smiling for now, looking over it all. He'd hang out with these people, be a good date. But this was going to be the *new* way to live; it was going to—

Something threw off his thinking. The blonde, from the picture, who'd been looking over things, too, was looking at him. Had seen *him* looking over things.

She smiled. Nodded. Like she knew exactly what he was thinking.

H e ran into Feel in the bathroom, hadn't talked to him since Gina'd pulled him up on the dance floor, soon as the music started—was one of those girls who danced without a break, Gina, swinging her perm around, her hands in little fists at her sides—he said to him, "Don't get concerned, Fee, but I plan to have a good time without Connie. Who wears a fucking shawl at a dinner table?"

Fee said, "She's cold."

"Why doesn't she dance and get warm?"—though he hadn't even asked her. But that wasn't the point. He said, "It's a fucking granny shawl. It looks like her granny made it. I don't want to see some girl wrapped up like an old lady, dying, at my prom."

"It's not your prom. Are you ready? We going back to the table?"

"Are we girls? Are we taking a powder?"

"We're *in* here already."

"We *met* in here. Pure chance. You go out first. And remember"—pointed at him, warning—"don't worry if I brush this girl off. Don't get involved."

"Do what you like," Fee said, and started back. "Gina already told me she wants to pretend she's a virgin again so she can lose it at her prom. I *have* plans. You make your own. We'll figure out rides home later," and was gone.

He looked in the mirror. Thought about it, again. Take his shot with the blonde, or was it all wrong now? Not ten minutes ago, he'd watched her leave Marco Duomo on the dance floor and head to the lobby, so he'd followed her. Kept way back, but tailed her. Watched her walk for the doors and go into her purse for a cigarette, step out into the portico, the lights bright on her, and pale, and she lit the cig and walked off, down the circular drive. Smoking and walking. Taking time to herself, checking her look every now and then in the limousines' windows. He'd watched her, decided he'd wait till she came back up, then he'd talk to her. He leaned on a column and listened to the sound of her satiny shoes on the gravel. Then the brother, Marco, came outside. After her. Said, "Where you going?"

"Just walking."

"Well, stop. You shouldn't go walking without me."

She stopped.

Martin looked around the column, careful. She was smiling, flirty, as far as he could see. She was teasing. Said, "Why? You seemed happy dancing with Sandra Ricci, slut that she is."

"You jealous?"—stepped in close to her, the guy.

"You crazy?"—she stepped back. Looked the limousine over behind her, dusted away something she saw, and sat.

"Jealous is good," he said, and did a little disco move—rolled his fists in tight, by his body. "Gets girls going."

"O my God, you're not crazy; you're retarded," she said, and took a drag and looked off, blew out the smoke and laughed.

The guy's arms went flat at his sides. He was still smiling, though. Still trying. She looked at him again. "You still here?" she said.

Then he wasn't smiling. Suddenly looked his age completely. He stepped in closer to her and tipped his head, studied her. Was emptied of humor, like.

She tried to keep cool, but after he stood there, a while, staring, she looked afraid to even swallow. Martin couldn't move. His knees, his arms, were weak. Like the guy was in *his* face.

"You put on a nice dress, you got limos all around you, you think you're in Hollywood?" the guy said. "You think 'cause this night ain't real I won't slap that fucking look off you? 'Cause I'm real, girlie. You think I won't throw you in this limo, tell the driver, 'Take a walk'—do what I want to you? Make you do it to me?" Stayed there, in her face. Cars passed on the road, below—headlights shafting through the trees. Three, four of them, going by. The guy said, "You should know better. Even at your age," and she nodded—a sudden, spastic agreement. "Tell my sisters I took the limo. If I feel like it, I'll send it back," he said. He looked, and spotted it further down, walked to it, got in. In a few long moments, it was making the turn at the base of the hill, its headlights cutting through the trees, was gone. The older guy was gone.

Martin looked at her. Still leaning on the car. She hadn't moved at all, staring ahead at nothing. Her pale, shiny dress soft-looking on the shiny black steel, her cigarette in her fingers, down at her side, smoke crawling up her arm.

He went in. Had to piss and met Felix in the bathroom. Had already made up his mind he'd forget about Connie and ask this one they were calling Penny to dance, if she came back inside. *"Do what you like,"* Fee'd said.

He looked his skin over in the mirror. Splashed water on his face, fixed his hair right. He went back to the table. Connie excused herself and left. He didn't care. He didn't watch her go. He hoped Penelope would come back. *Pen*ny, he corrected himself.

Gina said, "O God, give me a break, Connie"—barely looking up from spiking their goblets of Coke with the flask of rum she'd brought. "I'm sorry, Q. You want a sip?" and stretched a glass across to him. He thanked her, drank some, kept it. She worked on all the other glasses. Fee was smiling, keeping an eye on the chaperones. This Penny came in, came over, stood, by the table.

"I think I scared Marco away," she said. "He said he may send the limo back."

Gina looked up, smiling. Was waiting for the punchline, maybe.

"Sorry," this girl, Penny, said. Who'd just called a don's son a retard.

Gina said, "O my God, I don't believe this." She looked amazed. "What dingbats, my family, no?"

Felix looked at him, narrowed his eyes, wondering should they say something. Threaten something. Martin looked back at her. Penny. She was smiling. Distracted-looking, though. She sniffled.

Gina said, "You were crying?"

"For what? I got ash in my eye. I went outside for a cig."

"I was going to say. 'Cause don't cry over my brother. He's even dumber than me."

They laughed. Gina handed her a drink.

H e called her the next week from Felix's apartment and she picked him up at the train station. Bronxville. Westchester. "My mother thinks I'm shopping," she said; "we can't go too far." There was a seriousness to her, now. On the phone she'd been playing cool. Like she was painting her toenails, or something. It'd been fine, her wanting to work it that way. He'd just kept remembering how she'd been on the dance floor with him, for the rest of the prom. The strapless dress she kept having to pull up, and her eyes that were really a dark blue, up close. And the warmth that glowed off her. But this somberness now, though? He didn't like it. This was a long way to come if she was going to jerk him around.

They drove a few minutes. To a small park. With a little round lake. Got out. They walked. Her leading, but he kept beside her, in front of her, even, tracking her movements looking sideways. Without heels, she was smaller than he'd thought.

They came to a bench and she sat. He put a couple of feet between them and sat also, leaned on his knees, looked around at her, looked away. "Fee got your number from Gina," he said.

"She won't tell Connie. They hate each other."

"Good reason to tell her."

"She'll enjoy laughing about it. She'll talk about it behind her back. Connie'll find out anyway. Story of her life."

"You want to do that shopping?" he said. "I could just go with you."

"Take me five minutes."

She looked at her watch.

"You ever come into the city?"

She said, "Sometimes. With Gina. My mother likes her."

"Because of her old man. Big Mafioso."

She looked at him.

"People trust him," he said.

"Wouldn't you?"

"A certain way, I guess. She's a nut though, Gina."

"Yeah, she's wild. But her parents don't know it. And she's good with Felix."

"Yeah, he's crazy, too," he said.

Thought, Not crazy, just out for himself.

There was no point explaining it, though.

She said, "You're close. You like him."

He gestured he guessed so.

"You can say it. He talks about you all the time."

"We're close, yeah."

"But different."

"Different worlds."

"He told me."

"Told you what?"

"Where you're from."

"He talks a lot."

"I know all about you. And him, too. Mostly *him,* of course."

"Like?"

"His family. His brother being dead. His father."

"What about his father?" He'd meant for her to say what she knew about *him,* but he let it go. Kept his eyes on the lake.

She said, "Who he is. It's all around me. Look where I live. Fee knew I was already keeping secrets like that."

"What's your father do?"

"He owns a cement company."

He smiled. "He makes shoes?"

"My father's not in the Mafia"—she said it low, tightened her voice on it. "He works hard. He's a saint. He comes home exhausted, six nights a week."

"Gina and Connie's father owns half the cement in New *York,*" he said.

"Cement *com*panies. *Plu*ral. More than one."

He shrugged, to tell her okay. But he didn't see the difference. She wouldn't acknowledge what was right in front of her. It must be true then, he thought—the old-time guineas kept their business from their daughters.

She wasn't saying anything now.

He let a minute pass, figured he'd use the silence against her. Told her his father was dead.

She said she didn't know; Felix hadn't told her.

But she didn't ask how. And he could tell she wouldn't. He liked that. "Fee doesn't really *know* about it," he said. "Not the details. He doesn't know a *lot* about me. Makes me wonder what everything was he told you." He looked at her.

"That you come from the Village, from Thompson Street. Which I know all about because my mother first lived there when she came here. She lived upstairs from the social club. She used to ask Joseph Lamentia to help her make telephone calls. Couldn't figure the phone out, for some reason."

"I live over that club now," he said.

"You do not."

He nodded. "No lie. I know Lamentia's grandson, too. A kid named Bunny—"

"*Bunny?* Is his name?"

"Yeah, his real name's Pasquale, but—"

She laughed. Found that even funnier. "Easter Bunny," she said. "Okay. I got it."

He nodded. Bobbed his head once, like if she was filled-in now, he could continue. Though he'd never actually gotten the name before. He'd always freaking wondered. "Yeah, I went to school with him, Bunny."

"Grammar school."

"Yeah."

"You go to private school now, with Felix."

"Yeah, my mother sent me." He moved a twig with his shoe. Felt her looking at him, waiting for him to look at her. He did.

"You'd rather be in school with a bunch of meatballs?" she said. "Like Marco Duomo?"

He smiled, looked away. Because she was sharp. He'd been praying she was. That warmth on the dance floor and that chill in the parking lot both inside her.

"Felix told me," she said; "I know." Nonchalant. No big thing to her. He bit his teeth tight to not smile harder. "How you were really defensive when you showed up the first day of school. Fourteen, dressed like a guido. Matching leather tie and shoes. Totally out of place."

"They're all rich there," he said. "I'm not one of them. I don't want to be."

"Felix is rich. You stay over at his apartment like five nights a week, right? Eat dinner with him and his parents. Flirt with the Polish maid."

"He's different. What he knows from his father makes him different."

"Why'd your mother make you go?"

"Fee didn't tell you that part?"

"He said you got into some trouble in your neighborhood and your mother didn't want you going to high school with the guys you hung around with."

"That's it, basically."

"What did you do? What *trouble* did you get into?"

He lied—"I got pinched selling fireworks. One too many times. Family court called and said they were sending my case to juvey, and she freaked, my mother. She asked around her office, got me an interview uptown. A scholarship." The last part true enough for him to look her in the face. "That was it."

"Did you go to court?"

"Juvey? No. I must have fallen through the cracks. Unless they're still looking for me."

They smiled.

"Are you still up to no good?"

"Are you asking, or Fee told you?"

"He said you run some things out of your school."

"He wants to be a bigshot. He was trying to impress you."

"No doubt, but is it true?"

"We throw parties, and charge at the door. Rent out lofts and spread the

word the weekend before and print up flyers, buy the booze and quadruple
the cost. We run some card games. Those kids have money to burn, up
there. I tried a little numbers action, but no one knew what the hell I was
talking about."

"You sell pot?"

"No. He told you that?"

"I was just wondering. That's what people do around here for money."

"Drugs are off-limits," he said. "Bad business, in the long run"—giving
her the straight course of denial. Cradle to grave. Just like the wiseguys.

But she was looking at him. Flat. Like he was talking around the truth so
she'd keep waiting to hear it.

He said, "The Lamentias don't run the Village anymore. A guy named
Rocco DiNabrega does. He whacked out Bunny's father a few years ago."
He was more comfortable talking about Mafia things he knew. There were
a thousand good stories, and people always wanted to hear them.

She said, "What are *your* long-term plans?"

It took him by surprise. He looked at her.

"You want to be a *wise*guy?" she said.

"No, why?"

He did, more than anything, but the arc in her eyebrow made him hold
back what he would have said—that he was becoming one, but it took time
when you weren't Sicilian.

"You say you got '*pinched*'; that '*juvey*' called your mother; that you
wanted to run a little '*num*bers action.'" She laughed at that one. "'The
Lamentias don't *run* things no more. He got whacked out.'"

"I didn't say '*no more.*' I'm not a mook. Me and Fee are at the top of our
class behind a couple of geeks that have no lives. I can do whatever I want
in life."

"That's what I'm asking you."

"What's your beef with"—he stopped, glanced at her. She smiled and
raised her eyebrow again, had her wiseass comeback ready. "What's your
problem with me?"

"Nothing at all. I just don't want to be with a hoodlum."

"I'm not a freaking hoodlum."

"I know. I wouldn't be here."

"Neither would I," he said, and looked away from her. It made no sense, the response, but he couldn't think of how else to say it.

"Look at me."

He did.

She said, "Listen; I'm going to tell you something." He nodded—her tone sounding like if he *did* listen, they'd be on the level with each other; there'd be no issue between them. She said, "But you have to understand what I'm really saying. Because my father . . . *is.* Connected. Everyone around me is. But he's not a killer, though. He invests in their operations. Doesn't really have a choice now, I guess. And, yes, it's the very definition of racketeering, I know, and he has people on the street, I think, who run a crew for him, but . . . *but,* to be in that business you *need* a crew. You know that. You don't just bid for construction jobs." She paused. Her eyes were wide. She wanted a response. He nodded. Shrugged, like *Of course.* "But, he did *choose* it," she said—"I know. And that's what I really want you to understand. He might have known better, maybe not. Maybe he's a wised-up immigrant businessman, and I'm naive. But you and I are from *this* generation. The next one. We don't need to be that. I'm not going to want to be with you if you want to be that."

It was like that scene in *The Godfather* he'd never understood—Marlon Brando telling Pacino "I wanted you to be senator." Who would want to be senator if you could be don? he'd always thought.

She said, "Do you understand?"

He nodded. "Yes. Of course."

"So I'm going to kiss you. Okay?"

"No."

"Yeah, right."

She kissed him—took his face in her hands, turned it gently to hers and looked in his eyes, closed hers, kissed his lips. Opened her eyes again and smiled. He didn't smile back. "What's wrong?"

"You act like you know me," he said. Made like it bothered him, looked away.

"I do. I know you."

"Felix tell you when I first met him I threatened him? I walked in the wrong homeroom and he was sitting there with a bunch of rich kids and they looked me over and he laughed until I told him to shut the fuck up? And he did? Did you know that?"

"Yes. He also says you bounce at all the parties but that you never hit anyone. You talk them out of whatever it is. And that you've saved his butt in the street when he was drunk and being stupid. You took the blame when he stole a bottle of vodka from his father, and his father said you couldn't hang out with him anymore, and then let you back in the house and told you you were very loyal." She gave his face a soft jerk toward hers, so he'd look at her. He did. "All true?"

"It was scotch," he said.

She gave him a tap-smack with her fingertips, then kissed the spot. "So do I know you?"

"You've met me, sure."

"Don't crack wise. Do I know you? Say it."

"I know you."

"Say it."

And he would, eventually—*"Do I know you?"* *"Yes"*—would tease her for a while, then let her hear it. When it only seemed like words to him. But what he would always remember, after it, was that whether or not she *did* know?—the way that she'd looked at him, she'd seemed to. And it had made him feel that it could be good to let her know him from then on. That it would be right to. It would relieve something in him. Bring an end. And a beginning, maybe. It had made him feel, suddenly, that life was maybe something to really look forward to.

T he nun was moving around, straightening things, it sounded like. He could feel it was late. Sensed the sun was down.

He'd only opened his eyes a few times in the last few hours—few days,

maybe—and only to slits. To better hear Corso in the hall. Corso'd be forcing him to come around soon, he knew, if he didn't do it on his own. A
marshal outside the room, around the clock now.

The nun coughed—a short, constricted sound.

She was old and had an accent. He'd heard her talking to Corso, picked
up *she* didn't like the man either.

He listened to her moving.

Constant, and near silent.

Strange characters, nuns. Patient and humble. Had practically bowed to
him as a kid, when all of Saint Anthony's had been convinced he'd be off
to the seminary and into the priesthood. What else would a boy with his
grades be? He'd believed it himself for a while. Then the Italians had taken
notice of him. Had something much more fine to offer a kid. So the sisters
and fathers saw what he really wanted to be and forgot him. Simply cut
him off. Which had been just fine.

What's black and white and has a dirty name?

Sister Mary Fuckface.

It had been just fine. Running home from school to drop his books and
change his shoes, then sitting on a bench downstairs, outside the park, and
waiting in case the wiseguys needed him. *"Kid, come here. Get my jacket from
my car . . . Get me a sandwich . . . Go to Arturo's for an abitz . . . Get me cigarettes . . . Who else wants? . . . Two L&Ms, two Camel, one Parliament. And
whatever you want for yourself."* Though he never bought anything he really
wanted. He always came right back, ignoring any kids he saw on the street
who weren't hustling like him now. Would only take a slice of the pizza if
the lunch at school had been shit. Running errands September to May and
selling fireworks beginning of summer. Worked the stands at the feasts,
worked the basement casinos during the race and football seasons. Learned
the general art of getting over on people. Went to work in secret for Joe
Moon and Sweet Peter Hughes at fourteen, when trust was built, making a
hundred dollars a delivery, then two, when business took off. Three years
like that, until they disappeared suddenly, and Rocco called him onto the
carpet. *"You don't work here no more. The shop's closed."*

Spent the next week drunk in Feel's apartment.

Fee dressing every morning and warning him one last time that he was leaving for school without him.

Then beating that poor bastard in Jersey half to death before Felix pulled him off. Beating him thinking when he was dead there'd be no more anger, no more worries. Not worried about him or anyone else because he's going to die and I'm pounding on him. But Felix pulling, so everyone lives.

The nun paused her cleaning. She was standing over him. Suspected he was awake. She checked his IV. Stood there a minute. Moved away.

Felix pulled him off and got the money from the safe and got him into the car and back to the city, then was sitting there in the apartment counting the money on the couch while he drifted in and out of blackouts. Felix gone the next morning when he finally woke up. The maid brought him a breakfast. Set it up on a folding tray before him where he sat off the edge of the bed with his face in his hands. He ate a bit of it. Watched a war picture on the tele. Turned it off and took a shower and caught the train up to Times Square and joined the army. *Battleground,* the picture was, with Van Johnson. The recruiter looked over his enlistment papers, thanked him for his commitment, shook his hand, and wished him happy birthday— eighteen that morning, at the edge of the bed. With his face in his hands.

He was gazing at the black-screen TV.

"You are awake," she said. Old foreign penguin.

He nodded. It seemed proper not to answer her out loud. Like being at a funeral—anything he said might not be right. He closed his eyes again, then let them come open, stopped fighting it.

"They are not here," she said—"it's late," and tucked the bottom of the bed in. He looked at her. Like a stump down there. A dark, withered old stump in full habit. But healthy. Not steadying herself on anything. Had dark little eyes. "You are hungry at all?"

He said he wasn't.

"You are very thin, eating from this tube."

"It's tasty."

"Yes, I'm sure."

He turned his head to see the IV. Pain caught him, made him wince.

"You are still in pain. Not healed inside. But you are very lucky." She kept tucking, worked her way up the bed. "A CIA letter opener" she said. With difficulty. Phrasing it carefully. "What you were hurt with. The agent told me. Made from plastic. A government weapon."

He smiled and shook his head. Said, "No." He'd known, somehow, that the thing wasn't metal. No glint when the kid had raised it. The doormen at Anastasia's carried them, and plastic brass knuckles. *Polymer Paperweights,* they were sold as. Weighed three-quarters of an ounce. His own gun had been mostly plastic. Weighed as much as a mug of coffee. Corso probably leaning over some guy's shoulder right now in Forensics making sure that the prints were all consistent. "You get them from a catalogue, sister," he said. "The backs of magazines. Anywhere."

She clucked her tongue. Lifted his head and punched his pillow, set his head back. She studied the bandage, touched at it. A pinched face, she had. The infirmary nun at Saint Anthony's had once checked him for lice like this, he remembered—her face in right over his. And even *then* he hadn't trusted nuns being nurses. Patient, humble ignoramuses, they were. Aging, good young girls who never actually *knew* anything. Experienced nothing.

"It is much better, your ear. I saw it last night. They can give you plastic surgery, create a new one."

"Where are you from?"

"Hungary."

"How long have you been here?" She sounded like she just arrived—he was squinting to understand her. It was getting on his nerves. Like the effort strained his stitches.

"Fifty years."

"You ever heard of Maria Ouspenskaya?"

"No."

"She played the gypsy fortune-teller in all the old monster movies."

"No."

"No movie night in the convent?"

He looked away from her. Knew she wouldn't answer him. Attending to him now, but a side of her turning away from him, now that he was awake, was real. He said, *"Bevare of de verevulf."*

"They did not stab you, the agents?"

"No."

She walked away. Rearranged the small pillow in her chair. "Did a *vere-vulf*?" She sat, looked at him.

He smiled. "You're nosy for a penguin."

She lowered her eyes, apologized.

He said it was all right. He was sorry—his chest hurt. "You've been taking care of me," he said, "hunh?"

"Four days."

"You work here?"

"I am a volunteer. A trained nurse."

He nodded. Thanked her.

She didn't respond.

"There's other nurses, though? I've only seen you."

"One other. The agent likes me to stay."

"Corso?"

"Yes."

"Figures your heart won't get in the way."

She looked at him. Eyes trying to understand just behind their surface.

"You'll do your duty," he said. "Won't get involved."

She looked away from him. For something to get up and do, he guessed.

"Like right now," he said. Waited, a second. "I know nuns; it's all right. You don't get involved."

"You're . . ." She stopped.

"What? I've known nuns, sister. So has Corso; believe me. I don't hold it against you. I'd just rather be talking to somebody who knows who Maria Ouspenskaya is. Someone who doesn't only know Spencer Tracy flicks."

"You are a criminal," she said.

He smiled. "No, sister. I shot someone in self-defense. Keep your eyes on the papers, the next few months. You'll feel bad you judged me."

"You are, without judgment. I don't judge you."

"Yeah, I know; God does. Not your responsibility. Nothing is. Get the other nurse, though, would you? Take a break."

"You *are* a criminal."

"Jesus *Christ,*" he said—his chest starting to burn—"it was self-defense. Don't believe everything the priests and federal agents tell you."

"Beneath. Inside. Criminal."

He squinted at her. "Are you *kid*ding?" he said. "Get the other nurse."

"You are rude and arrogant. It is a fact. These tattoos"—motioned fierce at his forearms.

" 'These tat*toos,*' " he said. "Get the other nurse."

"I get the doctor."

"No."

"You are awake"—she was up again—"the doctor must see you."

"Sister, please."

"You cannot pretend to sleep anymore."

"Sister . . ."

She stopped.

"I'd be asleep if you . . . I'll see them tomorrow, all right? And every day, for a long time; believe me."

She put a hand on the back of the chair.

He said, "Just let me lie here. I can't think with them here. They hear what they want."

"You must be examined."

"I'm well. I can feel that. Let me get better. Don't send them in here. You know how they are, sister; I've heard you talk to them."

She looked at the door. Glanced at it. Like if Corso came in right this moment, she'd never interfere, but . . . the door was closed.

"Just sit down," he said, "please. I don't know you. I'm sorry."

He'd seen them pretend to be insulted when he was a kid—they could be as shifty as anyone. But this one was better than that, he suspected. Her eyes far, far more intelligent. Like a soul in there. A history. Maybe some doubting of the Word. It wasn't her fault she had just the right accent to crease him at the moment. That choked-up, Eastern Bloc lilt.

Finally she sat. Looked away from him and kept her mouth tight. Was half sitting on a folded newspaper tucked down between the arm of the chair and her leg. He'd heard her turning pages during his half-sleep, he remembered. "Am I in there?" he said. "In your newspaper?"

"You are unconscious and critical, it says. A murder suspect. An organized criminal."

He stared away from her, at the door. They both stayed how they were,
a while. He thought of Rocco and Peter Hughes and Joe Moon and Bunny
Lamentia. Terry Hughes. Thought of heroin and extortion and counterfeiting. Men beaten. Men snuffed. He thought of it all like a round, solid
mass. A mental picture of a tumor inside him that he'd never get rid of.

Plus, he thought, these tat*toos*.

But he didn't smile.

He looked over at her, let his eyes focus on her. Knew she could feel him
looking, and that he was about to speak. "I am a criminal," he said. But her
expression didn't change.

"We are all sinners," she said, her eyes not moving.

He was ten. His father was dead, a year. And two things were making him wonder. One, was his mother trying to outrun the ghost, because they'd moved three times now, and Two, what was the difference she was making when she spoke about two kinds of people—the families in their building, the Angottis, Polnicettis, Acumanos, were *Italians*, she called them, and the men downstairs, who sat in their beach chairs on the sidewalk in Hawaiian shirts, smoked cigars, and played cards on the hoods of their double- and triple-parked cars while they chatted or stepped into the club on the ground floor for a coffee *"Come inside have a coffee"* with its soupy green, painted windows and recessed doorway and the lights never on during the day so he could never see a thing when he passed—these people she called *the* Italians. He made his way through the beach chairs and around their legs three or four times a day, and they never seemed to notice him. *The* Italians.

One day toward the end of school, when the one he'd heard them calling Joe Moon was grilling things on a wheeled-out barbecue right there, by the front door, he went to go in, past him, and Joe said, "Wait, kid, here," and stabbed a sausage off the grill, gripped it with the end-piece of a loaf of bread, and handed it to him. He looked at it. Joe said, "What's the matter, you don't like the end of the bread? I thought kids loved that. Eat." Had muscles in his arms like the old black dumbbells at the Y, Joe. Cannonballs, like. Wore only sleeveless T-shirts. And, today, an apron.

All the Italians were looking over. They'd stopped their card games and their conversations. Even the one, Rocco, who the kids at school said ran things even though he was only thirty—always in sunglasses—he turned his head, a bit, and looked.

The nearest one, who'd been facing away straddling his chair, put his cards to his chest and looked backwards at them. Smiled, and said, "Kids hate the end, stupid. You liked the end when you were a kid?" He said to Martin, "He wasn't ever a kid." "Sweet" Peter Hughes, "Sweet Pea," had blue eyes like him, and blond hair that stood up. Like him. Was *half* Irish. His brother, Terry, in Martin's class. "You can eat it," he said. "It's okay."

So he did. Took a bite, eventually. But had held out, a couple of seconds.

He liked the attention, all these men waiting to see what he'd do, Sweet Peter Hughes smiling, looking at him level in the eyes, and Joe Moon enormous over them all and powerless until he ate—*"This fucking kid's going to hurt my feelings here"*—and then, when he *did* eat—and smiled, because it was good—Joe saying "See, he knows," to no one in particular, and turning back to the grill.

The whole summer he played in the park, then school was starting again. His mother made no mention of moving. She was buying some things—new towels, a sugar bowl, a vase. The weather got cool, and Peter Hughes and the rest of the Italians moved their card games inside, turned the lights on and closed the door, shut the blind that hung on the back of the door's dusty glass. He was happy. He played in the park every afternoon. His mother would come home from work, would pick up his kid brother, Frito, and they'd pass the fence. He would catch up to them and go upstairs. The days got shorter and colder. He was alone in the park sometimes. Had the jungle gyms, the swings, all to himself. He would survey things from the top of the monkey bars, give out orders, climb down and carry them out, every day leaving off his adventures to pick them up again tomorrow.

One afternoon, he was talking to himself, and he stopped. There were two girls in the park. Standing over by the benches. Older girls. From the eighth grade. He knew who they were. When they heard him, they looked, but he pretended he hadn't been. And they looked away. Were waiting for two boys, he guessed. They were still in their school skirts. Had their hands tucked up in their sleeves for warmth, their arms crossed. He could see their breaths. And his. The metal of the monkey bars cold to him, under his hands. He climbed up, hung off, and jumped down. Climbed up, hung off, jumped down. Couldn't stop looking at them now. Wondered if they'd look again. They didn't. They went foot to foot. Talked too quiet for him to hear. He climbed up and sat, and watched them. The real Italian-looking one that everyone stayed away from on the play street. She was mean, tough. And the *furlani*-looking Italian one. Lighter hair and eyes, personality. She was pretty. He looked away. Looking so hard would draw them to look around. The mean one would say something. *"The fuck you looking at?"*

Someone was coming in, behind him, on the Sullivan Street side. An older guy. Maybe twenty, or twenty-two. Bounced when he walked. Looking around at things. Like he knew where he was. Martin had never seen him before.

He saw Martin, walked by below him, and slapped his foot where it hung down. "What's up, little man? How you doing?" he said. His eyes were on the girls, though. Martin looked at them. They were looking over—had heard the guy—but they looked back. They didn't know him. Whoever they were waiting for would be coming from the other direction, Martin guessed. The guy was looking up at him. And smiled. Raised his eyebrows. Martin realized he hadn't answered him. Was that what he wanted?

"I'm good."

The guy nodded. Looked at the girls again. "Yeah? You're good? Well, that's all you need." And took a cigarette from his jacket. Went to the girls and asked them for a light. They didn't have. He dug around on him and found one. He lit it, and stayed there. He asked them the time, but they didn't know. He said it was cold and the nice one nodded. The mean one looked at him, a second, but didn't say anything, because they were freezing—obviously. Are you kidding or what? her face said. He offered them a cigarette and they shook their heads. Now weren't looking at him, again.

He looked them over. Smiled. Said, "Hey," like he'd just realized something. "Saint Anthony's, right?" He pointed to their skirts. They told him
yeah. He said, "Fucking A. I went there. Mrs. Musante, Sister John Bosco,
Mrs. Montemurro—"

"She's dead," the nice one said. Trying to be hard. Because the guy was
too excited now, having a real reason to talk to them, Martin realized. She
wasn't stupid.

"Who?"

"Mrs. Montemurro. She died."

"Really?"

He looked sad. She looked at him. Then nodded. Like to say yeah, she
knew; death was terrible.

Couldn't stay mean. Taught never to be, probably. Like the nuns taught
them *all,* but it was natural in her. Some people had that. Some girls did.

The guy was looking at her. "She was a *bitch,*" the other one said, and he
looked at her. Was confused which one to agree with, Martin realized. The
guy looking back and forth, between them. The lighter one said, "She *was*
mean," and the guy said, "Yeah, she was. She was a real *bitch,*" and the dark
one said, "That's why we *said* it," and went to sit down. Smoothed her skirt
onto the back of her knees and sat. Being cool. The guy wasn't looking at
her, now, though; he was looking at the nice one.

Martin Quinn turned around on the bars, locked his feet, and hung
upside-down, backwards. Watched to see how it would go—if the guy
could really get her to talk to him, and if he'd ask her out, then. He'd seen
stuff like this before, seen guys talk to girls they liked. This guy was no different. Asking her questions, saying little things quietly, in close to her, now.
Introduced himself, and she did back, and he said, "No," that he couldn't
believe it, that she was somebody's little sister, somebody's cousin. Now she
had to have a cigarette with him. His head all tipped sideways and she smiling back at him. But "No," she said, "not here," waved her hand around at
all the windows on Thompson. He said, "Forget them, come on"—trying
to convince her, and juggled his hands around like *What do I have to do?* All
in gestures now. All silent-movie-kind-of, to Martin, because he couldn't
hear a thing with all the blood in his head, but he could make out every-

thing. Could hang that way for hours. People moving like they were behind glass with a light bouncing off it. This guy here saying "Take a cigarette . . . come on . . . have a drink . . . well, then, how about you?"—and had a little pint bottle in his jacket, and the girls from eighth grade were all "No way . . . Now you're freaking *crazy*," and the guy was all "All right, come over here, then, by the monkey bars. No one'll see," because the buildings on the Sullivan Street side had no windows where they rose up over the playground, and the ones across Sullivan had far more in their way—the trees, a fence, the jungle gyms.

They came over. The guy gave them cigarettes. Martin curled up and turned around again, and the two of them were leaning in to where the guy was holding out a lighter for them—low, just out in front of him. Then they were smoking. Kept them down at their thighs and blew the smoke out sideways. "You smoke, little man?" Martin told him no. The guy said, "Good, that's the way it should be. We're old; it's too late for us," and they laughed—the three of them. The guy said, "I'll bet you don't drink neither," but before Martin could answer, the guy turned to the light-haired one and said, "I bet you take a drink, every once in a while," and she smiled. He said, "See, I knew it," and started to take out the bottle. She had blond in her hair this close. She said, "No. No way," and waved her hands, crisscross, in front of her. Walked away and came back. He said, "Come on." She said, "Not here." He said, "Come in close; no one'll see," and she thought about it. He took the dark one by the arm and brought her in close and reached and took the blond one the same way, brought her in. They looked at each other, the girls, then looked into his jacket where he was screwing the cap off the bottle. He said, "You first?" to the lighter one, and she shrugged okay, and leaned—to drink. He tipped it up for her and they all jumped back. They laughed. He'd spilled it. She was wiping at her lips. And her jacketfront. He said, "Another?" and she held her hand up— *Wait*—and kept wiping. He looked at the other one. She was waiting now. "And how about you?" he said, and she shrugged and closed her eyes like *Yeah, if you work a little harder to convince me, maybe,* and he shrugged, like *Forget it then,* and when she opened her eyes, he was back waiting for the other one to be ready again.

She was mad, the dark one. Her cheeks got purple. She waited for him to see how mad. He looked at the windows on Sullivan Street and brought the blondey girl close to him, because she was ready to try another time. She bent her knees a little, put her face right inside his lapel, and the dark one said, "I'm leaving. You coming? You're going to get in trouble."

The blond one looked out at her. Said, "Why?" But she knew—Martin knew that. And the guy smiled, looking at her, *knowing* she'd stay now, too, because she'd pretended to her friend. And it would *make* the dark one leave, Martin knew. And knew the guy knew that, too. Martin *wanted* her to leave. He'd wanted her friend to drink, and she had; things were fun. Everyone was happy but her. She was ruining things.

She said again, "You're going to get in trouble," and the guy said, "No, you won't; I'll protect you." He put his hands behind his head and made his muscles. He told the blond girl to touch them.

She did—just one—and pulled her hand back, like it was hot. "O my God," she said, "you got to feel them"—to her friend.

"I'm leaving"—she walked away. Out of the park.

Martin watched her walk the length of the fence. Then she was gone. He looked back again, and saw the guy down on one knee, pretending he was wiping at his shoe. Drinking, though. Had his bottom lip stuck out to keep the bottle from dripping. She laughed at him. He looked like a gorilla. Martin smiled. They switched places so the guy was blocking her from the buildings across the street. He put his arms up again, behind his head, and flexed his muscles, told her to drink. Told her again. Then—"One more time." She swallowing like it hurt to, every time. Stood up after a while. Maybe a minute. The bottle in her hand and the cigarette in the other, not bothering to hide them. She was dazed. Looked at the cigarette, burned down to the end, and took a drag on it and dropped it. She looked at the guy. He was smiling at her. He bounced his muscles. "How'd you get those?" she said. "My face is hot."

"Nine months of push-ups, sit-ups, and chin-ups," he said. "These are from chin-ups." He smiled. Stopped, then. His eyes somewhere else in his mind. He said, "First day in a long fucking time I didn't do any," and he looked around for something. Looked at the monkey bars. Looked at Mar-

tin. Started coming over. "Look out, little man," he said, and took the bottle from his jacket and sipped it, put it back. Was right below him now. "I
said look out," and hopped up, caught him by the jacketfront and yanked
him off, forward, and left him flying.

Martin landed on his face, his hands. Then the rest of him slapping
down. He smelled the blood in his head. Tasted black rubber playground
tile. He looked up. She was backed against the wall. Her face a girl's face. A
little girl's. Afraid. Behind him, the guy was doing chin-ups off of the
monkey bars—steady up-and-down. His breath seeping out. Little grunt-
ing puffs. "Motherfucker," Martin yelled, and ran. Toward Thompson.
Looked back as he rounded the fence, then out. The guy still going. He ran
in his building, ran upstairs. Took a pillow from the couch and walked up
and down the hallway, slugging it. Saw the blood he'd dribbled down himself, on his pants, his jacket. With his fingers, pushed at the ache in his teeth.
He went to the kitchen and turned on the faucet and stuck his mouth sideways under the water and saw her, down through the window. In the back
of the park, behind the poolhouse, through a sliver between two buildings.
He'd never noticed it before—how he could see a section of the cement
dead end at the back of the park that was formed by the backs of the three
buildings that rose up around it. Her hair it was, he'd seen. A glint. And
now the guy was there, too. Leading her. With his hand on her back.
Stopped and turned her around and kissed her. She flinched—hunched in
on herself, like, and he did it again. Her forehead, her face, her neck. He
took her by the hand and backed against the wall and brought her to him.
Took off his jacket and laid it on the ground between them, put his hand on
her shoulder and pressed her down. She went to her knees. He pulled at his
belt. Her arms were flat at her sides. Her hair was a lot darker with no sun
on it. Someone else was there, then—things moving, a second—she
whirling off the ground, her knees still bent. Rocco DiNabrega with her—
had her under the arms, swinging her around, then they were gone, Martin
sure that it was Rocco—saw the sunglasses and the limp-hanging lip-ciggy,
the bored expression. The kid still there. Still back against the wall. Flat up
against it with his throat held in somebody's hand, both his own hands
pulling at their wrist, then the other hand shooting in to hit him—Joe

Moon, Martin glimpsed—and the kid's body spazzing from the blow, then went limp. Joe stepping in, choked him higher up the throat, hit him. Then again. Someone else coming in—Peter Hughes—and started to punch, swinging, whaling, hitting as Joe let go, and following down, swinging, then started stomping. Joe joined him. They put their arms out for balance. Brought their knees up high and aimed with their heels, ten or twenty times, until it was done. Looked down. Waited. Joe pushed Peter out one-handed, looked down, another second, and left.

The guy was like a bag of garbage, spilled. His head like something Martin had seen once. The inside of a Chinese apple. A pomegranate. And no breath in him, now, Martin knew, or no electricity, like. The guy was cooling flesh. Blood spreading out of him. The pool getting larger, every few seconds, like watching the minute hand on a clock.

He had wanted the guy dead and they'd killed him. Like sudden heroes, they'd come. In leather jackets, velour tops. Monsters doing battle just beyond his imagination.

He didn't leave the window. Didn't shut the faucet off. There was no need to, he felt. No place else to ever have to go again.

Cops came. Were down there in the silence, after a while, moving, making the kid seem more dead. Martin wondered was he already disintegrating? And how long would it take? Would his clothes be the only thing left? And the small pint bottle?

Then they were gone, and the guy was dead there, like before. Just the light on him longer now.

Other men arrived. Two in suits and one in an overcoat—a tall man, who squatted by the guy's head and spoke without looking around, the other two nodding, answering, said a few things to him, after a while, and indicated things with the ends of their pencils, but he didn't look up, the man. Was thinking. Began to look around—at things close up, then further out. Swept his head wider—looking around over the cement everywhere and then up the wall. And further—to the rooftops—his neck pinching the back of his collar. He revolved on the concrete, tracing the roofs and the backs of the buildings with their single rows of windows on their stairwells. He rotated on the balls of his feet until his profile was clear—angular and long—thinking. Then turned his head suddenly, like someone behind him had said something, or he'd thought of a thing he'd once known but forgotten and was looking to check—looking back at the buildings behind him, right at Martin, finding the window and looking straight in, past the glare.

But Martin was gone. Reared-back, raced away into the hall and hit the floor, slid to the wall, and crouched. Waited till his mother was home. Which took a while.

She helped him clean himself and change his clothes. She let him tell her as best he could what had happened downstairs—happened to him and what he saw. She stiffened, straightening the shoulders of the sweater she'd helped him pull on, her hands hardening and that hardness traveling her arms to her face. "Men from downstairs? Martin, look at me"—though he already was—"The Italians?"

He nodded. Thought, Peter's half Irish. His brother Terry's in my class. I don't like him.

She stared off, squatting there before him, then looked at him, and smiled. The smile adults gave when they were thinking the things they wouldn't share. She said, "You tired, a bit? Do you want to lie down? I know it's early."

He did, though. Normally would never, but sleeping would feel right.

He dreamed the police came to the door and his mother stepped out into the hall, to let him sleep, but spoke loud anyway, though she'd always told him, "Speak softly in the halls," and "Be a good neighbor." She told them he hadn't been out all afternoon. He'd come home and gone straight to bed. He was sick. He was asleep.

Next morning, she stood with him in the vestibule. Held his hand. She was trying to see into the street, keeping back from the glass, trying to hide from him that she was looking at all. "I'm going to be late," he said, but let her have her fear. He knew he was protected. He'd dreamed the police wouldn't come back, so they wouldn't. The Italians, Joe Moon and Peter Hughes, did what he wanted.

She nodded, and opened the door, still holding his hand, and said, "Go, just . . ." and released him. And he stepped out onto the block and the air was cold. He hurried to school, and nothing happened. Ever. As he told Penelope, seven years later. Kids whispered about him on the play street, later walked home with him asking his opinion on this and that. On baseball players. If he'd seen this certain movie. They joined his adventures on the jungle gyms.

He told her, "West Fourth Street to Canal—going north to south—and Lafayette to Hudson, east-west, I knew who I was before I *knew* I did."

He'd become neighborhood.

8.

Libonati was fifteen, Raganisi was fourteen, he was thirteen. The black kids were their age, more or less. Maybe twelve to sixteen. But there were five of them. And they didn't seem to give a shit they were out of their neighborhood. They were from Chelsea, Ragu had said—knew because he'd played ball against two of them in City Wide League. Libby said, "We might as well keep close to them, 'cause you know what's going to happen." Martin didn't know what was going to happen, exactly, but he could guess.

He'd been at the far end of the festival with Tommy Ragu, pitching softballs at stacked milk cans for half price, because Philly O worked at the stand, and Libby'd come jogging through the crowd, told Ragu, "Come on," and Ragu had tossed his last shot and gone. Martin did the same, thinking if he wasn't invited wherever they were going, wasn't old enough, they would tell him; he could just come back and knock milk cans down, some more. But, now, they were hanging back from these five homeboys, who were too loud and too far out of Chelsea to be so comfortable—making stupid sudden movements here and there like they might grab a purse or some girl's butt—and if they turned on their radio, Libby said, that was it; he was going to talk to them right here, not wait till they were out of the feast.

Martin hoped they didn't turn on the radio.

Augie came out of the rectory, caught up, said, "That's that—Marzolino says we follow them a couple of blocks after they leave, throw them a beating." Martin thought, With Augie, there's four of us. That's better, at least.

They followed them. Not talking, not taking their eyes off. The kids slapped at each other, laughed when people lost the carnival games, challenged the ones who won, and said Nah, they were kidding, then, and kept on. Doing the stuff we would do at a street fair in *Chels*ea, he thought. They might even know we're behind them.

Libby said, "If Marz told you, that means Rocco told *him*."

Augie said, "So?"

"We're doing this for Rocco, that means."

Augie said, "You wouldn't do it for Marz? What, you think you got a choice?"

"I'm just saying."

"Don't fucking say—do."

The kids stopped at the barricades at the feast's end and ducked under them, to the Houston Street side, turned and looked back down Sullivan at it all, ran their eyes over them coming up. What do we do if they *stop*? Martin wondered; Marz had said to follow them a couple of blocks, *then* throw them a beating.

And how do you even throw someone you don't know a beating? he thought. They could throw you one back. They could *dog* your ass. Some of these kids looked tough. Then, some of them not so bad.

He tightened his mouth, narrowed his eyes a bit, tried to look badder.

The tall homeboy was looking at Tommy Ragu. Said, "What's up."

"What's up," Ragu said.

"You play on SoHo Fuel, right?"

"Yeah."

"Point guard?"

"Yeah."

"How'd you finish, last year?"

"Fifth."

"We seventh. Fifth damn good. After all them in the Bronx divide up the championship, and shit. You playing this year?"

"Nah."

The kid nodded. "How come?"

"Got other shit to do."

"Word," he said, "I know how it is."

"You do?" Augie said. "What do you know?"

The kid looked at him. Cocked his head to study him. Smiled. "*What's* up?"

"He's saying what do you know," Libby said.

"He know who he talking to," another kid said. The chubby one, with the radio. The one Martin had thought was twelve, maybe thirteen. He was older though, by his voice. Maybe fifteen, sixteen. Fat baby face, he had. Martin was *way* youngest here.

"So who the fuck *you* talking to?" Augie said.

"You talking to us, we talking to you," the chub said. "So what you got to say?"—rose up off leaning on his forearms, set the radio down on the cement, and put his arms out wide, like a big question What. "You got beef? What you got? What you got to say, homes?" He was their leader— Martin had judged them all wrong. Only the tall one looked nervous. The other three straightening, putting their popping-shit faces on. The tall one hesitating to even stand up full. And, when he did, his eyes roamed. Like a cop-horse in traffic.

Martin joined the chorus of questions and dares going back and forth. "Who the fuck you think you are?" "Go back to Chelsea"—not noticing how it all was kept general—"Go back to Italy," "Go back to Africa"— said, "Just go the fuck home, you fat fucking fuck," and the kid said, "What you say?" and looked at him for the first time. They were opposite each other, with the way they all stood, in two loose rows, maybe ten feet apart. The fat kid moved the radio aside and ducked under the barricade, put his hands out wide again, said to him, "You got beef, little motherfucker? Me and you. Nobody else."

No one talked. He wanted to look at Augie, or Libby. Even Tommy Ragu. See what they expected of him. But he knew what they expected— he just wanted to see if they believed he could do it. Just had to step up and swing, motherfucker; that was how it was done. If he tried to answer this fat-mouth, some choking squeak would come out.

And, if I run? he thought.

Keep running.

He stepped forward. Hoped he wouldn't start crying the way some kids did. He kept his hands at his sides. The fat kid stepped forward, arms wide. Martin whipped the right hand and cracked him, went to swing the left and got cracked. They both swung, then, made a storm of punches. He felt something pop inside his head somewhere, like a light going out, and heard nothing. Then heard yelling again. He was down on his hands. Under the barricade. Next to the radio. Sneakers all around him, stepping in, backing up—a wavy rhythm that followed the cheering above him. He'd toppled. His jaw was numb. He tipped himself back on the balls of his feet to stand, and the fat kid said, "What you getting up for?" and kicked him in the ass. His face hit the barricade. He scrambled not to fall. He tripped on the radio and went down, flat, scrambled up and took the radio by the handle, spun around, swinging it, and fucking *hit* him. The kid stumbled, looking confused and distracted, then mad. Martin followed him and swung again, heard the black kids and his friends saying "Oh, shit, run," and the flat slap of sneakers everywhere, the radio catching the chubfuck in the ear and he was out, falling. Martin swung three-sixty to hit him again, the kids all scattering and two cops steps away, coming on fast, and fatty hit the pavement, Martin swinging past where he would have been, and caught a cop in the ribs, not meaning to, but knowing, somehow, that he would. *Whomp.*

Then he was down, looking at sky. The cops with their knees in his chest. He'd been airborne, a second, he realized, before they'd slapped him onto his back. And it hurt. Like his ribs were all funny bones. He couldn't breathe. And had somehow started laughing. Couldn't stop. So, even more, he couldn't breathe. At least he wasn't crying.

Beyond the cops' pissed-off faces, people he knew from everywhere in the neighborhood were gathering. The cops turned him over and cuffed him. Stood him up, and led him off. He breathed and said, "Ow . . ." took a breath, said, "Ow," and laughed. Other cops over the fat kid now, sitting him up. Fatty rubbing his head. Looked around, said, "Where my radio? Fool hit my radio," but didn't look at him. Had forgotten him, it seemed. Didn't look even as Martin was pressed into the cop car and driven away. Didn't look again at the boy who'd decked him.

"Only cared about his radio," he told Penelope.

The cops were from Manhattan South Task Force, drove him east on Houston Street for blocks, and somewhere around Lafayette, he saw the tall black kid out the window, walking the same direction, alone and fast, like he'd just stopped running not too long ago. The kid crying. Tears just leaking down his face. People staring at him sideways as he passed.

From the head of his juvey bed—knees tucked up, sneakers on the blanket that not once yet had been turned down to sleep—waiting for the next little crazy kid to fuck with him, he thought he heard his mother's voice down on the street, on Hunts Point Avenue, calling "Martin Quinn? . . . Martin? . . . Do any of you boys know Martin Quinn?" addressing the kids standing in the windows yelling down to their families out there, yelling down to their girlfriends, down to the local kids who had a good time yelling up taunts at the kids from other neighborhoods dumb enough to get jailed. But, then again, clearer than those nonstop, screamed-out conversations, he'd been hearing all kinds of things—girls shrieking, dogs barking—like they were two feet away in the bed next to him. Six days now since he'd slept. But this was "Martin Quinn?"—his mother's voice. He was practically certain.

He rose and went to the chainlink-covered windows. He stepped up on the radiator and found a spot to hang on to and look down, beside the fifty other kids with their fingers in the fencelinks zoo-like.

She was down there. Not surprised to see him, it seemed. Like she'd known he would be here. So, he knew it was nearly over.

She yelled up was he all right.

He said, "Yes. Get me out."

She said she thought that she could now.

He yelled, "Get me out," and someone down the row of windows whined, "Get me out, Mommy." He ignored it, yelled, "Today," and she said that now that she'd found him, she would have to post bail but she didn't have all of it. He said, "Go to the Italians." She said, "We'll talk about it; I'm coming in," and he said, "Go to the Italians," and she said, "I'm coming inside," and she disappeared walking closer in, walking too far in for him to see. He stepped down off the radiator and headed for the door to the dormitory. The same voice down the row said, "Go to the Italians, Mommy, get me a pizza," and he turned to find the kid from the mess of laughing faces facing into the room now, looking at him. Though he didn't have it in him anymore with his mother in the building.

It was a kid he hadn't fought more than an hour ago, over one of the little containers of milk, stepping down now off the radiator saying "Mommy, Mommy."

Another kid came down, beside the first one, and said, up close to him, "Shut up, motherfucker, he mean Mafia; ain't talking about no pizza," and the kid was quiet, a second, thinking about it. Then smiled, weak.

So, it was done.

Martin walked to the door, looked sideways through the chickenwire-glass, and hoped they didn't bring her right here to see him.

A few minutes later, when a guard came and got him, he was kind of disappointed they didn't.

He slept, woke up at dawn and went out into the living room, turned on the TV. He lay on the couch, fell asleep again. Woke up that night. His mother said she'd canceled his enrollment at Xavier High School for the fall; she'd found a spot for him in a small private school uptown, the only school with room on such short notice. He was done hanging out with the kids from around, she said.

He didn't care.

His dealings in the neighborhood became only business dealings—Marzolino offering him a job on a beverage stand, next feast; Charlie Mirra putting him into a key spot selling fireworks at the Holland Tunnel outlet, giving him and a select few other kids first crack hawking to the inbound traffic from Jersey; and he couldn't go in or out his front door without some wiseguy or other sending him quick out on an errand—"Kid Quinn, get us the racing form . . . Get me some dessert . . . Here, go up my house—take my keys—get the nitro from the fridge. God *damn* this angina"—unless he was with his mother. They didn't know him at all, then, so slick they were. They never *asked* if she would care; they just kept his business his own. Would acknowledge her politely, nice woman in the building upstairs— "Hello. How you doing there, miss?" *"What interest could we have in your older son?"*—and she didn't suspect. Never had less than two jobs herself. She was never around.

He went to his private school. Had his one friend in it, Felix, who said his father was a gangster. *Did* have a house filled with guns, in drawers and cabinets here and there, but was so innocent and . . . weird and . . . honest about everything, it didn't matter if his father was Don Corleoneski; he was no tough kid, Felix. Hardly ever freaking left his apartment. What kind of a rep could be built like that?

■ ■ ■

Walking back from Felix's. That November. Stopped the Brooklyn guidos from heisting Rocco's DeVille, and nearly got run over for it. His reputation solidified.

Though he didn't know it. Not till a few weeks later, when, that one morning, there were Peter and Joe sitting in Joe's El D, parked at the curb near the top of the subway stairs near school, way the hell uptown. He thought it was strange—their having business here, and so freaking early. Went to pass them. Didn't even think of acknowledging them, interrupting, drawing any attention at all. And between the whoosh of two passing cars he heard the single word, not quite whispered— "Irish"—and stopped, turned, and looked at them through the thin reflection of the city across the windshield. They were looking at him. Waiting for him. Kid Quinn. Martin Irish.

Felix said it was because of his car accident. Because his brother'd been killed and *he*'d been in a coma, a few hours, then in traction for weeks, that his mother didn't want him out of her sight. But this was going on two years. Enough was enough, he'd told her. Had gotten his father, Lexi, Mr. Pasko, to take his side. A boy had to go out. "So take me out, man," Felix said.

Martin took him to Chinatown, got him a fake ID, took him to a boob bar, took him to a college bar, took him to an invitation-only loft party on Desbrosses Street, and before Martin had his money clip out, Felix, like he'd been doing it his whole life, said to the bouncer—a guy dressed like a beatnik, but packed in muscle—"Invites? Yeah, I think they're in this pocket," and opened his lapel to hide his hand from the people behind them. Greased the guy with two tens.

They went in. Martin said, "I told you I was going to take care of that," moving down the hall to the main room, Felix taking off his overcoat and looking around like he was looking for something. "I wanted to try it," Feel said. "Why, did I mess it up?"—looked at him, worried about it now.

"No. It was fine, I guess."

"Good. So, next time, you'll get them."

Already making plans for next time.

Martin thought, Do I mind his doing that?

But he didn't, he guessed; he would do this again. You came to places like this with guys from the neighborhood, some college kid ended up on the floor in a pile, his girlfriend screaming. It was peaceful hanging out with Felix. The way he was strange and funny in his house, he was that way outside. Always himself. Looking around now again, Feel—left, right, behind them, "Where is it?" saying.

"Where's what?"

"The coat check."

"It's a loft party, Felix. A city-wide. There's no coat check. They rent the place, one night. Charge a fortune for drinks. That's all. There's the bar"—he pointed to the crowd, other side of the dance floor—so thick a mob it shimmied—"a fold-down table. You want to check the wall behind it for a liquor license?"

They went further in. Smiled at the girls around, nodded at the guys. Everything civilized. Nobody of age. "I'm already sweating," Feel said. "I have to carry this thing around all night? There ought to be a coat check."

So, at their parties, they had a coat check. Had a lighting guy and a DJ. Rented six-foot speakers, portable bars, and lounge furniture. Sold cigarettes at a 100 percent markup—Marlboro Lights only, the brand and strength it seemed that anybody with a couple of drinks in them had no real problem smoking. And on the two TVs they hung in opposite corners they ran Russ Meyer movies. The mind, on a subconscious level, Felix said, would always enjoy the sights of gigantic breasts and violence—"I was practically locked in my house, two years; you think I don't know these things?" They'd been fifteen years old when they started, invested twenty-five hundred apiece. Martin's money from bodying smack for Joe and Peter. Felix's dough just always there, it seemed, like Lexi left it under his pillow. Maybe did. And on that first five-thousand-dollar night they'd netted two grand. By now they'd thrown over twenty. Nearly one a month. And the rush from it hadn't gone away. Felt like it never would. This was who they were now. They'd become it together.

But something was off tonight. Penny's being here, of course, had something to do with it. But Felix conducting other business during the party, by phone or not, was definitely another part of it, he knew, and it was making him edgy—Feel prowling the side of the dance floor, dialing again and again.

He watched him, another few seconds, then looked at her—sitting beside him on the table they used for collecting the money at the door. "You're having fun, right?" he said.

She leaned closer to him—over the music.

"Good time?" he said.

She nodded. Like a pleased little kid. Looked back at the people dancing.

He slid off the table and stepped in front of her. Spread his feet so he was eye-level with her. She smiled. She leaned and kissed him. Seemed to know he had something to tell her.

He did.

But he couldn't figure out what it was, exactly. All he had was a feeling.

He went back and sat on the table. She leaned and kissed his shoulder. Then he realized what it was.

It wasn't that he had something to tell her, really; it was that he'd wanted to see if she'd *do* it tonight—that was what he couldn't shake—but it would seem too obvious, now, he thought—this being the first time she'd come to the city at night in their six months together. He couldn't just ask her. Couldn't just get her alone, start making the final moves. He couldn't assume she was ready.

She'd told her mother she and Gina were going to Manhattan. For dinner and dancing with Gina's brother and a friend, Gina staying home to watch TV, and who knew where the brother was.

But, if this wasn't a signal she was ready to be alone with him, what was? he thought. She'd wanted to see one of his parties, she'd said. Okay. She'd been hearing about them so long. But she'd also just said she was happy just sitting beside him like this, and, shit, they could do that anywhere.

Christ, Felix, stop pacing, he said in his head. He couldn't stop noticing it.

He looked at her. Slid down. Got in front of her again.

"What is it?" she said. Gave a little frown at him.

"You mind if we go outside?" he said. "I know you came down for the party, but maybe we could take a walk?"

"I came down for you. Of course."

A good sign, he thought.

She said, "Can you leave, though?"

"Nobody really shows up this late. If they do, we don't charge them. Only for drinks. At this point, the parties go on their own till they're over. But Felix . . . He's all . . ."

"Yeah, what's he doing?" she said. "Who's he calling, a girl?"

"His new partner, in Jersey. Trying to start up a recording studio. They think the big money's in music. Don't even ask. So, you want to take a walk?"

She slid down from the table. Ready. He smiled. "All right, hold up, then. I got to tell Feel." He signaled, got his attention, waved him over. Fee signaled him to wait—held up a finger. Was on the phone, listening. Hung up. No answer. Came over. Martin leaned in to speak to him. Felix leaned in, gave him his ear. The way they always spoke now at the parties. When it was Felix's turn to speak, they would switch. It reminded Martin of how the wiseguys kissed each other—one cheek, then the other. Knew Felix thought the same thing, though they'd never discussed it. "Can I step outside for a minute? Can you handle things?"

They switched.

"Of course I can handle things. This fucking guy, though. He's supposed to be home."

Switch.

"It's Saturday night. He's probably out."

Switch. "He's supposed to be home. We had a date to talk."

Switch.

"A date to be gay?"

Again.

"If that's what it takes? To get my studio off the ground? Yeah."

Again.

"Can I step outside for the rest of the night?"

Felix backed away, gave a big shrug—*Of course*—and started dialing again, walked away. Waved backward over his shoulder the way he'd heard that they did it in the Hamptons. Knew it drove Martin crazy.

Martin took her hand. They went out. "Bye?" she said. Felix had left without saying it, he realized. Hadn't spoken to her at all. Too concerned about his deal.

They waited at the elevator. He said, "This was easier than I thought."

"You're not worried, not having two of you there?"

"He'll be fine. He's a good guy, Felix."

They waited, watched the numbers panel.

He said, "He didn't mean to be rude. That's what I mean, I guess."

"Oh, I *might* care," she said.

She did that, sometimes. Used expressions little kids did on each other. Things he hadn't heard in years. When she used them, though, they made sense. As a kid, he'd just heard them as insults; had never once stopped to think what they meant.

Again, though, now, they didn't talk—looked up at the numbers. And, when he realized he couldn't take his eyes off the panel if he tried, he understood they were standing here so quiet because they both knew they were free to go do it now. The elevator coming up—four . . . five . . . seven was their floor.

"I like the way you two talk to each other," she said. "Inside? With the music? Leaning in? You're like two supercool guys at a square dance."

He laughed, was glad she'd loosened things up. He leaned to kiss her on the head and she turned her face to him and went tippy-toe, in one movement, and kissed his lips, her eyes wide. Her blue, *furlani* eyes. Her mother's northern blood, she'd told him.

She leaned her head on his chest. The elevator opened. "Can you wait here, a second?" he said. "I forgot to tell him something."

She waited.

He jogged back in. Went up behind him, put both hands on his shoulders and leaned, said, "Give me your keys."

Fee didn't turn. "My house or my Jeep?"

He hadn't thought about it. He *would* have to drive her home—she'd be late. "Where's the Porsche?"

"My house or my Jeep?"

"Both."

Fee went in a pocket, took them out, held them up for him to take.

He took them. Told him, "I think I'm in love."

"I think I'm going to kill this guy," Fee said, and dialed again.

Pen hadn't seemed to notice it, but he sure as shit did. *"You kids can sit any-where you like. I'll be right there."* Not more than twenty-five herself, the waitress. Shit like that could ruin a good time. He told himself, Don't let it. Don't let it.

Penny caught him peering over his menu, watching her read hers. She raised her eyebrows at him—*Well, what do you think?*

He said, "I'm going to have a piece of pie. Cup of coffee."

"Sounds right."

"What kind you want?"—he flagged the waitress. The bigshot. She saw him.

"Not telling."

"I have to guess?"

"When I order, you'll find out."

"I'm supposed to order."

"Such a gentleman. I'll order for myself, Prince Romantic."

The waitress coming over. Smiling tight, impatient. So busy with her one booth and three counter customers. Pencil to pad. Was ready. "What can I get you kids?"

He looked out the window.

"Cherry pie and a cup of tea," Pen said.

He could see her apron reflected in the glass. If she called him "kid" again, he'd fucking—

"And you, sir?"

He didn't look around. Kept facing away. But she wasn't being smart, far as he could tell. "Sounds good," he said.

"Okay."

"Didn't you say coffee, before?" Penny said.

He looked at her. She knew something was wrong. Looked concerned, though. Like she'd done it herself.

"Yeah. Thank you. I did. Coffee."

"You bet. Coming right up for you folks."

He looked at her. Her smile the real thing before turning to go.

Because she thought they were fighting, he realized. Somehow that made them not kids.

He said to Pen, "I thought I saw someone out the window. Who I didn't like too much."

"It's okay. I thought you got mad I ordered."

"I would nev—" he looked at her, dead serious. Too serious to say it, somehow. I would never embarrass you, he thought. Be mad at you in front of people. "I would . . ." He shook his head. "No."

"Okay."

She reached into her purse and got a cigarette. Lit it and blew the smoke out sideways, into the aisle. She took his hand across the table and held it, and stayed like that—stretched, a little, toward him—and smoked. He guessed if she'd wanted him to stretch *his* halfway, she would have tugged, a bit.

Looking off into the aisle, now, her eyes out of focus. Kind of posing, he guessed.

The waitress brought everything. Pen didn't let go of his hand. Didn't move at all. Even acknowledge that the waitress was here. Then, when she'd gone, said to him, "The city has this energy at night that's so different."

"Busy," he said.

"No, more natural. During the days, it feels busy. People doing what they have to. At night they're doing what they want to. I like it. I think that if I move here after college, I'll sleep during the day and live at night. Like a vampire. But I'd be nice."

"Let me ask you something," he said. "Don't take it the wrong way. Have you ever been in the city *alone* before this."

"Without my family or Gina, you mean? No."

"Man. So sheltered."

"Nothing wrong with being sheltered."

"*Totally.* I shelter my brother all *over* the place. He doesn't know anything I do, none of my friends. He goes to school, takes his piano lessons, goes to other kids' houses to play. If he hangs out out front, the old goombahs'll be like 'Oh! Little Quinn! Walk my dog for me. Load my gun for me.' Like a year from now they'll be doing that. But every chance I get, I make out to them he's some little preppy wuss. *He* doesn't know, so what does he care? By the time he's old enough to run for them, he'll be lucky if they're not shaking him down for his lunch money."

She smiled.

He dug into his pie and ate a piece. They'd warmed it up. That was good. He ate more, drank some coffee.

She said, "I'm going to shelter my kids."

He nodded. Had another bite. Two more and his pie would be gone.

She hadn't touched hers. Maybe she'd offer him some, he hoped.

"Are you?" she said.

He split the remaining piece. Thought about it. Thought, really, it was definitely a good idea. Said, "Yeah, sure."

"I think what I want to do is live in the city, after college. Maybe go to college in the city to start putting down roots, and then live here in my twenties and have my good time, move back to Westchester when I have kids."

And then your good time is over? he thought. He said, "You don't want to be a mother?"

"I just said I did."

"But it wouldn't be good? A good time?"

"Different kind of good time. The best time in the world, I think."

Oh.

He nodded.

Finished his piece. She finished her cigarette, sipped her tea. He thought of something, said, "Then you and Gina can let *your* daughters lie to *you* and come meet their boyfriends down here."

"Right."

"You two are funny. Come in for lunch and your little shopping sprees. Like two suburban ladies."

"We enjoy our lunch and shopping, first of all. And second, if we didn't have receipts, they'd never let us go again."

"Lunch at Bendel's, sales at Bloomies. Tough life."

"Then I get to see you, who never wakes up before two o'clock, weekends."

"I *can't*. Now you know why."

"Yeah. I do."

He sipped his coffee. Leaned back in his corner. Let her look at him. Because she did know why, finally. She'd seen how hard he worked.

She said, "It was pretty impressive. Not a lot of people could do that even once, never mind once a month."

He said, "It's not so much. We've done it so many times now. But thanks. Let's not talk about it." He leaned forward again.

"Why?"

"I don't know. It's weird now."

"You talk about it all the time."

"Not anymore. Now that you've seen it."

She smiled at him. "You're satisfied with yourself."

He smiled back. "I guess."

She nodded.

He wanted more pie.

"You're a good provider," she said.

"A what?"

"You just work hard; that's all. It's good."

"A good earner, the wiseguys say." He reached for his fork again.

"I don't care what *they* say."

He stopped. Where he was. Brought his hand back. "It's just a way of saying."

"I know."

She was quiet. And sorry she'd snapped, he could see.

He said, "Gina still seeing that forty-year-old perv?"—off the subject. Maybe *too* far off.

But she smiled. Said, "O my God—last weekend, when we came down?— I meant to tell you this, all week, on the phone, but I kept forgetting—we're done shopping, and I go to meet you, right?—she goes to meet him?— boyfriend of the week? Okay, he's forty, but Gina's Gina and this is like the third week in a row she's seeing him, so it must mean *something*. I meet her at the train later? She says they went to a hotel. A little afternoon . . . you know."

"Delight. Sky rockets in flight."

"And he's forty. He had a couple of gray hairs. Down below."

"O my God," he said. "I was going to ask you for some of your pie, but not now."

They laughed.

The waitress filled his coffee. Penny lit another one.

"Gray pubes?" she said—"please. Not till I have them myself. That's total skataah."

He said, "You say 'skataah' in Westchester? I thought you'd say, 'grody,' or something."

"Everyone I know is first generation from the city. You could plop Gina down in Bensonhurst and what'd be the difference? She wouldn't know. She'd just need directions to the mall."

"She'd find it," he said. "Like a pigeon. *Zoom.* Right to it."

"Poor Gina. I don't know what she's doing. It's too bad she didn't last with Felix."

"Didn't *last*? Did they even get *started*?"

"I guess not. They just had sex, and that was it. It was enough for her, I guess."

"For him, too; believe me. I can't believe she thinks she dumped him—"

"And he thinks he dumped *her*. I know; it's so perfect. They're perfect for each other. We could have been double-dating all this time."

"Yeah, we could have," he said.

He *had* double-dated with Fee a few times, early on, with girls from the parties, but they were different about women now. Which was fine. It made the million other ways they were the same all the better. He was just quiet about his personal life; Felix liked to talk. That they didn't double-date anymore only gave Fee that much more to fill him in on. He banged the shit out of this one, video taped that one. Tied her up. She loved it.

"Felix talks, Pen. I actually kind of like it better that I don't know his girlfriends too well."

"What does he say?"

"It doesn't matter. You know. It's just a thing with me and him. I never tell him anything and he doesn't expect it, but, when it's the other way around, I can't shut him up."

She smiled. Looked down. She understood.

He was glad. He didn't want to get into it more than that.

She said, "Gina's a good girl. You know, all the crazy stuff aside."

He nodded.

She did that sometimes, Penny—said something nice before the subject was closed.

He thought, A Catholic girl thing. A girl thing.

He said, "If *anyone's* lucky to be sheltered, it's Gina. Dim like she is. And nice, like you said. But the world would swallow her up, man."

Pen nodded. "She's good at heart, though. She'll settle down, someday, be somebody's nice, scatterbrained mother. The other night, I got off the phone with you?—she called right as I hung up. Had been trying to get through? She asked me if my parents had a story they liked to tell people about me when I was little because they think it describes me so perfectly. I did—I had one, of course. But her mother had just *told* hers. To the head of some big charity who was over their house for dinner. We said the funny thing was we're both always like, 'Why do you *tell* that?' but by now, the stories actually *mean* something to us. They kind of say something that matters to *us* now."

He said, "What was yours?"

"Don't you want to know Gina's?"

"I'd rather hear yours."

"Do *you* have one, or is it a girl thing?"

He thought, Like always speaking last-minute-nice about someone? He smiled.

"You have one?" she said.

"No, I don't think so."

"You do."

"I don't. I don't think I . . ."—he couldn't picture one. Nothing came. His mind didn't work like that, he guessed, couldn't force something up. "What was yours?" he said to her.

"Hers is about cutting her own hair when she was three years old. She thinks she should *still* be cutting it, apparently. It's a cute story."

"The more you don't tell me, the more I'm going to ask."

She smiled, sat back in the booth. "Apparently? When I was three? My mother and the maid were off shopping. My father was gardening in the back. I was in the den, right on the other side of the garden door, playing, and in a bassinet near me is the maid's new newborn daughter, four or five months old. She's still swaddled up. A nice, peaceful day. Shopping, gardening, and children sleeping and playing. But my father hears the baby crying all of a sudden—*hard*—and he comes running in. Well, I'm there with the kid on the floor. I've got her out of her bassinet and I'm on top of her, slapping her around, like a bully in a schoolyard. My father said not only did he have a hard time quieting her down before our mothers got home, he said once he got me off, he had a hard time making sure I kept my distance. I had this *look* in my eye."

"Demon child."

"Spawned from Hell. And I don't really know what it means, even. They bring it up and I ask them why they always do. I'm like, 'Why do you tell that story? What does it mean?' But they just look at me and say, 'You know.'"

He smiled at her.

She smiled back. Looked at her cigarette burning down in her fingers. Looked at him, again.

She knew. Of course, she did.

He thought of one—the kind of story she meant. "When I was five . . ." he said.

She leaned forward. "You have one?"

He looked off, out at the street. "When I was five, I was playing outside. This was in Paris, before my brother was born. My mother was actually pregnant with him, I guess."

"You lived in Paris?" She exhaled her drag into the aisle, tapped her ash into the ashtray.

"Because of my father," he said. "I never told you that? He was popular over there; his album sold well. I was playing outside, though—listen— around the side of our building, and there's this kitten. Little, black. You know. Sweet. And after a while, the sun's going down, I have to go inside, I know, and I want to take him home, right? But I know I have to ask, and I know he's going to run off as soon as I leave, so I had to make sure he stayed there, right where he was."

He raised an eyebrow and looked at her.

"O God," she said. "What did you do?"

"I put a great big rock on him and went upstairs."

"Oh, no"—she put her head down—onto the table. Shook it. Then looked up at him—fast. She'd figured out the rest. "Your parents said *yes,*" she said. "You could have it."

"Of course. Who wouldn't want a kitten?"

"And you ran downstairs."

"I *raced.*"

"Oh! Poor you."

"Poor me."

"But you can hardly even remember it, right? You know it all from your parents telling you?"

"Yup. Same as you."

"That poor kitty."

"That poor *baby.*"

She laughed, opened her eyes wide at him.

And a week later, when he'd abandoned her, when he'd joined the army, tried to disappear, and, for a long time after that, he kept the rest of that night solid in his memory. The one feeling that had been there, in every moment after they'd told their stories, was trust. He didn't feel afraid of her at all anymore. Did feel some other kind of fear starting to grow. Something like urgency. But as for being with her?—for the rest of their lives? He felt she'd be as good to him as he'd be to himself, or better.

"You haven't tried your pie," he said.

She said, "You still flatten the thing you love? Or you learned your lesson?"

"By heart, I learned it; believe me. Your pie's probably cold now. It was warm. I should have told you."

"It's okay," she said. She crushed the cig. "I'll get it wrapped up. I should probably go."

"There's a microwave at Felix's," he said. "He lives just . . . you know. On Lafayette."

"Is that right."

"Yes."

"Okay, then."

A t the register she forgot her cigarettes. She went back to the table. The waitress—annoying still, just to look at her—he didn't care, though—said, "You made up, hunh?"

"Pardon?"

"You worked it out?"

He bit his teeth down, took a breath through them, and blew it out. "Sure."

"That's good. Six-fifty, please."

He had his money out just below the counter—had been waiting for her to ring the check; they'd left the table before getting it. "Six-fifty?" he said. He slid a finger in the fold of bills, folded them back the other way, twenties on the outside now, and brought the wad into view. Flipped past a hundred dollars' worth of them . . . two hundred. Near three, he hit the tens. "Good, I do have something smaller. You keep the rest, hon."

▪ ▪ ▪

He whispered the dining room was in the other apartment—Fee's parents' apartment—through this kitchen that they shared; Felix's place just the one enormous room, but a duplex, with the desk and whatnot up the stairs, and, down below, just the bed and the home gym and the fifteen-foot-long entertainment system.

She took her pie out, a second before the microwave beeped, and walked inside. He followed her. She lay on the bed on her stomach, her elbows at the edge. "Sit."

He sat. With his back against the bed, on the floor. Their faces beside each other. The pie suspended by his.

"I forgot to get you a fork," he said, and went to get up.

"Stay. I'll use my fingers." She took a cherry and fed it to him. "You said he had his own connected little apartment. I didn't picture this."

"I know. It's like six hundred square feet with the upstairs, but he never even goes up there—he does his homework in homeroom. The ceilings are like twenty-two feet, or something. The windows are twelve. I know that much for sure because we measured them so he could special-order some blinds. The decorator forgot. They're still making them."

"Eats all his meals with his parents."

"He eats in bed a lot, too."

"This bed? This is the one that you sleep in?"

"Uh-hunh."

"Both of you?"

"You see the size of this bed? It's a king-size bed. It filled half his room over in his parents' place."

She whispered to him—"Some people would call that gay."

"Some people would get their heads broken."

"Some people would duh-duh-duh," she said.

"That's right, duh-duh-duh. Some people would call that 'brothers.' "

She pinched his ear and kissed the fingers. "Hold this pie, please," she said.

He took it. Held it there, out before him, like an altarboy. He had a feeling he knew what she was doing.

"You can look if you want," she said.

He turned, and she was. Undressing.

S he started up suddenly. "My God, Felix'll come home," she said.
He told her to lie down again—he had Felix's keys. "He'll ask the doorman if we left and dropped them off. If we haven't yet, he'll wait in the coffee shop, flirt with the waitress."

She laid her head back on his chest. Like he'd hoped she would. Though it wasn't the most comfortable way to take a breath, he had to admit. It looked better in the movies. But the moonlight through the windows was nice. Was perfect.

He told her he'd been lying there thinking about things, and there was a different story he wanted to tell her. He wasn't sure it was a story that told who he was, or however she'd put it, exactly. He wasn't even sure he didn't wish it never happened, but he knew that if it hadn't, he wouldn't be here. "I was a little kid. Playing in the park. My father was dead a year"—and told her about the parolee and the blond girl that he'd tried to make, then Joe Moon, Rocco, and Peter; the detective looking back through the buildings. He went on and told her about running errands, selling fireworks, running stands at Pompeii Feast and Saint Anthony's.

"And San Gennaro?" she said.

"That's Little Italy."

Then the black kids—the little fat one and the tall one and the other three he couldn't picture anymore. And Tommy Ragu and Danny Libonati and Augie, who's last name he'd never known.

"What happened to him?" she said.

"Overdose."

"And Danny Libonati?"

"Crack rehab."

"And Tommy Ragu?"

"Raganisi. He gets out of jail in the nineties. Home invasion and murder."

Told her about Spofford and the kids yelling down to the street, hanging on to the grill that covered the windows, their families out there, and the local kids yelling up taunts— *"You* maricon, *when you get out you better never come to this 'hood, bee; I'll bust you ass"*—and how he'd argued with his mother in Visitation about going to the wiseguys for bail— *"You have to ask them; they won't come to you." "They're half the reason you're here." "That's why they'll help."* "Acting like bigshots," Penny said, "at all the wrong times." His mother using the phone on the CO's desk to call the number she'd gotten at the DA's office, and he went from Visitation right to a group home for the night, not even setting foot back in the dorm. She went to his father's old manager for bail, a guy named Sugar. "The next day I was back in court and they let me go, time-served." She wanted to sue the DOC, he said, for psychological hardship, but he said no, never; he'd been too ashamed. He would never get up on the stand and say he'd heard things. He was afraid that his father'd been crazy. "I never told *any*one that," he said. "I never told *any* of this, but I always thought I'd never tell anyone about being afraid of that." He didn't think his mother ever got that money back to Sugar. She tried, but Sugar was a good man.

Pen said, "He died?"

"No, my mother's uncomfortable seeing him. *He's* uncomfortable seeing us. Reminds them both of my old man. All their better times."

And now he knew he would have to tell her about him, that she probably wouldn't ask, but that he had to. Another thing he swore he'd never talk about.

Maybe all this talking was just a way to lead up to it, he thought.

He told her. The same pretty way that his mother told him. And thought, Now there it is again—John "Stinger" Quinn's story of fame and fall. Start, middle, and finish.

She cried. He'd figured she would. He said, "Now he's always in my head, even when things are going well. I'll be laughing or something, and I'll think I see him at the edge of my vision, and I'll turn to find him. In a crowd or an empty room, even. I've checked the back of Felix's car because I thought I saw him in the rearview. That sounds nuts, right?"

"You saw yourself, maybe?"

"Maybe. There's something more important, though. Since I met you, I hardly think about him. It makes me feel bad that I don't, but I can't help it. It used to happen when I was with Felix, sometimes. We'd be hanging out for days at a stretch and I'd go home and realize I hadn't thought of him once. But with you? I just told that whole story about him, I wasn't even thinking about him, I was telling *you* something, thinking about *you*. And me. Lying here. That kitten I told you about? I cried over it; of course—I was five. But I could cry over it right now probably if I thought hard enough, but I was nine when my father died and I stood there staring at him bleeding to death or already dead, and I didn't cry. I saw him in his coffin?—nothing. No tears. I didn't understand suicide, so I couldn't cry over it. And still. Now?—here?—the same." He shrugged. "When I hear about people dying, I think, People die. Someone else who won't be coming around." He said, "I need a shrink, I guess."

She looked up at him. Her eyes still red. "I think so." She smiled.

"So that's my story. Who I am. What about you? You want to change yours, now?"

"Slapping the maid's baby around?" she said.

"Yeah, beating up that baby."

She rolled off him. Careful not to let the sheet get below her nipples. She looked off at the windows. "No. That's me," she said. "I'll stick with that one."

H e gave the house keys to the doorman, drove her back to Bronxville, dropped her off at the bottom of her street. Dawn out. Gray light.

She crossed her arms and started up the hill, her eyes down. Either was cold and too tired to be walking uphill, or she was already trying to look sorry for being late, in case her mother was awake at the window.

Whatever the reason, he knew, she was happy. Inside her hunched-over shape, she was glowing like he was.

He drove back in the sunrise. Parked at the hydrant, let the doorman know, and gave him the keys. Walked home to Thompson. Went upstairs and let himself in, tiptoed to his and Frito's room, and watched him sleep, a while. Knew the kid would be in love one day, too, and that was nice.

He went in the closet for half the money in his old Saint Anthony's bookbag, and went back downstairs and sat in the park. At eight o'clock he started walking uptown. Was outside Tiffany's when it opened. The rent-a-cop wished him good morning and unlocked the doors while he stood there watching. A thin, solid-looking old black guy, ex-military type. A good, proud guy, he thought. Not at all worried about a young kid standing over him saying nothing. Knew the difference between a kid in love and a young stickup man.

N ext day she didn't answer her phone, and he figured she'd proba-bly caught heat.

Day after that, still no.

After three or four hours, he took a walk. Went back upstairs, and started calling again. Then sat, a while, and stared at the phone. He thought of call-ing Fee, maybe ask his advice. The phone rang when he reached for it. Fee said, "Come over, man. Now."

At the apartment he opened the door as Martin went to ring the bell. Martin followed him in, sat in the chair he pointed to. Watched him pull another one up and sit. The tips of their sneakers almost touching. "That business deal?" Fee said. "With the wanna-be-tough-guy in Jersey?"

"Yeah, I had an idea for you, actually"—he'd thought of it walking up Fifth Avenue to Tiffany's, how there was such wealth to be had in this life. "If you're investing fifty-one percent, all you have to do is expand into producing records—videos even—and if you invest the new difference yourself, you just buy the guy out. Legally. Forget your father's plan"—Lexi saying exploit the whole opportunity, keep it going, a while, make surprise visits to see the books, and then maybe buy the accountant, when the time came.

Fee said, "Well, thanks for the advice, but the guy fucked me. My whole seventeen grand. I gave it to him in cash and now he says it's gone."

"How?"

"He says the guy he bought the space from took off. The marshals locked it up for taxes."

"What guy?"

"I don't know—the *money's* gone."

"Does he know who you are? Who your father is?"

"I let him think he was the bigshot. Biding my time."

"The money all yours?" Martin said—"or your father's, some of it."

"Mine," Fee said. "Since my bar *mitz*vah I've been saving that money. Plus a bunch that we made on the parties. Mother*fuck*er."

He had a lot more, Martin knew, but that wasn't the point; Fee was humiliated, thrown completely. Martin wondered if the old man knew. "Who's this other guy? Who the marshals closed down?"

"I don't know. I don't care."

"You think he's real, I'm saying, or the wanna-be still has it? Or spent it."

"He better have it. If he doesn't, I'm taking whatever he has." Looking away, Fee said it. An empty threat.

"How, Feel?"

"I'm going to get it."

"How?"

"I'm going to walk in his house and take it."

"Robbery? Armed, I assume? And home invasion? You better talk to your father."

"I did."

Martin was surprised. And nodded, without meaning to. Then realized Fee'd only gone to the old man when that part of the story was in place— how he was going to get the money back. And that now he'd have to follow through. "What'd he say?"

"He said to take someone I trusted. Somebody loyal. Didn't want to know who."

"Me."

"Who else, the maid? You remember he said that to you? When you took the blame for me that time with the Chivas?"

"When do you want to do it?" Martin said.

"Soon. I want to do it now, but—"

"You got to calm down first—"

"I know that, but there's something else."

Martin waited.

"So you'll do it then?" Fee said.

"Yeah. What's the other thing?"

"Gina called me."

"So?"

Felix shrugged. Something he didn't want to say.

"What, she pregnant? It can't be yours."

Felix shook his head. Reached out a hand, put it on his knee. "Penny's father died."

He thought, Why she hadn't called. Or answered her phone. Her father died. "When?"

"Last night. That's when they found him."

"What do you mean 'found him'?"

"You remember Marco Duomo? Gina and Connie's brother?"

"Yeah."

"Three days ago, he got busted, selling a trunkload of guns to under-cover cops. He's going away. No entrapment or anything; they have him. Then Penny's father disappeared."

"He got *whacked*? Why, he ratted?"

"I don't think so, but he was probably involved. Shit, *def*initely he was; it's too much of a coincidence. He may have been the buffer to Marco's father."

"What buffer? Why didn't Marco just go to his *father* for a go-ahead?"

"I don't know. Either Duomo wanted no part of it or Penny's father was just a partner. Nobody knows. And probably won't."

"But Duomo killed him," Martin said. Didn't mean it as a question. There probably *was* no question.

Fee said, "Yeah," like there could have been. "*Had* someone kill him, I guess. But what's the difference?"

Martin didn't say anything. Thought, Different degrees of brutality, calculation—nothing that really mattered.

"You *are* still going out with her, right?"

"Yeah."

"We should go to the funeral."

"Yeah."

"It's tomorrow. Gina said Penny probably couldn't call you."

Martin nodded, was half-listening. "She didn't think her old man was like that," he said. "We had a fight about it once."

"They never do. Gina and Connie only know because their father's always on the freaking news. Penny's father was small-time."

He nodded again. Because it was true. Poor fucker. "They're always disappearing in my neighborhood, guys like him."

Fee said he was sorry.

Martin didn't answer.

"We can drive out together," Fee said. "Get the day off from school."

"Uh-hunh."

Fee patted his knee and stood up. Looked around the room. "I told my father about it, just before you got here. He doesn't think he can find out what happened, though; he doesn't really know Duomo. Only from Puerto Rico, but they don't work together. He says Duomo's such an idiot he might have gotten irrational over Marco going to jail and just killed the guy for being involved, for not being there to get caught with his kid. Marco's going to do a lot of time. They were fucking ma*chine* guns"—patting his pockets now, Fee, thinking what to do about his own situation.

"Why'd you tell me this after the thing in Jersey, Fee?"

Fee looked at him. "So your head would be clear. I wasn't sure if you and Penny were still close."

"She was at the party with me, Friday. I asked you for your keys."

"I know but . . . That was her? I didn't—"

"You're a fucking idiot, you know? You're all heart."

Fee said, "Business first, man; don't be mad. Your business goes bad and you don't *have* a life. No girlfriend to even worry about. Don't be mad at me."

"I'm not mad," Martin said. "You just . . . fucking . . ." he stood up to go and Lexi was there in the door, leaning. Something small in his hands. Bright. A peeled orange. Lexi split it, offered him half—

"Tangerine?"

"No, thank you, Mr. Pasko."

"In Russia sometimes, for months, there was no fruit. I was in the black market, at the *top,* and there was no fruit."

"I'm just not hungry—I meant no disrespect. About the . . . tangerine, or what you heard me saying just now."

"You two know very little."

"I meant no disrespect."

"Shh"—his finger to his lips.

Martin looked down, looked up at him again, more impatient than scared. Why the fuck would I want a tangerine? he thought. Eat your fucking fruit and get out of my way.

Lexi said, "You go to this man's funeral. You feel sad, angry. You're respectful there. Then you go to New Jersey—" Felix said something in Russian, nervous. His father shut him up. Said, "Why? Why do you interrupt me?"—looked at Martin again, said, "You go to Jersey. You wear gloves. You get *this* stupid's money back—"

"Don't call me stupid, Daddy."

"Do I love you?"

"Yes."

"Did you do stupid?"

Felix stayed quiet.

It was so crowded, the funeral, he only kept catching glimpses of her— up front, sitting with her mother. It was crowded and somber. Closed casket. A funeral was a funeral.

He and Fee stayed in back, Fee nervous Gina'd see him and that he'd have to be nice, take her out again, maybe. She'd been flirty the other night on the phone. Saying Penny's old man was dead, but flirty.

"She can't be any other way, Fee; take a pill," Martin said to him, low. She was coming back toward them through the crowd along the side, trying not to jiggle too much.

Fee said, "No, bull*shit,*" and disappeared.

She took Martin's hand. They touched cheeks. She was acting like a woman. A lady. Narrowed her eyes on the door, where Felix had slipped out. "What's he so scared of?"

Martin said he didn't know. Asked how she was. Wondered what to say about Marco, if she even cared. She didn't seem to. Wasn't really thinking about it, apparently.

She said, "I'm fine. You okay?"

"Fine."

"Pen's really happy you showed up."

He said he wished he could talk to her. He looked and could see her now, again. Had her head on her mother's shoulder.

Gina leaned in to whisper to him. "She wants to see you. In ten minutes. By the car."

She wasn't crying. Held him for less time than he thought she would, let him go, and leaned on the car and lit a cigarette. She looked toward the parlor. "I can't believe she's here," she said.

"Who?"

"Gina."

It hadn't even occurred to him. He guessed he'd thought that what happened between their fathers had nothing to do with them. They just went to the funerals when something went wrong. Innocent of malice their whole lives. Stayed friends.

It seemed to be how Gina took it.

If she'd even figured out her father's involvement.

"You think she knows?" he said.

"She's not that stupid."

True, he guessed. Nobody *could* be.

"I've known her my whole life," she said. "We wanted to go to college together." She went to smoke, and dropped it accidentally. Ignored it and took out another one. Brushed the ashes off her coat.

It made him happy, her doing that, her lack of embarrassment. Even her distance from him, leaning on her car, absorbed in thought. It made him feel they'd been together a long time.

He had the ring in the pocket of his suit pants. He wouldn't leave it in the house. Once he'd chosen it and bought it, he felt it had to be in either of their possession for the rest of their lives.

When she's over this, he thought—a while from now—I'll give it to her. Open up a whole new life for her. For us.

He closed his hand around the box.

"We're going to have to move," she said. "My mother can't afford the house."

"Where?"

"Not far." She smiled, looked over at him. "Don't worry. Someplace in Yonkers. Or Fleetwood, where we started."

Two stops closer on the railroad, it was. A different world though, completely.

"And I won't be able to see you for a while. We're going to be busy."

He asked if he could help. "Not at *all*?" he said.

"She's got enough to deal with. Maybe a month," she said. "I'll call you. Tell you how things are going."

He touched the back of his hand to her cheek. She forced a smile and dropped the cigarette. Took keys from her coat. "I got you something," she said, and went around to the trunk. Opened it. "Turn."

He did.

She shut the trunk, and came over, her feet not shy on the gravel. He felt her laying it around his shoulders. Heavy. He looked down and saw the purple-black leather and could smell it now. A car coat they'd seen in a store window in the Village. She'd said it was a wiseguy coat when he'd said he liked it.

"I got it for your birthday," she said. "I didn't know, though, now, when I could give it to you." She sniffled. He turned. She wiped her eyes. "Not really crying," she said. "It's just being at a funeral. People die, right? You said that."

"I didn't mean it like this."

"Like this. Like everything. Straighten your shoulders," she said, and told him he looked good. He rolled his shoulders. Felt awkward, young. "Yes, you do," she said. "I got it because you liked it so much. Up until this morning, I wasn't sure if I'd give it to you. But keep it. Makes you look like a wiseguy."

"Don't say that," he said. "Come on, Pen." Talking like she was giving up, he thought. Going over to the other side, like. What was the phrase? Conceding defeat.

But, he couldn't step any closer, either, couldn't put his arms around her. Something inside her was weird. He had a feeling she'd have to talk to set it right.

"There's nothing *wrong* with it, Martin. As long as you do it like a man. Like an animal. Don't be nice. Small-time." She wiped her eyes. Wasn't tearing anymore, though. "Marco made a pass at me once," she said. "I told him to fuck off, basically. I've been wondering—"

"No," he said. He started in toward her—

"No, I know that"—she put up a hand to stop him, to finish—"I know it wasn't revenge. But if I had said yes, I wonder if it would have helped. If he'd have gotten more clout, my father. Without even knowing where it came from, you know? But from his angel, it would have been, who gave his boss's son a hand job, or something." She raised her eyebrows. Shrugged—*Who could know?* "I have to go," she said. "I'll call you soon. I promise." He watched her go.

Didn't see her again for seven years.

■　■　■

They grabbed him a block from school, Felix buying a gyro on the corner and him reading the headlines at the newsstand, looking for anything on Penny's father or Marco Duomo, Charlie Mirra coming up and slipping a hand under his elbow—"Into the car"—the Eighty-eight waiting just the other side of the newsstand, the back door open, Tommy Marzolino behind the wheel.

Inside, he was glad he'd just pissed back at school, because his bladder opened up seeing the Olds. His briefs had a wet spot now where his penis was touching them. He adjusted himself. A toughguy move, either way. He asked Charlie where they were going. Mirra ignored him. Told Marz to take Ninth Avenue—"We're not fighting that traffic again."

When they passed the Lincoln Tunnel, he knew they were only going back to the neighborhood, and not to Jersey. That trip would have meant he was going to die, probably. And he'd have probably never known the reason.

In front of Rocco's restaurant, they pulled in. Charlie got out, waited on the sidewalk for him. He got out.

Inside, they went straight back, the dining room between lunch and dinner, nobody around but a few busboys. Rocco talking to the bartender. Only glancing when they passed through.

In the office, Charlie told him to sit, then stood behind him, back at the door. Rocco came in, passed him, sat behind his desk. "What'd you do for Joe Moon and Peter Hughes?" he said. He took his cigarettes out of his shirt, lit one. Past tense, he said it. So he knew. And, it was over.

Martin shrugged. A small one. "Nothing," he said. Like, Why, is something wrong? But his accent had come out like a kid's—heavy on the t-h. Showed his fear, he knew.

"They're gone. They're not coming back. Vinny Miniati neither. What'd you do?" Dragged on the cig.

Martin looked at him. Really couldn't think beyond just seeing him there, smoking. Dealing with someone who'd crossed him. He thought, Is this the end? This skelly fucking backroom guinea office? Holy shit.

"I'm not asking everything twice," Rocco said. "Show some balls."

"I did nothing," he said.

"Stand up."

He did. Heard Charlie Mirra coming up behind him, soft on the rug. Turned to look as Charlie punched him, side of the face. He got up from the carpet, stood there.

"Sit down."

He did, his knees about to give.

"You're not ratting; they're gone."

"Why?"

" 'Cause they were stupid. Don't you be."

"When?"

"Answer me."

"I just carried samples."

"Of *babanya*."

"Yeah."

"To Vinny."

"Yeah. To the candy store. On Mulberry and Grand."

"How often?"

"Every couple of weeks."

"What'd they pay you?"

"Two hundred. A hundred at first."

"For how long?"

"Three years, maybe."

"Maybe?"

"Three years."

It had been fall when they started. Them meeting him outside of the subway, uptown— *"Get in back,"* Joe said— *"we want to talk to you . . . Did I say you could open the window?—it's cold this early—put up your window. You, too, Pete." "I had to call his name, didn't I, you fag?" "Well, he's in the car now, fag you; put up the window"*—and it was fall now. Thanksgiving coming up. His birthday, too.

Rocco said, "Two months ago, you got a call. From Peter."

"Yeah."

"And?"

"He told me to run over into the courtyard, behind his mother's building, on Spring. Then he opened the window and dropped out a box, wrapped up. Like shirts from a laundry. Told me to run."

"Then?"

"Then the feds picked him up and let him go. The same day, I think. They didn't have anything on him."

"Where's the box?"

"Now? I don't know."

"Where'd you *put* it?"

"In a locker at the pool."

"On Leroy Street?"

"Yeah. I gave Joe Moon the key. He came by my school like a week later."

"Anybody ever ask you anything? Approach you?"

"Cops? No. Everything was easy. For three years. Except for the thing with his mother's house, and he told me not to even sweat that."

"You should've," Rocco said, exhaled. Crushed the cigarette.

"Are the cops coming for me?"

"What do you think?"—didn't look up, killed the ash off completely. Which meant that they weren't. *That* shit Rocco wouldn't allow.

You'd have been dead already, Martin told himself. Assured himself.

"The shop's closed," Rocco said. "You don't work here no more. Leave."

And he went to Felix's and got wrecked. Finished the bottle they kept behind the entertainment center, told Felix it was nothing—his getting picked up off the street, or the bruise in his cheek, his eye half-shot with blood. Neighborhood business. Didn't tell him that he was a kid who'd been up like a star since he'd come out of Spofford and now was down. That that trip was over. *He* was over, and really didn't know what he was going to do.

He went out later and got another bottle, didn't go home. Didn't want to be anywhere near Thompson Street.

∎ ∎ ∎

He'd worked out the details with Felix of how they would get back the cash from the toughguy in Jersey, planned what they would say and do—threaten him calmly and with assurance until he went to the safe around back of the wet bar that Fee had seen him put the money in, tell him, If you ever open your mouth, no one'll ever hear from you again—total disappearance—and they drove out Sunday night, Martin half-whacked still, and drinking in the car, not talking.

The guy opened the door with the freaking chain on and asked what the fuck they wanted, and Martin kicked his way in and caught him running, hit him and sent him down, hit him as he went down. Went to his knees and hit him more. Jumped up and stomped on him—his face, neck, anything above the shoulders. Tried to crush his hands when they darted in the way. Tried to stomp one, then, fast, to the other, then to the first again, his arms out for balance, like he was aiming for panicked little animals on the carpet.

Felix pulled him off and flung him, jammed the Baretta under the guy's chin. So shocked, at first, he couldn't speak, just stared back in some wide-eyed amazement. The safe did have a combination after all—*Jesus, man,* his eyes said.

Drunk. He stayed that way. Stopped going to school. Saw *Battle-ground* on the tele and joined the army, catching a class just before it started, was on a bus to Fort Hamilton two days later. He was becoming like them—like Rocco and Lexi. They weren't born hard, he told himself; they just refused to do things society said, and now they were good at it. But he wouldn't be that way. Monstrous like that. Killing guys he knew his whole life, over money. And pride. Leaving daughters fatherless. He didn't know *what* he would be, but he couldn't not care about things at all. So, for a while, he'd try being no one. Let the army take care of the day-to-day details till he figured out some new way to be. A man. A better one. They'd wake him up and keep him busy, the military. Penny could mourn, he thought, and he could clean up. Then, in a few months, he'd come back on leave and they'd start over again. She'd be proud he left the wiseguys behind and made moves to become something else. Proud of him and proud he'd come back for her though he'd left the rest of his other life in the past.

He looked out the bus window. Took comfort in the Shirelles, back of his mind, singing they'd be true to him.

D own in Georgia, they made him turn out his pockets. He handed over Penny's ring and found a wad of fifty hundreds in the inside pocket of the new car coat. He counted them quick. Realized it was his cut from the Jersey thing. Had no recollection of Felix giving it to him. Only one of him counting the money on the couch saying "There's a lot more here than my seventeen"—he lying on the bed, finishing the bottle.

The Pfc. looked up from the pile and took him in—leather jacket, yellow bruise and eye, perfect hair. Opened the ring box and looked in. Began to record the belongings on the outside of a manila envelope.

"Don't ask," Martin said to him.

"Don't give a shit, nohow," the Pfc. said.

W *hat he would remember from those early weeks and months? What he would choose not to forget? The mornings. The smell of the grass, just cut. Lawns everywhere around the base, and always so close-cropped. The healthy mornings. After waking again from another evening with no letter from her, one or two from Felix, a few from his mother, and dozens from Frito.*

He stopped writing to her. If she can't understand who I'm trying to become, I'll do it alone, was the idea.

He'd fly out of bed, straighten his bunk, and pull his boots on, stand at attention. He couldn't wait. Took good, deep breaths. Could not wait to get outside.

▪   ▪   ▪

S ister?"—he had the feeling she wasn't sleeping. Couldn't see her well in the darkness and she'd been still for hours, but he could feel her thinking. Some primitive sense, it was. Some instinct to pick up on consciousness. "You can get the doctor, if you want."

"Fine"—she began to get up.

"Tell me something first, though."

She waited, her hands on her knees, her body pitched a little forward to rise.

"Did your life ever . . . come apart? Nothing could be the same?"

"When the Nazis arrived."

"But did you ever ruin things for yourself?"

"It was this—the same—when the Nazis arrived."

He didn't get it. Said so.

"I left my country," she said. "Abandoned it to them."

"You'd be dead, though, probably, no?"

"Yes. I would be dead"—still waiting to get up.

He said, "Stay there a minute, would you? Lean back, so I can tell you something?"

She reclined, stiff.

"When I was a kid I saw these two guys kill this other guy," he said. "And I'd kind of liked this guy, too, for about a minute. He was bad news, though, it turned out. That's why they killed him. I liked the killers, too, by the way. A lot. And I mean they *really* killed him. They stomped him to death. But what I'm saying is, some people seem to have things coming to them. You ever think that? They live their life a certain way, treat other people bad, so what can they expect? And I know you're thinking It's God's role to judge, lest ye be. But a lot of times it happens so fast it's just done. They've been judged. And *you* have to look at the ones who did the judging then, and see if they know badness enough, themselves, to decide. And, if they did, who are we to judge them?"

Nothing—she didn't respond. He wondered if she would. If he *wanted* her to, even. "They're dead now, too, by the way," he said.

She raised her chin, and paused. In interest? he wondered. In judgment? "Not be*cause* of the guy," he said. "For other reasons. Years later."

She lowered it again. Had learned what she wanted to, he guessed. "Perished by the sword?" he said to her.

She didn't answer.

"I worked for them, when I was older," he said.

She looked up again. With no expression. Waiting for him to finish now.

"When I was fourteen I caught two guys—two Italians guys, from Brooklyn—trying to steal a car that belonged to the Mafia guy, Rocco, who ran my neighborhood. They were doing it for a joke, it turned out—a prank—but I was coming through a park nearby, and there were a couple of kids I knew there, and they saw what these guys were doing but wouldn't say anything or go after them. They were in shock, really. So I grabbed a knife from one of them and chased the guys away. And, as these things happen, the guy whose car it was didn't care—never thanked me, or anything—but a couple of weeks later, I was going to school, and those two guys I'd seen kill that other guy when I was a kid asked me to do a favor for them after school, and I did it. When I got back, they gave me a hundred-dollar bill. I was *fourteen*, Sister. My mother was a secretary and my father was dead. I'd run errands for people before—for Mafia guys—a lot of kids did, but this was different, working for them in secret. At a hundred dollars a time. More when things took off. I was working *with* them."

"Drugs."

"Heroin."

She blinked, he thought he saw, through the darkness. Then she nodded. Kept her eyes down.

He said, "Nothing surprises you."

"We used it after the war. To break the soldiers' addictions to morphine." She closed her eyes and kept them closed, the glisten gone from her face.

"It's not *your* fault," he said.

She opened them. Didn't smile, though.

"You, ah . . . got a lot on your mind, sister. You should go to confession, let it out."

"And yours is finished?" she said. "I'll get the doctor"—leaned forward in the chair again.

"There's one more thing," he said. She stopped. "My father was a junkie. A heroin addict. Kind of a successful musician for a while, but it didn't last and he killed himself. I think because he couldn't quit heroin and couldn't support his family at the same time. He couldn't bear that."

She came over. Lifted his head. Punched his pillow and set him down again. He couldn't read her face. She went a few steps toward the door, and stopped, turned. Had something to say, apparently, before she left. He thought, Don't answer me like a nun. *Please.* Don't change the subject and ask me what the fuck I want for dinner. " 'When I was a child, I spake as a child,' " she said, " 'I understood as a child, I thought as a child—but when I became a man, I put away childish things, and began to speak as a man, and understand as a man, and think as a man.' "

He knew the verse, had heard it a hundred times. "Ecclesiastes?"

"Corinthians."

"So it's in the past?" he said. "I put it behind me? I don't learn from it?"

"Think as a man. Act like one."

Later, Corso came in. Stood down the end of the room, quiet for a second, smiling. Clapped his hands and held them closed. Like he had news. "True bill, buddy; you're going to trial."

She left. Made no noise of contempt or disgust, just wouldn't be there. Corso said, "You won her over, hunh?" and walked to the window, looked out. "I told you to do the right thing, plead guilty, but nope. And, I'll be honest, your lawyer's getting the gun checked out by independents because our people found a print, a partial one. Could be Terry Hughes's, Felix Pasko's, mine. But you're going to lose. I'm tempted to ask you again why you killed them, let you mitigate your sentence, but part of me wants to see our prosecutors draw out all your bullshit—"

Martin ignored him—his game, his clown show. Knew what the man wanted.

He looked himself over. In bed like a cripple. Everybody would take turns dismissing him now, he knew, till he was better.

As a kid, the fact that he'd be facing this would have been inconceivable. He'd watched them near ruin the neighborhood once, the government, when he was twelve and thirteen. Some Sicilians going to war with the New York goombahs over heroin, and the bloodshed made the papers and the feds got wiretaps. Then the wiseguys started looking out for themselves—a lot of them—one after the other, for a while. A period there when you'd be sitting in the park and hear how one or another had turned over, and you'd think, Them *too?* Those *fucks;* you never thought *they* would do it. And then you'd think how things must have really been worse than you'd imagined, and now you'd never see *them* again, either, because they had cut themselves loose, too, in the end. They'd known they were dead otherwise. He would picture them disgusted and sad that they'd been turned—been made to fail—and he would sit there in Thompson Street Park and look around and try to see if there were other signs that everything was falling apart.

Then, that bad time had passed. After, the only guys that anyone talked about were the ones that had stayed quiet and took jail time. They were the backbone. The kind of men all kids who were striving hustlers wanted to become.

He thought now, Well, not everyone can be a hero. That fucking simple. That lousy. Sometimes you can just be a man. Who brings down everyone he knows. Everyone who *knows,* on their own, that they couldn't get away with it forever.

Because that heroin war was a long time ago. And the government was like the sixth family now. They were always in there playing, these days. Like some fucking expansion team you'd first thought wouldn't last.

He closed his eyes. If protection was a *choice,* he had no other. He'd *never* be some convict doing time. Maybe a fingerprint would set him free on the murders, yes, after he'd signed an immunity deal on the smack, then they'd have no choice but to let him go, painful as it would be for them. And then his soul-wife and his money were out there, waiting. But if not?—in the meantime, he'd send Lexi up. Why not. And the others. *Ev*eryfuckingbody. See what kind of future that traded for.

He opened his eyes. Knew this Corso was going to make him ask, though, would extend no hand, suggest no help. Would make him crawl. ". . . probably be the kind of thing you wonder how long the jury will take" Corso saying now, gazing out the window. Then silent. Had reminded himself of something. Or was beginning to enjoy his own bull- shit. Even believe it, maybe.

Maybe wisdom was compromise. Maybe that's what all men knew somewhere inside.

An idea that conceded defeat, he guessed. But he was defeated.

He thought, You shouldn't have tried to kill me, Lexi. You neither, Bunny.

And that peanut gallery of wiseguys all my life? They should have let me grow up like a man, not a boy at play.

"Mr. Corso?"

Corso looked back from the window. "Agent Corso."

"What did I say?—Mister?"

Nodded—a single drop of the chin.

"What do you know about witness protection?"

Mister Agent Corso asked him what he wanted to know.

The big secret location for a witness in custody? Floyd Bennett Field.

He said, "The place off the Belt Parkway?"

Corso said yes.

"Who was he—Bennett?"

Corso had no idea.

"What's at the airfield, then?"

"Hangers. Privacy. Lot of rookie cops."

Dolan smiled.

"They're going to protect me?"

"They're learning to drive," Corso said.

"What the fuck are you talking about?"

They brought him down in an ambulance. Twenty minutes into the trip he asked the attendant to knock him out with something, wouldn't be able to take three hours lying down and riding backward. South Brooklyn was no mysterious destination. He said, "Wake me when we get there."

Davis said he'd come down and meet him *pro bono* to talk about the legal options fresh. Had to do some more research first and make some calls. The story in the papers would keep saying he was in a coma, held for murder. Lexi probably still waiting to hear he was dead.

That afternoon, before they left, he asked Corso to bring him in a phone, didn't want his mother thinking he wouldn't be waking up. Sister Agatha sat quietly, in the corner near the door. Corso plugged in the phone. He started to dial and Corso walked down to the end of the bed and sat.

"She's not involved," Martin said to him.

"I can't leave. Just call."

"It's bugged anyway, right?"

"No"—shook his head. "A little give-and-take. A little trust. It's standard policy."

"You're full of shit."

"I'm not. We got to try and think of you as one of us, now."

"That's sweet, thank you. But you're still going to sit there, though."

"You're not going to be alone for a long time. You can't imagine."

She answered on the first ring. He said, "It's me, Ma. I'm fine. I'm not in a coma and I'm not being held for anything. For *mur*der, or anything."

Corso raised an eyebrow to himself—*Not exactly true*-like. Martin looked away, kept him out of view.

"Then what happened? Are you hurt at all? Are you in trouble still? Where are you?"

"In a hospital, upstate," he said to her. "But I'm fine. I'm in custody. I got hurt. It's complicated." *"The kid with the shank?—an illegal," Corso'd told him. Had come in from Canada, probably, and they still had no ID on him, no bail set.* "And I didn't do anything, Ma; we're working something out." *Corso'd said, "He's probably completely untraceable. Won't talk. Couldn't finger who hired him anyway, I'm sure—too many buffers—but you know who it was. And don't say it could have been anybody since you own a nightclub filled with Russians. You know, and I know, who it was." And he'd thought, Still, though, the old man had flown in the face of the feds in that courtroom and told them, "Fuck your suspicions—I'm untouchable. Catch me if you can," and they couldn't. Not alone.*

"What's to work out if you didn't do anything, Martin?"

"Nothing, Ma. It's complicated."

"Don't give me that bullshit, you. What is it? What's happening here? Are Frito and I in the middle—"

"No, Ma; it's over. We're working something—"

"Jesus Christ, what happened? Will you answer me?"

She was crying, anger making her come apart.

"Ma"—he wanted to tell her to stop. Corso still sitting there motionless. "Ma, listen to me. I think that you and Frito and Juliet—"

"Hello?"

"Frito?"

"Yeah. Are you okay?"

"I'm fine, buddy. You all right? What's happening down there?"

"Nothing. The papers said—"

"I know. Listen, I called for two reasons. To tell you don't believe the papers, and that I definitely want you to go away for a while. I'm going to testify. I decided. You don't tell that to anyone—"

"Jesus—"

"Whatever. You got to be the man there, now. Take charge."

"When do you testify?"

"I don't know. A year, maybe, I'll start?" He looked at Corso. He nodded. "Probably a year."

"We have to leave for a year?"

"I don't know. Just leave now and I'll figure the rest out."

"What do we do? Once you testify? Where do we go then?"

"Buddy, I can't . . . Just do this now, okay? I'm sorry. How's Mom? She all right?"

"She's fine."

"I don't have all the answers yet, Frito."

"It's okay," Frito said. "I'll handle it."

"Good. How's Juliet?"

"She's fine—"

"Good—"

"We're all fine. We've been calling."

"It's been crazy, man—complicated. I'm sorry. But get to work on shipping out, all right? I'm going to go. I'll call you later, again. Tonight or tomorrow. Tomorrow probably. See how things are going. But do me a favor. Frito."

"Yeah."

"I want you to answer the phone from now on. I don't want to talk to her right now. I can't. Okay?"

"Okay."

"I'll talk to you tomorrow."

"Okay."

He hung up. Lay back and stared at the ceiling. "Thanks."

"No problem."

"How many times did she call?"

"Thirty?"

He closed his eyes. Tried not to imagine her. "What did you tell her?"

"You were okay."

"And that that was all you could."

"Yup."

"Felix's people call?"

"Yup. For his body. And Terry's people. Autopsies are done. We gave them the case numbers. They claimed them immediately. Already been shipped. You got a girlfriend, Quinn?"

"What? Not really."

"We got a call. A phone from the street. Asking about you."

Her, of course. He shrugged. No reason to answer about it.

"Was it Felix Pasko's wife?"

"What? What kind of question is that? She didn't say who she was?"

"She gave a name. Run some by me."

"I know a lot of people. Lot of women."

Corso softened his voice, his chin on his chest—"You . . . ah . . . screwing her?"

"What?" He didn't look down, kept his face toward the ceiling. "You mental?"

"Are you screwing her, Quinn?"

"Give it a rest."

"Why'd you shoot Felix Pasko?"

"Motherf—don't start that again, man, please. Don't I even get to mourn that he's gone?"

Whispering—"You have feelings? Fuck your feelings. You know I still don't believe you. Why was she calling? Why'd she give a different name?"

"How do you know it was even her?"

"We'll run the voices through the system. Voiceprints are even better than fingers."

"That's a bit high-tech, no?—why not forget it? I have no interest in his wife."

"Say her name."

"Penelope. I've known her since high school. I introduced them, for Christ's sake. She probably thinks I fucking killed him."

"Why would she think that?"

"What did you tell her when she called?"

"Which time? From the house or from the street?"

"Give it a rest, man; let it go; there's nothing there."

"Penelope," Corso said, looking up. Dreamy-like.

"Penelope," Martin said.

" 'We'll be together once I ice him, dear Penelope.' "

"When are we leaving here?"

"Tomorrow."

"Can I call my brother before we go?"

"Yup."

"There'll be a phone down there, too, no? At Floyd Bennett Field?"

"Everything down there. All the amenities."

"Better food?"

"All takeout."

"Hmm," he said. Had to change the subject. "Do me a favor, would you? There's an Italian restaurant on the main street here. Can you get me something heavy. An Alfredo or a Carbonara. I have to get some strength back before we leave. I'm dropping weight by the hour."

"This minute you want it?"

"Is it a big deal? I just can't take this food. Five days on a drip, and then watery eggs and dry toast. I'd rather have the IV."

Corso stood up, said, "I'll be back, then."

"You want something, sister?" Martin said. Didn't look at her, there, in her corner—watching all this spin away beyond belief, he guessed.

She didn't say anything he could hear, though. Had simply shook her head, he figured. One pass, left to right. Two days ago he'd seen her eat a package of soup crackers and it took her an hour. Little oyster hexagons.

Corso smiled, his eyes still on Martin's. "I want to know about Pasko's wife."

"Don't insult me, Corso; she's a nice girl. I've known her ten years. I introduced them."

"Yeah, okay," and finally went out. Martin stayed as he was, eyes on the ceiling. The door closed. Corso talking to the agent in the hall, then. Then walking away, squishing his rubber soles down the hall.

Martin grabbed the receiver off the phone, bore the bang of the pain in his twisting around, and dialed with the same hand, poking awkward. Frito answered. "Go to France," Martin said, "to Juliet's house. And call Penny and tell her I'm okay. Tell her *not* to call again, that the phones are bugged, and to stay with Lexi Pasko. But to also pay her rent. Pay any rents that are due, tell her. I'll miss you." He hung up—reached for the cradle and pressed the small plastic nub, Frito's voice trailing, then gone. He set the receiver down carefully and rolled onto his back again. Listened. No one approaching the door. He raised his head a few seconds later and looked over into the corner. "Would you trust him?" he said to her.

She didn't respond.

Was gone, a little later, when they left for Brooklyn.

Reduced to simple necessities. It was fine. The DA's office upstate was holding his clothes; he had his wallet back, and his keys. Which were all there, Gotham Storage units included. They were all he and Penny would ever need again from that life. Till then, he'd do his duty and be patient. Day One in the Witness Protection Program.

Government Issue civies they'd provided him with. Which made him smile. Dolan carrying in a nice stack of new duds—piled high and held in place below the black shoes sitting on top. Flight jacket, officer's sweater, chinos, white T-shirts, some briefs, socks, a web belt. He'd lived comfortably in the same outfit after the army, then slowly weaned himself off of it wearing an article here and there from the civilian world again, trusting it didn't mean his new self-discipline would fly apart.

Young Dolan handing him this new gear, though? Like a surly quartermaster? Take it as an omen, he guessed. The time has arrived again to start over. Unadorned.

He put the jacket on a hanger in the gray, steel wardrobe in the corner. The sweater, second pair of pants, and all the underwear he refolded and put up on the short shelf, above it. He'd be fine in a T-shirt. The room was warm. And wide. Maybe thirty feet high, twenty deep, fifty long. Metal on the three sides that were the hangar proper, cinder block on the fourth, where they'd bricked up straight to the ceiling to create the place. Intended just for this, almost ten years back, built on a city contract, Corso said. The attorney general had gone on a mission to hunt wiseguys and corrupt cop officials, and a lot of goombah hangouts had been shut down. A few cops had committed suicide. A crackdown Martin knew all about. But which he kept to himself. Wouldn't say a *thing* now till he knew its worth precisely. He wondered, though—maybe some neighborhood guy had been here before him.

Two beds by the wardrobe. Wool blankets. Clean, white sheets. A pair of short couches along the back wall and an armchair at an angle to them, for conversation or television. A big television, but getting old-looking. Kitchenette, big fridge. A folding table and chairs, center of the room, and, down from the door, a desk with a phone and fax machine. Corso still on the phone, talking shorthand and taking notes on a yellow pad, nearly an hour now, by the clock on the stove, and Dolan still sunken into the armchair, smoking. Something he hadn't been doing any of before. Though Martin had smelled it on him. A young, hard character, Dolan. Younger than Martin was. And completely his job. Devoted to it. With all its good and bad. That commitment made him a solid, good guy. And, something of a chump. Chain-smoking one now, gazing half-dead-like at the TV, like praise God it would pop to life.

A lot of time in Protection was spent in front of a TV, Martin guessed. These fucking guys wanted to spend their days and nights with him as much as he did with them. But, it was none of their choices to make.

His one year in college, it reminded him of. Got put in a room with a seventeen-year-old. Told the housing administrator, "I'm twenty-four; I had a life before this," but all freshmen had to live their first year in the dorms. Then the kid—Todd? Ben? Ted?—changing within two weeks from a homesick momma's boy to a bong-smoking, shirtless fraternity pledge. Martin rented an apartment in town and swallowed the dorm fee. The added cost of freedom.

So long ago, now, that it seemed to have never been. That first year in school, he was nothing like the person he turned back into, in New York again.

And he had to admit that. He *had* become the same person he'd been when he left.

Now he had the chance to try again, he knew. There'd be no bongs *here,* though. No Introduction to Western Thought. No Freshman Psych.

There'd be agents with sidearms, meetings with U.S. attorneys. There'd be suiting-ups with flack vests for excursions to court appearances.

He rolled the IV over to the other window, see what he could see. The first one had offered just tarmac and sky. He got up close to the glass, looked out to the side, and saw what he'd hoped—the trainee cops learning to drive. He watched them. The lights and sirens on. The blue-and-whites weaving the pylon formations at high speed, one after the other. Back ends fishtailing once in a while. Good stuff.

Though after a couple of them, he could tell by the way they accelerated, the first few seconds, if they'd end up driving wild and nearly losing it. None of them ever really fucking it up completely, though, anyway. Wouldn't ever, it looked like.

Out beyond them, the bay and the Atlantic. Manhattan somewhere behind him, other direction. World Trade Center and the rest of it all in sight, maybe, if he were outside. Battery Cove and his apartment somewhere right below that. A National Preserve close by here, too—had a park official in a little booth. He'd spotted it driving in, when the ambulance attendant woke him up. *"What's to preserve in Brooklyn?"* he'd asked the guy. The guy didn't seem to get him—

"Ducks?" he'd said.

Martin looked at him. The guy was serious. Trying to be nice.

"Brooklyn ducks?" Martin had said.

Corso hung up. "Everybody playing catch-up. Un-fucking-believable, no?—the *has*sles?"—got a bit more New York when he was mad, Martin saw.

"Pain in the ass," Dolan said. No emotion in his voice. Only spoke cowboy style if he spoke at all. "You called them two days ago."

"You know it. I know it. They don't give a shit."

"You're off the phone?" Martin said.

"Yeah, you want it?"

"I wanted to ask what's next."

"What's next, Kevin?"

"We wait. Then we wait."

Being themselves more, the two of them. This element was theirs. "What for?"

Corso said, "Files. Paperwork. Other things. That I told them two days ago to have ready. The machinery of the Bureau warming up. There's supposed to be a doctor here, too, check you out. And one of our legal people. You, him, and your guy, Davis, getting things cleared up, whenever Davis gets here."

"I'm all right. They said I was good, up at that hospital."

"Not the point. Nobody cares, in fact. *I* do, of course. So does Dolan, with every fiber. But things have to be done accordingly. From now on. Done precisely. Protocols. We keep ourselves covered. Make sure your rights aren't violated."

"Yeah, 'cause I'll sue your ass."

"It's happened, chief, more than once."

"Get the fuck . . ." Martin said. Watched if he would acknowledge street shorthand, Corso. React at all.

He didn't. Except to keep talking. Acknowledgment enough—"We had a wop hit man one time"—he swiveled his chair out to face the room, remembering the story, a second. Dolan shook his head, Martin saw peripherally. "Used to change his tale every few weeks," Corso said. "On the phone with his lawyer every fucking day. Thirty-two murders he admits to. Thirty-two or -three, he says; he can't remember; he's been doing it twenty years, back and forth between here and Palermo. Hardly speaks English so we have an interpreter for him. He's racking his brains for details on a murder that he *didn't* commit—one of the few—that he was just there to witness. We figure this is the one we can pin on this guy in St. Louis we've been after. The greaseball, though?—he can't remember the shooter. He says he wasn't paying too close attention since he wasn't the triggerman; he was doing something else. Getting something from the fucking fridge, or something. They've got this guy duct-taped to a chair, cutting his fingers off one by one with little pruning shears until somebody finally pops him, but the Sicilian is in the kitchen. And he can't exactly remember everyone's name, either, anyway. After a while, I'm screaming in his face, but he's cool.

Talking past me to the interpreter. I'm thinking How the fuck do you say 'little pruning shears' in Italian, because I'm going to get a pair myself, and I say this to Kevin here, and walk away. I'm ready to bust. And the interpreter says something under his breath and the greaseball says, *"Como? Como?"* and he gets up and goes right to the phone and calls his lawyer. In Palermo, by the way—this guy he calls every day, checking every step he's going to take. Next day I get a call saying we're going to lose him. He's going to the Supreme Court. The Geneva Convention. Every fucking thing. They took me off him. Convinced him to keep cooperating, though. How many convictions we get out of him, Kevin?"

"Two."

"How many that stuck?"

"None."

"He flip-flopped again. The two guys won on appeal."

"What's he doing now?"

"Dropped dead of heart attack in a courtroom somewhere. He was three hundred pounds. I still wish I was there to see it. To this day."

He looked off, a long second, Corso. Then picked up his notepad, started reading. Dolan ran a hand over the couch arm beside him, tried the fabric out. So, either the hit man was something they didn't like talking about or they were over it completely. Martin said, "I'm pretty fit, you know. If you ignore this thing"—rattled the IV pole.

"We're not worried about you," Corso said; "you're still a young guy, memory's intact. And you know enough people, I'm betting, because we got nobody on the Russians. We take *you,* hear what you have to say, and grab somebody else. Little chain of information we build. Open a whole new area of investigation. It takes a fucking lifetime. A career. At least three-dozen unsolved murders in Brighton Beach since 1980, you know? In Little Odessa there? And the cops couldn't crack them and we thought there was nothing to crack—just immigrant violence. But we were wrong. It's emigré crime, we know now. Russian mob. *Organizatsiya,* right? *Mafiya?"*

Martin nodded. Thought for a moment how Lexi'd grown fond of saying the only Russian Mafia left was the Communist Party.

But, hadn't *stopped* thinking about this fat Sicilian hit man Corso'd mentioned.

The fact that the guy had lied meant lying was possible. Unoriginal, but possible. It was something to ask Davis about. Know the kind of sway the truth and the untruth had here.

He'd once thought he'd lie to these guys, himself, he remembered. Hadn't doubted it, back then. Not for a second. The idea seemed as long ago now as trying out college. "When do we start, Corso?"

"When everything's in order. All you have to do for a while is think. About everything you ever saw that something in your heart told you wasn't right. Everybody ever got duct-taped to a chair, got his fingers taken off knuckle by knuckle before somebody—distinct in your recollection—put two in him. Every chieftain to every nickel-and-dime frankfurter pimp. We got files and 302s coming on everyone we *know* you know, and maybe a hundred more on people you might. Just start thinking"—and back to his notes.

Had his shit together, in his way, Martin thought. Playing by the rules all the time was a pain in the ass, could break your heart. The army had been like that for a lot of guys.

Corso looked at him. Had sensed him looking, maybe. Said, "Flip-flopping occurs to every witness, by the way. I don't advise it. It's perjury at worst. You lose protection at best, go straight into the system. Why you smiling? You were just thinking it?"

"Not *just,* but."

"Don't at all, is my advice."

"Ten-four. Where are you from, Corso, by the way? If you don't mind me asking."

"A mile from here."

"And you?"—to Dolan.

"Ohio," Dolan said.

"Where's that?"

"Close enough."

"He's one of the best," Corso said. "Don't kid yourself. You're the one got caught."

"You got lucky," Martin said.

"I don't think so."

"Yeah. I'd like to see that narcotics case file sometime." He turned around, looked back out the window.

"What case?"

He said, "Yeah, 'a little give-and-take,' you said, didn't you? Everything up front? I'm not sure you're being completely honest with me, Agent Corso."

The rookies were done for the day, it looked like—an instructor collecting the cones, all the cars garaged. It made his heart hurt, the way a day could end when nothing was good. How many days would there be like this? he wondered. Fucking hundreds.

"Please, call me Paul," Corso said. Had some smile in his voice.

He kept looking out the window. Was tired. His wounds ached, a bit. He wanted to sit.

But he couldn't face all this, yet. Face sitting in a room with these two, twenty-four hours a day. Then, after these two, the marshals. What would it be like trying to sleep? Would people talk to him with the lights out, try to laugh about something that they'd seen on TV.

He missed Penny. Felix. Three years he'd slept in the same bed with him, in high school, like brothers, and now the sun would go down and he'd still just be dead, Fee. It would rise and he'd just be further gone. Days ago he was thriving. Eating life alive.

Would Fee have lied like the fat Sicilian? he wondered.

"Something I meant to ask you," Corso said.

"Something *I* wanted to ask. Excuse me"—he waited, listened. Corso silent. "You think I could do a murder—plan it and do it—but you'd let me off, more or less, to testify against gangsters. What is that shit?"

"Another thing every witness thinks. Like it's *our* fault. I'll tell you my feeling on it. Speaking for myself, the constant, insidious robbing of innocent, ignorant people is what rankles. The knocking each other off never bothered me. In fact, I'm a believer, in some ways, in the old-fashioned code. Doing your own laundry, cleaning out your own closets. Being an agent for the government's like that—I don't want to answer to anybody either. But I *do* get pissed when the knocking off interferes with my investigations. Not that this here did. Only to let you know."

So Corso, too, wanted things back how they'd been before. No bodies. Nothing sloppy.

Everyone here wanted everything back how it had been. He shook his head. Fucking tragedy, he thought. Said, "What were you going to ask?"

"How long you been playing toughguy. Fifteen years? Why no adult sheet? You've been running with the bad guys a long time."

"Four years in the army, some time working, some in college. I came back when I was twenty-five." And he saw it all, suddenly—the engagement announcement, the road going home, the neighborhood after so long.

"Who were you with?" Corso said. "What was your MOS?"

He focused hard on a barge out in the bay, wanted his mind clear, not flooded up with shit from the past. He said, "Listen, Corso, I got to tell you something. About the Russians. They're not glamorous like the Italians were. They're the embodiment of fucking greed. With a vengeance. Most of them in cheap suits—no camel hair. You and Dolan there go after these people for your life's work?—it's just a crusade, man—a mission. No glory. Just a place in Heaven, maybe, if you don't get weak in the meantime and let some pierogi in polyester pay your mortgage or build you a pool, showing you the only thanks you'll ever get."

But . . . no reaction. Silence behind him. Couldn't see their reflections, either. He said, "What time do these rookies start driving every morning?" Heard Corso flip a page on his notepad. Dolan turned on the tele. "Am I ever going to get to go outside?—just walk around?"

"Sure"—Corso. "Maybe we can plan a few field trips. Take a picnic."

He said, "I've never been to the Statue of Liberty." Wasn't exactly kidding; he really hadn't been.

He thought, How could I come from New York and never see Lady Liberty?

He looked for her out the window.

Mrs. Adria Potenta Anzone
joyfully announces
the engagement of her daughter,
Penelope Amiata Anzone,
to Felix Pasko,
son of Mr. and Mrs. . . .

He knew where it was, still. Tucked into the jacket of the copy of his old man's album. The copy Penny'd found in Paris on the honeymoon.

Dolan was asleep. Had moved to the couch and lain down, drifted off. Corso lowered the sound, went back to reading the pages the fax machine had started curling out an hour ago. Sat half on the desk, with a foot on the floor. Dolan and Corso both with their jackets off now, guns on their hips, ties loosened.

A buddy in the army had said Alaska was the last frontier. He'd liked the sound of that, gone with him. Figured in the hardship there'd be further peace of mind, a calm of spirit. They put their names on a list for oil-rig work, and in the meantime took their spots beside the other new-arrival pioneers on the assembly line at the salmon cannery. His buddy lasted a month—through the noise and the red-line-paced repetition and the stink—and went home to Pennsylvania, left him their copy of *Let It Bleed* and permission to see Kate, the girl they'd gotten to know, but who his buddy knew better. She tended bar in the place downstairs.

Soon enough, she was staying over. Brought food up. And then moved her TV in. They needed something to do after eating and rolling around. A nice kid she was. Young, but on her own for years. She drank too much and was always suspicious that he didn't drink at all.

After a while she was dating somebody else, same time, and the guy came by. Martin opened the door and he was there with a thirty-eight. Nothing dramatic, just showing it low, hands-up style. Katie flew off the couch and got between them, Martin saying it was okay. Wanted to say, "Take her, man; I'm easy," but Kate saying "We were just watching TV. It's all we ever do. He's my friend. He ain't got a TV," and the guy said, "You ain't friends no more, and the TV's coming with you," and Martin shrugged, waved the guy in, and let him take it. "I'll see you, Kate," he said, and went back to the couch.

The guy said, "No, you won't," and Martin stopped, looked at him.

"I won't?"

The guy sized him up, a big enough fucker himself. And older. Near forty. Said, "So, if I didn't have the piece, you'd toe the line? That what I'm supposed to think?" and he put the TV down, handed the Special to Katie. She looked at it—held it in both hands, out in front of her—like a kid with a bag of groceries she was too tired to carry anymore, wanted to hand off. Martin smiled at her. Looked at the guy, looked back into the room. Empty-seeming now, with the TV gone. Said, "No, you're not supposed to think I'd toe the line."

"Come on, Larry," Katie said, and they went to go, and she closed the door behind her, said, "Good-bye, Martin."

He said, "I'll see you, Kate."

"God damn it," Larry said, and started back through the door.

"God damn *you*," Katie said, and blocked him. "You got me, you got television. Leave it alone."

And, after a heavy-breathing few more seconds they were gone. Martin didn't even look over. They hadn't closed the door but he left it as it was.

Violence? he thought. Man, in the army, he'd seen packs of guys sneak across the barracks at night and baton down, under blankets, some kid or another whose poor performance was making their own days longer and harder—another hundred push-ups for them all, another mile to run in full gear—and they'd converge on the poor dumb fuck while he slept, slink up from all sides, secure him down, and beat him. With their fists, with socks full of bars of soap. The guy screaming but no one would come. The DI would flip on the light in his room down the row and the little punks would scurry off, and it would be over, the kid crying. Sometimes cursing, but usually not. Too fucked-up to form real words. So violence? His own, back in New York, may not have been justified, but it hadn't been fucking cowardly. He'd *seen* how other young men practiced it, and he slept just fine now.

And as for Katie being gone? he thought. Shit, a little monastic self-denial might do some good for a couple of weeks.

In spring, he went to work on the rig—big, skeletal, rusted, top-heavy island city—and learned to fear huge brute machines and the very ground beneath his feet, slick with the earth's own ooze. He'd lived in near poverty at the fish-plant job, and now made thirty-two grand in nine months. Was too tired to spend any of it, though. He quit. He traveled. Found he was heading more east than south and thought about going home. But to what?

He was back in New York State, after a while. He stopped and settled for a bit, where he was—in the middle, more or less—and let himself try school again. Decided to believe it was a means to a better future. Not the distraction that it had become when he was a kid tapping his feet and watching the clock till it was time to go back downtown and run for the wiseguys.

By his second year, though, he was burning, some nights, with loneliness. Thinking more and more about his old man. Waking every morning with something like a hangover from the dreams he could never recall but figured were the same ones he'd had every night for years after he died. Except for the nights spent at Felix Pasko's, of course. Waking up there with his head clear. The light that came through the tall windows there always good, even when it was raining out, somehow, and Felix chattering from the moment his eyes opened. Throwing himself off the side of the bed and coming around yanking all the covers off on his way to the john.

So this living far away from home?—it was like a trance, he decided. America saying the house in the country—with the cars, the isolation—was perfection. No. He wanted to be part of something again. A neighborhood. Get himself a sound union job and spend his nights at the bar of a good local place. Friends around him. None of them more than a few blocks from their homes. More and more he thought about it, his mind wandering further and further in the new round of fall courses. And then it arrived— *Mrs. Adria Potenta Anzone . . . joyfully announces . . .* —like Felix was calling him back. Gilt letters on a thick, cream-colored paper. Felix's lousy, child-ish handwriting unmistakable on the envelope in shitty ballpoint. Never able to cheat off Feel on pop quizzes, he remembered. Always chewing him out after class. Would tell him, "Make an effort at least. Write something at least half readable when we're under the gun like that." Feel always saying "I was cheating off *you*, though."

He gave the invitation a week's thought. Then spent another weekend alone. He broke his lease, threw the little he had into his winter-rat Plymouth that refused to die, and was on the road, day before the party.

How Felix had changed, he didn't know. Or, if they'd have anything in common again—a lot of fucking time had passed. But the trance was lifted. The nightmares on hold.

And what about this marrying Penelope Anzone? he wondered. The girl I slept with once and then wanted to marry, boy-ass that I was.

But, he couldn't just flat-out knock that now, he knew—that innocence. A girl like she was—young and no bullshit about her—she let you sleep with her, she already had no doubts you'd want her forever. And when someone that much better than you inside had that kind of certainty, who could question it? Who would even want to?

He drove.

What would she be like, now, though? he thought. After all this time. What did no-bullshit goodness like that turn into when life set in?

Near the New York/Pennsylvania border he opened the windows of the car to let the smell of burning wood from the tiny houses in. Knew he'd never go back to school or see this countryside again.

He checked the closet quickly and saw he would have to pick something up tomorrow, early—Frito's clothes were like a rack at a secondhand place. He searched the floor and then the shelf above, more carefully. This had been *their* closet once. His closet. Frito so young back then he needed next to nothing. "You seen my old Saint Anthony's bookbag?" he called. His mother finding him something to eat in the fridge. Was on her way out the door, herself.

"Saint *Anthony's?*" she said. "That was twenty years ago."

"Not quite." He couldn't find it.

She was in the doorway now. "We have cheese, and some chicken I made. At the beginning of the week, though."

"I'll get pizza, thanks."

"What are you looking for now? That bag?"

"I guess it's gone. And my car coat, too, now that I think about it. My three-quarter leather." Frito had come up to visit him at school last year, saw it by the door and asked to wear it, took it home, then—Martin bringing him to the bus station and taking it off and handing it to him. The kind of article of clothing an older brother should share with a kid who suddenly showed signs of catching up with him. Frito seeing it more as an antique—a costume. And that was fine. Because for *him?*—*per*sonally? By then, it was a uniform for a contest he'd forfeited a long time ago. He did want it back *now,* though. There was security in it. And, he was wishing that his hair was longer, too. That he wasn't buzzing it anymore. He felt strange back on Thompson Street looking still so GI, nothing to style.

He straightened, looked at her. Palms-up and a shrug, to ask her.
"Can't find it?" she said. "He's probably wearing it."

She said some club on Union Square, she guessed—Frito was there
every weekend. Martin went up and found the place—a cave of an
entrance that led down to a joint that sprawled back, like an underground
town. He spotted the kid on the dance floor and watched him, a while.
Spied on him in his world, like. The kid—the *guy*—still innocent, though—
not drinking or smoking; just dancing. And with one girl. Spinning around
a lot, a bit silly. His hair bleached-out so pale it glowed like a lightbulb. And
he liked this girl. Kept close to her when he wasn't spinning. Black girl.
Short, short hair. Young skin but an older face. And taller than Frito.

Martin moved to the edge of the dance floor. She noticed him first.
Seemed to pick up his being there for them. Or maybe'd seen a picture. A
few laid-back seconds later, she got Frito's attention. Frito looked up and
stopped moving. Everyone still grooving around him. He took the girl's
hand, weaved his way over. Martin said, "You're sweating up my threads."

They hugged, backed away from each other. Frito took the girl's hand
again and introduced her, like he wasn't himself unless they were touching.
Crazy in love with her. "This is Juliet," he said, and looked at her, a long second, before speaking again. Just looking at her. "This is him, Juliet."

She put out her hand. Straight and confident, from the shoulder. Martin
shook it, glanced at Frito's hand still holding her other one. "I'm pleased to
finally meet you," she said.

He had known, somehow, she would have an accent. "Martin Quinn,"
he said.

She was looking at his eyes. Wanting to like him, he guessed, but trying
to determine was he good or bad, here in person, for his little brother. Her
shock-haired Romeo. Loved Frito back, Martin saw, but different than
Frito loved her. And the kid needed a guardian, he guessed he understood
now. Going to college in the fall—with no major in mind at *all,* his mother
said—and still dancing around like a child.

They talked all night, in the lounge. Frito bringing him up-to-date on what was what, Juliet sitting pretty-much quiet beside him, watching him as he talked. Trusting Martin enough now to stop studying him, going back to enjoying this young man they both felt they had to look after. She was French, Frito said. They met at orientation at Columbia. Her mother was at the UN. Had heard their old man play in Paris in '69. Martin told them why he was home and they listened carefully, didn't speak. Were two teenagers to him, then. They said nothing when he was done. In love and thinking they would always be, and had no idea what to say about the lives of adults. He reminded himself that when he was their age he'd carried a ring around everywhere, waiting for the right moment to propose to Penelope. Remembered how close they'd gotten in just six months. Remembered, he guessed, how it felt to believe you would never be any older and would never find, suddenly, that you felt different about things. It was college that would probably split these two up, he thought.

He said he would need the coat tomorrow. Might start wearing it again and maybe nobody would notice he'd been gone.

Frito laughed. "You haven't changed; believe me. Your letters, when you were traveling, were about different things, new things, but you were the same in them. Always."

Outside the club, he and the girl, Juliet, waited while Frito used the bathroom.

"You love her still," she said. Was looking at the entrance, past the crowd of kids lined up to get in. Had her arm hooked into his, her other hand lying on his forearm. Something he'd have to get used to. Her sophisticated affection. What was meant by "continental," he guessed. He said—

"No." And smiled. Because, aloof as she was on the surface, underneath she was still hoping to hear something romantic. "I've been away too long for something like that. Any nervousness you're getting off me is just me wondering what it means to be back. What people will think. Will I want to stay. Things like that. I've been away a long time."

"You were in the army?"

"A few years ago."

"Well, *that* doesn't even show in you. So you shouldn't worry. You look like you've never left. New York." She waved her hand out before them. To show where she meant. Laid it back on his arm. "Here he is"—Frito coming down the steps.

"You know where he got his name from?" Martin said. She raised her chin, listening, eyes on Frito. "From the corn chip. Delicate. Crispy, I used to call him, when he was a kid. From Christopher."

"Crispy," she said, as Frito came up. "He would never tell me."

"That's right," Frito said. Stood there and looked at them, a second. Uncomfortable they'd been talking about him. "You ready?"

"He's a piece of work," Martin said.

She reached out and touched the kid's cheek. Moved her hand to his forehead and brushed the damp hair off it. "I think he's beautiful," she said. " 'What a piece of work is a man.' "

A few blocks away, they hailed her a cab, and said goodnight. Martin opened the door for her. She took his face in her hands and looked at him, a moment, kissed him on the lips. He didn't kiss her back. Could tell she didn't expect it. Making some smart teenager point and he guessed he had to let her. "He loves you very much," she said. Earnest. But with respect in her voice. Like she'd kiss her own father this way. Talk to him like this when she was most serious, then maybe stand his collar up, to make sure he stayed warm.

She let him go. Went to kiss Frito again. And then hugged him, a while more, and got in. Martin let the kid watch the cab till it was out of sight. Frito said, "I'm going to marry her." Martin said nothing. "That doesn't surprise you?"—the kid looking at him.

"We'll talk about it."

"Is that right?"

Martin smiled. "You want to walk home?"

Frito said yes.

They walked.

"You spend my four thousand dollars on her?" Martin said. "Or you just move it out of the closet?"

"On her and other things," Frito said. Without a pause. "Mostly her."

"That means I got to get a job sooner than I thought."

"You wrote me you made a bunch on the oil rig."

"It's gone, mostly."

"On women?"

He said, "Yeah, and other things. Mostly women."

He didn't hear the alarm and woke up past eight, ran downstairs to move the Gran Fury. It was alone on its side of the street, had a ticket under the wiper and a big green fucking sticker on the driver-side window saying the block couldn't be cleaned because of him. Everyone else already doubled-up across the street from Prince to Spring. He left it parked there and took the train down to Delancey and bought a suit. Went with a blue-gray, single-breasted. Autumn-weight.

The whole Orchard and Delancey Street scene had changed. Half the stores were Korean and the old Jewish guy he bought the suit off kept calling him "Homeboy." Martin talked him down to two-fifty, with a pair of shoes, paid full for a shirt and tie— *"Egyptian cotton. Two hundred count. Chinese silk. I don't pay rent?"*—walked home and took things in. The changes were everywhere. Little Italy was reduced to just Mulberry Street. Thompson Street had boutiques and tiny, one-room bistros in every other storefront. They flanked the club and the other joints. All the cars were foreign.

Even back when he was a kid, though, the Italians had started to park in garages, all the old arrangements with the cops sacrificed for new ones—for a more important, deeper-buried secrecy. But, still, there was no evidence that *any* Italians had ever lived here, with the exception of the tricolor painted on the wall of the handball court.

He thought of an old-time wiseguy named Speed who used to say all the time, "It ain't the fifties no more, fellas; take nothing for granted." It was looking like he was right.

Spent the last few years of his life in and out of the clink, Martin remembered. Did six, eight months at a time for contempt. Died in there, mouth shut, no deathbed confessions.

He hung the suit up and put the shoes on to break them in. Ironed the shirt and hung it separate. Got a razor from the medicine cabinet and went downstairs to scrape the sticker off the car. The door to the club was closed. Kids ran around in the park, yelled like savages. The Twin Towers rising down the end of the island still, like Thompson Street led right into them. It all felt right. He could stay, a while, he knew. Needed a job, though. Soon. Maybe sanitation, he thought. Slap stickers on cars. He smiled. Scraped. Someone was crossing the street, middle of the block, behind him. He clocked them coming in the blotched-up reflection.

"They got you, hunh?"

He turned.

Bunny Lamentia. Still too laid-back to have to smile. A good person to see, your first day back, he thought. A good side of the past. The old loyalty beefs too petty for him even when they were young. "Easter Bunny."

"Win-with-Quinn."

"What's up, Pasqualie?"

"Nothing. Where you been?"

"The army."

Made a sideways noise through his lips, Bunny—he'd have *none* of that. "Fucking . . . why?"

"A little structure."

"You got that here. Nothing ever changes."

"Yeah, well."

"Oh, that's right—Rocco bounced you. I forgot about that."

And iced your old man, Martin thought.

Bunny's mother not even moving off the block. Knowing her kid would have to pay Rocco back, one day. Take back what was theirs.

Bunny caught his image in the rear-door window, touched at his 'do.

"You still brush your hair a hundred times a day?" Martin said.

"You still dig men?" He straightened, satisfied with the styling. Spoke looking up the block. "You left 'cause of him?"

"Rocco? Fuck no."

"Yeah. A million reasons, I guess, right? What you doing back?"

"Don't know yet."

"You staying?"

"I think so."

Bunny stepped in, a bit. A car passed. "Working?"

"Got here yesterday."

"This your car?"

"Yeah."

"Piece of shit."

"Needs work."

"Needs a fucking priest. It brings down the whole neighborhood."

Martin smiled, started scraping again. He'd always liked Bunny. He said, "These fucking shops are ruining things, no? Boutiques? Bistros? What the fuck is a bistro?"

"A hole in the wall. No liquor license. B-Y-O-Vino, you yuppie slaves. I heard it was Mirra picked you up off the street," Bunny said. "Threw you a beating."

Martin shook his head, looked at him, to let him see the disbelief. Said to him, "Why would you remember that, Bunny? *I* don't remember that."

"In-like-Quinn. He got old, you know, Mirra. Did some time and it aged him. Marzolino, too. The joint's tough when you're older, people say. And Richie Jinta's dead. And Fischetti. Bobby Stella. Morello. Ray Balls. Mikey Ha Ha."

"Bunny."

"What?"

"I don't care."

"Okay."

"You're alive. What more could I want?"

"True."

Bunny came around, lowered his ass onto the fender. "You need a job?"

Martin looked at him. Went back to the sticker.

"Oh, you want to stay out of trouble," Bunny said.

"If I can."

"Big if."

Martin straightened, leaned on the car. "You going to just stand here?"

"I got nothing to do"—and shrugged. Turned his head and looked at something across the street. Carefully. Martin looked. Saw a kid hustling out from the pizzeria. The kid stopping at the curb and popping the top on a soda, sipping fizz, and starting to run again, back across, to the park. "Stop," Bunny said.

The kid stopped.

"Look both ways."

The kid did. Ran across and slowed as he was passing them, sipped the Coke. "It's only one way," he said, didn't look up.

Bunny cuffed him on the back of the head—batted out sideways, soft—not looking. The kid ignored it, knew it was coming. Kept going into the park.

"So, you need a job, or no?"

"Doing what, man?"

"All kinds of shit. They don't know." He motioned back toward the club—a quick head-flick.

"Building up the empire?"

"Takes time."

" 'Royalty in exile,' " Martin said.

"You remember that?"

"I just did."

"Rumble Fish," Bunny said. "Good flick. Coppola."

"A *paisan*," Martin said.

"Fucking A"—looking off at things, his chin raised, a bit. Even better-looking in his twenties, now. Girls used to follow him, stop when he stopped. He'd turn the corner, a few seconds later, they'd be bringing up the rear. Bunny always pretending they weren't really there. Said now, "That Mickey Rourke, though? What's with that guy? 'I whisper all my lines, so I'm a toughguy' or what? He's like a fucking . . . weird fag tries to talk to you in mensroom."

"He was good in that *Pope of Greenwich Village,* though."

Bunny nodded. Bobbed his head. "True enough." Was quiet.

Kids hollered in the park.

"They filmed that here," Bunny said.

"No shit? Right here in Greenwich Village?"

Bunny said, "I'm going to go," and came off the car. No change in his voice, his face, anything—ignoring him. Martin smiled. Looked away before Bunny turned. Bunny said, "I give this piece of shit a week. Transmission. Starter. Few hundred dollars' worth of work. Come see me then."

"Where? For the sake of discussion."

"My father's restaurant."

He'd always called it that, Bunny. It was down the block from Rocco's.

"You'll put me on waiting tables?"

"Please; I got actresses for that shit. Enough for a whole prison flick."

"Chained Beauties."

"*Chained* Heat," Bunny said. "Linda Blair. You see her tits in the scene with the warden, in the bathtub. *Nice.* Look at that." He reached in a pocket, took out a pager. Read it. "The day's business begins."

"You got a beeper now?"

"And a phone in my Japanese fucking car, yo—this is the twentieth century. You think only the homies carry these, you been away too long. They carry them for show. Get beeped by their caseworker, go down and use the phone on the corner 'cause they can't afford one in their house."

"My man."

"That's right, blood. Not everybody drives a fifty-two fucking De Soto. I'll catch your sorry, white ass later." He started over toward a car. A deep-blue, four-door Mitsubishi, tinted windows. A grill like an owl's face. Sharp as hell.

"Much later," Martin said.

"One week, Irish"—not looking back. "I hope you don't get stranded in the Bronx looking for a nice legal job with the fucking phone company." The car chirped, the headlights flashing on once. Bunny held up his key ring. "See that? Progress. Oriental know-how."

He got there late on purpose, parked far down the street. Stepped out onto the pavement and heard his shoes echo up under the trees. Which were so big they blocked the moonlight, arced together out over the center of the whole, long block. He got his suit jacket and the car coat from the back, and put them on. He studied the house. All the lights on on both floors and cars packed into the driveway and at the curbs, along both sides, for a hundred feet. Expensive cars. American and German. The house looked familiar. He couldn't place why.

He breathed deep, a while. Thought over again the kinds of things he might have to say. Where he'd been, why was he home, that he was good, really good.

He closed the doors, started walking.

A dozen yards on, he stopped and went back, took off the coat, threw it in the car again. Might never even *see* Feel and Pen after this, he told himself—he didn't want to walk in like he hadn't changed at all. Like he'd been waiting all this time for them to call him up.

He approached the place—stepped into its ambiance, like—and someone was there on the lawn. Had come out from beside a tree. Dressed in black. Leather jacket, turtleneck. Young guy. Foreign face. Midtwenties. Another one moved by a tree further back. Martin took a few steps more, toward the first one, stopped. Said to him, "How are you."

"I can help you?"

Russian.

Took another few steps, friendly. "Yeah, I'm going in."

"You have invitation?"

"Yeah, in my jacket."

The guy stiffened, somewhere down his spine. Put his hand too slow in his side coat pocket.

"You want me to take it out?" Martin said to him.

The guy nodded—a nervous jerk of the head, no particular direction— his eyes on Martin's chest. Martin opened a lapel, reached in for the invite, held it up for him. "All right? You'll let me in?"—put it away.

"Why did you go back? To your car."

"What?"

"What did you get? In your car."

"I put my topcoat back. I didn't need it. You going to step aside?"

"Put your hands out, please. Your arms up."

The other *byk* took a step. Had a small machine gun. A short, industrial silhouette it made, out of the light. Martin said to this one here, in front of him, "You out of your mind, Ivan? You try to search me, your ass is in the fucking street. I'm going to put it there, and the old man's going to make it stay. *You understand me?*" Said it in Russian, the last three words, the phrase just coming out. Like *byk* for bull, for bodyguard. Hearing the accent sparking up the bit he'd ever really known. "You want to walk me inside, go ahead, but you keep your fucking distance. I'll tell you that much for free. Anything else, it's going to cost you." He waited. Looked past him at the house. Laughter breaking out into the silence. And me in a scene on the fucking lawn, he thought. Halfway to ruining everyone's night already.

"You go"—the one in front of him, jerking his head again. Cooler this time. Martin went up the path, up the stoop. The guy staying behind him. He opened the storm door and held it and knocked, felt the guy take it behind him. The front door opened. Felix's mother, Ariana.

"Well," she said. Martin smiled. She offered her cheek.

"Congratulations." He gave her her kiss.

"Yes, it's very nice." She looked past him. Asked the bull something in Russian. He didn't answer. She dismissed him, impatient—waved him off. "Come inside, Martin." She closed the door behind them, came and stood beside him where he stopped. Didn't take his arm. Touch him at all. Cold. Like his own family. He'd always wished she wasn't, he remembered. "Come, into the living room. He misses you."

They walked, and his heart started up as they got close to the noise. His color rose. They went around past the staircase, turned, and were in the doorway to the living room. His hands jumpy. He stuck them in his pockets. Fee was there by the mantel. Was already seeing him. Then coming over, fast. Martin put out his hand. Fee ignored it and grabbed him, hugged him, hard. Everyone was looking. He thought, A little scene on the lawn, now one inside. He couldn't take looking back, though, trying to smile, and closed his eyes. Fee wouldn't let go. He pried himself away, felt panicked all of a sudden that he could cry.

Fee *was* crying, he saw. Was looking him over. Top to toe. Fee older, but the same, really. Thicker in the shoulders. Fleshier at the collar. Healthy.

Happy. "Jesus Christ. You made it." Took off his glasses and wiped his eyes. "I'm all emotional today."

His mother smiled, left them, began explaining to people who he was—the faces all on him still, and smiling. Then, one by one, back to their own conversations. He didn't see Pen anywhere. He scoped, casually. Scoped. Realized Fee was looking at him.

"How are you, Felix? Thanks for the invite, man. And congratulations, of course." He couldn't get any life in his voice.

"You okay? What's the matter?" Fee took his shoulder, shook him by it. Reserving the affection now.

"Nothing. I'm nervous. I been away a long time."

"*You're* nervous."

"Yeah, I guess you're right."

"I missed you. Every *day* I missed you. I *still* do, because I can't believe you're fucking *stand*ing here." Shook him again.

"It's been a while."

"Your big disappearance," Fee said. "I'm buying a gyro on the corner and the next thing you're gone."

"Don't exaggerate."

"Exaggerate? *Barely*. You going to explain it all one day?"

"Christ, not now. Not tonight."

"No, not now, not now. You want a drink? Come and meet everybody?"

"Of course."

But he didn't move, Fee—kept staring.

"What? What is it? I owe you money?"

"You'll give me a hug?" Fee said. "A little one?"

"What's the matter with you?"

"Little one?"

"Just one."

Martin returned it, though. Thought it felt all right to be missed so much.

They went in, met people. Handshakes with the men, a kiss with both cheeks for the women. Walked over to see the old man where he sat in an armchair, smiling at everything. Or at nothing, Martin thought when they got close. The old man's eyes slow and glassy. He thought, Lexi Pasko's drunk. He'd never seen that. Seen Lexi allow things to be out of his control.

His face was the same, though—round and brutish. No older really. "How you doing, Mr. Pasko." Martin leaned down to him, extended the hand. "I'm Martin Quinn. From Felix's high school."

"He knows who you are," Felix said. "He's just drunk. Happy and drunk. You all right, Daddy?"

Lexi took his hand. Went to say something, but started in Russian. Stopped. Closed his eyes and turned his head. Smiled, looked back, said, "How have you been? It's been a long time. You left my son"—his eyes almost clear, completely.

"Yeah, I left him. And my mother, my brother. Everything. But he's doing all right, no?"—Lexi looking up at him closely. Not fully listening, though. More like he's listening for what I'm saying underneath. What I'm not saying.

"You have to leave sometimes, a man," Lexi said. "But you have to return"—gripped their handshake tighter.

He squeezed harder back. Said, "Yeah. Yes. I agree."

"You've returned"—his English better every second.

"Yes. I'm back."

"You're back?"

"Yes."

Let him go, the old man, and looked around for something. His glass. Took it. Drained it. Looked up at Felix. Like an old, old man. Said something sticky in Russian, and Felix leaned and kissed him. Straightened and looked at Martin and raised an eyebrow. Shrugged. "Freaking hammered," he said.

Lexi looked from Felix to him, then back and forth again. "He's missed you."

"I know, Mr. Pasko. Me, too."

Lexi nodded.

Felix smiled.

They waited.

"You're back? You'll be friends with my son?"

"Daddy, Jesus Christ—"

"Yes? Q?"

"Yes, sir."

"Good."

"Yes, it's good," Felix said. "Daddy, you want a drink?"

"Da. Spaceba." ▪

"All right. We have to meet some people; I'll bring it in a minute."

"Scotch."

"I know, Daddy. I'll be back."

"Nice to see you, Mr. Pasko."

Felix said, when they were a few feet away, "Chivas Regal."

"I figured."

"He still remembers that, you taking the blame for me. 'I drank it, Mr. Pasko.' You were such a nut. He mentioned it when I told him I was inviting you."

"Yeah, I've thought about it myself, a few times."

They stood next to each other, a while. Didn't talk. Looked around at the other people. "You remember that girl Daniella?" Fee said. "That I introduced you to? In the blue?"

"Yeah."

"You remember her?"

"No, I mean from what?"

"I didn't either, at first. The house, it doesn't ring a bell?"

"It does, but no."

"That junior prom," Fee said. "Before it. The preprom party was here."

"Holy shit."

"Yeah, holy *fuck*ing shit, right? How big a scope does life really *get*? It all *start*ed here, for God's sake." He put his arm around his shoulder.

They looked over the room.

"I'm glad you're here, man," Felix said, looking at him close. He could feel it—the gaze. "You really look great. Lean, like a *man*. You lost weight."

"From missing you."

"Yeah, well, that's over now." Pulled him tighter. After a moment, said,

"This guy goes to the doctor, right? Says he's having a sexual problem. A problem down low—"

And she was there. Came in the room, in the far doorway. Dressed in white. Went straight to her friends and didn't see them standing across. Her hair all swept up off her neck. A woman now. Thicker at the hips. Not a girl's bony angles. A woman's curves.

He kept himself loose, worked hard at it. Seeing her and feeling the weight of Felix's arm. Hardly breathed. Tried not to at all. He was afraid he'd shudder.

From her *face* to his *face,* he looked, not at their bodies, the one figure that they made. Her arm around Fee's waist. His arm down across her back, hand cupping her at the hip. She smaller-looking now, beside him, than when she'd first come in the room. She always was a little small. He said, "This is incredible. I got the invitation, I said to myself, 'Yeah, this is right.' I'm really happy for you," looked from her face to his face.

"You missed a good one," Fee said.

And she—"Oh, please—"

Martin echoed her. "We were kids. Right?"—looked at her. Smiled. A difficult thing suddenly, because his teeth were setting. He wanted to take her by the hair, hit Felix in the throat. But there was nothing in her face to say she *could* be taken. He swallowed. Worked hard to grin easier. "So, what's the story? Where'd you meet again, finally? Something good?"

"Yeah, not bad, I guess." Fee hugged her into him.

She rolled her eyes. "Not too bad."

Fee said, "My fraternity had this Miss Sorority contest and I looked up onstage and I thought, I know her. Could I possibly know someone that good-looking?"

"Stop it," she said.

"It's true, Pen; that's exactly what I thought. I told you that story."

"I know your dirty mind."

"No"—he looked at Martin for support. Said no again. "She was like a vision."

"Sugar, sugar," she said, "yet my coffee isn't sweet."

Fee beamed. Said to him, "She likes her Russian expressions."

Martin said to her, "You won."

"Yes," she said. "I won."

"That's the *story*. I went to one of the brothers on the committee and told him to let me give her the trophy or I'd kick his ass all over the frat house. I got up there on the stage. I said, 'Congratulations. You remember me?' "

"I didn't." Pulled him at the waist, then. "I'm kidding."

"How long ago?" Martin said.

"Four years."

"Long years," she said.

"She knew I was going to ask her; I just had to get set up first. Get going in law school."

"Business first," Martin said. "No business, no life."

"See, he knows."

"Thanks, Martin," she said. "That was very helpful."

He smiled.

And none of it awkward, somehow. Like it had always been this way— the two of them together and he the close friend of both. Of the long-time couple. And of course it had been four years, he thought. Four years ago, when he was in Germany, Feel's letters had stopped. He'd written a half-dozen postcards to him about all the Russians everywhere over there—the soldiers, the hookers—and got nothing back. Ever, again.

Now you know why, he thought.

Had always assumed Fee was just pissed off he hadn't shipped Stateside when the option came.

"You were both in school all that time, you didn't run into each other?"

"I transferred in, junior year," she said. "It was hell."

"Had time for the pageant, though?"

"Senior year. All my applications were out. I spent half my time in the gym."

"She's diesel," Fee said, squeezed her biceps.

"I can see. Applications for what? Law school?"

"Oh, yeah."

"Jesus Christ, everybody's a lawyer?"

"I guess," Fee said.

Then silence. Penny fixed her eyes straight ahead. Fee swallowed. Forced a closed-mouth smile, letting something pass. Some ongoing beef between them, Martin got. "Did I say something wrong?" he said.

"No"—Fee shook his head. Slow and benevolent. And smiled. Something he'd tell him later, if it still mattered, the look said. Nothing important.

"Well, it's a nice story, anyway," Martin said. "A little romance, a little threat of violence. Where's the trophy?"

She warned him with a look. "Don't start. It's buried. No one will ever find it."

"Miss Sorority."

"I'm going to leave."

"I was Mr. Platoon. I still have my thong."

"All through?"

"Yes, ma'am."

"You want a drink?"

"Sure. Soda or something."

"Shit," Felix said. "Can you get my father a scotch? I forgot."

"Of course."

Fee released her and they watched her walk away, get pulled into more conversations before reaching the bar. Martin trying to give his look a bit of condescension. The little bride-to-be. Let's admire her. Wanted to take her under the arm and pull her outside, take her away. Put her in the car and begin their life like that, with drama. *"What the fuck is the matter with you? You couldn't wait a little longer? We've always been together. Always will be."*

"You okay with this?" Felix said.

I'm staring at her. "Yeah, what are you, crazy? It's incredible." He looked away, shook his head. In dismissal.

"I know I should have written something to you before sending you a fucking invi*t*ation—"

"Believe me, Felix, seven years and you're not the same person any-more. You think I spent my time in Germany and fucking Ko*r*ea thinking about high school? You get old fast. You meet *women,* you know? They age you."

Fee nodded.

"You don't think about *high* school," he said again. "I don't mean any offense by that, by the way. To you or her. She's great for you, but." Christ, he wanted to get out of here. Now.

But, that last bit seemed to take care of it, though—he saw it on Feel's face. Fee actually frowning, looking over at her. Uncertain, for a second.

"No, no offense, no. I know"—looked back. "So, the army. What was that like, hunh? What the *fuck* did you join the army for? Really"—his mood coming back around.

"I don't know why. I don't. I don't even *think* about it anymore. Three years I sat by myself in fucking radar booths around the world and read books. It's a blur."

"College was like that for me. A big blur. The first three years. Stupid shit."

"Then you got serious."

"I guess."

"What does that mean, then? What happened before?—just a minute ago. She got pissed."

"I'm working for my father."

Looked at him, a second, Fee. To catch his feelings on it. Raised an eye-brow.

Martin nodded, noncommittal, nondiscouraging. Nonanything.

"There, see?" Fee said. "You, too."

"Me, too, what? I don't care. You always wanted to be a gangster."

"That's the thing—it's not *like* that anymore"—he exhaled, heavy. "It's all real estate now, and gasoline. It's legal. It's nothing. It's *money,* is what it is. I'm not busting my *ass* in some law firm. I did that for six months, my last year. I'm at the top, like this." He lowered his voice—"My father's getting out, bringing in a guy from the gulag to run things. A career con. A prisoners' rights advocate. They call him 'Little Mongol.' 'Azarchik.' "—Jesus, Fee, Martin thought, you haven't changed at all—your loose tongue, your wide eyes—"He's going to come and organize things. Get all these little criminals in line—these *mafiyatchiks*. But he's a puppet. My father sprung him with bribes to a judge and Brezhnev's son-in-law. He's bringing him over so *he* can step away, himself. He says there's no chance of keeping things organized anymore. He'll take what's kicked up to him and keep his back turned. He's got his legitimate investments now, and his ties to the Italians on the highest levels. He's untouchable. And I'm stepping in at that level, beside him. Right at the top. For the rest of my life. But Penny . . . she . . ."

Her father. The small-timer.

Who got disappeared for a Bronx don's moron son.

Martin didn't say anything.

"You remember what happened to her father?"

He waited. Narrowed his eyes. Said, "Oh, shit, yeah, I see what you mean."

"Yeah, well, I can't forget it for a second. She's got this fucking list in the back of her mind of who knows who. The lines of allegiance crossing all the time. Parallel lines running together, you look far enough ahead. That Sicilian thing goes *deep* in her. And fear, of course. She has that, too."

"Right."

"But, anyway . . ."

"Everything's legal, though, right? Real estate, you said. Gasoline."

"The real estate's a hundred percent. The gasoline's soon to follow. It's nothing."

"But money."

"But money."

"What's with the badguys, then, outside?" Martin said. And smiled.

"Who, Vlady? And the little guy?"

"That his name? I called him Ivan."

"Close enough."

"What's up? He should be wearing a black hat, for Christ's sake. He's like Jack Palance in *Shane*."

"In what?"

"What's up with him?"

"There's been some excitement."

"Some excitement? What are you, kidding?"

"It's nothing; believe me. A precaution. Tell me something else, about you. What's with telling my father you're staying?"

"I am."

"What about school?"

"You my mother? I'm not going back. I'm fucking twenty-five."

"You dropped out of high school."

"You want me to be a lawyer?"

"Hell, no. I don't wish that on anybody."

"So?"

"So, what are you going to do?"

"I'm looking at some things."

"Nobody gets anywhere anymore without a degree."

"Put me on with your father."

"I will."

"I'm kidding."

"I'm not."

"Don't be so serious, man, Felix; it's a joke."

"I know—" He stopped. "I *know* you can feel it, Q," he said. "That you were meant to come back. It's like you never left."

"Felix—"

"And don't . . . What's with this?—with 'Felix'?"

"What do you want me to call you, Fi*lush*ka?"

"I know what you're feeling. You're just in shock."

"Oh, yeah? That what it is? How long's it been since you even *wrote* to me? You think I wasn't lonely over there?"

"I *told* you I was sorry about that. Plus, *you* fucking left, in the first place. And *would*n't come back. You said you chose not to be stationed over here. Even though I *asked* you to come back."

"I had reasons."

"I *know* that. But you're here now. And none of that matters anymore. You're my brother."

"You *are* emotional. You going to hug me again?"

"I'm going to *crack* you."

"Behave yourself. Christ"—smiled at him.

Fee looked off.

Martin thought, It's amazing. Like I never left. The guy's got his soul opened up to me—"Felix . . . Feel, what's with Ivan? Everything's not cool here, man. Something's . . . what's the word . . . *nalevo?*"

"Will you come to work with me? It's all up-and-up."

"I'm flattered, but no. What's with the *carabinieri,* Feel?"

"You come here tonight, when my future is finally starting. It's like a return of some purity from the past. It refutes the whole march of time. I got seven years back when you walked in here. I got innocence back. I don't want you to go and take that with you."

"What happened, Feel? Will you talk, God damn it? Is everybody all right?"

"Everybody's fine, yeah. Thank you. Everybody but my uncle, Monya. But he doesn't count."

"I forgot about Monya. He died?"

"No. Well, yeah, in a way. The Italians shot him up. Six times in the back. But he was too thick in the head for it to do him in. He's paralyzed. Collecting disability."

"Why?"

"He's got no money."

"Why'd they *shoot* him?"

"Same reason he's got no money—he's a loser. And a *stukatch.* Well, not really—I should be fair—he owed some guy on Staten Island twenty-seven grand and fingered my father instead. Said *he* owed it to them. Then they shot him anyway. And my father squashed it. That's all Monya had to do— tell my father. My father called the guy up and smoothed it over. Now they're partners, and Monya's out."

"He smoothed it over, or the guys on the lawn did? Your father always did his own work, I remember."

"He smoothed it. A little talking-to, he gave the guy. These *byki are* crazy, though—this new generation? They grew up with nothing. Children of poverty, so, nothing to lose. Will do anything for reputation. They'd die for him, I think. It's creepy."

"That why they're still around?"

"I don't know. I guess. Why send them away?"

"If it's over? No more Staten Island threat?"

"They were around anyway. We just gave them machine guns."

"Jesus."

"Yeah, I guess it sounds bad when you say it."

Martin thought, Not by your *at*titude, no—but Fee's mind moving on, already. Looking at Pen coming back. Bride-to-be. "He's dropping out of college" saying to her.

"Good move, Mr. Platoon."

"Thank you."

"It's Coke."

"It's perfect, thanks." Took the glass.

"Your mother wants to talk to you. About food."

"What about it?" Fee said.

"Too much Italian on the menu. She's talking about flying your old *chef* over in time for the wedding." She looked at Martin. "I think she's purposely trying to spend more on this thing than anyone ever spent, ever."

"Our old chef," Fee said. "I still remember him. From twenty years ago. Big sweaty guy. She's still upset my father didn't smuggle him out with the rest of us. This is her excuse."

"*Glasnost,* baby," she said.

"There's enough freaking Russians in this country. Don't you think?" He said it to Martin.

"You're the only ones I know."

"And Vlady."

"And Vlady."

"There's a thousand more like him in Brighton Beach right now. A thousand more by the end of the month. Plus that many nice decent suckers to prey on. The place is filling up with *Homo sovieticus.*"

"God bless America."

"God bless Gorbachev."

"Go talk to her," she said.

"Russian food sucks."

"Well, go."

He leaned, kissed her head. She looked up. They kissed lips. He left. "Two months, the wedding," she said, watching him walk away.

"Wow, soon."

"He didn't mention it?"

"The date? No."

"So he didn't say anything."

"About what?"

"Being best man."

"Jesus Christ, what's the matter with him? I could be a fucking nut, for all he knows. I could have joined the Moonies. He's telling me it's like I was never gone. But I was; believe me; I was there."

"He misses you."

"How many people going to tell me that tonight?"

"You shouldn't have left. He loves you."

"I'd be dead or in jail, the way I was going."

"Yeah, well." She sipped her drink. He watched her. Realized he might have just missed something. Couldn't try to bring her back to it now, though. Couldn't say something stupid. *"What did you* mean *by that?"*

He took a drink of the soda.

She said, "He really grew up." She smiled, friendly. "I didn't like him at all in high school. You remember?"

"That you didn't like him?—no."

"He was conceited."

"We both were. Everybody that age."

"I know. That's what I mean. He was *great* when I came to school. I had no money, no plans, really. He was a prince. Supportive. My mother got sick, he used to drive me to the hospital. I didn't have a decent car. Then he drove her to the doctor twice a week."

"Is she okay?"

"She's right over there. You didn't see her?"

He pretended to glance. "Is that what she looks like?"

She laughed. "O my God; that's right."

"Never seen her face." Only the back of her head at the wake, he thought.

Penny shook her head, like she couldn't believe it—the way things were so long ago, he guessed. "I forget things like that," she said.

"Me, too."

"So? How was the army?"

"Tidy."

She laughed.

"That's all I remember," he said. "I was working for a while, after, and traveling. It's like being in a cult out there, though. Go to work, eat fast food, watch TV, into bed. If you go to the mall on the weekend and every-one's smiling, you feel like maybe it's all as good as they think it is. But it's not. It's b-a-d, bad."

"And school?"

"I don't know"—he shrugged. The subject was going to make him mad if people kept asking. "It was all shit I figured I could learn when I got out. All these professors saying what the real world was like. I would think, When was the last time you were even out there, man? You know? They were just collecting a paycheck. I'd sit there and try to *respect* them. What the hell is that?"

"What are you going to do?"

"Any ideas?"

"Nope."

"Work with Felix?" he said.

She looked at him.

Something there again.

Either something she wanted bad or not believing he'd said it at all.

She said, "What did he tell you?"

"He's not becoming a lawyer. Got other plans."

"Where is he?"

"With his mother. Other side of the room."

"I wish I had a cigarette," she said.

He thought, Let's go outside. But didn't say anything.

"Eight months ago, he got in an accident," she said. "Serious. It didn't bother *him*—they put pins in his shoulder, popped his eye back in his head. But his parents flipped."

"Because of his brother. That crash."

"They closed in on him, yeah. Wouldn't let him out of their sight. The same thing they did to him the first time, I guess; I didn't know him then."

"Me neither; I met him right after."

"Well, they started spoiling him all over again. Doting on him more than usual. Doting on me. Then one day his father sends him off to do some errand. He's got the bar exam in two months and his father sends him off to Long Island to collect God-damned swag gasoline tax. Now it's his, the business. He runs it."

Martin didn't say anything. Had questions. About everything. So many he had no words for them. But there'd be time to get them all answered, he knew—he wasn't going anywhere. Ever again, maybe. Life, right now, was right fucking here, he was sure.

She said, "He asked me to marry him right after. Like he'd crossed some line in his mind. Become a man in his father's eyes. I said yes. He *was* taking steps. He swore it wasn't the job. He said it was the accident. Realized he wanted to marry me now no matter *what* the future. But the money *was* rolling in, of course. And, who am I blaming here, him or me, right?— things *were* looking good. That was that. And, then, he passed the freaking bar anyway, to show me he could do anything he really wanted. Or, he did it like an afterthought." She shrugged. "I'm still not really sure. He studied for like one more weekend."

"He's a smart guy. Always was."

"Yup."

"He's coming back."

She nodded. Lifted her drink. "Don't get involved," she said.

He didn't say anything.

"I didn't invite you tonight," she said. "He did." She sipped it, didn't look up at him.

"What does that mean?" he said. Hardly moved his mouth.

"I was telling him about your eye," she said.

"Yeah, this one," Fee said, pointed up at it, absently. "It was hanging out, they told me. The car was history. My Porsche. I miss that car."

"I have to pee," Penny said. "Oh, *excuse* me. I mean, 'I'll be back.'"

She left. Went up the stairs. No kiss this time.

"Going for a cigarette," Fee said.

"So, you're good as new?"

"Yeah, sure. They put a pin in my shoulder. My vision's fine. It's the car that bothers me. I drive around the city in the four-by-four now. I look like a yuppie."

Martin nodded, mellow. Looked around. Felt like something had turned on inside him, though. Like he'd been drinking. When she came back down the stairs, he knew, she'd be more aware of him than Felix. They were already having problems.

He looked at him. Said, "Brezhnev was an ugly dude. How's his son-in-law?"

"Not *half* so bad," Fee said.

"That's not saying much."

"Yeah, he's a hound, too," Felix said.

"You still got the spots in the garage on LaGuardia?" They were halfway between Fee's place on Lafayette and his, on Thompson.

"Yeah."

Martin nodded. "You still live next to Mommy and Daddy?"

"Yup. Maid still does my laundry, too."

"You looking for a house?"

"Maybe. We may buy something in the building. Or keep both places if they move to Canada. My mother thinks Toronto's more sophisticated. My father's putting up buildings all over the place. Apartments, hotels."

"In Canada?"

"Yeah. You want one? We could run it."

"I'll think about it."

"Good."

"I'll tell you what, though. If you're not buying another car, I'll take the parking spot."

The feds would have to take another look at the partial print now, Davis said. And if they found it to be Terry's like the independents had, it was undeniably important corroboration. It pitted his case solidly against the government's. "You could rethink your decision to testify if the lab has the same conclusions. Then, let the state take you to trial for murder two. Face the feds on the heroin. Which you can probably beat, as well. I think your instincts were correct from the beginning, with that—they'd probably just begun their narcotics investigation. And, if you didn't kill Hughes and Pasko, I should be able to *prove* that. Which is a shot I'm willing to take, when the time comes. If you are. Months away, I know. But it's more than just wishful thinking now. It would mean you'd lose protection, but you know that. Just . . . We have to start thinking that way again. I'm going to get more coffee. You want a little? No—you still have"—he got up, Davis. Went to the kitchenette.

Martin smiled, and lay back on the couch. Looked at the ceiling. Thought, If *I* didn't kill them. If I didn't, who did? Something he'd been going over, a lot, these last few days. How he could have let Terry walk away. Hadn't known for sure if he was coming back or was leaving them there for dead and dying. Assumed he might come back, and shot him. But a man's life couldn't be weighed against a split-second assumption. *Any* assumption. And as for killing Felix? Fee? Who'd never lived the uglier sides of life, till then? Didn't you want to ruin him?

Maybe.

Maybe they were all just wanting to be gangsters, though—Terry Hughes and Fee and him, and everyone that the feds were going to want him to deliver—so they were all taking their chances. All grown men.

It was the one place Lexi was still so wrong, though. Influencing Fee and him when they were only just boys. Cultivating them to be hardguys. Making them want to prove they were like him all the way through. Making them scared of him so fucking young.

But, then, was it even so bent, that? he thought. *So* amoral?

Who could figure it?

Not me.

Not tonight.

People died and life went on and it wasn't fair. That was all he knew. Wasn't fair and it was even a little embarrassing. Lying here, not only getting well, healing at a decent clip, but looking at getting off the hook. Some people had left this life not too long back, others would be facing the slam, and Davis saying now "your instincts were correct." He wondered. If since you were a kid most of the guys you knew who got close to H were dead, didn't it make you an asshole for going into it? Didn't it put your best friend's death on your head? Or did it make you both just a couple of drug dealers? A couple of guys who had tried to fuck over a lot of serious people with a quiet heroin deal and it just went south. Made you, he thought, what you always wanted to be. A risk-taking earner and a killer. Made you a wiseguy. By fucking definition.

All of it feeling so long ago now.

But so close, in another way. Like it was stuck to him. Couldn't be brushed off. He understood, these days—after twenty-seven years a Catholic, finally—he understood what was meant by a "soul." The record for all time of who you were, what you did. How, if you killed a guy, your soul was stained. And when you saw that, you realized you hadn't ever known it was *pure* till the stain came. You realized there were things that had made it glow in the past. Beautiful things. But, now, with that stain that could never come away, if Hell existed, you'd be there with the rest of the unforgivable.

Still, he thought, it was better to be one of the ones who when he got his chance to admit his faults, did it. Better to wander and burn with the honest than the eternal deniers, and the sneaks.

And Terry's? he thought.

Where was old Terry's soul?

Where did *it* get sent? he'd been wondering. Where did I send it?

Because he *had* sent it. He thought of Felix alive. His own father, dead eighteen years, he thought about alive. Their times above ground were stories you could tell. But Terry Hughes's story was *his* now. Terry's flesh his. Their souls were linked up for eternity. Christ, they'd gotten tat*toos* together, once. They and a half-dozen guys from the neighborhood. They were linked for all time since *boy*hood, with that. Stained themselves with their toughguy images of choice.

He laid his arm up carefully on the couchback, glanced at Christ ascending the muscles there—hazy ink, pale skin. Glanced at the tiger coming on through bamboo on the other. That one from a few years later. A ten-day leave in Korea. Terry had waited like an animal around the side of the house to pounce on Fee and him. Had listened to their conversation and didn't give a fuck if it was important. Waited there till he was the only one with a gun in his hand, then blamblamblam.

He'd been strong that way, Terry. Thinking too hard could be a weakness. A profound incapability.

But who was dead, and who was kicking back wondering when he'd be free and rich again?

He turned his hand over, looked where the shunt had been, the burn there getting less and less. The doctor had come and gone, taken him off the IV, changed his pills. The pole still standing by the door now. Waiting to be picked up by some specially designated agent. The last bag of electrolytes sucked thin, the tube coiled-up and hanging from one of the hooks on top. A tiny puddle had formed on the ground below it, he'd noticed, while the doctor was doing the paperwork. He'd looked past the guy's waxy head and watched it form, wondered who would clean it up.

Raining outside, now. Corso and Dolan playing cards at the table with two agents who had shown up in the afternoon, apparently had nothing to do with the case, and now wouldn't leave. He imagined the rain glistening on the curved metal roof and running down it. Thought how if you set a marble inside a round bowl, it would go still at the one center point where there was no slope at all. That point existing on the exact opposite side, too, in theory. But who could balance a marble on an overturned bowl?

Davis sat, careful not to spill his new coffee. Sipped it.

"Protection's still most important right now, counselor."

"Agreed," Davis said. Sipped.

"And, on that, you have what to tell me?"

Davis leaned back, still kept his voice low—"What we knew from the beginning. Beyond a violation of your civil rights . . ." he shrugged, tipped his head.

"I belong to them."

"More or less."

"And fuck the Thirteenth Amendment, or whatever."

"More or less."

"Oh, fuck you," Corso said. "Whose deal, mine? Good."

Davis squinted, tried to ignore him.

"And what if they can't use what I tell them?"

"It's their problem, I guess. But—" concern in his eyes, Davis. "I'm not sure what you mean, exactly."

"They're like a couple of priests expecting me to confess. They're taking it for granted."

"Okay . . . And . . ."—he needed more.

"They were telling me about a guy who kept changing his story. Some Sicilian hit man."

Davis went to come forward, stopped, leaned back. Sipped the coffee. Was staying cool. "They can charge you with perjury, Martin"—trying not to whisper. To keep the tone of simple privacy. "They can convict you for it."

"If they find out."

"Obviously."

"I'd be where, in the meantime?"

"Where they put you."

He didn't say anything.

"What are you thinking about?"

"Nothing."

"This is the safest thing for you. We know that. We have to assume Lexi Pasko will try again."

"That's not my concern."

"Then . . . your family?"—trying to read him. A consistently considerate guy. Martin stared at him. Instead of nodding yes. "I just don't know what to tell you, Martin. People have tried, but the criteria are strict. Are fixed. Only spouse and children."

"They're safe for now. They're gone. I just got to wonder where all this will go, though. Do I trust bureaucrats to protect my people?"

Davis said nothing.

Couldn't know, Martin knew. "I'll stick with our plan, counselor," said to him. Changed the tone, then—the subject—"So, what about you, then?"

"What."

"You going back to hicksville?"

"I'll be here for a few more days, then back. Going to do some more research, tell you what I can. Better libraries here."

Martin nodded. Realized he found it hard to thank the guy. Would have to be thanking him again and again. "Tell me something, man. Why do you work in that little town?"

"Our summer house was there, when I was a boy."

"You graduated top of your class at Georgetown, you said. Why'd you go upstate?"

Davis smiled to himself.

Because he'd been seen into?

"My father was a lawyer," he said. "Very successful."

"You became one for him."

"Correct."

"Found it wasn't so bad, took it only so far. Proved you could do it, then burned him, a bit?"

Davis looked down. Smiled, took a good slug of coffee. Couldn't lie.

"My old man was a musician," Martin said. "I never even picked up a kazoo."

"To hell with them, right?" Davis said. Looked up.

"Right. I just wish mine had left some *money*—I could pay you. You've been a lot of help."

"Please." Davis shook his head.

"You've got more than you need. Going way back. Before your father, even."

"My great-grandparents made a fortune. Furriers. It shows, hunh?—that I come from money?"

"Not how you think. Don't sweat it."

He took a breath, Davis. Then glazed, thinking of something. "They came from Russia," he said. "My people. The turn of the century. Had nothing, then they built a little empire."

"Tough people. You can imagine what I'm up against," Martin said. "My adversaries."

They smiled.

Davis said, "Who would've thought it, ever? A Russian Mafia."

Martin shook his head, looked at the ceiling. Thought, Why did Lexi only come after me, though? Why not do Bunny, too? It wasn't fair, that shit.

Though—of course—he knew why.

Be honest, he told himself.

It was personal, not professional. You don't get mad at a shark for biting, but you do at a loyal dog that turns.

"People love to think there's a Mafia of their people," he said, remembering Davis there, beside him. "Thinks it shows they could be bad if they wanted to."

Davis not answering.

Martin looked at him.

Davis saying "It's true"—embarrassed. Worse—was ashamed.

Martin said to him, "Hey, man, I spent my life pretending to be bad. *You're* embarrassed? The time for that shit is over. What to do *now* is all I care about. Life's only so long, you know?"

Davis nodding. Finished his coffee down. Set the cup on the end table there by him. Was still bothered, though. Had shown something he didn't want to.

Funny how fast men become boys again, Martin thought. "And it's not your fault I got stabbed, by the way."

Davis said, "Jesus," and shook his head. "I was acting like an . . ." He breathed in, held it.

"Like an asshole," Martin said. "You can say it. I won't be offended."

"Like an asshole."

"No, you weren't. I'm swimming with sharks here."

Davis took it in, that.

Exhaled, let his shoulders come down.

Martin listened to the rain. "You should get going, man," he said. "Go to the movies or something. Get a good meal while you're down here. The food up there's terrible."

"It is; that's true."

"But you're coming back, though."

"Before I go, yes. I'll fill you in on everything. You have my number there, at the hotel, if anything comes up, before then. And keep notes on what the U.S. attorney's people tell you, remember. Then we'll work with the feds until the issue with the fingerprint is resolved. Either way, it's to your advantage, playing along now."

Martin nodded.

"I spoke with them on the phone, as I told you," Davis said, "and they say there's no need for them to be here until all the dossiers arrive and you start talking." He corrected himself—"'Giving them information,'" he said. "I sound like you now."

"'Start talking, buddy,'" Martin said, and made a gun with his fingers, aimed it sideways at him, from the waist. Shrugged. "New York, Hollywood, it's all the same now. I've seen guys do things right from the movies. I swear to God. I could have told them on the spot. 'Hey, *Godfather . . . Scarface.*' All the same."

Davis nodded, put his hands on his knees, ready to stand.

Martin put his hand back on his stomach, glimpsed the tiger tatt again, stared at it. Felt again at the new bandages beneath his T-shirt. Said, "That guy Terry?" Didn't look over.

Davis paused—"Yes"—his breath catching, a bit.

"When I was a kid, a teenager, me and the guys I hung around with used to bring the little kids in the neighborhood to the movies. Our treat. Like twenty kids, sometimes. See whatever just opened. But Terry would never go. He said everybody in the movies was a pussy. His old man was doing life upstate without parole, and his brother Peter was an earner without equal, so he had nothing to prove, old Terror. And we all said what he did, too; believe me—'They're pussies . . . They're fags.' But we studied them. That's the truth. Terry, though? He meant it. He had no interest. We just told him he was cheap, wouldn't pay for himself, even; forget the kids. He'd just smile. Maybe hit you in the face if he felt like it." He remembered something else, shook his head. "I once told a friend of mine I was going to call him out, Terry. Just fucking fight it out with him, once and for all, put an end to it? We were like sixteen. I'd had it with him. You know what he said, my friend?"

Bunny.

"What?"

"He said it wasn't worth it. If I fought him once, win or lose, I'd have to fight him every day for the rest of my life. Freaky, hunh? I should have fucking called him out back *then,* you know? I'd still be lying here, but I could have just gotten in a few good shots."

Davis nodded, looked at the floor.

"I don't mean to be funny," Martin said, "but there was a lot of stress when I was a kid. It never ended. Even at the movies, like I was saying. In your head, *you'd* be the toughguy on the screen, but you'd get back to the neighborhood, and you'd see the wiseguys doing it for real. And you'd wonder if you'd ever be up to it. Because if you weren't, who knew what would happen to you. You had to be so tough to be like them. Like how they'd get stony when the cops came around. Their hands in their pockets. Leaning in the doorway to the social club. Cool motherfuckers, you know? Hard, hard guys. And *hat*ed cops. I mean *hat*ed them. Saw them as just the enemy. Never thought, for even a second, that they might be right. Never admired them for a second as being the goodguys. And Terry was like that. Would have turned into that. Saw the world as a fucking annoyance. Not something you should maybe hide your face from, once in a while, if you thought about it." He could feel Davis staring at him. He looked over. "What?"

"Are you . . . okay about . . ."

"Shooting him?"

Davis nodded.

"He interrupted an important conversation. You have no idea. Conversation was everything to Felix. It was his weakness. Even if Tee had interrupted and said, 'You guys are pussies to talk so much,' I wouldn't have minded. Relatively speaking, of course. But he just walked up and got right to his executions. So, yeah, I'm okay about it. I should have done it at fucking sixteen."

A little flourish of bravado at the end there, he thought. But if you're going to lie, lie big, no?

Corso said, "That's right. Turn them over, baby; let me see them."

Martin smiled. Said, "See, he knows."

"Yeah, *let* me deal again. Keep your eyes up my *sleeves,* if it makes you feel better."

"Real piece of work," Martin said.

Davis said, "You can put it that way."

"He works hard. He saved my life. You'd have been history. That little *mafiyatchik* would have carved you up, if you'd interfered."

"Very true."

Corso dealt loud, enjoying himself—whapping the cards down hard as he could.

"You should go, Counselor," Martin said.

"I should. All right, then," Davis said, stood up.

"Get a meal, get laid. You're not married, right?"

"Right."

"Hey, you know what? You're in Brooklyn. You should go to Anastasia's. My club. My *old* club. I ran with Felix. You could take a cab. It's like ten minutes from here."

He cocked his head to the side, Davis. Ready to say no. "Thank you, but."

"Yeah, maybe not. You'd probably get your wallet lifted. You should see that neighborhood though, one day, if your people were Russian. Everything's Russian there now. All the stores, all the signs and awnings, the language you hear on the street. It's like you stepped off an airplane to get there instead of the subway."

Picked up his briefcase, put out his hand. "Maybe."

Martin shook it, said, "Okay. Maybe. I'm not going to get up; this feels too good."

"Please, don't."

"I'll see you, man. Two days."

"Two days," Davis said.

Terry Hughes just sitting there, down the empty dining room, looking back at him. With Peter's face now, at twenty-five. Still a young Terry's mean, dog eyes, though. Mouth turned down forever. Sitting there. No patience in the world, but nothing to do.

Bunny said, "You eat lunch? You want something?"

Martin told him, "Sure." Broke Terry's gaze and looked up at the waitress. "Yeah, something light. White clam sauce. No bread. Thank you."

"You want anything, Bunny?"

"No, thanks, sweetheart. Just put that in and finish setting up. Marjorie's still not here?"

"Nope."

"Well, do what you can and leave early tonight, split the tips the same. But put that order in, though; it's quarter to fucking five."

She went back, toward the kitchen. Said something to one of the busboys on the way and he nodded, kept smoothing down the tablecloth he'd just thrown open. *"No bread,"* Martin guessed.

"I only keep three on, Mondays. No manager and a late waitress, comes at seven. This fucking Marjorie, though." Bunny shook his head. Martin nodded like he cared. Thought how logical it was that Bunny was an owner now, an operator. And Terry a hood a few years and a dozen pounds away from being universally feared muscle. Slots opened up in the world, and people filled them—the neighborhood was no different. It was what they'd really all hoped for as kids, anyway.

But, coming to Bunny Lamentia for work? he thought.

He didn't know. It was strange, sitting here. They used to goof together at the movies ten years ago, make all the little kids laugh.

He thought, There's definitely things in life to look back on and miss.

He motioned toward Terry with his head. "Nothing for him?"

"Terry?" Bunny said—"no. Only health food. Grains and shit. Leafy greens."

Like an ape, Martin thought. "He just going to sit there?"

"Yeah, why?"

"He involved here at all? Can he hear us, even?"

"I don't know. Who cares? He's always sitting by himself."

Martin shrugged. Like it was done, then; let him sit there. "Terrible Terry," he said. "It's pretty bugged-out, the people still around."

Bunny said, "Yup," and stretched—reached up, and back. Way back. In no hurry. Same as in grammar school. Always getting yelled at for it. Was who he was, though, Pasquale. His body in low gear, his brain on high. "Got out of the joint the last time, he came to work for me. It was breaking his heart working for Rocco before that, Rocco doing the work on his brother, and all, but"—shrugged—"there was nothing else. He sits there and thinks deep thoughts. How many curls tonight at the gym. Is he getting enough vitamins. What's the best way to choke a guy, use your hands or a cord. Lot on his mind. You all right back there, Hughes?" Terry nodded. His eyes on Martin's. Not exactly listening. Bunny not bothering to turn around anyway. "See? He's fine." Bunny rolled his neck. Lowered his voice. "Before he got out the last time?—the guards held him down, shaved his head. So, even if he tried going legit"—he laughed. Picked something off the tablecloth and dropped it on the floor. "How's he going to get a job looking like he's in the Aryan Brotherhood? So?"—his voice louder— "What happened?" He opened his hands, guinea-benevolent. "The De Soto die?"

"It's holding up."

"Couldn't find a job?"

"I got one."

"Doing what?"

"The phone company."

"Get the fuck out of here. I was kidding when I said that."

"Yeah, well, it sounded like a good idea."

"Maron."

"I tried."

"You tried."

"Two weeks in the classroom, though? Then a month out on the street, with that fucking belt on . . ."

"That's a nice belt they have. You can wear it with everything."

They smiled.

"So I'm here."

"Good"—he nodded, Bunny. Pleased. Serious again. "I knew you couldn't hold out. Once you've been on the inside of things, you can't live otherwise. Fuck that."

Martin said, "I just want the money."

"Don't we all. Lots of it. And *still* I say good. You're just in time, 'cause I got something right this weekend coming, down in Maryland, and I can't go, and Terry neither. You're going to pick *up* money. If it's all there, I know I trust you. You want wine? Marjorie, where the fuck you been? Bring a glass of white over here."

"I'm good with water," Martin said.

Bunny told her forget it; get to work.

He checked an atlas, calculated the miles, figured he should get the car looked at. He drove to Tenth Avenue, got the hoses replaced, the brakes reset, got the pads changed, the transmission flushed. He spent the last of his money on new pipes and a muffler. The scream of the engine was plain embarrassing anywhere but the highway.

His mother had his first phone company check, for the rent. He'd opened a mutual fund with the second two. Was waiting for the fourth, the last. He kept his fingers crossed everything went smooth. Hoped Bunny would pay him first thing. *"You're back? You're paid."*

Baltimore was hot. He got in at dusk and they had mosquitoes. Like in

Queens. He had to close the windows when he hit downtown, going stop-light to stoplight. Decided a new AC was the next thing to get.

And Bunny's man was all right. Made a decent first impression. Dressed all in denim and his hair too long—looked a bit like a porn star in that regard—but he was a pro; the operation all for real. Martin hadn't realized, though, the cash to be picked up was fugazi. A federal pinch twice-over if he got caught—taking it, in the first place, and then bringing it back. The guy had a full photo lab and an offset press. Blueprints of plates and two lighted drafting tables, architect slides. A sleek-looking computer. The only thing missing were the clotheslines with wooden pins. Martin stood there and looked the room over, the guy saying "Two more minutes, man. I'm sorry about this. I'm usually ready"—and running the last of it through the counter. A long, steady fall, the sound. The bills tumbling through like a dealer shuffling cards for Twenty-one.

Martin said, "No clotheslines."

"Nah. You throw them in the dryer now. Put them in with blue and red poker chips, get the tiny threads of plastic fused on with the heat. Like the security threads the mints use. It's sweet, man—new advances every day. One more." Lined up another stack in the machine and ran it. Pulled a rubber band around the first one and placed it—evenly aligned—in the small, canvas duffel bag. Looked at Martin and smiled. Genuinely. Smiling over the noise of money counting. A sound to sing and dance about, Martin guessed, and smiled back, nodded.

The guy bound the last stack and zipped the duffel, handed it over to him by the straps. Like a well-mannered grocery clerk. Said, "You're good to go."

"And we're square, no?"

"Yeah. This is left over from the last one. He's a good guy, Bunny. Said to hold the difference for expenses. I was waiting for the paper, though. Paper's everything. Crane Company Original. Linen and cotton. Levi Strauss sends them denim scraps, 'cause it's like a cult, you know?—you worship the paper. But the downside is there's no substitute. These bills for you guys are raised. Bleached-out singles. It takes forever. But the results"—he kissed his fingertips—"*magnificante*. It's all going to end, though. All this. In about a decade. Government's changing the money."

"What do you mean *'changing'*? Why?" It *both*ered him, the idea. He didn't know why, but it did.

"They want to make a *s*upernote, they're saying. Raised threads, watermarks. Shit like that. We'll go under for a while. Get back to the drawing board. We'll crack them."

"It's still going to be green, you think?" It was bugging the *shit* out of him, this. What if they had colors, he thought. Like foreign bills? The thought made him sick. No colors said money was no game in America.

"Shit, I hope so," the guy said. "Jesus."

They stood there, a moment. Martin tried to push the image from his head.

"Bunny's a good guy," the little counterfeiter said again. Dressed all in denim. From the cult of the paper. Martin nodded at him. "Tell him I got even more paper, though, all right?"

"All right."

"Excellent."

He looked around, the guy. But didn't move. Like they were waiting for something. "You, ah . . . you want anything else?" the guy said.

Martin looked at him, a long second. Thought he might be up to something. Putting it out there, maybe. Suggesting. But there was nothing suspicious about him. Just friendly, like. "Such as?"

"Come outside."

They went out on the pier. The tide-stink blew around them. The guy closed the padlock and lit a cigarette, waved his hand down at the rest of the lockups. The row of single-garage-bay warehouses stretching way down, out over the water. "There's fireworks, fake Calvin Kleins, a case of Turkish rifles. No joke," he said. "Exotic animals"—laughed. "*That's* a joke." He flipped the collar up on his jacket. Still a young guy, really.

Martin said, "I don't think so. I'll just follow you back to the highway."

"Cool enough, man. Good doing business with you."

They shook hands.

"You know what?" the guy said. "Bunny still have that restaurant? 'Cause I got something. Just follow my car, like you were going to; I'll put you on the highway, after. All right? It's cool?"

Martin followed him, picked up the tribute.

Crabs.

Two coolers of them.

They stunk up the car and he opened the windows, despite the mosquitoes. Drove to the highway swatting and wafting.

Bunny told the manager, "Tell the busboys get the coolers from the car and stick them in the icebox." Told Marjorie, "Put softshells on the specials tomorrow." In the office, he counted the money and opened the safe, paid Martin a grand. About a 15 percent whack of the score, Martin figured. Though he didn't know how much the first part of the take had been. This was enough for a decent wedding gift, though. And to pay for his own tuxedo. "I got to move this starting tomorrow," Bunny said. "You're free, no?"

"In the morning, I am, yeah."

"What time you come by?"

"Eleven."

"All right, then, eleven. I'll tell Terror."

Martin told him, "The guy says he's got more paper. The Baltimore guy."

"How much?"

"Didn't say, but he's looking to do business. He's got everything for sale."

"I know—I'm getting my fireworks from him next month. He's undercutting everybody down there. He's going to end up dead. Or incorporated."

Martin smiled. Said he'd be back tomorrow. Walked out through the now-busy dining room and thought, In life, you had those three choices— dead, incorporated, or working for the fucking phone company.

Bunny's wait staff, maitre d', bartender, all gave him a nod. Respect. Too bad being a kid again wasn't the fourth choice, he thought. Because everybody—he, Bunny, Felix, Terry Hughes—were all grown way the hell up now, and weren't going back.

It was the same tuxedo place. He couldn't believe it. And this time, Fee with his own bodyguard. Vlady. The thug from the lawn at the engagement party. Had dropped them off and gone to park the car before hurrying back to get fitted for one, himself.

Again, Martin's sizes were easy. The tailor measured him and went to double-check the registry for cummerbund and tie. They stood there waiting for him to return, measure Vlady. "We have a month, for God's sake" Fee saying; "I want to do all of it. Dublin, London, Brussels, Amsterdam. But she only wants to do the standard ones."

"France, Italy."

"Yeah, of *course* Italy. All over Italy. But Paris, Athens, freaking . . . little . . . Malta. Everyplace hot."

"France isn't hot."

"It isn't Copenhagen."

Vlady leaned toward them, to interrupt. He looked nervous, said something low. Felix cut him off, squinting—"In English. And louder."

"I can*not* take off my jacket," Vlady said. Bugged his eyes. Said something more in Russian.

"Jesus Christ," Fee said. Looked at Martin. "He's got his new shoulder holster on. I don't believe this. I'm not coming back here; I was here last week. I have enough shit to do. Why didn't you get yours when I got mine? Remind me."

"I was with your father. Working."

"You were following him around." He said to Martin, "He bought a club in Brooklyn, my father. He's interviewing management level, and *host-esses*. Vlady sits there staring at them. Tries to get laid."

"I could put it back. In the car. Bad to leave it, but—"

"It's six fucking blocks from here. I'm not waiting. How much money do you have on you?"

"Two hundred, I think. Two hundred."

"That means fifty bucks," Fee said. He shook his head, took out his roll. Thumbed off three hundreds and gave them to him. "Pay for both—yours and Q's—and bring them downtown. Take a cab home. Come on, man, let's go."

Vlady said something else.

"You speak fine," Fee said to him. "It's not like they're going to screw you, for Christ's sake; it's a reputable place."

But he'd said it too fast—Vlady didn't get it all. Fee said, slowly, "It's not Odessa."

Martin said, "Why not keep it in his jacket? Go in the room there, put the piece in one pocket, the holster in the other. Fold it up. Then *you* hold the jacket."

Fee stared at him. Thinking about it. Said, "Fine. Okay. Did you get that?" He repeated it in Russian, quick. The soft push of the language still nice, even with the impatience.

Vlady went back to do it. Fee looked at his watch immediately after the door closed. "I'm not waiting," he said—"he took the three hundred; let's just go. Vlady?"

"Shtoah?"

"Hold on," Martin said. Vlady looked into the hallway. Martin said to him, "Nothing. Go ahead. Keep changing." Vlady looked at Fee, closed the door again. Fee hadn't looked around at him. The way Bunny didn't look at Terry, Martin thought. "Feel, you carrying?"

"Yeah. We're fine. We can leave."

"We're fine? What about me?"

Fee looked at him, a second. And puffed his cheeks out. Raised his eyebrows, hiked his shoulders. Didn't know what to say. "I didn't think of it. I'm sorry."

Martin nodded. Then shook his head at him.

Fee said sorry, again.

Vlady came out, the jacket on his arm. Walked over. Cautious almost. Was embarrassed. Martin liked him this way. Better to see uncertainty in his face than the arrogant look that he now realized why he'd been feeling like he knew so well. Germany. The Russian Regular Army guys. Out and around, or on guard duty post. It was the smile they gave American GIs. It said, "You're spoiled babies. You'll never last a day in conflict. You'll see, someday. Soon." Packs of soldiers eyeing each other as transport trucks passed embassies, random jeeps flew past barracks. International games of chicken that they'd all played. He'd caught Vlady with that look on him a half-dozen times since the party.

Fee looking at both of them now. Looked out into the display room. Said, "Screw it. I'm still not waiting." Walked behind Vlady and half turned him sideways, patted the pockets of the coat and found which one he wanted, took it out—the gun. Came over to Martin and slid it into his side jacket pocket—"Come on, let's go. I'm hungry. I didn't even eat breakfast. All these freaking errands." Looked back at Vlady and told him again to pay for both tuxedos. Vlady just standing there now, looking helpless. Foreign, mean, lost.

Outside, Martin said he'd wanted to pay for his own rental. "But you're not going to take my money now if I pull it out, right?"

"That's right."

"Then let me get breakfast."

"Good. We'll go someplace expensive."

At the garage, he slid cautiously into the Pathfinder, held his lapels tight to him so the bottom of the coat stayed close. When they were moving through traffic, he took the gun out and released the mag and put it in the other pocket. He opened the chamber, made sure there wasn't one in. "This thing clean?" he said.

Fee said, "Yeah. I got it myself for him in Canada. He's never used it; believe me. He's not allowed to without my father saying so."

With the shells out, it was impossibly light. Matte-finished black. "This a Glock?"

"Yeah, it doesn't say?"

It did—he found the name etched in the slide. "I heard rumors about these, in the army."

"They're all true," Fee said.

They unloaded the counterfeit in two days. Worked it through two restaurants and a deli, four pizzerias, a wholesale meat and poultry plant in Staten Island. Then, most of it on a Puerto Rican kingpin in Washington Heights named Crazyhorse. Fives and tens, all of it. It was why the guy needed so much paper all the time, Bunny said. "But nobody else deals in small currencies. Everybody thinking too big, too greedy, too fast. And I buy the fins two-to-one over the sawbucks. Takes more time for the profits to build, but it's safe. Like you wouldn't believe, it's fucking safe. It's not like some nigger crackhead's going to put his money in Manny Hanny."

End of the second day, Martin got another cut. A much better shake this time. Bunny said, "I feel like throwing a party"—on the other side of his desk, looking down at his own share. "You up for a party, Tee?"

Terry said, "We going to throw one every time this much comes in?"

Bunny smiled. "That'd be a lot of parties, no?"

Terry bobbed his head to say that was his point.

"Yeah, it's going to be coming in like this from now on, fellas," Bunny said. "I'm going to have to keep hiring. But only Italians from now on; you micks bring me down."

He couldn't sleep. Crawled out of bed, careful not wake Frito. Went out on the fire escape. The sky dark. No stars. No stars ever over New York, he guessed—New York it's own universe. The Twin Towers down there, down Thompson Street. Red light blinking on the top of the one of them.

All that day, traveling around the city doing business, making money, he'd felt free. He'd sat in the back of the car, kept quiet, Bunny doing most of the talking—chatting, really—and never before had he felt so good. Finally understood what it meant to be packing. Filled-up. Fortified, it meant. It meant replenished from some former weakness. The Glock light and solid, and his, from now on. Filled-up and fortified, and ever weakening again an impossible thought. Bunny talked, and talked. Spoke for Terry at times—"Terry said this or that . . . went here or there"—Tee's head always just facing away, a bit, out the window. *Aware of me, or not?*

But who knew?

Just give him the benefit of the doubt; figure he never thinks twice about you.

They were both just carrying now.

Christ, you been afraid of him so long, he thought.

Already could see Bunny's favoritism shifting.

But you're not working for Bunny forever. Get rich with him, go on your own. It won't take long, like this.

A car passed, below. The first since he'd come out. No more coming that he could see. Peace-off-in-the-distance-like. More of the same beyond.

He went back inside.

∎ ∎ ∎

Friday, another trip to Maryland, another duffel-bag-full—twice the size, this bag—and, Saturday morning, to the bank. Got a grand in new hundreds, an envelope for the wedding with golden bells in the corners, a little oval cut out beneath the flap, for Benjamin's face. Knew Fee would get a kick out of that. Two grand into the mutual fund. Opened a savings account. Drove out Sunday morning, following the Pathfinder, and he and Fee changed in Penny's bedroom. She was at Daniella's. On the dresser, there was a photo of Fee and her. A Salvador Dalí crucifixion-in-space type picture over the bed. Single bed. He wondered if Fee had ever been in it.

At the dais he remembered it was a full mass—he'd have to receive—everyone would be watching. He exhaled a fast Act of Contrition and took the wafer in his hands. He put it in his mouth, chewed fast, and swallowed. No lightning struck. No blink of an eye and he was down in Hell. *"Only say the word and I shall be healed."* But no feeling of grace either. Like in childhood. It had been so long since he'd been to any service. He wondered what anyone really felt anymore.

He checked all the people up there with him, what he could get from their faces. The bridesmaids had received but hadn't changed. Same dopey looks. Big grins. He could shag one later if he tried, he knew. Penny'd received but she just still looked attentive. Like what the priest was saying was transforming something she could actually see but she would keep watching close to make sure the changes *took*. And Fee seemed to take it all in stride. Part of the day, it was. A little stop at church. The kneeling, standing, avowing—it was all just a good time to him. A good day in his life.

Wait a second . . .

He asked him about it later, stepping onto the dance floor with him after the best man speech and the half-dozen spotlight dances. "I converted, brother," Fee said. "Getting a tattoo next. Like yours," took his hand and spun away from him, spun back under it. London Bridge. Put his arm around him and led, rocked them back and forth. Martin remembered something Fee'd told him when they were younger—Russians were Russians first, Jews second.

"And what's your mother think of your conversion?"

"She couldn't give a shit, man; look what she got in exchange." He reached out, Fee, and caught Penny's arm, pulled her away from some cousin or other. Brought her into the pair the two of them made. A trio, now. Kissed her. Then broke off with her, alone. Put his arms around her tight, and danced. So grateful, Fee, that she'd actually gone through with it, it looked like. Grateful that she'd have him, Martin guessed. He and Felix hadn't really talked about anything like that.

She was blocked off from his view, now.

Except her face, suddenly—they'd turned, a bit. Her cheek pressed to Fee's. Her eyes closed. She put her hand up in his hair.

Martin found a bridesmaid and danced with her. Had a good time, after a while. Then was dancing with her and her friend—another bridesmaid. Went on with that for a bit. One song, two, four. Thought could he take them *both* someplace for the night. Shit like that happened either in the movies only, or after parties like this, when no one was quite themselves because they were more themselves than they knew how to handle.

He didn't drink. The urge was strong. For the first time in *years*.

He worked hard to keep smiling for the bridesmaids. It was impossible to miss Pen in that dress, though. Anywhere in the room, for fuck's sake.

It would be all right.

He didn't drink.

H e was coming out of the loo, drying his hands, looking around him for a garbage can, going back to the reception, and he stopped. She was there. Sitting in a phone booth. Old-fashioned bank of three of them opposite the rest rooms. Big dress filling up the cubicle. Rising around her. Staring at the wall, she was. Staring at nothing, but was waiting for him, he knew. Even if she didn't know it. He stretched his hand in her direction, snapped his fingers. She looked up. Got up. Steadied herself on the door. Tried to. Looked at it with disgust that it wouldn't quit collapsing. "You okay, Pen?"

She stepped into the hallway. The wide red carpet. Her white dress. She wasn't answering. Came toward him—up to him—stopped. Jerked her dress in behind her and stumbled. He put his hand out to steady her. On her arm, he put it. Which was bare. She looked down at it—his hand on her arm. Then shirked them apart. Blind drunk she was.

"Don't touch me."

"Okay."

She looked up at him. After watching him take his hand back. Her eyes thick-looking—opaque irises, red in the whites.

"You look a little wobbly," he said, "but, okay."

"You're a motherfucker," she said, her head weaving with the effort.

And he knew, then. And knew there was nothing in the world to do about it.

His throat tightened.

"What is this?" she said. Took the paper towel from him. "What . . . is this?" Studied it. Like a dead animal.

"It's a napkin."

She tossed it away. It sailed. It dropped to the carpet. Spot of white on the red, corner of his eye.

"Out of my way"—her eyes still down. On nothing. Lids half-closed. "You motherfucker."

He took a step, back, stayed in front of her. Didn't want her to go. "Get *out!*" she said.

"All *right*"—he stepped aside. Looked down the hall. No one there. "Don't yell." She walked past him, her dress taken up. "That's the men's room," he said.

"I know . . . what it is."

He listened. Her dress rasped on the tile. The stall door banging. She started to puke.

He left her there and went back to the party.

▪ ▪ ▪

On Wednesday, he stood on the corner waiting for Bunny to swing by and pick him up. At four, supposed to be, but Saint Anthony's ringing the hour a while ago, now. He thought about her coming for him drunk the other night. Drink let your mind speak free, he knew, so maybe she cared for him still. Or maybe it was just the hatred talking. A girl as good as she was, for the rest of her life she would hold either emotion, sober.

Plus, now, the dream had come a second time. He'd had it that night, after the wedding, after slipping into bed beside Frito as usual, no two bridesmaids with him *What an ass you are, thinking that,* and then last night, again. Which meant his brain wasn't through with it. Through working it out. Dreamt of her coming up to him, then was right in his face telling him "Pick it up"— the napkin, a splash of white on the wide red carpet. His brain distilling the whole thing down to that—would he pick it up, or no.

In the dream the other night, he'd left it where it was and walked away. In last night's dream, he'd held out. Stared at her. Couldn't leave, but wouldn't do what she said. "Pick it up, Martin, God *damn* it!" she'd told him.

Today was the third day of their honeymooning.

Bunny's car pulled up. He got in. It was Terry at the wheel. No one in back. "What'd you, steal his car?"

"Change of plans," Terry said.

They went up the West Side. Were supposed to be going to Staten Island, but he didn't ask—showed no concern, no interest. Terry offered nothing. They stayed quiet, up the length of Manhattan.

At a stoplight between two bodegas in Washington Heights, Terry took a small automatic out of his sock and put it on the seat, between them. Said, "Niggersville."

Down a side street, further in, he stopped, and said to switch with him. Got out, came around, and got in the passenger side. Told him to drive down two more blocks and make a left onto the avenue. Then, to pull up in front of the sneaker store. Asked if he had something on him.

He said yeah.

"Keep it in your hand."

Terry hid the automatic in his beltline and got out, went around the front of the car, up onto the curb, into the sneaker store.

Martin loaded the Glock. Couldn't imagine what else to do—what they were doing at all. He laid it in his lap, his finger outside the trigger guard. Terry came out a half minute later, smiling. Nodding at something someone coming out behind him was saying. It was the P.R. Who they'd given the swag money to the week before. Crazyhorse.

Terry brought him around the passenger side. Martin tucked the gun between his leg and the door. Had no fucking idea now what Terry wanted, but they were laughing, the two of them—the gun should probably be hidden. Terry opening the door and the guy put his foot in, ducked down, was laughing. Then convulsed. Every muscle in him. His shoulders drawing up, like a puppet's, toward his starked-out face. He fell in, his head into Martin's lap. Terry still laughing. His head up out of view. Hooked his shoe under the guy's free leg and laid it in and closed the door. Martin saw the stun gun in Tee's hand.

Terry got in back. Martin shoved the guy's face away and pulled calmly from the curb, like a citizen. Drove off. Didn't know where he was going but knew they couldn't stay. Terry leaned into the front and shocked the guy again—set the conductors against the muscle running out from his neck, and the guy's head went back and his fingers closed.

"Up there, on the corner," Terry said. "Pull in."

He pulled to the curb. Put it in Park. Nothing around. Just rows of buildings, gutted-out. Terry took the guy under the arms and hauled him into the back before Martin could even help. Set the guy against the door and raised one of his lids, pulled a pair of gloves on, looking up every few seconds, checking, worked fast. Told Martin to switch seats and put his gun on the guy, "Not too close." Put a hand firm on the guy's chest and took something from another pocket, closed his fist around it. A walking fucking armory. Waited for the guy to wake up. Looked in his face. Waiting.

Martin couldn't swallow—had to work to.

He blinked, the Puerto Rican. Fluttered his eyes weird. Opened them completely. Looked sleepy. Took in Terry, the gun, Martin behind it. "What the fuck, yo?"

"You awake?"

"Yeah, man, what the fuck?"

Terry hit him. A muffled crack into the face. Everything in the car seeming to jump, a bit, with it.

The guy was out, a second. Then came back, and freaked to fight back, to not be held. Terry hit him again. Leaned him forward as he came conscious a second time coughing, drooled blood and teeth. Terry leaned him back.

"Don't hit me again." Brought his hand up to wipe his mouth. Terry let him. Said—

"You packed?"

"No. Not in the store."

"You knew we were coming. That Bunny was."

"I thought it was business. Don't carry in the store. Cops be bringing me in every week. That's my place."

"He's going to frisk you. If you're carrying, I'll kill you. You won't leave this car alive. Think about that, a second. This interior's the last thing you'll see."

Martin leaned forward, stretched a hand to start patting.

"Go ahead, man"—sleepy still.

"Forget it," Terry said, not turning.

Martin backed off.

"What is this, yo?"

"You fucked up. We figured you didn't have to be told you only sell to niggers and your own, but you fucked up."

"What you talking about, bitch?"

"You passed to Rocco—you're fucking stupid."

"Who?"

Hit him again. A thump in the forehead. More a shock than a blow. The guy took a second. They waited. "Rocco DiNabrega," Terry said.

"So? I said don't hit me no more."

"He's coming to kill you."

"Then what the fuck you doing here?"

"Letting you know. And that you got the money from a nigger. Somebody. I don't care who."

"Fuck you, Irish bastard."

There was nothing left of his face when they dumped him out, Terry keeping up beating him when he was unconscious. Rolled down the window as they drove away and broke open the roll of dimes, let them fall into the street. Threw the gloves away, peeling them inside-out, like a surgeon.

No one followed them. No souped-up gangster rides or sudden lights and sirens. It was just over. And as easy as Terry's original calm had suggested it would be. A real pro now, Terror. He'd had some practice. Said, after a while, "Fucking car's a mess." They were back on the Henry Hudson. "He's going to have to trade it in."

"Why's Rocco buying money?"

"He's not; he's selling *yeyo*. Your man back there bought it with the funny money. Stupid motherfucker. Threw everything off for a couple of hours."

"And you're sure he won't rat you to Rocco."

"Guaranteed." No question in his mind. Looking out at the water. "Or let him. It doesn't matter. It'll never get back."

Martin thought, a second. Saw it. "There's someone inside for you. Whoever Rocco gave the hit to. It's how you knew in the first place."

"Everyone hates that fuck. Nobody stays in power that long."

Everyone *did* hate Rocco. Nothing was truer than that. And there *did* have to be guys in the neighborhood still loyal to the memory of Bunny's old man. Guys who just didn't know what else to do for dough. Terry'd *been* one of them, for Christ's sake.

"What the fuck did we come up here for then, though?"

"They're not going to kill him," Terry said.

"He gets another beating from Rocco's guy?"

"*Our* guy. That's right. More of the same. Stupid motherfucker."

"You gave him yours to let him know Bunny knows all."

"Knows *ev*erything. He'll never forget that now. If he does, he's removed. A nice clean head shot I'll bless him with from my Sig. Then, time for us to find a new buyer."

"Meantime we keep doing business with him."

We. He didn't like the sound of that.

No impact on Terry, though, apparently—"The only way," Terry saying. Eyes out the window still. "Let things cool a while. Let me see that piece."

Martin handed it to him. Terry looked it over. Sighted at the floor. "They don't melt, hunh?"

"I guess not. The slide's metal."

"You never fired it."

"Nah."

"We should try it out."

"I don't think so"—didn't look at him. Terry was staring at him, though—he could feel it.

Terry handed it back.

He put it away.

"You remember that time, we were kids?" Terry said.

"What time?"

"I pulled the gun on you?"

"Yeah."

"Yeah."

"You finally ready to apologize?"

"Yeah, sure," Terry said.

Martin looked over. Terry looked out the window. Wouldn't meet his eyes. Ever, when they were alone, Martin realized. "You were an asshole," Terry saying.

Martin said nothing.

"A half-a-wiseguy is what you always wanted to be."

"I had the money, Tee."

"No fourteen-year-old gets his own fireworks drop. They were laughing at you."

"Then why'd you pull the gun?"

"You were an asshole. I just said. An annoyance."

"Fuck you, an annoyance." But smiling, he said it. Couldn't stand up completely.

Terry said, "I'll explain this as best I can to you, college. I don't like you. You're *still* an annoyance. One sunny day, I'm not going to worry about you no more. That's it."

"I'll remember that."

"Do what you like. That a fact's a fact is a fact. The girls on the playstreet used to say that. You'll remember it that way, I bet. From your young girlish days."

They didn't speak again. Drove in silence to the restaurant. Martin angled in at the curb and turned the engine off, pulled out the key, opened the door, Terry making no moves to get out. Said something as Martin stood up outside the car. Martin sat back down, brought one foot in. Didn't turn. "What?"

"I said one of these days you're going to tell me what happened to my brother."

"I thought one of these days you were going to get rid of me."

"You'll tell me first. So-help-me-God—"

"You're asking the wrong person," Martin said. Got out. Terry followed, fast. They looked at each other across the top of the car. Both doors open. *All* eyes now, Terry. Martin's legs got weak, a bit.

"You're going to tell me," Terry said. Talking lower. Harder. *Seeing fear?* "You are . . . going to tell me."

"You're what now, hypnotizing me? Do me a favor, Terry. Never fucking say another word to me. How about that?" He could collapse, he felt. Or go berserk. *But do* some*thing.* He'd never really seen Terry mad. Terry calm still, yes, and his eyelids mellow, but his pupils blaring.

"How about I shoot you right here?" saying. Was serious.

"Open fire on Prince Street? You won't make it five blocks. They'll drop you before you hit the corner. You won't make it nowhere." *Nowhere.*

Like he was eleven again. And he felt that he was. The hollow cold in his balls. Terry crazy enough to do it just to make his point, not be shown up.

"You're going to tell me or I'll fucking beat it out of you. Your private school, GI ass."

"You're the one that worked for Rocco after it, motherfucker, not me." He threw the key on the roof, and shut the door. Walked away. His legs jumpy but tough to bend. He looked to find him in a window somewhere, see his movements.

What would a bullet in the back feel like? he wondered. Would you feel the thump and the tear of it, or would your brain just try to stop you from falling first?

He turned the corner onto Thompson, walked faster. Guessed he wouldn't be finding out, just now.

S oldiers sneaking across the barracks to beat the slackers, the laggers, the retards. Beating their piss out in the darkness. He pushed the thought away. But, Christ, he wondered, some of them had it coming, didn't they? *Some* of them? He turned around in the booth, faced the sidewalk, said, "I'm not a fucking torturer, Bunny."

"Me neither. Where are you, the street?"

"I took a walk. Did you send him?"

"Of course. It's business."

"Did you tell him to pick me up? Where you and me were supposed to meet?"

"Yeah, I got no one else. I told you I got to start hiring. It was a two-man job."

"Well, I'm not doing it again. Not with that fucking whackadoo. I'm not working with him. It's not worth it."

Silence.

Cars passed.

Bunny's office chair squeaked on the other end, so he was fidgeting. Thinking. "All right, whatever," said. "You don't got to see him for a couple of days, anyway; we got to cool it this week. Stupid fucking spick fucked everything up."

"I'll call you in a couple of days."

"Yeah, take a break. Go down the shore. Spend some of that money and get some color. But come by late, Sunday."

Martin hung up. A little too hard, but fuck Bunny anyway. He stepped out of the booth and looked around. Like maybe something might have changed. His senses calmer at all? Every stimulation not so shrill? Down the avenue the Twin Towers sat, rose, loomed in the sky. So peaceful down here where the city started up. He didn't know any hoods who lived down here. Didn't know *any*one who lived down here.

Something in him still wanting to run, though. He'd wanted to since he left Terry standing there. Run, and sweat the fear out completely, like an illness. But his strength was gone now, every bit of it.

With a blind hand he found the booth behind him and leaned back, lowered himself to the pavement.

He waited for his courage to return. His resolve, at least.

Where are you *call*ing from, for Christ's sake?"

"I don't know. Someplace hot. And the men are all short."

"Who is it?" his mother said.

"It's Felix. He's calling from his honeymoon."

"Is that a good sign?" She said it quietly.

"Is that your mother? Hey, Mrs. Quinn."

"He says hello."

"Hi."

"She says it's a bad sign, you calling from your honeymoon."

She held her breath in, swatted him on the shoulder. Fee was laughing. She hit him again, said, "Don't . . ."

"Stop, he's laughing."

"No, things are great," Fee said. "That's why I called."

"To fill me in? Give me the itinerary?"

"No, man, with good news. Good, good news. We got to the hotel here? My father'd sent a wire. My wedding gift. The club in Brooklyn? You remember?"

"Yeah. With the hostesses."

"Yeah, the hostesses."

"It's yours?"

"It's mine."

"Congratulations."

"Will you run it with me?"

And there it was.

He had known Fee would ask.

Fee said, "Come on. We'll show Russ Meyer movies, like in high school."

He didn't respond, though. Just listened to the hollow rush that passed for silence, speaking overseas. Felt like the new life they would have was already starting to break over him.

Bunny'd been right. Knew you couldn't just live in New York. You'd have to get back inside it, be one of the people who reinvented it every morning, for everyone else. Jesus *Christ,* he'd missed it. The action. Being connected. Upstate, he thought he'd want something quiet, coming back. A favorite joint. Meet your friends at the bar. But he wanted a place of his own. His spot at the bar. His table in back. From the moment he'd seen her, he'd wanted that power, just hadn't admitted it. He'd run to the army because he was too scared to fight to build something new up for himself. Far too young then to take things in control and face whatever came. But everybody felt fear, he knew now. And he was ready to finish what he'd abandoned. Take another shot at being the man he'd once imagined. Who she'd expected he would be. Even if he'd never have her. Even if he'd just be sticking close.

"Please, Q, this is an expensive call. No dramatic pauses."

"Yeah, man. I'll do it."

"Fucking excellent. He'll do it, he says."

Penny there in the room, listening, he guessed. What was she wearing? Sitting there nonchalant? Knees crossed, and leaning on them with an elbow, smoking one of her Parliaments?

"Yeah, I'll do it. Definitely." Didn't say to say hello.

"Tremendous. Go see my father, then, all right? I'm going to call him. Then you go see him. Right away. Tomorrow."

"All right."

"Definitely."

"Thanks, Fee."

"My pleasure. I'll see you in three weeks. Keep Vlady away from the quim."

W ho?"

"Lexi Pasko."

Bunny shook his head. Took his feet down off the desk. Martin kept his up. Bunny looked at him. Something serious coming into his face. "You were there," he said.

"Where?"

"In the Heights."

"Bunny, don't threaten me, man. You're not listening."

"I'm just saying you were there."

"Don't threaten me."

Bunny looked at him. Long. Martin smiled. "You listening?"

Put his feet up again, Bunny, crossed his ankles. "Tell me again. The name."

"Lexi Pasko."

"I don't know him. No."

"You got to stop dealing with Puerto Rican drug dealers. And meat warehouses."

"Who is he?"

"He's the head of the Russian fucking Mafia."

Bunny thought about it. Said, "Okay."

"Okay?"

"Sure, I'll buy it. How do you know him?"

"I went to school with his kid. We're tight."

"That fucking private school."

"Yeah."

Bunny nodded. Shook his head. "Smart, sending his kid there. I'm going to send mine to private school, if I can. It's tough to get in, though, right? Well, fuck, you did."

"What I'm saying is we're opening this club, and things are going to happen out of it. We're going to make money, and we're going to want to invest back *into* it. Diversify."

"Okay, when?"

"When what?"

"Are you going to fucking di*ver*sify? When do *I* get to start earning?"

"We got to open the place first."

"So, you're saying you want to buy yourself out from working for me, but you don't want to pay me nothing. *La botte piena e la moglie ubbriaca.* You want a full barrel *and* a drunken wife."

"You'll *get* your money back. Your security."

"And you get what, up front?"

"I get money, man. And freedom. No offense, but I don't want to be working for you, the rest of my life. Three weeks is enough. I'm sick of you calling my house."

"So you'll make money off the both of us—me and the Russian. Set your*self* up for something down the line."

"Yes, but I'm being up front with the both of you, from the get-go. That's my angle. And *every*body makes money, man; don't play innocent. You keep building the empire, I go out on my own, come the time. The Russians do whatever Russians do. I don't really know."

"Pasko?"

"Lexi Pasko. He has no oath or debt to anyone. He's right at the top by himself. No five families to clear things with. He owns Brighton Beach. And half of Toronto."

"So how come I don't know him?"

"I don't know, man. I'm kind of surprised you don't, really."

"Fuck you, you're surprised. You surprised I had work for you? You surprised I'm thriving right here around the corner from the motherfucker killed my old man?"—no anger in him, though—just questions. Things were always face-value with Bunny. Martin shrugged, shook his head to say no. "I don't know him 'cause the feds don't know him, I bet," Bunny said. "And if the feds don't, the news don't. Then nobody knows. That's how shit works now. More money in a story than your average decent score."

Martin nodded. "That's true." Though he knew *Rocco* knew God-damned well who Lexi was. And that Bunny was probably thinking that, this second. But, if he had to convince himself, fine. "Everybody makes money with him, Bunny. He's got so many legitimate fronts, you wouldn't believe. He's unreal, this guy."

Bunny nodded like Yeahyeah, he'd heard it the first time. He leaned back and moved the curtains, a bit, with a finger. Stared at the street. After a while, said, "People aren't loyal like they should be, no more. I don't mean to *me*. I'm not like that whack-job around the corner. I just mean to the things that made them strong. While you were in the army, somebody painted over the Italian flag on the handball wall in the park? It was there my whole life. Let you know the neighborhood was in control. Somebody just blanked it out. White paint. The wiseguys too busy trying to move to the suburbs, reading the real estate pages. I put the word out, and some local kids found out it was a rival basketball team, Lower East Side. I sent them down there to kick their asses. I bought new paints, a fucking ladder, got kids who could paint the flag back nice."

"It's an Italian flag, Bunny—I don't care."

"You don't care. You joke, but the Italians made you, Irish. You talk like one. You dress like one. You always wanted to fucking—"

Martin put his hands up, palms out—*Okay*—"I was kidding, we just said, Bunny, no? Finish the story, for fuck's sake."

"It's finished," he said, and shrugged. "That flag's a symbol. Of order. Safety. You come in this neighborhood, you know it's peaceful."

"*Peace*ful? I got scars from—"

"You got scars 'cause you wanted them. You could have grown up getting them without a *choice*. Like if there'd been niggers around? Every time you weren't checking your back? At least there's no niggers."

"'No niggers.' Everybody's always bugging-out over niggers. Every-

body's so scared. You ever even know one? You know what one is, even?
Describe one to me."

"Your mother's one, no?"

Martin smiled. Bunny looked at the street again. Shook his head.
"When are you going to open it? Your big fucking club."

"I'm going to talk to him tomorrow."

"And you start making money right after?"

"You know what *glasnost* is? Gorbachev? You know who he is?"

"Yeah."

"Well, he told the Russians last year they could leave if they wanted to,
and they're coming in by the thousands and moving to Brooklyn. The bor-
ough's booming."

"And he runs it."

"All the Russian part of it, yeah."

"For a while."

"Yeah, probably; there'll be competition. It's how this country operates.
But there's tens of thousands of people coming in every year. We're talking
about world politics. Things bigger than anyone can control. All you can
do is guess, dip your hand in, take as much out as you can. Then, send your
kids to private school. Then die."

Bunny nodded, listening, thinking. "You're seeing him tomorrow?"

"Yeah. What is it, man? What's the matter with you?"

"Just figuring."

"You want all the money back I made from Baltimore?"

"No, I don't fucking . . . Keep it. And get your feet off my fucking
desk."

"I can't do that, sheriff."

He sighed, Bunny.

Was giving in more and more, though. And knew he would prosper, of
course.

"They're going to be big, you think, the Russians?"

"They already are. It's time you met some of them. Plus, further down
the line, I'm in there as your *per*manent connection. You're gaining here,
man, not losing—"

"Don't fucking . . ."

Too far, that bit. Telling him his business.

But he *was* cornered, Bunny. Had no options anymore.

Except killing. Everyone. Michael Corleone style. The only way to stop the world turning for a while.

"Then I'll talk to you tomorrow, Irish. Get out."

Martin took his feet down. "All fucking right, then."

Bunny looked at him. Smiled. "You want to say goodbye to Terry before you go?"

S aw Lexi and got his consent, called Bunny and gave him some in-the-air dates. Then took his original advice and rented a place on the shore for a long weekend, put Frito and Juliet in the Plymouth and spent the three days on the beach, eyes closed. Listened to the waves crashing in and the two of them whispering in love. Got on the road early Monday, but still hit commuter traffic. Frito and Juliet sleeping in the back all the way through it.

He dropped them at the apartment and made it to Brighton by ten. Just made it. Wearing shorts and sunglasses, still. Pulled in behind Lexi's Continental and went up in no hurry, made sure Lexi caught him coming in the sideview. Lexi got out, up-and-downed him fast. They went in.

Men were tacking in new baseboards—the floors newly finished. Men were remortaring exposed brick walls for a West-Side-Manhattan-joint look. Staining two long and two horseshoe-shaped bars. Setting in stained-glass panels. Hoisting chandeliers. The place went on and on, turned corners, opened up again. Was tall and vast in some parts, cavernous in others. Lexi walked him through, pointed out details, introduced him to foremen, envisioned outcomes out loud. Led him, showed him, made everything clear and set him straight. Said, "This is your office" at the end of a hall at the back of the building. Martin opened the door, looked in. It was empty still. Hollow. It would be perfect. He could see the boardwalk out the window, a half-dozen blocks away. Lexi said, "You'll be spending a lot of time in here. Do what you want with it. Filushka can work hard, but he'll want to play. He'll spend a lot of time out *there*. Decorate it how you want."

Martin said okay. Like there was no boon in what Lexi was saying, just more facts to absorb. But he was thinking that the old man was still comforted, now, seven years later, at Felix's choice of business partner. "We'll have our files in here?"

"And your safes."

"We'll do wainscoting. Wood a quarter way up the wall? And an old-fashioned desk, like you have in your apartment. Royal-looking. They'll give a sense of tradition, those two things. A couple of leather sofas. One a fold-out. Some armchairs"

"Carpets? Caucasian? Persian?"

"Shag," Martin said.

"Like the seventies?"

"They're making things like that again. Bell-bottom jeans, neck pendants, Day-Glo Afro wigs."

"The staff will see you as young."

"Hip," Martin said. "But with a taste for elegance. A sense of humor."

"They'll think they can be honest with you."

"Their mistake to make."

Lexi nodded, saw it immediately.

They looked over the room. No talking. The tour was over, Martin guessed. Work ready to begin. Lexi said, "They will all be here at eleven, to meet you."

"We'll meet in here." He pictured it already. Saw himself. Leaning back on the window sill, facing them. Uncrossing his arms and coming forward, pacing, casual. Addressing them like troops he could care for.

He should have a coffee with him, he realized. Symbol of hard work. Show them he'd been here since early. "Let's get a coffee. Before they get here. I was up at five."

They went out.

Down the hall Lexi said, "It's good for screwing, I'll bet, shag carpet." Eyes straight ahead. Thinking aloud.

Martin said, "I'll let you know on that."

They would open on time. It had been questionable, the last week. Plus, he and the old man getting on each other's nerves. Too many years between them. But they pushed through, the last night. Before Fee and Pen's return. Finished late. Or early. Four, five in the morning.

In the lot, they shook hands, smiled at each other. Relieved. Proud of themselves. Lexi said, "Wait," went to his car and opened the trunk, moved the rug back and took out an envelope, gave it to him. "You can live on it for a while. Have a good bankroll in your pocket. From the beginning. All part of the decoration."

"Finishing touches."

"But the last. No more. We're finished."

Martin thanked him.

"I ordered a car for them," Lexi said. "At the airport. A stretch. With Champagne and chocolate. Some strawberries. Make the vacation, you know . . ."

"Go as long as it can. Not end too abruptly"—Lexi nodding as soon as he'd started filling in the words for him. Something the old man rarely needed.

And, now, his mind going somewhere else. His own honeymoon, maybe. Or that place where fathers felt their sons' happiness like their own.

"Feel's going to be amazed, Mr. Pasko. He's going to be blown away. He's going to thank you."

"He'll work hard. He'll see what we've done. He'll be honored to work."

"Shit, I hope so. Let *him* break his ass for a while."

They smiled. Said all right. Went to their cars. Didn't ask where they were going, offer to buy the other a breakfast, anything like that. Knew they'd see each other at the opening tonight. Which was what this had been about from the beginning, no?

"You'll be lucky you stay awake for it," he said aloud to himself, pulled out of the lot. Thought, It's good we're sick of each other. There's respect in that.

He didn't want to be the fucking guy's *pal,* for Christ's sake, right?

In Manhattan, he had breakfast at the all-night diner on Tenth Avenue. Opposite the repair shop. Watched out the window for it to open. Ordered a new engine and a custom color paint job when it did. Left 50 percent down for the deposit, and drove back home. He showered and shaved. Dressed up, sharp but casual. Got a coffee from the bakery and sat in the park and drank it. Then got back in the car. He had a last loose end to knot up before this new rest of his life got going.

My old man's manager? he thought looking at him. How do you manage
the unmanageable?

Sugar said, "I thought you'd look more like him. You *do*. You always *did*.
But your eyes are different."

He shrugged. Shook his head. Didn't know what to say to that.

"And you didn't think I'd be so old," Sugar said. "Exiled to Riverdale.
Land of the nursing home. Say it—I look like shit."

They laughed.

"Sugar, the last time I saw you I was ten. I'm not going to say something
mean."

"But you'll think it? That's fine. I got my answer. Thank you."

They laughed again. Martin shook his head, put his hands up to say, *No,
wait,* until he could speak. "I mean I couldn't even *joke* it."

"Shit, I was old when your daddy first came to me. Old compared to
him, forty-five. He was twenty. You're what now, twenty-five?"

"Twenty-six."

"Twenty-six he was doing well. That was when it all took off for him."

Martin nodded, looked at the floor. Comparisons inevitable in some
people's heads, he knew. His old man had jammed with Monk and Mingus
by twenty-six. Had released his only album. The first reports coming back
that it was selling in New York and Chicago. It was about to break big in
Paris. By twenty-six, he'd discovered and already once kicked heroin. Had
his famous tattoo by then. Fat little yellowjacket on his inside forearm.
Bullet-shaped head, bugged-out black eyes, oversized stinger pointing into

the elbow crook. His worn-out mainline. Everyone calling him Stinger after that.

It was in Paris that he went back on the needle. Where the cops didn't give a damn and the women begged to watch you fix. At least as his mother described it. How they lived there three years and she got pregnant with Frito and the old man sent her home and kicked again, in a chalet in the south he rented from some *nouveaux riches.* Then he came Stateside to again try being a papa.

Sugar's nurse knocked on the half-open door. Came in, handed Sugar the paper. She'd pointed Martin down the hall when he got off the elevator. *"He's my number one guy,"* she'd said. Young, Hispanic. Filled out her uniform, and then some. Gold on her neck and both her wrists, her fingers already too chubby to ever get her engagement or wedding ring off again. "No gambling today, Sugar," she said.

Already he'd put on his glasses, turned to the sports. Had been looking at the door when her shoes were squeaking close. He said, "No, no," and folded the paper where he wanted, laid it in his lap. Looked up again. Dropped his chained glasses back on his chest. Winked at him. "She thinks I gamble."

She said, "I'm worried about your heart, Sugar. Too much excitement. Even when you win all the time, which I know you do, you know what happens." She looked at Martin and winked. Looked back at Sugar, and frowned. "I'll check on you later." Pulled the door closed, a bit, behind her. Squeaked down the hall. Her little white sneakers. *"Hello, honey . . . Hello, sweetheart . . . Mrs. Kelly, you got your hair done. Que linda, it's beautiful . . ."*

"My girl," Sugar said. "She's twenty-two. Three kids. Knows I keep thirty grand in my strongbox downstairs behind reception. In case I lose my touch, suffer a catastrophe. I told her my earnings the last ten years? Winning fifty-two percent of the time? I told her I'd teach her to read the line for basketball, help her place her bets, but she won't do it. A shame." He held the glasses up closer to his face, a second, and glanced the paper over. Shook his head. "The spread on New York, you know? It's painful. I'll bet them the same as I would anyone, but." He set the glasses down again. Looked at Martin. Smiled, after a second. A fresh look, like.

"You want to call your bookie?"

"I got a few hours. I feel better now I got my paper. You look good, too, by the way. At twenty-six. Things look like they're good for you."

"I'm opening a restaurant."

Sugar closed his eyes. Nodded. "Beautiful. I wish you luck. You here for advice, then? Got to be a reason you come to see me after fifteen years," and opened them. Waited. Martin looked at the floor. "Find out who the wiseguys are," Sugar said. "Go to them first. That way, you don't have every guinea in a shiny suit coming asking for his. More important, once you feel comfortable enough to leave before closing, if you *ever* do, turn your phone off when you get home. Make your staff learn how to think for themselves. Otherwise they'll be calling you asking where the key to the booze lockup is 'cause they ran out of vodka. Or where their dick is, they got to take a piss. The rest?—you'll figure it out."

Martin nodded, looked up at him. Sugar opened his hands, fingers wide-spread.

"That it?" Martin said.

"How much can I tell you? You must be doing pretty well for yourself to be opening your own joint. And, if you're as smart as your father was, you'll only listen so much anyway. Unless you went on the street for the money. But you didn't, right?"

"Right."

"Then, okay. Plus, I know part of you's only here to show me that you're doing well. I appreciate that. You kids and your mother had a tough start. She tries to keep me up-to-date, though. I know you're good. Healthy. Working." He smiled.

Martin smiled back at him. Opened his own hands up, shrugged. "When does it arrive?" he said—"wisdom like that."

"When you stop getting laid. Enjoy your ignorance."

They laughed.

"Seriously?" Sugar said. "The only other thing is where you're opening it. Maybe I know the people around. I can get you an early break on your garbage haul. Get them to charge you an old-timer's rate."

"Brighton Beach," Martin said. "A couple of blocks in from the board-walk."

Sugar shook his head. Didn't know. "Not a soul. But I'll tell you some-thing. That neighborhood's growing, as I'm sure you know, and they got people of their own. Their own little underworld figures. Not a lot of peo-ple know that, but it's there. Has been, a long time. I was in the Riviera in the fifties? Listen to me. Monaco, Nice. Then I'm traveling, a bit—Mont-pellier, Marseilles. In Marseilles, at the waterfront, I see these guys in among everyone else, but all wearing fedoras with red hatbands."

Martin smiled.

"You *lis*ten to me," Sugar said. "These guys were a crew. Russians. But . . . hold on . . . ten years after, I go out to Coney Island. I'd met this ladylove from out west—she wanted to do something New York, so I take her on the Cyclone, a stroll along the boardwalk—son of a bitch if I don't see them again. Burly little guys in fedoras, with red hatbands. Almost thirty years ago, I know. But that neighborhood's coming around again. Looking good enough for you to want to open a restaurant. So *they*'re going to come around again. They always will."

Martin couldn't get the picture out of his head—Fee and him in fedoras.

Sugar said, "You can laugh, but don't dismiss this."

Martin said, "No. If you could see in my head, Sugar. It's just the oppo-site. You're one of the only people that knows they do exist. But I'm good. I'm cleared to operate. I grew up with the son of one of them." The heir apparent to the whole fucking thing, he thought.

"Well, then, shit, what did you come see me for?"

"You know . . ." He shrugged. "My mother told me she talks to you. I wanted to show you I was doing okay. At twenty-six." He raised his eye-brows. Shrugged again.

"*Now* you look like him," Sugar said.

He looked down again.

Sugar said, "That's how he came to me. When I had my club. Wanting to please. Twenty years old, in the seminary, and he hears on his contraband radio that the trumpet player in my house quartet died of a heart attack.

Your father sneaks out after Vespers and comes to the Village and begs me to let him audition. I ignored him. Too deep in mourning. He's out on the street looking in through the window with his hands pressed together saying Please. He's got his horn with him, there in its case. I just waved him off. Kept taking chairs down off the tables, I remember, setting up. And the next thing I know, I hear this note. Long. And rich. And clear. The kind of note lets you know what a trumpet was made for, and he segued into 'Round Midnight.' "

"And it started raining on him. That's how my mother tells it."

"Like his playing opened up the floodgates of Heaven. It poured."

Martin nodded. Kept his eyes down hard. Couldn't look at a man who'd ever cared that much for Stinger Quinn.

"I put him up in my apartment. He hardly ever went back to Brooklyn. He became a new man. Showed us his genius for a while."

Martin nodded. Again. Wanted to do here now what he'd really come for, then get out. "You should call your bookie," he said, and went to stand. Waited to see if Sugar'd protest. He didn't. Martin stood. Looked down at him. Smiled. Forcing it now. So hard it hurt. "I just wanted to stop by, Sugar." Sugar looking at him closely. Quiet.

"You don't forgive him," said.

"It's not really important to me anymore. I'm sorry; that's just how it is. But there was another reason I came."

But Sugar wasn't done with it, he could see. Had figured he probably wouldn't be.

Sugar saying "We'll never know what . . . Sit down."

"I feel like standing, if you don't mind."

"Sit down."

He did.

"He came back from Paris clean, and being clean for Frito's birth was the greatest thing he'd ever accomplished, he felt, so I don't know why he went back on. I don't know why he killed himself after. He had another record deal lined up. He had you boys. He had your mother. Things were better in his life than they'd ever been. But in his mind, things were over. So, how can we fathom that? How can we ever know how someone else suffers inside? That's what I learned when Stinger died. And, to be grateful I didn't hurt like that—"

"Sugar . . . I . . ." he twisted in his seat. Don't *fight* with him, he thought. Don't ask him what kind of a man opens his veins in a bath, with his family in the house. "You knew him as a kid; I knew him as a father. So I . . ."—he stood. "Forget this. I don't talk about this. Thirteen years ago, my mother came to you for bail money. For me. Five hundred dollars. You gave her twice that, then wouldn't take it back when she got it together to repay you"—he rattled it off. Something close to how he'd rehearsed it. "I wanted to thank you for that and to pay my debt." He put his hand in his pocket, to get it. Sugar shook his head. Saying no, Martin guessed—but also saying that something he was seeing here was regrettable. Truly.

"Martin, don't offer an old man money; it's bad form."

"I appreciate all you've done for my family."

"But now you'll take over—is that it? It's honorable. Consider your paper burned. But I haven't really done all that much, you know. Your mother handled everything fine."

"I'm just saying."

"I know what you're saying." He put his glasses on, took up the paper. "Keep in touch, once in a while. Let me know how the place does."

Martin said, "Okay." And didn't know what to do now. Sugar acting like they were done before he'd actually left. Had his little half-pencil out. Touched the tip of it to his tongue. Was reading the line . . .

Downstairs, Martin told the reception clerk, "Put this in Mr. Burton's strongbox, please. He asked me to drop it off on my way out," and handed the guy the twenty hundreds.

What he found was he was trying to read them. Caught himself looking from one to the other like this was some stupid comedy bit, his life. Trying to tune Fee out, hear something in Penny's silence. They kept unpacking. Their bags on the bed. The two of them back and forth from the bags to the hamper, or to the pile piling up for the dry cleaner's, or to the closets for the shoes and sweaters. An umbrella. Up the stairs to drop the camera and the travel guides. Felix talking without a break. Yakitty-yak, he was going to summer in London, winter in Greece the next few years, retire at thirty, in Monte Carlo. Took him by the shoulders—"I'm serious"—close, in his face. "You're just going to have to come with us, make it your home, too. You'll love it." And she smiling the whole time. Tired-smiling after a long day's traveling. Smiling at Felix when she was listening. Smiling to herself when her mind was somewhere else. But gave no secret look that said, "You were there, in my mind, the whole time. I never left you." For a moment, he wondered if she'd ever broken down at the wedding at all and cursed him. Had he imagined it? Misunderstood? She passed him, to get to a cabinet, smiled pleasantly. Like he was some old friend of Felix's she'd always liked.

This *honey*moon, he thought. This *trip* that a husband and wife took. It fucking changed things. He'd lost every bit of her. He thought, This is when a person faints, no?

It made him have to smile, the thought. His neck, his shoulders, his legs, felt every minute of the forty hours or more he'd been awake. He walked to the bed, and cleared aside a suitcase, sat at the edge and lay back. Stared straight at the ceiling. Dim, flat, white. "Two days, I been up," he said. They worked around him.

Fee said, "You look it."

She said, "Sleep. We're not due in Brooklyn for hours."

"But first look at this," Fee said. "We got you something."

Dropped his head to the side, looked. Fee drawing something carefully from one of the smaller cases. Handed it to him.

In some instant way, he already knew what it had to be. Fee saying "We found it in Paris. This is it, right? That's him?" and turned his hand for him so he was looking at the back of the album. The photograph on the back cover. The old man at work. Stinger Quinn. Standing behind the sound technician, with the other four members of his group, looking down at the mixing board. Cigarettes burning, everyone smiling, happy with the take. His old man who was never old. Not even twenty-six here. Not *my* age, now. Not lying back on a bed, worn-out. Just cool, and happy with himself. In a turtleneck, and sideburns. Looked nineteen, or twenty. Looked like Frito. Had one young son already, and another on the way.

*Ev*erywhere today, the old motherfucker. I'm fucking sur*rou*nded.

"Thanks."

"You're welcome," they said.

She went around, toward the hall closets. Had a bunch of shit on hangers.

Fee leaned down close to him, said, "She found it, man; thank *her,*" and Martin nodded okay, he would.

Thank *her,* man; she found it. *Fuck* her.

He closed his eyes. Crossed his arms across the album and held its edges. Like a schoolgirl holding her binder. Had no affection at all for it, just the instinct to keep it out of the way while they worked.

He would force himself to sleep, he guessed. Let himself. Let it come. Christ only knew what life would be like when he woke up *this* time.

■　■　■

WEEKEND. DINING OUT.

ANASTASIA'S

3010 Coney Island Blvd., Brighton Beach, Brooklyn. (718) 555-1234. *Part supper club, part nightclub, part formal dining room. All kept separate by speakeasy-ish ante-rooms, with leather-covered double-wide doors and leather-sporting double-wide bouncers. The place is much to tackle in one night, but give it a shot. The bar/lounge/supper club has vodka, full table service for dinner available, vodka, and a floor show with high-kicking chorus girls who cover Sinatra, Presley, Diamond (Neil)—all in Russian—and then pull diners out to join them in a free-for-all. Boogie a while, then move on to the official dining room. The decor is borderline baroque, the menu equally indulgent, excessive: there are thirty cold appetizers. Try the latkes, the blintzes, the herring in wine, in horseradish, in sour cream, the pickled watermelon. Consider the Georgian lamb dumplings with cilantro as entrée, or the sturgeon fillet in sweet-and-salty fig and caper sauce, or the Siberian borscht with veal, white vinegar, and sour cream. Sample around for dessert. There are cakes, tarts, meringues, jellies, candies, cookies, and chocolates. With every course there's vodka. An iced bottle is brought with the menu. Drink what you can and move on to the night-club (separate entrance on Ave. X). Revelers are sixteen to sixty, and attire ranges accordingly, from halter tops and tracksuits to rhinestone-studded gowns and shark-skin suits. The dance floor is huge, packed, and ringed by a balcony, also packed. The music is almost up-to-date, the special effects are not—lasers and strobe lights—but you'd never know it; the patrons—mostly Russians, mostly from the neighborhood, which is growing so fast it sprung a nickname, Little Odessa—know how to have a good time. One might suspect they're having it with a vengeance. Party with them till closing, if you can keep up, then exit onto a deserted Avenue X and hear the seagulls waking up not six blocks away.*

ANASTASIA'S

Food: ★★★

Atmosphere: ★★★★

Vodka: take a guess.

◾ ◾ ◾

A move or two each, per day, was all their brains could handle, but it was enough, it turned out. Enough to clear their heads of anything for a couple of minutes, and every few months, one of them would have the other in check, or at least have his king on the run. Some nights, they'd take out the game, he'd swear he never saw the layout before. Couldn't remember how things had gotten to this point only twenty-four hours or so ago, and he'd have to figure out all over again what he'd probably been trying to do— the club could overwhelm you so fast like that. But, then, he and Fee would get silent, a good few minutes, and there'd be nothing but the game, the game, and he'd make his move or two. Feeling good that he'd gotten something started. Or shut something clever of Felix's down. They'd put the board back, then. Out of the way, on the end table by the couch. Beneath the framed write-up from the paper, which he knew by heart, and the photograph of them in front of the entrance. The recessed Gothic door and the small, script neon sign, ANASTASIA's, in pink above it, the night they opened. Fee proud and laughing, and he smiling, too, but looking a bit like maybe he didn't get the joke. But it was just the fatigue. He liked the picture. He loved it, in fact. Would lie on the couch, beneath it, the game by his feet, already forgotten, and put a hand beneath his head. Fee'd sit at the desk and recline. Then they would run things. Troubleshoot employee problems. Talk food orders, entertainment changes. Business in general. Which always turned out to be a good subject.

His title, as far as he let the staff be concerned, was general manager, but his pay was commensurate with Felix's—he earned like an owner, pulled down twenty-five hundred or a flat three grand a week. All cash. All quiet. Was the first one in, before noon, every day, and the last to leave every morning, predawn. He earned and deserved. Started pricing new cars but then heard word of the groundfloor apartment opening up on the promenade down Battery Cove, and dropped ten grand on the managing agent. Was in in a week. Tinted the windows on the Plymouth instead. Put in a new dash, stereo, suspension, got a tune-up every 150 trips or so to Brooklyn, plus the times driving all over Long Island collecting receipts from the gas stations involved in the old man's fuel scam, and the car did more than hold on; it got better. Like some piece of his past he was making perfect.

Penelope disappeared into some law firm Felix hooked her up with. Frito got married.

Around Easter, Vlady got locked up for beating a guy half to death. Out in front of the club. With one of the poles that held the velvet roping. Before the cops got there, Martin did his best to help the guy breathe—sat him up against the wall and tipped his head so his throat stayed clear, the blood just keeping up running out of him—his nose, his mouth—and Vlady smiled. Couldn't help it. So amazed at the damage he'd done, like— the guy was broken-up—a big, sad doll. Martin said, "You're going to jail for this, you fucking asshole. Do you know *that* word? '*Asshole*'?" And Vlady looked around. At the crowd that was hearing it all. Martin slapped him. Said, "Look at me, motherfucker. I'm talking to you," but barely got it out before Vlady was on him. They rolled on the cement kicking the piss out of each other. Headlocks, bites, gouges. The whole schoolyard nine- yards. Martin wishing he'd had the Glock just then, so he could have beaten him with it. Knew Vlady never got over never getting it back after the tuxedo shop. But he'd thrown it in the safe when he'd heard there was a fight.

The broken guy left with the paramedics, Vlady with the bulls. Felix paid his bail, canned him. Some lawyer for the victim served them with papers. Felix said, "You're not a success until someone sues you."

New tires next, for the Plymouth. And a new electrical system. Frito and Juliet found an apartment not far from his. He paid their first six months up front, and got Juliet's mother to cover the rest. Felix bought them a car, unannounced. Would hear of nothing but a thank-you card. Penelope started coming around, some nights. Brought people from her firm with her. Nice people. Good people.

Time passed. The nonstop, no-rest madness of the joint got routine. Became his life. He dug it. Felix got him in check. He got Felix in check. Then they troubleshot. Every night. Time flew.

Except, after a while, the few hours he was home. Staring out the living room window onto the promenade, the water. He'd watch the day come up. His mind would be his for a bit, but he'd begun to have trouble sleep- ing. Then came to expect it.

So he started taking home waitresses. Hostesses. Dancers. Bought condoms in packs of twelve. Sometimes got up to shower right after. To rid himself of the girls while they slept and he still didn't. Russian, all of them. Fun, and nice enough. But with their bodies too thin and their eyes with sunken, dark circles so often—a bit undernourished-looking, so many of them. But flirtatious like they were under a spell. Plus vain, and overconfident. Very different from Italians. They would ask for the best and expect it, the Natashas. Never expected to have to accept any disappointment besides, like Italian girls got taught to.

Sometimes, in bed with them, he'd think of Penelope or Juliet. Not screwing them, just someone he wouldn't want to wash off of him. Someone he'd want to stay up with and talk to, talk to, talk to. The girls from the club, if they tried to say much, always ended up asking him to teach them better English. Any English. And all he could think of, those moments, was the kind of shit girls said in porn flicks. So he kept the lessons to himself. Most of the time. More and more, though, some mornings, something was welling up in him. Some darkness that spread forward from behind his thoughts. He'd say to them, "Tell me, 'Come on my tits,'" or, "'Fuck me from behind.' Can you say that?" Though they never really seemed to mind. Some would practice, even. Nice girls, really. A complete mystery to him.

And those mornings, the insomnia was worse. No desire to sleep at all. Just fear, he had. It spilled up into his throat. A fear he'd never sleep again and that he would die from it. He'd wake her up, his girl, and drive her home so she could finish her sleeping alone, and he'd drive to the club, then. Make himself breakfast in the empty, bright kitchen. Eat standing up. And wonder where the ugliness came from.

But he knew. It came from the way that other people got inside your life and then fucked it up for you. Just enough. So that after a while, you weren't thinking anymore what was right in your day, but what was wrong. What was right in your *life,* what was wrong.

It was Bunny moving too fast from running just grass and Ex through the club to adding coke and crank and acid to the menu without ever asking. It was the arrogance of the not ever asking. The presumption.

And it was the Sicilians he was hiring, Bunny, straight off the boat. Who followed him around, at first, like the girls in the neighborhood used to, but then came in on their own and partied. "Bunny send-a me." "*Send*-a you for what? To order drinks on the house?" Zips they used to call them, when they were kids. Back then, they were guys you would laugh at. But these boys were young and carrying. And sooner or later, gave *some*one shit. Gave everyone some.

It was the old man's business associates coming in for drinks and dinner, not two weeks here from Russia, then their scams would start piling up in the office. Literally. Mail from petroleum lobbies, health care operations, credit unions. All of it in preparation for the execution of one swindle or another. To get them on their feet till they were comfortable enough to steal on their own in this new, chosen home of theirs.

It was Penny stopping work suddenly and hanging around all the time. Having no reaction to his constant screwing except for something he couldn't prove but became convinced of when she stopped smoking suddenly. She wanted a kid. Fee was loaded. She was going on twenty-seven. And there was just something maternal about her already. Though maybe that was just his looking so hard. But either way, he got this twisted hope that if she was trying to conceive, it was to spite him.

Then there was Sunnyside, he guessed.

Of course there was. Being there for the murder.

The sharpest crimp in the paying-out of what had been starting to feel like the good life. The death of a man he'd only ever seen twice. The first time, back in high school. Eating dinner at Felix's place, Lexi shows them a Fabergé piece. A small, desktop snuff box. Blue enamel, gold edging, solid little gold claw feet. After tea and strawberries, Fee, the old man, and he get into the Lincoln with it. Drive out to Queens. Fee continuing a conversation from dinner and Martin along for the ride, holding the heavy little thing himself in the backseat—Lexi had wrapped it in a napkin from the table. They drove up, into the building's crescent. The guy came out. Said a few words in Russian and the old man lowered Martin's window. The guy reached in with both hands. Like Boris Karloff. Lexi nodded. Martin gave it over. The guy went back in. They drove home. Fee still chatting.

Ten years and ten Lincolns later, the old man drives up to the club, and sends a bouncer in for Fee and Vlady, but Vlady's in Riker's, so Martin goes

along. When they pull off the BQE, he remembers it all—sitting in back
with the box in his lap, wondering what it was worth while Fee talked and
Lexi smiled—and now they drove through the neighborhood again, Martin
near certain they were going to the same place. No one talking this time,
though. No one smiling. Just darkness in the car. No smuggled museum
pieces. His mind keeping wanting to wander. They pulled in the crescent
and Felix crawled into the back, and Martin shrugged to say, What the
fuck? What's wrong with the front? But Fee didn't look at him, kept his
eyes on the old guy. Same guy. So, Martin watched him as well. Coming
out from his building. The passenger window went down. The guy and
Lexi speaking normal enough. Though something was missing, Martin
realized. No head bobs or shrugs, like you saw with the Russians. Just
words now. Something cold—some kind of distance—there, this time, ten
years on. Which he figured was the fact that the old man was closing in fast
on a half-billion dollars' worth of Canadian real estate and this guy was still
living in Sunnyside. Then the guy backed up. So fucking fast that the brain
knew to look around for something wrong. *But what? But what?* And the
sound blew through the car and he was gone, the guy. Leveled out on the
sidewalk. Face all pulpy. Sucking and bubbling. Lexi tossed the gun onto
the passenger floor, and drove off so fast the Lincoln jumped from the pavement. The sound of the tires all faint and distant beneath the deafness
thumping inside the car. The upholstery on the ceiling above the
passenger-side window was in flames from the muzzle flash, and Felix
leaned up to pat it out. "Holy shit," Martin said. Fee and the old man
turned to look at him. He said, "My *ears,*" and widened his eyes. Hoped
there'd been no lying in his voice.

Now, he dreamed about it. Came to work and got the set-up crew on
their way for the afternoon, told them to buzz him if they needed him, then
went to go lie down in the office, to try to nap, and he'd see it again—the
guy's face like a split-open pomegranate—and *fuck,* he just wanted to sleep,
and if this *was* sleep, what fucking *good* was it?

Not that he judged Lexi. Fee said the guy had fucked something up, a
few days before, and instead of making amends, had panicked. Gone right
to the source of his fear to blot it out. Had summoned Lexi to Queens, was

going to pop him right there, in another second, himself. So that was fine. It was just the instantaneous permanence of the thing. That was what made it so incredible. One man's existence extinguished by another man's choice. Beaten to the draw. Robbed of life. Chiseled out of it, in fact, because he sure-as-shit wasn't getting it back.

Basic bloodshed like that had to have some equal and opposite good, though, no? he kept thinking now. Some logical, Isaac Newton balance, to even it out. But what? "God is love and loves all things"? There was that, the church said. And John Lennon—"Love is all you need." And "Love . . . love will keep us together," said Toni Tennille in the summer of seventy-four. So they all made the same kind of point. Warm, cozy feelings were the only thing holding back a world of shit. The only thing working for the Sixth Commandment was Aquinas, the Beatles, the Captain & Tennille. Was words.

The Russkies' mail kept coming to the club. Insurance fronts, tanker companies. He knew all the names, after a while. All the scams, the scamsters, their partners, their wicked half-brothers. He met, and helped to entertain, Victor Badguy, Ivan Ivanov, Azarchik "the Little Mongol," and dozens more like them. Fee pulled rubber bands around the piles of envelopes, brought them back over the bridge to Lexi. A hit in every one, Martin couldn't help but think now. Old bastards lying dead in Toronto, Chicago, Moscow, Odessa, Omaha. And in all the five boroughs. Leveled-out in every direction. Their faces gone. The guys in V-neck T-shirts and an old leather jacket that had once looked sharp. Pulled on one night for a trip out to the curb to meet a man you *had* to look sharp for. The only defense you had left against him.

He couldn't shake it. Or bear it sometimes. He'd stand in the window, look out at the water, bounce up and down on his toes suddenly, and roll his neck. He'd never even spoken to the guy, never heard him speak English, even. Or met eyes with him. Didn't exactly care about him. And, maybe if he had known him, wouldn't have liked him anyway. And, then, fuck him. Of course. Of course, then, fuck him. But it was too late to even know *that* now. Know if he'd like the guy better gone.

He brought the Russian girls home. Drove them there fast; figured he'd try to get a little clearheaded sleep after. The sex getting darker, getting more demanding. They put their hands on him as he walked through the club, now, the girls. Sometimes two and three in an evening. The hat-check, the hostess, the perky MC. They knew about each other and plied him. They vied.

Fee locked the door, said, "Your move, right?"

"I want to go out to dinner, Fee"—he sat down on the couch. Stood up again. "A nice place. You, me, and Penny. Someplace French."

"All right. When?"—Fee taking the board from the end table to set it down on the corner of the desk.

"Fucking . . . now. Call her up. I keep thinking we been doing this almost a year."

"Ooo, my anniversary's coming up. Got to plan something. Can you move that shit out of the way?"—motioned with his chin at a tax schedule, some other shit.

"You celebrate that one alone"—made no move to clear the desk. "To-night a little quail, some cold soup, a little *bistek* and hollandaise. Come on, call."

Fee held the game out toward him. "No chess?"

"Fuck chess. What good did it ever do me?"

"'Cause you're losing?"

"Who could tell? Like either one of us ever has the faintest fucking idea what we're doing."

Y ou can't have one drink?" Fee said. He was going to start to press—Martin could feel it. "It's a celebration."

Pen saying "He doesn't want one; leave it alone."

"One drink," Fee said.

"Not unless you want me to beat the waiter to death."

"I'd *pay* to see that," Fee said. "'Ve dun't *haf* steak knives, monsieur.'" Still creased about the guy's response. "What an asshole. If it was *filet* I'd understand."

Martin said, "Would you let it go? You want me to cut your meat for you?"

Fee threw his hands up, said no, resigned. Very French himself, there, for a second.

Martin looked away, looked over the dining room. They'd been there an hour. A short wait at the bar, then over to the table, which was round, too small, and had them all too close to each other. He kept switching back and forth from feeling he was seeing them together, or they were seeing him alone. He hadn't pictured anything like this when he'd suggested the plans. Plus, there was something about Penny. He couldn't get a read off her. This was the longest he'd been around her since the wedding, and she was distracted. Content, but entirely elsewhere.

"One drink," Fee said.

Martin looked at him.

"Come on, Q. A toast. You honestly can't keep control, or you're just making a point to yourself?"

She said, "Drop it, Felix, hunh?" She reached, put a hand on Martin's forearm. "Ignore him. You do what you have to. Do what you want." Her hand not leaving. He burned, not looking at it. He looked steady at her eyes. Said—

"I'll do that."

Her eyes pleasant, distant.

She took her hand back. Put it back in her lap.

His forearm hummed where it had been. It fucking *sang* there, under his shirtsleeve.

The asshole waiter brought the second bottle. Poured without a word.

Martin raised his glass of water, said, "To a big year. A couple of marriages. Couple of business ventures." Couple of fucking other things I want to talk to you about, Felix, he said to him in his mind.

They drank.

"Speaking of anniversaries," she said. "Where you taking me, Feel?"

"Someplace hot, don't worry." He winked at Martin. Said to him, "I have no clue."

"Get one, fast," she said.

"Puerto Rico?"

"So you can gamble all day? I think not."

Fee poured more for himself. Raised his glass to drink. Paused. "How about Q and I go?"

"Excuse me?"—she staring at Feel. The side of his face. He didn't look at her, though. Kept his eyes on Martin. Said—

"The guy's burned out." Smiled at him.

"You're serious," she said.

"Yeah."

"When?"

"Shit, I don't know. Tomorrow. This little dinner was his spontaneous idea. His treat—"

"My treat? You ordered two appetizers."

"That's right. Tomorrow we go to P.R. My treat. My spontaneous idea."

She looked at Martin. "He serious?"

He didn't answer her. The buzzing in his arm was fading. He'd been hoping it would spread all the way through him. He'd never felt anything like that before.

"We'll be back in, what—four days?" Fee said. "I'll make our anniversary plans from down there. In a week, we go somewhere else. I'll surprise you."

"You're just living the life," she said, "hunh?"

"That's right, sweetheart, 'Like sands through the hourglass. So are the days of our lives.' "

She uncrossed her arms, sipped her wine. Looked at Martin over her glass. Shook her head at him about this.

Felix said to her, "You mad?"

"Please."

She wasn't. Not at all.

Every couple took breaks.

A bad sign, in its way.

Or a good sign.

Bad sign, good sign, he thought—what's the difference.

Fee said, "We should get Champagne"—looked around. "Where is this guy? I'm going to kill him myself." He waved.

"You remember Tours?" Penny said.

Fee signaled, turned back around. Said, "Tours? . . . O my God, yeah."

"We had this waiter," she said. "Who brought the maitre d' to the table. To translate for him. He didn't like Felix's French. His message?—'Keep the tip.' He didn't want our money."

"We left without paying," Fee said.

"My new husband figured, Let's take it literally. Dine and dash."

"Only, no dash," Fee said. "We went strolling. Passed a couple of *gendarmes.* Said *bon soir,* kept going."

"Nice," Martin said. "Romantic."

Then silence.

Should have smiled saying it, he thought. It had come out snotty.

Fuck it.

Fuck *all* of this, he thought.

Fee said, "I'd had too much to drink. You do stupid shit, you know?"

"Yeah, I know it well."

Fee looked up, past him, said, "Champagne. Clicquot," looked down again. Looked at his hands.

Then the silence, again.

Martin looked at them. Was pretty sure, when they looked sideways at each other, that one of them was waiting for the other to say something, but they couldn't decide who would say it. "What the fuck?" he said. Didn't like them having something between them about him.

Fee said, "Ah . . ."—starting.

"At the reception," Penny said.

He thought, Jesus, what the fuck is *this* now?

She said, "I'm sorry."

He squinted. Didn't mean to. His arms got cold. Now his hands. "For?"

"Cursing at you."

He kept his eyes on her. Tried to figure her. Saw Fee watching him, furthest periphery.

"You remember?" she said.

"I remember."

They sat there. Waited. For what was next.

But he got it now, what she was doing—God damn her. He told himself, Lead it. " 'Cause I left," he said.

She nodded.

"After . . . your father . . ."

"After my father died."

"Right after," Fee said.

Martin looked at him. Fee widened his eyes, sorry he'd said it. Would have sunk in his chair if they were alone. Martin said, "I'm sorry, Pen," and looked back at her. Shrugged to say, That's it. "I was young, you know? That's all I can offer you, kiddo."

Her eyebrows went up. "I know that, squirt," she said. Her eyes on him alone. And focused now. Sarcastic, but on him alone—no more distraction in them. She smiled. He looked away.

Fee said, "She told me a couple of weeks ago. I said you should talk about it."

She said, "You were distant. I felt it. In the office. I was, too."

Your point's across, Pen, he said to her in his head. You covered herself.

She'd probably told Fee because she was nervous it'd get mentioned one day. "I want to drop this," he said. "It was my fault. It's why I wanted to come out. But it's finished. We're square."

"It was his idea to call you tonight, Pen."

"Well, I just didn't like how things were," she said. To neither of them. To herself, almost. Like *she'd* been the one was insulted. He thought, You're playing it to the fucking hilt, hunh?

She looked at him. Eyes half-elsewhere again. Said, "You're not mad, Q?"

Q.

I'll hurt you for that.

"No. You?"

"No."

"I'm just tired."

"All that screwing you do," Fee said.

The waiter came with a magnum. Set down the flutes. Opened and poured. Martin looked at her. She smiled at him. They raised their glasses and he smiled back. Said, "Confession's over, Pen; you can drink," and sipped his water. He eyed her over his glass. She'd dropped the smile.

H e watched them in the street, a second. Saying goodnight, the door to the cab still open, Fee leaning in and saying something more to her. Some married thing between them. Household thing. He looked away. Up the block. Walked. Till he couldn't hear them at all, and waited there. Heard the cab door close and Fee coming up as the cab drove away.

They continued alone, found a small place up the street that had a quiet bar. He knew Fee would ask him again if he'd drink and this time he would, he decided, because Fee'd had a point before with his stupid questions. To take a little anesthetic in control was the only real way to be the son of an addict. Plus, he'd stopped drinking in the first place, when he was younger, because he'd failed in so many ways, but this time, he'd set out to get what he wanted and got it. He could treat himself right, for that.

A shot and a beer, he ordered, tapped glasses with Fee—who said only, "There you go"—and took a drink of both of them and enjoyed how the whiskey seared, the beer tasting almost too heavy, too filling after the meal. Immediately, he realized, he'd relaxed. A nine-year tightness in his muscles was gone before he'd felt it passing. He smiled. He drank the beer in a long draught. Ordered a second. For nine years he'd wanted to drink down a glass of beer.

The bartender returned with the second one, and the change from their hundred. Walked down to his regulars.

"Two things bothering me, Fee."

Fee sipped his beer and nodded. "Shoot."

"Long Island."

"Uh-hunh."

"Penny, at the engagement, told me the business was yours."

"Yeah, well . . ."

"That's what you told her. It's not."

"Correct."

"You see any of it?"

"Not directly. It's not like I can sit down and count it. Whatever trickles down is mine. Ours."

"Whatever trickles. Right."

"We can't not do it, Q."

"It's a fucking pain in the ass."

"But that's all it is. We can't stop. He's the chief."

"I know."

"Everything we have is his."

"My stinky *dick,* it is."

Fee shrugged. Like, Think what you want.

But it was true enough. He just didn't like to think of it. The old man up in Canada half the time and they were roaming in his kingdom. Protected in it. Like a prince and his loyal good man. Hunting in the royal woods.

But Anastasia's was *theirs,* by now, he thought, wasn't it? By *rights*? They broke their asses seven days like citizens. Took their sideline risks themselves with Bunny's enterprising.

"When do things become yours, then, Felix? You ever wonder?"

"They are now."

"Do you understand what I'm saying to you?"

"Not really, no. What do you want, more money? *That* I understand."

"You know that's not it."

"Stock up on as much as you can in this life. We have an expression— The house is burning and the clock is ticking."

"It's not about money. It's humping for somebody else. Lugging some other guy's shit. You feel like someone's still getting over on you."

"He's my father."

Martin nodded. Looked at his hands folded on the bar. Put them around his glass. "I know that, man."

Maybe that was what it was, then.

"He thinks of you as family, Q. You know that."

"No"—he shook his head. "A, that's not true. Just because you do, doesn't mean he does. Be honest with yourself about that, man; he thinks of me as your old friend and business associate, not his family. B, I don't want him to. I never needed it, for one thing. And, it'll make it easy when I leave."

"Where are you going?"

"Nowhere. But I'm not waiting forever. I got to go on my own sometime."

"Where are you going?"

"I'm not going anywhere, Fee; I'm just saying. You finished with that? You want another?"

He ordered for them. Slid a twenty off the pile.

"What's the other thing?" Fee said.

"The mail."

"His?"

"Yeah."

"You're just all over him tonight."

"The club is booming, man. The IRS is going to be all over *us* by the—"

"Everything's clean."

"So to speak, I know. But still."

"They can't go through the mail."

"They can do what they want. Tell him to get a PO box."

"You tell him."

"I'm serious, man. It's in everyone's interest."

The bartender poured, brought the change from the twenty.

"And tell him it was your idea," Martin said. "He scares me."

"You wish."

They smiled. Clinked glasses. Fee said, "Nothing's going to change with the island."

"I know."

"I'm not even going to mention it."

"I know."

"He's making millions of dollars a quarter at a time. If something's not broken . . ."

Martin nodded. Shook his head. Drank for a bit. Because the scam did make sense; he had to admit that. Sell fuel wholesale to wholesalers, because no tax had to be paid till it retailed. Then, fake-sell it to a paper-ghost retailer saying he'd paid the excise tax, sell the fuel for real then, at more than wholesale, to real retailers. Keep the difference. Twenty-seven cents a gallon. Minus two cents to the Italians to keep off a war. Ten million a year it left.

Then he and Fee running all over Long Island to collect receipts from random, on-board gas mart owners, who were always rigging their pumps to jump a few pennies at a time beyond the posted price. What gas buyer's eye would spot the difference if the posted price already made him happy? That was their thinking. It was all a kind of sleight of hand.

But stealing *tax*? Off *gas*oline? Who would ever conceive of something like that in the first place? he'd always think. It was like robbing a practically hypothetical thing.

The mornings he actually slept, it made him not want to get out of bed, because he knew he thought so small himself.

"Fee, man, seriously," he said. "How the fuck did he think of it?"

Fee shrugged. "He's a genius. It goes back to Russia. Selling state gas to private car owners. They had to buy gas in secret because they weren't supposed to *have* cars. He paid off the guys who drove the trucks for the state, made his little increments of rubles. It was like a hundred fucking rubles to a *pen*ny back then."

"That's what I don't get. That patience." He flagged the bartender, finished his drinks as the guy came over.

"It's vision" Fee saying.

"It's an eternity."

"Didn't take him that long."

Martin smiled. Said no, he guessed not. They ordered another round. Fee wanting Sambuca and a coffee this time. "Like your mentors on Thompson Street," he said. "For the digestion."

"If you mean for the vomiting, yeah."

Fee said, "How's Bunny?—speaking of Cosa Nostra. He's still all right?"

"Yeah, why?"

"Just asking."

"He's still a guinea, I mean—we don't let him do what he wants."

Though they already were.

That fucking Bunny.

"We should look into him, maybe?"

"Be my guest," he said. "Pay one of the zips?"

"I was thinking, yeah," Fee said.

"Fine. Don't get caught. We're making lots of money with him."

They got their drinks. Sat with them, a while. Fee finished his coffee and pushed the saucer away. Something displeased-looking about the gesture.

"No good, the coffee?"

"No, I was just . . . No."

"What's the matter?"

"Something bothering me, too. I've been meaning to bring up."

"I can take it if you can."

"It's something else that *I* did. I wanted to apologize, I guess. I told you at the engagement . . . about Monya."

"Yeah. How is he?"

"Still paralyzed."

"That's good; I hate miracles."

"I told you my father squashed it with the Italian—"

" 'Quashed.' Your wife corrected me on that once." Shut *up,* a second, he told himself. What are you, already drunk?

"Well, there was one last thing before he quashed it. A situation, okay? You understand? He defended himself."

"Okay. Obviously. When was this?"

"I don't know, exactly. Just after Monya. Then my father drove down to the club in Staten Island, walked in with his hands showing, and settled it for good. *Po ponyatiyam*—gave them a piece of some other deal he was launching. That was it"—staring down at nothing, Fee. His fingers still pinched around his shot glass, not drinking it.

"So?" Martin said. "What's bothering you? That he did that?" We've already seen that, he thought.

Fee shook his head. "Of course not. No."

"Then what's your problem? Weren't you supposed to be apologizing to me here, for something? You going to tell me Bunny's connected to these Staten Island guys. We got to quash him?"

"I'll look into it, maybe; but no. Not that."

"Then, what? What's this look on your face, man? Talk."

"I lied to you. Things weren't safe when I asked you to come in."

"I don't give a shit."

"I know that, but I should have told you. I'm sorry."

"Fee, I *do not* care. I'm not a retard. Vlady was dead serious when I walked up to the house that night. I knew."

"Honesty's everything to me. But I . . . keep things to myself. And they make me *sick*. It's important to me that you under*stand* that, Q."

Martin looked away from him. Said, "Fee, fucking . . . be cool, man. I *do not* care. Get that crazy look off your face."

"You forgive me?"

"Of course, but make your face normal, man. Don't look so fucking . . . *earn*est. I'm going to piss myself, I look at you again."

"You'll give me a hug?"

"I won't, no."

"Come on. You'll tell me you love me? A little 'I love you'? Come on."

"I don't think so."

"I love *you*."

"I know that."

He did. Didn't know why people felt they had to say it for, though. Or why they had to hear it. Why do people need to *hear* that shit? he thought. You fucking *know* I love you; leave it alone.

"Q, come on. Give me a hug."

"Fee—"

Fee came off his stool. Grabbed him. Hugged him. Told him again.

"Yeah, me, too," Martin said. Thought, Say the words. Just speak them. See what happens.

But didn't.

They ordered another round. Fee said, "I like this song," and held still to listen. Martin didn't know it. Something slow. Fee said, "No, it's not the one I thought. I don't even know what this is. You know what this is?"

He shook his head.

Fee said, "Hey, you like that album? You never mentioned."

"My father's? Yeah. Sure."

"You play it?"

He had. Once. Forced himself through it, beginning to end. "Yeah," he said.

"What's that like?"

"It's cool. Nothing really."

"Yeah? Good."

"Yup," he said. "Listen, Fee, you remember in high school, your mother would go to Switzerland for her spa weeks, your father would get all lonely? He'd mope around?"

Fee nodded.

"Don't you think that's funny? His being such a badass, but he couldn't function with your mother gone?"

Fee shrugged, nodded. Didn't really respond, though.

Stupid thing to bring up, Martin thought. Teenage thing. You're drunk. Don't say anything so stupid.

Fee took a breath, loud. Sighed letting it out. Looked at him suddenly. Something had come to him to bring up. "You know, you owe me an apology, too, Suzy Q."

"For what?"

"Think about it."

"I don't want to think; I'm drunk."

"Yeah, me, too."

"So?"

"You never told me. About your father."

"I don't tell anyone."

"Not true."

"Penny."

"That's right."

"I was seventeen when I told her. Trying to get in her pants."

"Well, tell me."

"I'm not trying to get in yours."

"*Tell* me, man. You never tell me anything. *Told* me anything. Still you fucking don't."

"I try not to think about it. Back the fuck off."

"Because it's painful? If it is, life's painful. That's all I have to say. 'Life is suffering.'"

"I'm getting that feeling right now."

"Talk, motherfucker. Life's too short."

"No shit, motherfucker. In two years I'm going to be older than my old man *ever* was. You don't have to tell me shit like that."

"My brother died at six*teen*. Don't forget that. And I told you about that in *high* school. That wasn't easy."

"You talk too *much* about personal shit. Plus . . . and *plus,* you didn't even *like* your brother."

"I *loved* him—fuck you."

"You said he was an idiot."

"He *was* an idiot. *To*tally separate thing."

"You had no respect for him."

"I needed him; he was my brother."

That why you latched on to me? he thought.

Had always suspected that was the reason.

And, you, Q? What's *your* excuse?

"Did *you?*"

"Did I what, Fee?—for Christ's fucking sake."

"Respect your father?"

"I hardly knew him."

"How old was he?"

"Twenty-nine."

"Had you when he was twenty?"

"And Frito at twenty-five. Married young."

Like Frito did.

And like *I* wanted to.

"You'd be like brothers now," Fee said.

He nodded. Had thought that himself, more than a few times.

"Why'd he do it?" Fee said. "Do you know?"

"He was a junkie."

"He was an artist."

"Same thing."

"How?"

"I don't know, man. It doesn't matter. He did it with a razor blade. In our bathroom. Then we moved. Life changed. I'm here."

"Your brother's an artist. We saw him play that time." Hadn't listened about the razor, Fee. Too drunk now. Good. "That recital. He was like ten, Frito. He was incredible. He's not a junkie. You said it was the same thing."

"You're making my head hurt, Feel. For real. Just shut up, a while."

He went to say more, Fee. Stopped himself. Looked straight ahead. "I'm not an artist," said then. "When I was ten I could play anything on the piano, and my mother wanted me to be a genius, but . . . there was no art. I saw your brother that time, and I knew. I was right to quit. She thought I was going to be the next Van Cliburn. Because I have his hair. She thought the genius was in the hair. I'm sorry, Q. About your father."

"No sweat."

"He had his reasons, right? He loved you a lot, I'll bet."

"Of course."

"Suicide's strange, you know? In all my philosophy classes, we used to talk about what people were capable of. The good in them? I would always say, 'What about suicides? Because if it's love thy neighbor as thyself, what if you don't love thyself?' And someone would always go, 'They're a special case. Mental illness plays a part.' And I'd go, 'You just said deep down, even murderers know they're wrong. It should be the same thing. What about suicides?' "

"I got to get you home."

"Your father almost got me thrown out of philosophy class."

"My apologies."

"Penny," Fee said. Not hearing anything now, apparently. "She told me about your father and started crying. *Tried* to tell me. We were in college. She couldn't even talk. She made *me* cry."

"Well, now you know."

"You think he loved her?"

"Who?"

"Your mother, who else? Mrs. Quinn. The fucking greatest woman."

"He loved heroin."

He looked up, Fee. Was mad. "That's bullshit. He loved her. That's the part of the story Penny told me. How she used to sit there in that club. What was it called? Tell me, man!"

"Sugar's. Keep your voice down."

"Sugar's. She used to sit there and watch him play, and he saw her one night. Saw the music in her face. Right?"

"That's how my mother tells it, yeah."

"She drew the music out of him. Fucking . . . pulled it."

"So, you know the story. Drop it."

"That's *all* I know. She fucking breaks down and cries right there. That's what she wanted." He closed his eyes tight, Fee. "Music in her face or whatever. Fucking beauty contest I meet her at."

Martin shoved him in the shoulder, one-handed. "Don't be a fucking asshole, stupid." Shoved him hard, again. Fee putting a foot down off the stool, to get steady. "What's this God-damned weak bullshit, hunh? Felix? This sorry-ass shit? You want to fucking kill yourself, see if she talks about you nice when you're dead? You got everything to give her that her father punked-out on. I'm going to kick your ass tomorrow, you sorry mother-fucker. Straighten up. You asshole."

Felix recoiled, slow. Smiled. "Ooo, you're mad."

"I'm not mad."

"You're mad. Real mad."

"Don't fuck with me, Felix."

"Give me a kiss."

"Don't. Quit that shit, now."

"Bartender. I just pissed off my best friend. Give him a drink. Something expensive."

"Chivas?" the bartender said.

Felix stood up. "Holy shit," he said. He laughed. "Holy shit." Reached and touched Martin's cheek. Then slapped it, soft. Looked like Lexi for a second. Spit and image. The bartender poured, and Fee stayed standing. Told Martin to shoot it with him. Put his arm around him as they did and banged his glass down hard, and went off to the bathroom.

Martin sat. Felt his wits slip around, come back. He looked behind him toward the bathroom, looked at the bar. He pulled a quarter from under the stack of bills and walked toward the telephone. Then was dialing. Concentrating on pushing the buttons. Leaned his head against the phone and saw her coming. Throwing off the covers. A white cotton nightgown. Bare feet. Rubbing her eyes. Walking across the carpet to the desk and the ringing, old-fashioned, ivory-colored phone. Three rings. Four. Picking up. "Hello?" He loved her voice. He closed his eyes. "Hello?" Could hear her say just that to him, again and again, if they were alone. "Fee?" He opened them. "Felix?"

"No."

"Martin?"

Yeah.

That's right, Penelope.

"Martin?"

"No."

He hung up.

Fee was passed-out standing at the urinal. Was leaning on the wall with one hand, his dick still pinched in the other. Martin flicked it with a finger. Told him, "Zip up."

Put his arm around him in the street, hailed a cab. Put him in it, and got in behind him. Fee said, "My dick hurts," and looked down at himself, looked over at him. Martin shrugged, said he had no answer for him.

Brought him upstairs. Dug the keys from his pants in the elevator, figured them—car, club, country house. Lurched down the hall with him. Got the one for the apartment, second try.

Pen was in the doorway to the bed/living room. Standing. End of the hall. Lights on behind her. He carried him past her and she stepped aside, Fee walking in his sleep. He dropped him in the bed and threw his legs on. Pulled off his shoes. Looked at him, a moment. Had slept beside him for three years here. His heavy smell. Thin legs and too-thick arms. Used to throw them off. Wouldn't ever be doing that again.

Slept with her here, too, once, he thought. Turned, and she was still in the doorway. Facing in this way now, watching him. Arms crossed. His monitor. Not looking like she was in the mood for reminiscing. *"Remember that time we screwed here, Pen?"*

He walked over. Put a hand on her shoulder. Said, "He's all right. Bad hollandaise," and patted her, went past. Remembered the keys and turned, handed them over. Looked at her, a second. She hadn't moved. Just standing there, hand out, keys in her palm. Her arm propped on the one wrapped across her ribs. Like there was something *else* he'd forgotten. But he didn't know what. He shrugged at her. But got no help.

"Penny," he said,

> "There once was a young man named Bloom . . .
> who slept in a lesbian's room.
> They argued all night
> as to who had the right
> to do what
> and *with* what
> to whom.

Goodnight." Went to go past her.

"Did you call me?"

He smiled. "What? When?" Her hand was still out. He should take it, he thought. Give it a good shake. "Must have been Fee. He fell asleep taking a piss. He's crocked."

"Did you?"

"When?"

But she said nothing—her face just set. The white nightgown had folds, and shadows. Her hair so beautiful down. He breathed deep through his nose. Waited. Would hold out longer than her, if she—

"Goodnight, Martin."

"Did you call *me*?"

Her eyes got sharper. Narrowed down. He looked at the floor. Her feet. The boney tops of them. And the veins that surfaced and crossed each other and disappeared again. Her toes. "Fucking . . . ever?" he said. Looked at her. Color rising from her chest up through her neck, right as he watched. It swarmed her face. Her eyes glaring now. Nostrils wide.

"Goodnight, Martin."

"Goodnight, *Pen*."

"Lock it before you leave. On the knob."

"I know."

She shut the light. The hallway disappeared. He heard her crossing to the bed. Then stopping. He waited. Listened to her listening to him across the darkness. He walked to the door and opened it, closed it again. A minute. Two. He waited. They both listening. He breathed in the dark. She wouldn't lie down. Then was coming at him, drifting in white down the hall.

A nd everything was cool. He'd always wanted to go to the place in P.R. but it had been off-limits for years. Since the gas-tax scam summit there with the Italians, when they got their two cents out of the deal. Lexi'd laundered the place after that. Rented it out to legitimates—stiffs—for a decade, to let it wash clean, but, now, it was safe. A small beach-front villa down Playa Luquillo. They gambled in Old San Juan to avoid the crowds. He lost two grand. Stayed sober. Got a bit of a tan and a bit of a burn.

Had no trouble at all around Felix. Because it wasn't so much that he'd been with his wife; he'd been with Penelle. He could still look in Felix's face, watch him as he talked, hear what he said. Fee and she were distinct in his mind. Plus, she'd come to *him*. Had *made* her choice. Couldn't deny anymore what was meant to be.

Back at work, he told the girls he needed time to himself, and took it. Found when Pen and Fee were in the same room, though, he had more trouble with the looking at him, taught himself to mind him intently instead. To not look away.

And he and Penny? Solid. Strange, but solid. At first having nothing to say. Had been away from each other so long, it didn't feel like there was any rush. In the hallway that night all she'd said in his ear was yes, so he walked around everywhere now still hearing that. Thought how it meant yes, she'd been waiting. Yes, she was his. Yes, she loved him forever. And it was enough.

With Anastasia's, the old man's scheme letters stopped showing up. His apprentices, subcontractors, still came around, but all the fucking mail was gone. That, too, was enough. Fee did the Long Island runs himself, and never mentioned it. The summer went by. Half the college-age kids disappeared, and Bunny's Ex and coke sales dropped hard. "Bunny," he told him, "you got to look at it demographically." Bunny told him to shove his demographicals up his Irish ass. Said they had to figure something else— that he'd get back to him—and he enjoyed the time that Bunny stayed gone figuring. Enjoyed the quiet and the slow-down. Shrugged about the loss in his own total profits. Told himself he had plenty for now. Don't be so greedy. Though the sting wouldn't leave every time he got paid. Paid himself.

Penny's mother put a down payment on a new place in Bronxville. Took a short mortgage, and Penny began spending her time up there. He took the early trains up to see her. Moved through the rush-hour crowds in Grand Central, rode near-empty cars, stood up the whole trip. Too young to sit down, he felt.

They'd settled nothing. Made no attempts. But it was fine. He met her in the parking lots of hardware stores, houseware and home decorating chains. Accompanied her. She ordered her mother new dishes, curtains, patio furniture. He didn't ask about St. Kitts—the anniversary trip with Felix. Knew she'd picked up he was keeping off women, though. She's just married, he told himself. Things like that took time. What it really meant anymore, though, marriage, he had no idea.

Breakfast in diners, they ate. Some coffee, maybe a corn muffin to share, and she'd keep her eye on the door, a minute, take his hand and kiss it, set it down again. He told her he was happy.

One morning she brought him back to a park that he'd always remembered. It had a dark, man-made little lake. She told him all she'd been able to figure, up to then. How Fee was still Fee but things were strained badly sometimes. Had been, since the beginning, weren't getting any better. "You'll always be in the way, Martin. You always have been. Always are. Somewhere close in my mind. The front of my thoughts. I can't ignore that, you know?"

He thought, You never should have.

"I thought about you every day," she said. "No exceptions. That's crazy, don't you think? Don't you think that's strange?"

"I guess."

"And dream about you. *Some*times about us—we're together. But other times, you just show up. Belong there for some reason, but the dream's about something else."

"You going to divorce him?"

"I guess I might have to."

"Might?"

"I'm Catholic, Martin."

"You're Catholic. So's Madonna, for Christ's sake."

"Well, she says she can't watch that *State of Grace* movie because of the sex scene with Sean Penn and Robin Wright. She's like, 'Hey, that's my husband.' "

"So?"

"So nothing."

"So I don't know what that means."

"It means that if I do, it carries responsibilities."

"You don't want him seeing other women, after?"

"Forget the whole Madonna thing. A bad example."

"Then make your case, counselor."

"I don't have a case."

"Just a crime."

"I guess."

They sat a while. He knew what she meant, though. What her problem was. Ignoring a sacrament, the church would call it. She'd still be married, in God's eyes.

Whose eyes? he thought. He couldn't believe his mind would still use the phrase.

A bunch of ducks coasted by, disappeared further on, in the reeds. "You going back to work ever?" he said.

"I guess so. I can't stick around Anastasia's anymore."

"We could put you on as a waitress."

"Then you could screw me all you wanted."

"Hey, I been good," he said. "I've been fucking *chaste.*"

"You're lucky you don't have a disease."

"I've been careful."

"Fabulous."

He kept what he was thinking to himself. *How many times a week you fucking do it?*

You do it with a camera? Fee used to like that.

She lit a cigarette. "I'm not jealous," she said.

"Don't be."

"Well, I am."

"Don't be. I'll fire them all. When'd you start smoking again?"

"Don't know. I was off, six months. That's enough."

"Proved you could do it?"

"Something like that."

"Were you trying to get pregnant?"

"Yup." She exhaled. Didn't look at him. Not at all surprised he'd known, apparently.

"What happened?"

She shrugged.

"You give up?"

No response.

"He shooting duddies?" he said.

She smiled.

"You tell him to get checked? Get him a little cup and a skin mag?"

"No."

"You get yourself checked?"

"Yup. I'm a fertile turtle. Always have been."

"Good."

She looked at him. Pissed-off, suddenly. "Oh, yeah?"

"Oh, yeah."

"I'm glad you're happy."

"Good. Because I want you to divorce him."

"I'll take it under consideration."

"Do that."

"I will." Looked away again. Dragged, exhaled.

"They say there's a psychological factor in trying to get pregnant," he said.

But she didn't answer it—she let it go—"How long you going to wait?" she said.

"For you? A few more days."

"Then it's back to the coat-check twat?"

"Jesus Christ, what kind of *word* is that from you?"

"The appropriate one."

"Well, maybe I will."

"Maybe?"

"No."

"Okay." She nodded.

"I'll wait," he said.

They sat. She finished the cigarette.

"What about you?" he said.

"Don't."

"What about it?"

"Don't ask me that, Martin."

"Oh, that's right—you're a Catholic; it's your duty."

"Something like that. It's not so great anyway."

"Fuck you," he said.

"Excuse me?"

"Nothing."

"Fuck *me*?"

"Forget it."

She drove him to the station. Waited on the platform with him. Said, "Do you ever feel badly for him now?" Had forgotten their silence. Fee still on her mind. Being told to fuck off the kind of thing she didn't dwell on.

"Not really."

"Is it revenge, all this?"

"Come on."

"Valid question."

"I just don't think about it, Pen. You know better than that."

She nodded. "I guess so, yeah."

"He's an adult." He thought, Never had any respect for women anyway.

"He's a sweetheart. You know that. He's not a bad guy at all."

"As far as things go. No violent tendencies. No addictions."

"I grew up with freaking *wise*guys, Martin. *Gui*dos."

"He's still a criminal."

"And you?"

"No argument there."

"But . . . Martin . . ."

"What?"

She breathed out, loud. Didn't want to say it.

"What? You love him? I know. Me, too. What's the difference?"

"It's not just about divorce. It's about marriage. You make a decision, maybe you just—"

"Well, don't. Don't *stick* to it. This isn't your fate, for Christ's sake."

"It was my decision."

"Free will, Penny-lope. You jump in front of this train, it's your choice. Someone pushes you in front of it? Still. You shouldn't have been standing so close. Your fault. No difference."

She nodded. Was looking down the track. Not watching it come, though, the train.

People moved toward the platform's edge.

"I'm going to wait, Penny. Penny, I'm *sev*enteen with you, in my head. You know what I mean?"

"We never talked about you"—not looking at him still. "All the time you were gone. Only once."

You told him about my father, he thought. "What'd you say?"

"That we were together because of you. Because we both missed you. We shared that between us, always. Something in common. Saw you in each other, I guess."

"But that passed, though."

"In a way, I suppose. It had to. We've been together five years. Things change between people."

"You can always stay friends."

"It's not funny."

"I said I'll wait. I meant it"—one foot in the train. The conductor looking at them from the next door, waiting. Saw they were serious.

She said, "You better get on."

"Talk to a priest, Penny. If you have to. I'm serious."

She nodded.

"A Jesuit," he said. "They don't believe in anything."

He stepped in, let the doors close. The train pulled away, seemed to leave her there. She not looking up.

He went and sat down. Felt sick. About it all. The whole fucking conversation. This life they were living.

In Grand Central, he turned his pager on, and it went off in his hand. Surprised him. He nearly dropped it. He didn't know the number, walked to a phone, called it.

"Martin?"

"Mom? Where are you?"

"I've been calling since last night. A hundred times—"

"I turned my pager off. Where are you? What's wrong?" She sounded shaken. Old. It was freaking him out.

"O God, Martin, Frito's been shot."

"What?" he said. "He's alive?"

"Yes."

"He was mugged? Who did it?"

"He was in your apartment. Through the window, they shot him. Right in. From the promenade."

He got the name of the hospital, hung up. Before she could start asking him things. Like why.

There was a cop in the hall—a detective. Standing across from the room. Waiting for me, Martin figured, and walked right up to him. Introduced himself. Asked how Frito was. Trying to seem innocent. Shocked, even. More blown away than anything else. Asked where the doctor was. Realized he didn't want to go in yet.

The guy said, "Your brother's fine. The bullet went in and out, through the shoulder. Damage to the bones. He didn't lose much blood. It was a strong weapon. A hunting rifle. We think it was, anyway."

"A what? Jesus Christ. Do you know who did it?"

"Not at the moment. He's sedated. He was alone in the apartment."

"Is my mother in there?"

"She was sleeping, last I saw. It happened early in the morning. Three-thirty, around."

He'd been in Brooklyn at three-thirty—in the club, still. Entertaining some Hollywood people who were going to film in the place. He'd been trying to charm his way into a walk-on part. Turned his pager off around one, when they all started partying. Had gone straight to Bronxville in the morning to see Penelope. Seven o'clock, around.

How long did Frito lie there? he thought. "What time did you find him?"

"He phoned, himself. Officers responded to a shots-fired call, though. Got there before the ambulance."

"Jesus," he said . . . "Jesus." They stood there. "Well, thank God, right?"

"Yup. Do you hunt, Mr. Quinn?"

"Hunt? No. I'm a restaurant manager."

"You own a gun?"

"No." It was in his belt. Around his back. He'd had to park on the street, wouldn't leave it in the glove box.

"You know anyone who does?"

"No. At least, I don't think so. No one ever said anything. Some people own them, though, I guess. For protection, whatever."

Fee owned a hunting rifle. A thirty-aught-six. Unregistered, like the rest of them. Kept it upstate, in the shed. Left Anastasia's around two. Dog-tired. Said to get him a part in the flick, if he could, but had to get some sleep. "Can I see him? My brother?"

"You're going to be around, I assume."

"Not going *any*where, man. Officer."

"You work in Brooklyn?"

"Uh-hunh"—kept his face flat. Innocent. Headed for the door to the room. Understood that *Okay,* they'd begun to investigate him. He was clean here, though.

The detective moved toward the door with him, leaned past him, opened it, quiet. Said, "The brother's here," and let him pass.

Another cop in the room. Behind Juliet. Where she stood. At the side of the bed. She didn't look up. Frito was out. Tubes and wads of bandaging. His shoulder a half-foot high with them. Their mother asleep in a chair, beyond.

He nodded to the other detective, went to the bedside. His mother didn't stir. He studied Frito, a few minutes, but wanted to get back out into the hall. Had to talk to Juliet. Whispered to her over the bed. Asked her to come outside.

"There's a cafeteria downstairs?" he said to the cop in the hall.

"Mezzanine."

Thanked him, and walked toward the elevators, Juliet following, right beside him. Looking down, ahead of her feet. Wouldn't look at him. Hadn't once, yet. He pressed the button, and faced her. Had to find out what they'd asked her. Knew it was wrong, but. He was too tired to try to be clever, polite. "You okay?" he said. Stepped closer to her. "Tired, I'll bet." She looked up at him. Slapped him. Kept her eyes steady on him. "Okay," he said. She slapped him again. To show the first one wasn't a gesture, he guessed. "Enough," he said. The elevator opened. Empty car. He stepped in. She stayed out, looked in at him, her arms crossed, now. "Come on."

"Are you a *gang*ster, Martin?"

"Keep your voice down, all right?"

"It is down."

It was.

"Just get in," he said.

"I'm not afraid of you."

He put his hand over the door when it went to close. "Don't be stupid," he said—"this is you and me, not a fucking movie. Can you get in, please? Juliet?"

They rode to the main floor, went outside. There were benches up the block. Patients visiting with their families on them. He went to a free one, stopped, asked her if she wanted to sit. She stayed standing. Crossed her arms again. Against the cold this time. Cold out, though the sun was bright. He untucked his shirt so it covered the gun, and took off his jacket. Put it around her. She didn't resist. He felt the cold immediately. And wanted to sleep. But he had to settle this, a bit, before he did. "What happened?" he said. "The cop said Frito was all right."

"He's alive."

Be patient, he reminded himself. "Is he okay?"

"He's fine. He's been shot."

"Were you there?"

"No."

"Talk to me, Juliet, would you? Please?"

"I want to know why."

"I'll find out. I don't know now, though, all right? Where were you?"

"Then you'll take *care* of it, I imagine." Her accent so interesting to him, right now. Normally it made her sound like an actress, today it just made her sound foreign.

"Where were you? What was he doing in my apartment?"

"We'd had an argument. He went out for a walk. Then didn't come home. Then they called me."

"Who?"

She looked at him. Disgusted. "The po*lice.*"

"And said what?"

"He'd been shot. They'd taken him to hospital."

"What else?"

"Are you even sorry?"

"Am I sorry?" he said. "You want to start trading slaps, I'll let one go right now, for that." Her eyes changed. Got less intense. So she was there, then—with him, now. "Are you hungry?" he said. "You want to go some-place and eat?"

"I'm fine." She sat down. He sat beside her. "Do you know who did this?" she said.

"No. I don't. What did they ask you, Juliet?"

He watched her. Said to her in his thoughts, *Think*—don't miss a detail—and she went through what she could, remembering carefully. Speaking fast, efficiently. None of it meaning anything, though. The investigation all preliminary, it sounded like.

"What did they ask about me?" he said finally. "If anything."

"Where you were. What you did for a living."

"What'd you say?"

She turned her eyes on him.

"What did you tell them, Juliet?"

"That I didn't know."

"You *do* know. I manage a nightclub and restaurant, in Brooklyn."

"Oh, that's right."

"Don't do anything stupid, hunh? Whoever shot him thought it was me. That's all."

Unless it was Fee, he knew. Had maybe woken up that night they were together in the hallway. And so there'd be more of this coming, till Fee was satisfied.

"Frito's out of danger now, Juliet. So are you."

"He might not *play* again. Piano. He's not out of *danger*."

He looked away, nodded. "He'll play," he said. Knew this wasn't the time to tell her that that couldn't be his first concern. "How's my mother? And you? How are you?"

"We're fine. Thank you."

"You cold?"

"No."

"I'm freezing."

She didn't say anything. Looked at the pavement. Moved something with her foot.

"I manage a nightclub—"

"In Brighton Beach, Brooklyn. New York."

"That's 11235."

"D'accord."

Her language. Some kind of okay.

Won't agree in English, he thought, but it was enough. *D'accord.* "I'm sorry," he said. "Juliet, he's fine, and we're going to figure this out."

"Are you going to work with the police?"

"Yes."

Maybe. Use what they knew, if he could. They'd be all over him anyway.

He tapped her leg so she'd look at him. She did. He smiled. She looked past him at something. He turned, and saw the detective coming toward them in no hurry. He nodded at the guy politely, looked back at her. "What'd you fight about with Frito, last night?"

"He wants to leave Columbia. Become a painter. Move to Williamsburg and live in a basement, because *all* art is coming out of the Brooklyn waterfront, he says. I told him he should take art classes at night and not sacrifice his opportunities, but he wants to be free of all institutional thinking."

He shrugged. "He thinks he can do anything," he said. "And he *can*"— got afraid suddenly he sounded jealous. She nodded. Didn't hear it that way, he guessed. She looked up at the detective. He looked up, too. Said to the guy, "Got some air, instead."

The guy nodded.

Martin asked her if she wanted to go in. Watched her stand and take off his jacket. He stood, rolled his shoulders to keep his shirt off the Glock. Accepted his jacket back and put it on. Told her he'd be up in a minute.

She walked away. He said, "Newlyweds," and looked at the guy. Shrugged. "I told him he was too young, but she's great. They're in love. What can I say? I hope it lasts."

He nodded again, the guy. Said, "Your brother has keys to your apartment?"

"Yeah. I have a VCR. A view of the water. Their place is empty. They have bookshelves and a bed on the floor."

"You going to cooperate with us?"

"Of course."

"Are you Russian Mafia?"

"No, I just manage the place. I'm Irish, for Christ's sake."

"Uh-hunh. You have a record?"

"A juvenile arrest. For assault, since you're going to ask. I beat a kid up with his radio. He wouldn't turn it down. It was a long time ago. An honor thing"—the detective nodding the whole time. Had stopped looking at him. *What?* Martin wanted to say. *Speak.*

"It comes back to *you,*" the guy said. "At this point in time, I'll tell you that. Whatever the reason, my money says it comes back to you."

"That's fine"—he shrugged again. "But come out to the club, then. Ask around. Shit, lock up some illegals."

The guy looked at his watch. Said nothing, though.

"Can I go see my brother?"

"Of course."

And he left the guy there, walked back down the block. Thought, *"Come out to the club."* Fucking stupid, he knew, but it had to be done.

H e sat with his mother and Juliet for a while, then said he had to go home. Had to change his clothes, take a shower. He called Fee from the street and woke him, told him about it. More worried at the moment about the old man's reaction to his inviting out the cop to the club than if Fee even did it or not. And, as for that, with the one phone call, he didn't know anymore. Fee starting to cry, he apparently got so mad. Held it back, but Martin heard his voice quaver.

They agreed on spreading the word that anyone with a warrant out had to keep clear of the club. Fee would make sure the office was clean. Martin would talk to Bunny.

He drove downtown, pulled up to another phone, called Bunny's pager, hit the asterisk. Bunny called him a few minutes later, from the phone on LaGuardia. Martin told him to keep the zips in Manhattan. Bunny said, "Someone take a shot at you? Shooting down where you live."

"They missed."

"You're serious? It was your place? News said someone got taken to the hospital."

"Yeah. My brother. He's all right, though."

"*Maron.* Cheeto? Dorito?"

"Frito," Martin said.

"He's all right?"

"He's fine."

"Good."

"Yeah."

"Where'd he get that fucking name from, anyway?"

"You hear anything about it, Bunny? Know anything?"

"Nah. But I will. Can't have people taking shots at family. It's *infamita.* Jesus. I'll bet it was Russians."

Hard to tell with Bunny.

Martin said he'd be talking to him.

At his mother's, he made himself a sandwich, showered, went out on the fire escape to think. But the feeling that he kept getting was that he was fine. If someone was after you, he thought, you'd feel it. The electricity around you would be different. People on the street would see you were marked. He knew there was nothing different to see about him.

He went down to his place around six. A couple of uniformed cops in the living room. Glass everywhere. Blood here, there. Yellow plastic cordoning. The detective he'd talked to was out on the promenade. Saw him and came back to the empty window. Twilight starting up, behind him. The apartment getting dark. Martin walked to the window. "Anything?"

"Canvassing joggers," he said, and Martin realized he'd forgotten the guy's name. But had a feeling he wouldn't be needing to remember it. This all already seemed to be done, somehow. What would a fucking jogger know?

"We'll find out something tonight, three or four. Their schedules are usually pretty regular," the guy said.

"And they keep their eyes open, I'll bet, exercising that late."

"They should."

Martin nodded.

"Pulled the bullet from the wall in the bedroom. Went right through that one, there."

He turned. A smear it looked like, from where he stood. Just a blotch over the couch, the way the light was changing.

"Thirty-aught-six," the guy said.

Martin breathed in. Carefully. Turned back. "That a hunting rifle?"

"You were in the military; you know guns."

"I know M-16s. Did know them. You forget that stuff."

The guy called past him—"Turn a light on in there." One of the cops crunched glass. Then—light—a moment later. The detective's outline disappearing, a second, then coming back. "You manage that club? Anastasia's?"

"Yeah."

"Pays for this place?"

"Bitch of a job."

"How much you make? The rent here's twenty-one hundred."

"I'm not on salary. Kind of a pilot deal. See how the place does."

"You got records?"

Martin laughed. "You with the IRS, too?"

"Just curious."

"We do pretty well."

"I'll bet."

"You going to come out?"

"We will."

Martin put his hands in his pockets, took a step toward the window. Looked around the frame. "Can I call a glazier?"

"Tomorrow, probably."

"Someone going to be here? My alarm's no use with this"—he waved his chin around, at the damage. "And I got to go back to the hospital."

"Someone'll be here."

"Well . . ." he said. "There's nothing in the fridge I can offer you."

"We'll survive."

"I'm sure. I got to change my clothes, if you'll excuse me." He found the guy's eyes in the darkness and met them. Waited.

"Go ahead."

"Then I'll see you in Brooklyn. Here's a jogger coming."

They came out two days later, the one from the apartment and his partner from the hospital room. The place was a mess with how the Hollywood people had rearranged it. Tables stacked up out of the way. Cables taped down over the floors, running over the walls. Sound and lighting equipment on scaffolding. Assistants' assistants hurrying back and forth, and the director walking around with a crew, making suggestions, hearing them, stopping every once in a while, and staring at the rooms from a new perspective. Martin sat at a table, back out of the way, and knew the investigation was history in another week. He'd take over from there.

The detectives didn't sit. The one from the promenade wanted to know what the hell all this was—why Martin hadn't told him they'd be filming a movie. Martin said he'd completely forgotten. Called out to the director and asked when they'd be done. Knew the city wouldn't spend ten more man-hours on a bodiless shooting. They'd open a file, file it. Things would get back to normal. Maybe the detective whose name he'd known would come by on his night off, sometime, if cops were anything like they were in the movies. But he doubted it. He clocked the director looking the two of them over. Said, "You figuring a *part* for them? What about *me*?"

"We talked about that"—the little talking beard. With the constant headset. Eyes on the detectives.

"What's the movie about?" the cop said.

"Russian gangsters," the little beard said. *"Doctor Zhivago* meets *Mean Streets."*

"Cutting edge."

"Nobody knows about them."

"We do."

"Yeah, I'll bet. But not much, right? You ever act?"

"I'm acting right now."

"You should think about it. I get some of my best work from authentics."

"I'll think about it. But I got to keep talking to Mr. Quinn here, at the moment."

The director moved off. Thinking so hard he bumped into the bar. The entourage drifting with him. A couple of them looking back, studying the scene.

"Where's Felix Pasko? He here?"

"Felix? No. He's never here. I run things."

"He's the owner, though."

"Right."

"He's twenty-seven also?"

"Yeah. His father's loaded. Owns real estate in Canada."

"Same name? Pasko?"

"Yup. Alexander. He's been here twenty years. Works like a maniac. I never see him."

Fee had assured him way back, *"Anyone ever asks, just tell them about the hotels. He's spotless."*

"You have any arguments since you been open? With staff? Or customers?"

"Gangsters?"

"Specifically, yeah."

"No. This is a haven for them—I'm not going to lie and tell you they don't hang out. But they treat this place like their home."

"You know their names?"

Martin smiled. To tell the guy, You're kidding, right?

The guy looked at him straight, not giving in. Said, "I'm just going to tell you this—the rate of violent crime in South Brooklyn has risen a thousand percent, this last year."

"Okay."

"If bad things start happening out of this place, it's safe to say that they'll get worse before they get better. Also, I don't know if we can clear up what happened to your brother, but I'm extending our help if there's anyone you know is after you. Maybe we can protect you. That's it."

Martin nodded. "Fair enough. You want something to eat?"

"Thank you, no. So the club's closed down? No one's going to be showing up?"

"Not till these jokers are done. And have cleaned up everything. Goddamned tape better come off my walls"—he raised his voice, looked around him. Twisted comfortably in his chair, took his place in, smiling.

And never talked to them again.

They called Juliet, a few times. For one detail or another, said they would keep her abreast, then stopped calling her, too. Had finally questioned Frito in the hospital room, but he didn't know a thing.

Every day, Martin sat with him. Asked him about it when the time seemed right. When Frito was smiling again. Chatting, reading, listening to his Walkman. Had been walking through the rooms with the lights off, he said. To better see the water. Twisting a Rubik's Cube, listening to music, thinking hard about his fight with Juliet, and he saw the window start to spider as the bullet slammed him. He may have heard the shot, but he couldn't be sure. It may have been why he looked up at that second. He hit the couch and bounced off it, hit the floor. Heard the glass showering down, then tinkling. Then the last big shards falling down all at once, a moment later, as he reached back above him for the phone on the end table. Saw no one outside. Heard nothing—no footsteps, no whine of a bicycle chain—couldn't have with the music on. He just heard the glass.

Martin asked Juliet to go out for some food. He pulled the chair up to the bed to be closer. When she'd gone, he began to tuck Frito in. Had some things to tell him, he felt like, but he didn't know how to start.

"*Watch*," Frito said "—the IV," and brought his hand up to free the tube. Martin saw the tattoo. Frito saw him look at it.

Martin said, "That what I think it is?"

"Uh-hunh."

"Let me see."

He turned his forearm out. Martin leaned closer. The yellow jacket. Head toward the wrist. Fat body. Oversized stinger pointing in to the crook of the elbow. The old man's tattoo, near exact. "You ever see his?" Martin said. "Old '*Sting*er's'? You remember it, or you were too young?"

"Too young."

"Well, this is damn close. It's nice work."

"Thank you."

"And it scabbed up nicely. Didn't run. Two hundred?"

"Two-fifty."

"Fair. Spend your loan money on it?"

"Maybe."

"Shame on you."

Frito brought the work up and looked at it. Ran his eyes over the details.

Has the old man's talent in him, Martin thought, but no real memories of him. "Mom see it?"

"Yeah."

Martin nodded. Said, "You ever try heroin?"

"No."

"Ever will?"

"No."

"Good lad."

"That's right. Good boy, I am."

Then Martin cried—it coming on him slow, so he thought he could stop it, but then he realized he couldn't; he'd reacted too late.

But it was all right. He laid his forehead on Frito's ribs, and sobbed, told

him he was sorry. Frito stroked his head. Told him it was fine. Was asleep
again when she came back in, Martin sitting quietly in the chair, reclining,
elbows on the armrests, fingers laced. The room in peace again, he knew, for
her return. He signaled her to wait at the door, got up and joined her.

In the hall, they sat, and he asked her if she knew about Stinger. Knew
the story that their mother told. She didn't, she said. He said the silence ran
in the family, but that he figured she should know, that he'd fill her in on
things in her husband's head, whether Frito liked it or not.

Fee and Penny came by in the morning, just after his mother, and he and
Fee went out in the hallway, Penny staying inside, started catching up with
his mother and Juliet before the door even closed on them. Had met them
only once, at Frito's wedding, but all three of them were good at awkward
shit like that. Most women were, it seemed to him.

"The cops still here?" Fee said.

"It's over. I think they're done."

"*That* part of it is." Dead serious, Fee. Eyes on the door.

"What's up, man?"

"I'm not sure."

"Talk, Felix."

"The only thing I can figure is the Italians in Staten Island."

"That your father had the problem with? Why me, then?"

"I don't know. Either it wasn't a sanctioned hit—was just some soldier
pissed off at my father for the old open wounds—or, it's bigger."

"Why me, though? Still."

"If it wasn't sanctioned, they were just scared to go for my father or me.
And if it was, it was a warning."

"Is your father fucking with them?"

"Because of this?"

"No, before."

He wasn't, Fee said.

"Not that you know of?"

"I asked him. Everything's kosher."

Martin shook his head.

"What?" Fee said.

"It doesn't make any sense. Have they even been in the club? You never pointed any of them out to me."

"Yeah. They've been there."

But it didn't seem true—Fee never said anything he couldn't prove on the spot.

Martin let it go. Stored it. "They could have just seen me outside, I guess," he said.

"Yeah, whatever. They've been in there, though."

"Point them out to me next time."

"Of course."

"So that's it, then?"

"Either that, or it's something I don't know about."

He considered the phrase. Checked Felix's eyes. Saw something there, but not something hidden. "Bunny?" he said to him.

Fee said, "Maybe."

"No reason."

"What did you do for him, that month?"

"Ran money, shook up some drug dealer in Washington Heights."

"Maybe him."

"I doubt it. I just drove the car."

Maybe Terry, he thought.

It was something to consider.

He wondered how attached Bunny was to him. What Bunny'd do if he ever disappeared.

I could kill Terry Hughes. Easily.

"Well, then," Fee said, "I don't know. We just wait now. Buy bullet-proof vests. Fucking things are two grand a pop. I can still ask on the street, I guess."

For vests? he thought. Secondhand? "What? What do you mean?"

"Ask *Homo sovieticus* if they know anything. And the sixty-odd *aparatchiks* working for us."

He said no—"Not yet. Wait until the thing's dead completely. Maybe five or six months without cops. Till we're sure that they're finished."

Fee shrugged—that he guessed he agreed. Said, "No Russian will offer unless someone asks him. This thing will disappear in total silence. Will *ever* offer information, a Russian—good or bad information—about someone in charge. But if someone in charge asks *him,* having info's a favor he wants returned. Usually just in cash, of course. Mercenary little bastards."

"We just have to wait," Martin said.

Thought Fee's mind drifting off the subject was evidence in the opposite direction. Carefree Felix, uninvolved, no longer interested in anyone else, again.

"Something still doesn't fit, Fee."

"It's all just a shock now. Things'll fall into place. Then we'll take care of it"—met Martin's eyes. Was Felix-the-All-Confident-Gangster, suddenly. Martin raised an eyebrow at him. Looked away. "We'll get them, Q. Have to wait at least a year, regardless of when we find them—it was just too public. But we will."

Martin didn't say anything.

Almost six months they wore those vests. Back and forth to the club. Then finally just let it go. He'd let Penny stay in the dark about his suspicions—had known as soon as he walked back into the hospital room that morning and saw her smiling so honestly, talking to his mother and Juliet, that she had no secrets from him, felt no guilt. The idea that Fee had done it hadn't even occurred to her. And as for himself, he just hadn't known. Would stare out the new window onto the water and try to figure it—who had done it; would they try it again; was he maybe in danger right now, standing here? He'd go out on the promenade and into the bushes to try to see from the shooter's perspective—like maybe something would come from standing in his place. And then, after a while, when the threat seemed gone, the past seemed to disappear with it. The whole incident becoming the kind of thing he found himself wondering if it really happened. And if it did, did it matter still? Did he really still care?

Memory was a liar like that, he knew. The way it told you your own story back. You had to listen close behind it to understand for sure what it really figured.

Like why was he going to kill Felix?

Why did you go upstate with him, charge your weapon, switch the safety off, walk with him into the woods. Follow just behind him to put the muzzle to his hair, time the triggersqueeze on a downstep, Felix saying without turning *"It wasn't the Italians." "What wasn't?" "Who shot your brother"*—like he'd read your mind, knew why you'd come upstate.

And escaped his death, a while. Long enough to walk back through the woods, into the clearing, and talk, a bit. While Terry waited for the right moment.

Smell the rain.

Hear, from your Government Issue couch, the currents of it dragging across the tarmac.

He wondered if the windows opened. Wanted to ask Corso.

The card game on for the third night running. Three wet coats hanging beside Corso's and Dolan's, now, by the door. Two of the agents with mustaches, the other one balding and tall. Must have once been blond. Corso'd said don't worry about their names. He didn't. Corso saying to them now, ". . . they're just boring to most people, the Russian crimies. The Italians make their money off what people want; the Russians do it off what they need. They don't deal in vice too much; they're just better with the white-collar stuff, crimes of deception. Insurance fraud, counterfeit documents, tax scams. But making *millions*. Maybe *billions* already, we think. So they have to be redefined. They're not like Cosa Nostra, at all, really. Fewer men doing more damage. And more . . . fucking . . . insidious, they are." Tossed his bet into the pile. "Plus—and this is the real thing we're going to have to live with—it's not just the gangsters. It's the average immigrants, also. The average Russian man and woman? They have the Social Security courts so fucking backed up with disability claims, it'll take a decade to sort it out. And *then*—just something to think about—the commissioner of the fucking *Park*ing Bureau wants the secretary general of the United fucking *N*ations to tell the Russian diplomats to start behaving themselves or pay their parking tickets, because since they got here? three years ago? they've run up two million dollars in summonses. No shame, they have, these people. They give a shit about no one. It's not the land of opportunity to them; it's just an easier system to crack." Tossed more change in. "Quinn."

"What's up?"

"Is Pasko fully legit now, or he's still got street-level shit going on? Had to, at first, I'm sure. He was the pio*neer* for his bunch." Said to the table, "The one Quinn worked for, as soon as we even *knew* about him, it was obvious we wouldn't get near him. It would take a year to get a tap warrant, his crimes were so far in the past, and everything rumor. The fucking magazines found out about him the same time we did. Well, is he?"—to Martin.

"You tallying racketeering counts tonight? According to my lawyer, that U.S. attorney, Ferguson, isn't even on board yet. This isn't really cleared, this cohabitation, here; I'm unofficial."

"It's cleared; believe me. You can ask him tomorrow. When you sign on the program. He's got my word we can use you. Meantime, just answer me that. Has Pasko got any vice shit going on? Drugs, or maybe whores coming in from Israel? Guns from Pakistan? Anything like that?"

"Meantime, answer me *this*. How'd you catch me? What were you doing up there? Upstate."

Corso shook his head, bet again, the other agents looking over. Looked back at their cards. Not Dolan, though. Wouldn't look up. Tough Dolan.

Corso wasn't going to answer.

"We wait for Ferguson, Corso?"

"I guess so."

"And then you'll tell me?"

"You're the one's going to be answering questions. The minute you open your mouth operation Red Devil goes into effect. We start making arrests, knocking doors in, freezing assets. I don't have to answer anything; you do."

Martin stood up, stretched. "Very mature conversation this is—I learned a lot. Thank you."

"You're the one started playing games. Call. What do you got?"

Martin looked. They put down their cards, eyed each other's hands. Corso raked change, again. His third hand in a row. Looked over, raised an eyebrow. Like his streak meant something that they both understood. Martin shook his head, walked to the windows. Stretched again. Couldn't stretch enough, it felt like, the last few hours. A mild withdrawal being possible from the morphine, the doctor had said. Some patients got it. He'd be one of them, he knew. He was sluggish and edgy, couldn't stop thinking about stopping thinking, getting out of his head. He thought, Maybe old Stinger was right, the approach he took. Something hurts you? Numb it. Confuses you? Numb it. Pleases you?

"Quarter," Dolan said. *Clink*—tossed it in.

"A quarter." Clink.

"Quarter." Clink.

"Quarter"—Corso—clink.

Clink. "Your quarter. How many cards?"—the red-mustache agent, dealing.

Why'd you want to kill Felix, man? Come on. Let it out. Because it sure-as-shit hadn't been over Frito. Even when Frito was a kid, would fall and get bloody, you didn't freak. You'd think, even then, So you fell—that's the worst thing ever happened to you.

The rain came sideways, heavier. "Corso, man, do these windows open?"

"Vacuum-sealed."

"Can you open the door, then?"

"For what?"

"So I can make a fucking break for it."

"Wants to play in the puddles," the red-mustache agent said.

"Do I know you?"

He looked up from his cards, the agent, looked over. Cop eyes, he had. Standard ones—sarcastic but easy to humiliate. A haze of smoke hanging with him while he stared.

Martin looked back out the window. Didn't bother.

They kept playing.

The wind pulled the rain around.

"It wasn't the Italians . . . Who shot your brother"—and he tightened his grip on the Glock.

"Corso, open the fucking door a minute. You can cuff me to something." He looked around. "The doorknob."

"You serious?"

"I'm getting nuts in here."

"Read the paper. Or start writing down what you want to tell Ferguson. Get your brain working."

"I can't think. You remember what that doctor said."

"You're with*drawi*ng?"

"No bugs on the walls, but I'm a little bit cagey, yeah."

Corso looked at him, a second. Thinking about it. Martin looked away. Didn't like being thought about, there like a child. Heard Corso get up, say "All right," and come over. Not "All right" like "Why not?" or "All right" like "I'm warning you," just "All right." Just a decision a man would make.

Pulled hard on the knob and the cuffs, Corso. Told him not to do anything stupid, and opened the door. Went back to the table, the rain blowing in. Martin closed his eyes to it, opened them. The drops cold on his forehead. His face flush underneath. "Quinn"—Corso again. He turned and blinked, saw them all there, clearly. With their five guns pointed at him. Cards held in their free hands, still, turned down. He looked back into the darkness. They laughed. He heard them lay the revolvers on the table and heard two metal snaps. Two holsters being closed up. Corso's and Dolan's, he guessed. *They* had no doubt he belonged to them.

That long, good period. When everyone else started falling apart and he stayed together, cool, made their choices for them. Learned he worked best showing off his strength against their weakness. That period.

Had started with Bunny. No question.

Yes, Frito had recovered, and Fee and Penny weren't getting along. But when he talked to Bunny on the phone that night, Brighton Beach alive all around him, the Q train banging overhead, he could have marked it right there on a calendar—"Future clear suddenly." Not ten minutes since the zip had approached him at the end of the bar. Shook his hand, being respectful. Said Bunny'd instructed him he should introduce himself. Carlo something, his name was. Martin hadn't seen him before. His English a mess but he was humble about it. Apologetic. Not defensive and contemptuous, like the rest of them. Said if they could do business together sometime, it would be an honor. Then left. Graciously declined a drink and was out. Had been there three minutes, maybe. Then Bunny calling, a few minutes later. Asking Martin had he met him. Martin saying yeah, and asked if he was family or something. "Yeah, probably he is," Bunny said. "I don't know. What did you think of him, though?"

"Why?"

"Sharp? Polite? What's your impression?"

"Yeah," he said, to both—a proper little greaseball gentleman the kid had been.

"Fine," Bunny said. "Good. I got to go outside, a minute. I'll talk to you later."

Martin told the hostess he'd be back in a bit, went outside to the avenue. Over to Brighton, to the phone three blocks up, down the stairs from the train. Waited another two minutes and called the phone on LaGuardia. Bunny answered—"You?"

"Yeah. What's up?"

"He's a character. Connected to my family somehow, back in Castelvetrano. Did time in Palermo for a hit he didn't do, when he was sixteen— then got exonerated. Kept his mouth shut for the whole fucking jolt. They asked him what he wanted, when he got out, he said to come here."

"How old is he?"

"Twenty-two, I think."

"Acts forty-two."

"I know; he's serious. He's a regular stand-up motherfucker. The joint in Palermo's no picnic."

"When did he get here?"

"Yesterday. Some distant cousin of mine calls me up, says this kid is coming and could I get him at Kennedy. Like he's some honored guest. I get there and he's still got zits, the little fucker. Wearing a suit too big that my cousin gave him. I brought him back for dinner at the restaurant. Over coffee he tells me he wants to work something out. This wet-ass youngster."

"Something he hatched in the clink."

"Something he overheard, night before he left. You remember Peter Hughes? Joe Moon?"

"Yeah."

"Good businessmen."

"Yeah."

"Carlo the zip says with a dollar and change, he could turn our lives around."

The train came in, up above, the phone shaking. "Hold on," Martin said.

Bunny said no. "We do the rest of our talking in person. You see what you think."

But Martin had known, already, that he'd do it. Would think to himself a year later that that was the night he'd stopped thinking too hard about Frito's shooter, started thinking about only himself again. "Tomorrow?"

"*Domani,*" Bunny said. "We'll talk early, before, make a time."

He kept it all quiet. Just the part about Bunny's phone call, at first, when he got back to the club and saw Fee, but then, later, all of it. When the score was swinging in full and was all he thought about. Decided he'd do it alone, fill Fee in when the time seemed right.

Carlo was at the bar, the next night, when he got there. He shook the kid's hand and ordered a Coke. Bunny came out from the kitchen, came down the room. Asked where the fuck Terry was, then said, "Here he is," and stood, waited for him. Martin looked, watched him come in. Had another zip with him, Tee. Another one Martin didn't know. There had to be ten of them by now. Tee took off his jacket and gave it in. Asked for it back, a second, and got keys out of one of the pockets and said something to the zip in Italian, gave them to him, and the kid went back out the door. He came over, Terry. "*What*'d you say to him?" Bunny said.

"To lock the car. I forgot to lock it."

"I think you told him, 'cook the cat,' " Bunny said. "Or maybe I heard wrong."

"Maybe you did."

"He's working on his Italian," Bunny said. Martin nodded. Terry leaned on the bar, with a gesture ordered a drink.

Martin said, "You in on this?"

Terry said, "Yeah, you?"

"Don't know yet."

"You talk to him?" Terry said to Bunny. "About everything?"

"Nope."

"What's everything?" Martin said.

Bunny said, "I'll get to that," and waited for Terry to sip his drink and give his approval, dismiss the bartender. Said, "Everyone has a drink, then?"

and Terry nodded. Martin lifted his Coke an inch, to show he was set. Bunny told the kid, Carlo, to explain it. Began to translate while he talked.

Soft, the kid spoke. Like he was describing something that had happened a long time ago. Something he didn't want to tell, but would, if Bunny wanted him to. Kept his eyes on the bar. Shrugged here and there.

"A new guy came into the jay, over in Palermo, the day before Carlo here got out, and said he was in for some package of heroin the cops never found. They locked him up for conspiracy and?"—asked something in Italian, to clarify—"contempt, I guess. Because he wouldn't tell them where it was, the guy. Because his old man had it"—kept listening, Bunny—leaning toward the kid. "He was protecting him. The father was old. Going blind. Blah, blah. Loyalty shit." The zip looked up, suspicious Bunny was mocking him. Bunny told him continue.

The father knew about the heroin, though, the kid said. Was an old-time gangster over there. And here. Got deported back in the fifties. A real-life Mustache Pete, Bunny said. Black Hand, the whole nine yards. Playing senile for the last ten years and pulling strings for his son when he could. The son talking on and on, the way guys did their first night inside. And Carlo listening to him, got the details that mattered. Then made the approach to the guy the next day, on his way out the door, practically. Said if he could get the *babanya* out of Sicily and into the States and get the money back there to the father, could the old man get the son out of stir himself? Pay off who he had to? And could Carlo keep the difference, if so? And the guy said sure. That the heroin would go nowhere, otherwise. You couldn't trust anyone over there anymore. The old man was afraid to make a move.

The kid shrugged. A lament for the sad state the old country was in.

Martin said, "Why'd the guy trust him?"

Bunny asked it. The kid answered. Two words.

"They trusted him," Bunny said. Smiled, shrugged. Like apparently that was all the kid figured he needed to say.

"He's a stand-up cuz," Terry said.

Martin nodded. "I heard." Thought how Sicily was more than another world; it was another century. They fucked things up and did their time, and there was always another greaseball to take your place. They lived by loyalty first, careful planning second. Success by attrition, it was.

He kept listening.

The kid had contacted the old man when he got out, and told him he could work it right. They'd agreed on a price. A route. The runners. Old connections that were lying asleep but were ready to wake again.

"He just said that?" Martin said.

"Yup."

"Jesus."

"And that all he needs now is bankroll," Bunny said. "Twenty'll get you fifty."

"Or twenty years," Martin said. "Right."

"Fuck that noise," Terry said, his eyes staying on the backbar. If he went away again, Terry, he wasn't coming out a young man; he'd do maximum, whatever the charge.

Though that wasn't exactly how he'd said it. It was more like, Fuck your chickenshit ass; it won't happen.

"Either way," Bunny said, "we got to make a move now."

"Why? What's the other shit that Terry was saying?"

Bunny gestured the bartender to pour for them. Raised his glass when he did. Said to toast. Martin clinked with them all, kept his eyes on him. Waited. Bunny said, "I had a sit-down with Rocco last week. He sent Charlie fucking Mirra in here to tell me come see him. I had to go over *there*." He nodded to himself about it, Bunny. Thinking for a moment, apparently. Put his glass down and pointed to it, waited till the bartender was gone again. He was trying to control himself. His face getting darker.

All their lives, Martin had never seen him angry.

But, then, there was a decent chance Mirra'd done the work on Bunny's old man, himself, going back twenty years.

Bunny sipped his drink, folded his hand, looked at his fingernails. "He says whatever I got coming in is his, from now on. He let me get myself set up, he says. Now his percentage is going to come to him. He's my skipper."

How much? Martin wondered, and wanted to ask. But knew it had to be more than fifty.

"But he doesn't know about Carlo here," Bunny said. "Right, Carlo?"

He nodded, the kid.

"And Carlo's got beefs going back a hundred years with that motherless hump's fucking people. So everything's good."

Martin nodded, and drank. Kept still. Kept listening.

"Everything's good," Bunny said.

"I just made the first fucking payment," Terry said.

Bunny said, "A duffel bag. We had to go to the bank. He wants back payments, too."

"He's asking to die," Martin said.

It was out before he'd thought about it.

One of those things you didn't say to Italians.

Either because they were superstitious, or hypocrites, or afraid of wire-taps, he'd never known. They just had their rules. Which were hard to always remember, sometimes.

Only the zip looked up, though, a second. Making sure he heard right, Martin guessed.

A few seconds passed. Bunny said, "You in, then?"

"For which?"

Bunny shook his head. "Fucking Irish," he said. "Killer Quinn. Just the money. That thing you mentioned, I'm going to have to forget. Terry, too. And little Carlo."

"Twenty large?" Martin said, and looked at his drink. Left the Irish comment alone. He was probably right, Bunny.

"Twenty."

"When?"

"A week."

"And the return?"

Bunny asked the kid. Nodded when he answered. "Two months."

Martin bobbed his head.

"You'll cover your rent till then?"

"I'll manage."

"Yeah, I'll bet."

"And you?"

"I got enough," Bunny said.

And Rocco? Martin thought. How long till he realizes you're not going bankrupt on schedule? How long before Mirra goes to work?

But he didn't really care about that—it had nothing to do with him. Bunny had plans that went back to childhood. Come into power sideways above Rocco, probably—go to the commission direct, and get straightened-out with them then, despite him. It would cost Bunny millions in tribute, come the time. And it's not my business. Backroom, old-world politics. Finger-pricking, holy-card-burning ceremonies in some old guinea's unfinished basement. In the 'burbs.

Didn't matter because here, again, was that thing he'd been thinking about so much, the last few months—he was picturing it again, suddenly—Juliet, standing there, in the hospital hallway refusing to follow him into the elevator. *"Are you a gangster?"* she'd said.

My God, if she knew about this, she'd need to sit down. A genuine wop, a neighborhood guinea, a half-dago thug, and the Irish kid from over the club going in on a heroin buy.

Killer Quinn. Kid Quinn. Suzy Q, he thought. I love this life.

He regretted Fee's not being there for just that, he guessed. To tell him, "I love my life."

And your wife.

He broke a smile and raised his glass to drink it and stop himself.

They stood there in silence, a while, all of them. Drank.

The kid, Carlo, was the only one to disappear, in the end, three months down the line. Collected his finder's fee and went back down to Florida to hang with one of the Sicilian runners, never came back. Never called or left word. Bunny sent Terry down to ask the runner about it. Terry came back and said Carlo was over in Sicily. Had gone to take care of the guy who did the hit that got him locked up six years before. Went home to clear his reputation in high, greaseball style.

Maybe he'll grow himself a mustache, Martin thought. And didn't ask about it again.

Because it was a real detailed account of the kid's whereabouts that Terry'd brought back. Which meant maybe Terry'd tortured the guy in Florida and gotten the truth, or tortured him and got a good story because Carlo was in a swamp somewhere getting torn apart by gators. Or, Terry never went down to Florida at all because Bunny had punched his little cousin the zip's ticket just after the money came through, and figured Martin was better off in the dark.

Every big score had its casualties. Just like with the old man's mail.

And, his twenty *had* turned fifty.

He didn't ask again.

Said, "I hope he gets the guy, from six years ago."

Bunny said, "Keep your eyes on the Italian papers. Me? I could give a shit."

He left Bunny's and drove to the club, went back to the office. Smiled at Fee behind the desk and waited for him to hang up. Took out the packet he'd prepared—fifty hundreds—and tossed it on the blotter. "What is this?" Fee said. Picked it up and riffled it. Estimated. Guessed right.

"Big Harry, Felix."

Fee squinted.

"Elephant."

"Big Harry the elephant?" Fee said. "That's a *real* person you're associated with?"

He smiled wider. "Scat. Schmeck."

"Heroin," Penny said. Was standing in the doorway to the bathroom. He hadn't realized she was around.

"*Caballo.* Brother."

"Stop," Fee said. "Answer me. That's annoying."

"You're such a foreigner, man. You can quote the soaps, but a little slang and you're out to sea."

She asked him—what was the money. Fee looked at her, then at him again. Wanting his answer, too.

He said, "Bunny came through."

"With what?" Fee said.

"*Babanya,*" he said. "You got any on ya?" An old, neighborhood line. He just remembered it.

Penny said, "*Heroin?*"

He hadn't planned on ever telling her if he didn't have to, but he felt too good now to care. "That's right, lady."

"When?" Felix said.

"Three months ago. Got paid three weeks back. Made sure everything was quiet. That's your cut. Your tribute, Don Pasko."

"From Bunny?"

"From me. So, you can be sure it's GI."

Fee looked at it. Penny looked at Fee looking at it. Then back at him. Thinking it all through. He was going to hear about this from her.

He looked at Fee. "What's the matter, you don't want it?"

"It's kind of weird, don't you think?"

"You set me up in this place, man. I laid down twenty grand, thanks to you. That's ten percent of what I got back, there. It's not a fortune I'm giving you; it's a gesture. A nod in your direction."

Fee said, "Well, then, okay . . ." Looked down at the packet again. "Thank you."

"Thank you?"

"Yeah."

"You're welcome. Give it back." He put his hand out for it.

"Why?"

"Because I don't fucking like your reaction."

"What are you talking about? What's the matter with you?"

"You think I went behind your back?"

"No. What the hell—"

"I didn't want to put you at risk. I took the chances myself."

"That's not what I'm saying at all—"

"But, Martin," Penny said, "what about . . . ?"—but that was all. Still in the doorway, still leaning on the frame. Looking at him closely. "What about your father?"

"My *what?*"

"Yes," Felix said. "That. That's what I meant."

"What about him?"

What about *your* father, Penny? You married another fucking *gang*ster.

He stared at her, thinking it. Wanted to say it.

Knew she *knew* she'd crossed the line, though.

She said, "Never mind," and looked down. "I'm sorry. It's none of my business."

They stayed how they were, all of them. He with his hand outstretched and his eyes on her. She with her eyes on the rug, arms crossed. And Fee, he saw, was half-reared, holding on to his envelope.

He brought his hand back. Said it was all right. "The money's yours, Fee. You staked me well enough so I could do a little something on my own. I'm thanking you for it. That's all."

"Okay"—Fee nodded. "Of course." Twisted his mouth, stood up.

"Don't hug me. I'm serious."

"A little one?"

"No."

The phone buzzed.

Fee made no move for it, kept his eyes on him. Frowned, thinking something, now. Said, "Heroin, hunh?" It buzzed again. "Did you cook it yourselves? Things like that? You *failed* chemistry."

"*We* failed. You were cheating off *me*."

Fee picked it up, third ring. Covered it, a second. Said, "Did you?"—his voice lower.

"Process it?"—whispering. "Course not."

Fee nodded, said hello. Sat down and started talking in Russian. Penny left—walked past them, and out. Martin took out the Glock from his waistband and laid it on the desk, and sat. Watched Felix from the couch for a while. Because there was something in his voice. It was the old man on the phone, but there was something more. Fee's eyes on his across the desk. The call had to do with both of them.

She came back in. Had drinks. Handed Martin his and stood over by Fee. Fee hung up, didn't look at her. Took the glass she held out for him, but didn't drink.

Would she lay a hand on his shoulder or something? She was standing right next to him.

She looked at *him,* though, on the couch.

He looked at Felix. Asked what was up.

"Have to go to your old neighborhood tomorrow."

"Do we."

"Just me. You know Rocco DiNabrega? You used to work for him."

"I know him."

"My dad and I are having dinner with him at his restaurant."

"Okay. Why?"

"I don't know, but my dad says Bunny's out."

They were filming a movie in the neighborhood—Thompson, Prince, and Spring all closed off to traffic—so they had to park down on Grand, walk back. Found spots for both cars, though, right across from each other. Penny riding with him. Along for the night because she and Fee were going out afterward. *He'd* been instructed to come so he could get the details, soon as possible, get over to Bunny's, and cut him loose. Fee and the old man riding alone, so they could talk. Though, walking up ahead now, they didn't seem to be speaking at all. Both with hands in their pockets, like they'd riffed over something. Keeping their distance. Himself, he guessed he hadn't said much to Penny, either. Even though they hadn't talked more than ten minutes in weeks. Since her mother got finished the house. This bullshit with Rocco was too much on his mind, now, though.

He looked at her, walking beside him, winked. She smiled, winked back. Was just giving him space. His girl.

Thompson was blasted with light despite the darkness of the sky up beyond the buildings. He brought her into the park and sat with her on a bench, back away from it all. A bunch of kids were horsing around by the pool, daring each other to jump in. Some teenagers he didn't know were drinking in the handball court, listening low to a radio. "I spent half my life on this bench," he said.

She smiled, looked out onto Thompson. "What happened with the movie they filmed in Anastasia's? When's it coming out?"

"Next year, sometime. I'm not even going to see it. I watched them do a couple of scenes?—it was just like a movie about wiseguys, but everybody was named Ivan or Boris. What's the diff?"

"You're just mad they wouldn't use you," she said.

"Damn right. I couldn't play the bartender, or something? I could have just stood there."

She pushed his face away, gently. "Silly."

He looked around. The monkey bars glowed, over by Sullivan Street. A little hump of steel rainbow. He said, "How's work?"

"Lousy. Unnecessary."

"So, do something else."

"Like?"

"Don't know," he said.

"Exactly."

He opened his hands, shrugged.

"You ever make out with anybody on this bench?" she said.

"I did my share, I guess, sure."

"You want to now?" Didn't look at him.

"You out of your mind?"

"I miss you."

"Yeah, well, that choice is yours."

"I'm still thinking about it."

He nodded. Knew she was. It wasn't like they could shack up, or anything, anyway.

"How's Frito?"

"Good. He's playing again. Taking the year off from Columbia to find himself. Something like that."

"You're so different."

"Not really."

"Please. How?"

"Can't explain it."

"Can you play piano?"

"Probably."

" 'Probably.' That means what?"

"It means I wouldn't be surprised if I could. I have this feeling I already *can*—but I'll never try it and I'll never know. Listen, what's on Felix's mind about this Bunny thing? Did you talk to him last night?"

"Not really."

"He doesn't care?"

"He's got a lot on his mind."

"Like?"

"Real things."

"You pregnant?"

"No."

"You still trying?" He couldn't tell anymore, recently. Too distracted with the Palermo thing. And she was so on-and-off-again with the cigarettes.

"Slim chance," she said.

"Which means what?"

She shook her head. To say never mind it. "We think Lexi's having an affair," she said.

"The old man?"

She nodded.

"How do you know? *Do* you know?"

"Felix asked him. Yes."

"Jesus Christ," he said. It was a bit of a surprise. He could still remember the old man mooing around the house whenever she went to Switzerland, years back. Devoted to her, he was. What changed in people?

"They've been fighting every time he comes back from Canada. We can hear them in the other apartment. Felix asked his mother, then confronted him."

"What did he say?"

"He's lonely. She's always away at her spas, or he's always in Canada."

"She's in Switzerland three times a year. He's making excuses."

"I know."

"Total bullshit he's giving her. I'm surprised Felix didn't tell me."

"He's wrecked by it. It doesn't show, but."

"And he tells *you* everything now. Doesn't vent on me."

"You're lucky."

"I know; that motherfucker can talk. How long's it been happening?"

"A year. At least."

"Jesus Christ," he said. "The same woman?"

"Yup."

"That's bad. That means something."

"Yes, it does. It's someone he knew back in Russia. Thirty years ago."

"Man, that's bad."

"The worst. As we know well. Who will it *be*?" she said. "Which couple will be first to divorce?" Like the big mystery question.

He thought, again, What *changes* in people? Why would an old guy start make excuses like a young guy?

And when did a man ever hit a point he quit looking somewhere else to be happy? "Should you be telling me this, by the way?"

"I think so."

"Did Fee say to talk to me?"

"We were up in the air about it."

"Well, tell him you told me. Don't forget."

She nodded. Said, "Things may start to change."

He said he guessed so, yeah.

"We're going to need all our money. If Fee confronts him again," she said.

"You think he'll take the club away."

"I doubt it. But still. Things may start to change."

"I'll keep an eye out," he said.

"Yeah, we all will. You want to make out, or no?"

"You're serious," he said. "For Christ's sake, where?"

"Your mother home?"

"Probably."

"Well, it's your neighborhood; think of something."

To Hudson and Leroy Street he took her. Quaint. Quiet. They compared time on their watches. Five minutes out—five back it would be. Took twenty for themselves. To tongue like teenagers. Then waited for ten outside of Rocco's, leaning on a car, gutter-side, watched the flick getting made up the block. Every couple of minutes, the crowd going silent, and someone saying "Action," then "Cut," ten seconds later, and the crowd breathing again. He turned, checked the restaurant every time he heard the door open. Penny didn't bother. She'd held his hand from Hudson back to Sixth.

Finally the three of them came out—Lexi and Rocco smiling, Fee looking over at Penny and him. Looked more like he wanted to get over to them than he wanted to be where he was. Which was involved on the highest level, Martin suddenly realized. Clearly he saw it. Three underworld figures they were, standing there. With their minimal interest in the world at large but feeling they could own it if they gave a little bit more effort. Fee just looking like a kid, again, was all. Like the height was making him dizzy. The silk suit he'd chosen especially was hanging too large.

Or, shit, maybe something was *really* wrong.

Christ, is Bunny getting finished? he wondered. Are we getting the contract?

"It might be worse than we thought," he said to her sideways.

She didn't answer, was looking over—square at the three of them. Chin up. Knew her role here. Comfortable in it.

Lexi called out to her. She went. All confidence. Took Rocco's hand, put her cheek, got kissed. Martin looked away. Tried to focus on things he knew—the candy store, the bakery. But his thoughts bugging out. They going to tell me to go by his office and blast him? Midst of this moviemaking shit? In the window and out again?

"This is the kind of night that you could do it," they'd say. *"Reality backs off on nights like this."*

Saying goodnight, now, the four of them.

He came off of the car, got into step with them, stopped when Lexi slowed to watch the filming, a second. Rocco called him. By his last name only. Made the *q* sound ugly. He turned and went over. Kept his hands in his pockets. Rocco lit a cigarette and took it in his right hand, put his left away. Smiled.

"Rocco. How are you?"

"Good."

"What's up?"

"You a bodyguard now or a bigshot?"

"Neither."

"You Lexi's driver?"

Martin smiled. Wanted to close his eyes at the insult. Opened them wider, instead.

"Oh, you're a player, then? Own part of that commie club?"

"I do all right."

"I think you're a driver."

"Think what you want."

"Oh, yeah? You're a toughguy now? Say that again."

"I'm going to go."

"Don't overstep yourself. I was your age I had three, five hits under my belt, but I'm looking at you, I can see you don't even want to do nothing but leave."

"Yeah, I'm going."

"Yeah, 'cause your people left you. Your partners. They're already around the corner."

He turned, walked. And they *were* already gone. The door of the restaurant closed, he heard.

They'd stopped, a dozen yards in, around the corner, on Thompson. Penny standing back and the old man and Felix up close to each other. Up in each other's faces, almost. "You're taking orders from him," Felix saying.

"He works for me," Lexi saying. In English. For Penny's ears, Martin guessed.

"*You're* taking orders."

Lexi pointed. His finger an inch from Fee's lip. "Understand what you see."

"I told you, Bunny has rights to this neighborhood. When he's in, we're out because of this."

"Bunny is a boy. And you are. Understand what you see."

"Would you freaking listen to me, God damn it?"

Lexi thumped him in the chest, shot the hand up and took him by the cheeks. Squared Felix's eyes on his. "I don't listen to you, my darling; you listen to me. This Italian, Rocco, listens to me. And works for me. Like you. Now, *who* do you work for, Fila? I just told you. Me or Bunny?"

Fee looked away, his mouth staying twisted in the old man's hand.

Lexi let him go. Started walking.

Fee stood there. Nowhere to go, really. His suit looking droopy. Penny crossed her hands behind her, leaned back on the building. Martin went over to him. Figured he'd make things worse. Asked him what to tell Bunny.

"That he's out."

"You sure?"

"Just do it."

"I'm asking you again."

"Fucking . . . Why? Why are you asking me *anything*?"

"She told me about the bitch in Canada."

"And?"

"You may have to start making some decisions. Of your own."

"Don't . . . freaking . . ."

"He won't take the club away."

"Oh, no?"

"I doubt it."

"You don't know anything."

"What's his connection to Rocco?"

Felix squinted, shook his head. Asking what his *point* was.

"What's the loyalty?"

"Money."

"Come into the park, tell me what money."

"He'll fucking cut us off."

"I don't think—"

"He will fucking *cut . . . us . . . off*, Q; don't—"

"Let him," Penny called over.

They looked at her. She said it again.

"What does that mean?" Fee said. "What's with you?"

"Come into the park," Martin said, "and tell me what money. Come on. Felix."

Hatched it that night, the three of them. Though Fee wouldn't go for it, right there on the spot. But that long good period started rolling.

Detail after detail Martin asked him. Thought back to all he'd ever known or overheard where Rocco was concerned, tried to match it up. Hits that made the news or got whispered in the neighborhood. Gambling circuits. Loansharking chains. Drug rings. Hookers. Counterfeiting. Construction booms and union overhauls. The lenient times, the crackdowns. When the neighborhood wiseguys hung out with confidence and when they'd disappeared for a while. Then, who had emerged when the stories were out of the papers, and who was dead, who was in the can. Fee told him Lexi and Monya's tale, and he listened and matched. Like playing Concentration, it felt like, as a kid. Turn up a strawberry, turn it over again. Five cards later, turn another one. *That fucking strawberry. Top right corner? Where* was *it?* He said, "Slow down. Say that part again."

He repeated it, Fee.

"So Monya might have introduced them?"

"Maybe formally, yeah. To do business."

"So Monya got here first."

"Yeah. In the sixties. He's been illegal the whole time. That's why his name is different."

"Why?"

"He took my grandfather's real last name."

"What's Pasko?"

"It's Polish Catholic. My grandfather ripped the dog tags off a dead soldier in the Black Forest. Stalin didn't like Jews."

Manhattan had to be *Para*dise to Lexi, Martin thought. Like fucking . . . kid stuff. *Kin*dergarten.

He shook his head, looked off. The park empty now. The film crew packing in silence. Their lights off, finally. It was his again, the neighborhood. He took a long breath. Let it out. "He came straight here, Monya?"

"Worked in France."

"Doing what?"

"Black market. Barcelona and Algiers."

"Where'd he live?" Himself, he barely remembered Paris. Was only four, five.

"Marseilles," Fee said. "I think."

But he knew—Martin saw it. "Mar*seilles, Felix? In the sixties?"

"Yeah, I know."

"That's the height of the French fucking Con*nec*tion, Fee."

"I know."

"That was his business, your uncle."

"Maybe."

"'Maybe.' I think you underestimate him. And I think your old man was involved."

"That's a movie," Pen said.

"It was real. The opium out of Southeast Asia into Marseilles. It went on forever. Ten, fifteen years. Then it changed its routes."

Fee nodded.

"Yes?" Martin said. "You know all of this?"

"Yes."

"The Pizza Connection?"

"Asia to Sicily to Florida."

"To Bra*zil,* to Florida. Then New York. Cleveland. St. Louis. About a dozen guys here and in Little Italy disappeared over that. In less than a month."

"When was this?" she said.

"A few years back. Not too many. Less than ten."

"Was Lexi involved?" she said. "Felix?"

"No."

"Is he now?"

"I don't know."

"Yes you do, Fee," Martin said to him. "There's a big heroin problem in Moscow right now. Why was Monya shot?"

"Monya's history. It wasn't over anything like this."

"Like what? Where does Moscow get its shit from?"

"Afghanistan."

"Motherfucker," he said. "I could trace the fucking route right now. Kabul to Moscow to Castelvetrano to fucking Brighton Beach, USA."

"He just wants Bunny out," Felix said. "He's just getting too *big.* Rocco's afraid of revenge."

"He doesn't want Bunny out; he wants your father in. If he was afraid of revenge for killing Bunny's old man he would have *killed* Bunny already. What did your father say to you? What did he say about dealing with Rocco from now on? Felix?"

"He said I wouldn't see him again. And didn't know him. Rocco just wanted to meet me. To tell me to my face, with respect, that he would like me to stop doing business with someone."

Martin shook his head. "They're so fucking smart," he said. He couldn't believe it.

Pen said, "And greedy." He looked at her. She got up off the bench, walked away. Came back. Didn't sit—crossed her arms and leaned her ass on the backrest. "A billion dollars," she said. "Looking at a billion dollars in real estate by the millennium."

"But he's got to deal H?" Martin said.

"That's right."

"Don't be naive," he said. To dismiss the subject. There was no point even going into that now.

She said, "Greed is greed, Martin. Screw you." But didn't look at him. Knew he was right.

"Heroin's on the rise again," he said; "it's that simple. The guineas go where the new commerce is. Bottled water? Gangster rap? Heroin again? Welcome *back,* they're thinking. There was no new market for it, the last few years, with AIDS. But now everyone's getting tattoos again, and . . .

fucking . . . nipple rings, and trying a little *babanya*. And if the Russians have the fastest trade route? Shake hands, comrade; we're partners, is Rocco DiNabrega's opinion. I'll bet everything I have on that."

Fee put an arm up across the bench-back. Crossed his legs like a gentleman, ankle on the knee. Hadn't moved before that in twenty minutes. "Something on your mind, Fee?" Martin said.

"I was just thinking that Joe Kennedy was a bootlegger."

"Yeah, well, you can't be president—you weren't born here."

"My kids can."

Martin glanced at her. She didn't turn, though. Wasn't listening, even. He looked off at Thompson. "The first Jewish commander-in-chief. I'd hold my breath to see that."

"Catholic," Felix said. "Second Catholic one."

"Oh, that's right—you're a papist," he said. "Name the Holy Days of Obligation."

"The what?"

"What are we doing about Lexi?" she said. Was still pissed. No patience now at all for distraction.

"I got an idea," he said.

"Then spill it."

"We parallel them. Get Monya's help. Use Bunny's and our money, use Monya's connections."

"That's . . . fucking . . . re*tar*ded," Fee said.

"It's fucking smart. And it's right there in front of you. That's why you can't see it. What are you so fucking scared of, Fee?"

"Nothing. We'd just get caught. Well, okay, that's what I'm scared of. I wouldn't call that an ir*rat*ional fear. Would you?"

"That night we got drunk, before Puerto Rico, you said we needed vision. That's what this is."

"This is copycat shit, man. You don't even know what you're *talk*ing about. We're still *kids*."

"For Christ's sake," she said. "Jesus, Felix, does every fucking thing Lexi says go right in your brain?"

"We're still young."

"That's *bull*shit—"

"Now *that* is stupid," Martin said. "Rocco took over this neighborhood at twenty-nine. Lucky Luciano—"

"Lucky Luciano?"

"That's right. You got no sense of history anymore?"

"Didn't old Lucky get killed?"

"He got deported. He died of old age."

"The exception."

"Your *father* ever do time?"

"You know the answer to that."

"Well, Rocco neither."

"I'm not doing it, Martin."

She said, "Fee—"

"And would you . . . just . . . I'm not too comfortable with your opinion about all of this right now, okay?"

"You're not *com*fortable? Who cares?"

"Who cares?"

"Another time, please?" Martin said.

He kept staring at her, Fee. A few seconds. Then looked at his watch—brought his hand up off the bench, an inch. Said, "I'm not doing it. Please tell Bunny he's out. Tonight."

"Let me tell you something, Felix. Your father thinks he's a kid, but if I tell him he's out—"

"*Fuck* him. Let him try it—"

"If I *tell* him, we're at risk. You're at risk."

Fee shrugged.

"And I'll tell you something else, Fee—you already are. This thing with Rocco is going to go down, and your father put you out there tonight like a chess piece. A show of balls and trust. But *Rocco* asked to meet *you*. It's his way of going 'Yeah, I need you, Lexi, but I'm still the kind of guy who'll snuff your kid.' You're at risk and your father *put* you there, Filushka. Even *if* it's because he's not afraid. Thinks Rocco works for him. He *put* you there. I'm telling you to take your *own* God-damned risks. Because your father's never going to be out. I see that now. He's never going to be fully legit. He can't be. He *has* to stay tied to the Italians. On the dirtiest fucking level. They'll never trust him again, otherwise. They'll never let him leave. Another thing I'll tell you—"

"You're on a roll—"

"Your old man wouldn't even care if he found out you pulled this off. We'd be competition for him in a big fucking bottomless market. He'd be proud. He'd be *proud* you took a piece."

He was quiet, Fee.

It got to him, that one.

Martin watched him.

"You're both sick," Penny said.

Martin looked at her. "Why? I thought you were behind this?"

"You're both fucking sick," she said.

He said, "What the fuck does that *mean,* Penelope?"

Fee looked at him.

Fuck it, he thought. Kept looking at her.

She didn't answer him.

H e outright lied to Bunny to buy the time to get to Felix. Said the cops were around again about Frito's getting shot and had files on people. Not Bunny *personally,* but either way, "Keep your distance. I'll be in touch." Snagged a library card from a wallet in the club's lost and found, and got every book he could on heroin. Brought them to the office, sat on the couch and read them. Read the important parts aloud whether Felix listened or not. Printed articles off of microfiche and put them under Felix's nose. CHINESE TONGS RELUCTANT TO FILL GAP IN HEROIN TRADE. TURK- ISH TYCOON KILLED IN BELARUS. MUJAHIDEEN USING U.S. FUNDS TO TRAFFIC OPIUM.

"Ripe, Filushka," he'd say. "I'm not talking about taking over. Just pick- ing some of the fruit. No hostile takeover of the orchard."

"He won't even leave you that damned couch to sit on."

"I'll buy my own."

"He won't leave you your neck to sit your damned *head* on. That's something I worry about, too, for you."

"You would. I don't."

"Me, he'll just beat my ass. You . . . ?"

"I'm trembling. Can I go back to my reading here?"

"How many people you know who are no longer with us thanks to heroin? Pardon my bluntness."

"Including my father? A truckload. More than I could name. What's the greatest fortune maker in the world, let me ask you?"

Fee stared at him. Knew the answer and wouldn't say it, so just stared.

When you're right . . .

"What business, more than any other, makes men's fortu—"

"War," Fee said.

"Get a couple of truckloads dead with that, too, no? Risk to reward? You know the phrase?"

"I know the fucking phrase. But why do I get the feeling, Suze, you're trying to convince yourself here, too?"

"No idea. I'm trying to convince you because you're a wealthy young man. I need your money. If you, me, and Bunny go in, we'll need a half million in bankroll, first time out, maybe more. But if we unload it at even *dealer*-level, we'll make eight times our front. From just a half-million dollars. We could raise it right now."

"Tell your friend there to *print* it up."

"We can raise it. You, me, and him."

"We could do a lot of things."

"But we could *do* this. You admit that."

"We could do a lot of things."

"Twelve times our money if we see the whole product straight through, down to street-level. To the pushers. Your father started out street-level. Selling protection, peddling gas, and ass. I'm more like him than you are, I think. That's clearer and clearer to me, now."

"Is it?"

"That's right."

"Nice try."

Every conversation they had eventually going something like that. Then Fee'd go back to whatever he was doing. So, it would take more than money to convince him. That much becoming more and more obvious every time.

But the instinct to stack him against his old man was right, it turned out.

The way it got proved, though, had just been unforseeable.

Help from outside, it came as. Reaping gain from others' misfortunes. But he squared it with his conscience in minutes, come the time. Told himself the simple truth that he'd never outright wish it on anyone. Still, it was cancer. And though they caught it early, it was what it was. And she was vain, Fee's mother. Getting sick again at all was enough to half wreck her. But, it all just continued the chain of things that made life feel like it was unfolding before him—Fee spending all his days with her, and a good deal of nights; the old man disappearing for weeks at a time, went to Canada, for business, he said; then Penelope just coming downtown. Cabs to the back of the apartment, mornings. In through the service door, up the elevator from the basement, and into bed. Would walk around the place, after, naked, stare out at the water. Come back again and lie down with him, a while, and talk, before he had to go out to the club, keep an eye on things. She wasn't working. Was happy. No guilt in her. None in him, he realized. He asked her about it.

"*Mea culpa,*" she said. That was it.

"*Ego te absolvo,*" he told her.

She crawled on top of him, sat up. The room all bright, and warm. Her flesh tight across her belly.

"You feel nothing?" he said.

"We don't even sleep together anymore. It's over."

"That's what decides it?"

"No, big baby, it's an example. We hardly talk. We're like friends."

"Buddies?"

"Not even."

"You told me once it was no good with him."

"What?"

"This. Before."

"Sex?"

"Yeah."

"Say it."

"Sex."

"Again."

"Did you say that, or not?"

"Yes. You remember. You told me to go fuck myself."

"*Why* was it no good. What was wrong with it?"

"Nothing was wrong; he was just . . . respectful. That sounds awful, I guess. It's hard to explain. He's got a virgin/whore complex."

"Madonna mia," he said.

"Yeah. Not anymore, though."

"When was the last time?"

"We've done it. Recently. *He's* done it, anyway."

"What the fuck does that mean?"

"It means, now that his mother's sick, I'm the whore."

"Enough."

"You shouldn't have asked."

"Fine." He looked away from her. Sideways saw her pull the sheet up on her head, wrap her face, like in a habit. She began to sing. Slow. The "Ave Maria."

His second hard-on was gone. It had started up beneath her when she told him to say "sex" again. He wondered if she'd noticed it.

"Men are idiots," she said. She dropped the sheet.

"Excuse you?"

"My mother despises all of you."

She pushed her breasts together, let them go. Played with the hair around his navel. "I've been wondering a lot lately. How it would have been if you'd never left. I wish I could see it. For just a moment."

"You'd see Sing Sing's visiting area."

She shrugged. Didn't look up.

"The day I nearly beat some guy to death," he said, "I go to *your* father's funeral. Who probably died over no more than twice what I'd beaten my guy up over. Someone was telling me something. It was a sign to leave, I took it as."

He drew her hair back from her face. Let it go again when she didn't look up.

"It was a sign to stay," she said.

He didn't say anything.

What to say?

"You remember Marco Duomo?" she said, concentrating—twirling his hair. "The guy I took to my junior prom? The guy who got my father killed?"

"Yeah."

"He's out of jail."

"How do you know?"

"Because I know."

"You keeping track of him?"

"Maybe."

"Why?"

"Let's just say I saw him."

"Did you?"

"Yes. Shopping with his mommy, in Cross County Mall. Carrying her bags for her."

"Nice boy."

"I asked Felix to kill him." She looked up at him. Widened her eyes. Pulled on the hairs she had in her fingers.

"Are you serious?"

"As a heart attack."

"What'd he say?"

"I was crazy. Which I'm not."

"I didn't say anything."

"He said I'd be the first person they looked at."

"Probably right."

"I told him to wait until old man Duomo was in the papers again, then do it. Confuse everybody."

"Be that simple, hunh?"

"Nobody cares when gangsters die. Believe me."

He nodded. Squeezed her leg gently. "I do."

"The cops asked my mother the same questions for a month. Then dropped it. Put it away in some file. They figure the only way they'll ever solve anything anymore is if somebody turns over."

"*Omertà,*" he said.

She said, "They can stick it up their asses, hypocrite cocksuckers," and lay down on him. Turned her face away. He wondered who she meant—the cops or the wiseguys? It didn't matter, though. He'd never understood how she really felt about it all, anyway.

He said, "You still thinking about doing it? Popping him?" Moved her hair off his mouth.

"Not really. No."

"I could take care of it. Find the right person."

"Forget it. I don't even blame him."

He nodded, relieved.

"When I was at the prom," she said, "he made a pass at me, Marco. I turned him down. I used to wonder, if I'd said yes, maybe my father—"

"No, Pen"—he'd heard this before, he felt. She'd told him, but he didn't know when. Or he'd thought of it himself, maybe.

No. At her father's funeral. Out in the parking lot.

"Maybe he'd have been moved up," she said. "Had more pull. Instead of being the kind of guy who got killed so other people could stay comfortable. Like a prostitute I was thinking. At seventeen. You believe that shit?"

He didn't say anything.

She swallowed. Heavy. Her whole body moved with it.

He said, "Did you ask Fee to do it himself? About Marco?"

"I don't know. I don't remember."

"He's never killed anybody."

"I guess," she said.

"You guess?"

"He hasn't. I know."

"It's not like asking him to go out and buy you Tampax," he said.

He felt her smile.

They lay there.

"Let's do it again," she said. "Can we?"

He said, "Okay. If we have to."

"Martin? It's Penny," she said. Familiar, cold. Someone in the room with her.

"Penny Pasko? How are you?"

"Can you come out to my mother's house? In Bronxville?"

"You all right?" he said.

"Everything's fine. Felix and I want to talk to you."

"About what?"

She stayed quiet.

"Penny?"

"Take the Henry Hudson to the Cross County. Then the Bronxville Road exit. The house is on Bronxville Road. Number 366. On the right."

"Are you fucking *okay*?" he said.

"Of course. Yes."

"Yes you're *okay*?"

"Yes."

He drove past the house again, see what he could. But got the same picture—Fee's truck in the driveway, the old lady's Buick in front of it; both garage doors open, no cars inside.

He circled the long, steep blocks, saw nobody else. No one walking or driving. No one parked on the street, even. Everyone pulled into their garages or alongside their houses.

He parked up the block, walked down to her place. Went soft up the steps. He looked around the side, at the patio. Looked up at the master terrace. Quiet, everything. Quietquiet. He rang the bell. The old lady answered, and he followed her in. To the living room. He kept his gun in his hand in his jacket pocket, his other hand in the empty one. Fee there, far side of the room, sitting. With his nose all bandaged. Both his hands showing, though. Resting on the arms of the chair. Penny on the couch, sitting sideways to him. Up straight. Her hands proper. Laced together in her lap.

He stood in the doorway. Waited. Eyed them. Her mother waved a hand up, walked out, past him. "I'm in the kitchen," she said.

"Thanks, Momma."

He looked at her on the couch. She forced a smile, looked at Felix.

Felix looking at him. Face swollen. His eyes fat, black, angry.

"The fuck happened to *you,* chief?"

"Lexi."

"What about him?"

"He broke my nose."

"Your father?"

"Uh-hunh."

"When?"

Over Bunny? he thought.

Over me?

"This morning. In the hospital room. She's back in the hospital."

His mother. The cancer. "She okay?"

"She might be."

"Radical mastectomy," Penny said.

"I'm sorry."

"He broke my nose."

"Why?"

"Because I called him on it. Said I'd personally throw him out if he didn't stop seeing her."

"The one in Canada."

"Uh-hunh."

"And he hit you?"

"We traded a few words first."

Martin nodded. Tried to think about it. Couldn't stop still thinking this was about him, though. He looked at them. Penny with no expression, really. Fee just ugly. "You okay, then?"

"Yeah, he did it in a hospital; they set it, right there. I want you to call Bunny. Arrange a meeting."

"About?"

"I already spoke to Monya. Call him now."

"Wait, slow down," he said. The fear wouldn't shake off. He couldn't shrug it. "I'm sorry. Wait. I have to go to the bathroom. I drove straight here."

"There's a phone next to you." Fee motioned. Toward right down beside him.

He looked. Saw a blue trimline that he and Pen had picked out. "Wait," he said. "The bathroom."

"On your left," Fee said. "Down the hall. Where you came in."

He went down the hall. Went in, flicked the light on. Closed the door. Turned on the fan. He took out the gun, careful, and snapped on the safety. He sat on the lid of the toilet, and opened the chamber, dumped the round in his hand and released the magazine. And pressed the bullet back in and slid the clip back up again. Checked the chamber once more. Put it away. He flushed the toilet. Ran the sink, and turned it off. Looked in the mirror. He watched himself breathe. Turned on the water again and filled his hand up and drank it.

Christ, he thought. Jesus Christ almighty, man.

onya they ended up buying, kind of. For a hundred grand. Buying his connections, his services. Buying him off. "My treat," Fee said. Meaning he'd take care of the bill alone. Meaning he wouldn't be asking that it come out of the final half million they'd have to compile to finance the score when the time came. His first go at the old man, it was, Martin knew. The first slap in his face. Contracting with the enemy.

Though that didn't seem to be Monya's interest in it, getting back at

Alexi for not taking his side against the guineas and then letting him rot in a wheelchair in a shitass apartment on Avenue U. "I could not be a part of things again if I *want*ed to" Monya saying. This was a *bless*ing, money in his *lap.* That was all he'd expect from it. No jump start to make an attempt at a second career. He was tired all the time, he said. Could barely take care of himself. He needed a better apartment, a membership at a spa, a nice nurse to come in, look after him, do a little housecleaning and maybe let him suck on her chest if he asked her nice. He said since Felix called him he'd made the first few dozen calls himself. Of reintroduction, reassurance. *"My nephew's a toughguy now. But he's still my nephew. Treat him right."* After that, he said, "the rest of the calls are up to you." Said it took about ten phone calls back and forth before any single move could be made in a heroin deal. By the end of the operation they'd have made half a thousand of them. And morphine base came out of Pakistan now, he said; Afghanistan was closed.

In the hallway outside the apartment, heading for the stairs, Martin whispered, "That's it? We're all through with him?" Wondered if Monya had a fedora in the closet. Red hatband.

Fee flashed the list of phone numbers again, buried it back in his pocket. Said, "I'll bring him the balance of the money? Any luck, we never see him again."

Martin said nothing.

Though the idea made him happy.

Smiling–hard–to–himself happy.

Because the apartment had stunk like piss. And Monya had stunk like piss. It had made him start to think that if things went wrong, that was how they'd *all* turn out.

They jogged down the stairs.

They ended up bringing in Bunny with not too many problems either. A little hedging he did, Bunny. A little gesturing, here and there, like nothing was ever really cut in stone. Playing coy. Wanting the attention. Like a schoolgirl. Like a wiseguy. But Martin left *that* meeting feeling his life was on a tightrope now. At the end was all he'd ever want, and down below was who-fucking-cared-what, because he wasn't falling off. Three hours into it—the meeting—the dining room filling up suddenly with staff who were setting up the night shot—it seemed to be done. There was nothing more to explain or say, for now. Bunny shrugged, Felix waited, Penny smiled. "All right, bro," Bunny said—"Start making your moves, then," and Fee took his hand. Bunny put his out to Penny, then. She took it. "Never done business with a girl," he said. She answered him in Italian. He smiled. Said something back brief. He liked her. Saw already how smart she was.

"Terry in on this one, Pasqualie?" Martin said.

"You see him here?"

"Good."

Though Terry was always involved, Martin knew. Just something to keep in mind.

"Private Quinn here don't get along too well with my right-hand, going *way* back," Bunny said.

She said, "Why not?"

" 'Cause Terry's older brother, Peter, may he rest, *loved* the Quinn. Made him a little bigshot in the neighborhood at fifteen years of age, and wouldn't give Terry the time of . . . fucking . . . the time to have a kick in the ass for himself. He *hated* him. But the Irish are like that, right? Got no real family loyalty. They like who they like. Nobody else. They forget them."

"Your right-hand man is Irish?" she said.

"Half Sicilian"—winking at her.

"We're good, then?" Martin said. He wanted to go.

"We're good."

"We're good," Fee said, and stood up. "We have to get out to the club anyway. We're running late now."

"My boys miss that place," Bunny said. "All they talk about is Russian girls."

Penny said, "We hire the best."

"Oh, yeah? You hire them?"

"He runs them past me, sometimes."

Bunny smiled at her, big. Looked at Felix. "She give you that?" he said. Raised a finger off the table, to point at his nose.

"Bounced it off a steering wheel," Felix said.

Bunny said, "Try a seat belt," and smiled wider.

Penny went to use the bathroom.

Fee went over by the bar, got on his phone. His back to them. Calling his mother, Martin figured, and took a breath, looked around.

Didn't like these personal little details interfering now. He wanted to be talking business or be out of here. Bunny standing now, beside him. Watching Fee. Said he didn't like it.

"What. Like what?" Martin said.

"You threw this on me."

"You said you were *in,* just now."

"I got time. We all do. Four or five months till we get all the money together. I don't know this guy, hardly. He don't know me. We got time."

"I've known him my whole life."

"He's going against his own old fucking man. I don't know what his loyalty's going to be, year from now."

"His father broke his nose," Martin said.

Bunny looked at him. "Really."

"In front of his mother. And Penny."

"Really."

"They're done. Long time coming."

Bunny said, "Okay." Nodded. "I'll take that under consideration."

Splitting fast to the phone across Brighton Beach Avenue. A new roll of quarters and the safe mouthpiece in one pocket, the Glock in the other. The list of coded phone numbers wearing soft at the edges. From unfolding and refolding. He'd want to remember his life like this, he knew. This nerve. This busyness.

The part about the calls had looked like a bitch. A no-joke, fucking pain in the ass. But they got masking mouthpieces to cap on the phones in the street that they decided to use, gave them all names, those phones, and wrote them down. With their coded addresses. On a cheat sheet that they each got a copy of. Silly, bullshit names you could drop in a conversation. Cars none of them drove. Foods none of them ate. Girls they'd never known. Audi, Spaghetti-Os, Miranda. On and on. And Penny went out to a few different sites around the boroughs and wired the first payments abroad.

They waited, then. For the next round of phone calls. As Monya had said.

The pattern from the word go, it turned out to be. Hear nothing for a month, then the dope would get stepped on, one more stage, and the next bunch of couriers would feel they could move it. You'd spend half your week on the phone by the stairs underneath the Q. Or in the shadows of the streets down the bottom of Broadway. All of them narrow and tall, those streets. Like the sun never hit them directly.

Almost four months like that, he spent. Passed his off-hours in the library. Read all he could. Stuff on production. On cultivation. History. Folklore. $C_{17}H_{17}NO(C_2H_3O_2)_2$ . . . *More soluble in fats. Less time into the Central Nervous System. Became morphine again in the bloodstream . . . Thailand, Afghanistan, Turkey, had whole regions that were covered—blanketed—in flowers. Uninterrupted for miles . . . The British got half of China addicted, nineteenth century, then cut them off so they'd have to spend more money internation-*

ally. He thought of Garland and Margaret Hamilton. Lugosi. Keith Richards. Felt like he was heading toward something. A meeting with a child from some previous marriage that his old man had had.

Penny shared her time between her mother's place and his. She bought a cellular phone in case Felix called her. He didn't. Was spending all his time with his mother. Helping her to recover. Lexi moved. Into a place in a high-rise way the hell up on Third Avenue somewhere.

He split quick across the traffic. To the phone under the Q. With his quarters, his phone numbers, his pistol. Told himself, Remember this.

The call came that it was coming. Would be into Florida inside of two weeks. He couldn't sleep. Kept thinking what to do that he hadn't done yet. How to ready the ground, not get slowed up. For his own part, he saw just the personal things to take care of. Fix up the past to step into the future, like. Find out what happened to Frito, or at least make an effort. Close that up, best he could, before Juliet had kids and wouldn't let him come see them, or something. He called Bunny from the street, told him the cops said whoever shot Frito was connected to the club probably. Was staff. A petty beef gone wrong. His hands were tied; he couldn't question even one of them. "Will you ask the zips? They know the girls." Brought up divorce again with Penny, but that didn't go smooth. "What do you think, Martin, you have to clean up your life before good things can come?" Knew him well. She said, "Tell him yourself. Make your full confession." He said that wasn't what he meant. He said, "I just want to see how things are going to play when this is over. This next phase here. If we're rich, we're not going to want to wait. You're going to have to talk to him about it." She said, "You're going to have to grow a spine and talk to him yourself." Was dressing, down the end of the bed. Putting on her shoes. Ready to leave, almost. They'd already said that this was it for a while; they would have to be cool, keep separate till the package had come and been dealt with. He said, "Don't fight with me, Penny, you know? We're not going to see each other, a while. You're not making things easy." "You think that's what telling me to bring up divorce is?" she said. "Making things easy?" So that took care of trying to clean up his personal life.

As for the shipment, the last thing was storing the money. The detail they'd decided to wait till the end to cement. His original idea still seemed the best, though. They couldn't make a deposit in any bank, and these self-storage places were popping up everywhere. Plus, what if the package arrived late at night? They were open all the time, these joints. There was one a few blocks from his apartment. Driving home from the club, before dawn, the glow coming from the Plexiglas guard booth was the only other light in the neighborhood on besides streetlamps.

They rented the smallest size. Bought a padlock, and they all took a key. Put their money in a Yankees duffel and tossed it in, and locked up. Bunny squared off in front of the thing and blessed it with the sign of the cross. They walked to the elevators.

30.

He couldn't sleep. Went walking. Walked past the storage joint. Walked back to it. There was just something about the place he liked. The way the loading dock glowed in the light from the guard booth, and the building rose up in the darkness, above it. All full of things that were sleeping-like, because someone was downstairs watching out for them. Like the Italians had guarded Thompson Street every night while he'd dreamed, upstairs.

He walked up the ramp. Crossed the dock to the booth. Smiled at the kid inside.

He put down his book, the kid. Pushed his hair back, came over. "I need ID if you don't have your card," the kid said, hit a key on the computer.

"No, I was wondering," Martin said. "Because . . . I like how you do business here. And I was thinking if my partners and I have a space, but I personally wanted one for myself, what's the chance of there being a confusion, them getting in?"

"To yours? None, man. We couldn't even say you have one if they *ask*."

"If I *had* one," Martin said. "I don't have anything yet to *put* in one. I just like how you do things. Everything's so peaceful here."

"Yeah," the kid said, "I know. It's nice to have a place. A good place to put your stuff. When you finally have something to put."

Martin nodded. "It *is* good."

The kid nodded. Slow and steady. Five in the morning and this all seeming perfectly normal to him. Like the sun would never come up again, or real people come around. The real world would never start over.

"I mean, that's what I was thinking," Martin said. "That's why I asked."

The kid said, "It's good to have your space." And they nodded, a while.

"You know what?" Martin said. "You sold me." He went for his money clip. "You got something near where I am now, with my partners? Around the corner, maybe, or the next aisle over?"

"I'll see"—looked at the computer screen. Hit a key again, and waited. Said, "What's your present unit number?" and got ready to type. His fingers poised. Like Frito, a second, when he sat at the piano to play.

The brunch hostess got married. None of the night girls would take the shifts. He hired Masha Kofman. Arrogant and beautiful she was. Was just a climber, if he really thought about it. Got to him in less than a week, but he guessed he let her. Maybe got to him right at the interview, even.

She was bland in the sack, it turned out.

He kept it just business after that.

"You're out of your *fuck*ing mind," she said, trying to meet his eyes, a second. Like if Fee'd just look at her, he'd stop packing. But he crisscrossed the room again.

"We'll be back in two days. Maybe tomorrow. We've got a *week,* still." Pulled a sweater from the shelf.

"Seven *days,*" she said. "Maybe *less,* we have."

"It's two hours away. Pick up a phone."

"Martin, tell him. Don't go. Not both of you."

"It's two hours away, Penny."

"What are you, in on this together?"

"In on what? It's two hours," he said.

Fee said, "It's two hours. We drive down, Q picks up the money, makes the exchange, it's over. We're loaded."

No pleasure in his voice though. No smiling at all from him today.

A handful of boxer shorts. Some socks. Into the bag.

Had paged him, asked him to come over to help with something. Martin just walking around the neighborhood anyway, unable to sleep. This, though, was bad. Was fucked way up.

She said, "Don't do this."

Fee said, "I'm going out of my head here, Penny. I need to go upstate, walk around in the woods. Smell the grass with my new nose. I'm going nuts. I can't sleep. I keep thinking how everything's going to change after this. Q and I are going to grow apart. Other things. I'm nervous about *every*thing. All the fucking time. I can't sleep—"

"What about me?"

"Go see your mother. It's where you've been for half of our marriage. Or go—"

"Go see *your* mother. You have nerve, accusing me."

"My mother's sick; yours is lonely. There's a difference. But, go see her. Or watch TV, eat everything in the house, like you've been. It's what I always wanted, a fat Sicilian wife."

"I'm leaving," Martin said. Started down the hall.

"I'm coming with you. Look, Penny, I'm packed"—zipped the bag— "I'm packed."

She didn't say anything.

Martin opened the door, held it for Felix. They walked to the elevator.

F ee dropped him at his building to pack. Had to drive out to the club first, get last night's take to deposit it. Would swing back, get him in an hour, pick up some bagels on the way. Martin went upstairs. Walked in, answered the phone. "Is it that fucking Masha?" she said.

"Is what *what*?"

"Felix told me you fucked her. I think he's jealous, for God's sake."

"You're out of control here, Pen. Use your head for a second. The only reason I'm going is to keep an eye on your husband." Who you can fuck anytime you want.

"That's bullshit. It's fucking *bull*shit."

"He's fucking up everything with this. It's *not* bullshit. I can't just let him leave."

"You can, Martin, please. Don't go."

"I have to."

"I'm scared."

"Pen, the only thing I'd do if I was here was keep an eye on Bunny. I'd fucking park across the street and follow him every fucking move, until the . . . presents arrived. God damn it." He sat on the couch. "That's what

I'd be doing if Fee didn't come up with this shit. I don't *like* this. I can't think."

"I'm scared."

"Fuck scared."

"Leave me your key. Tell Felix you forgot your wallet here, and come by again."

"No chance. If the call comes while we're upstate? What, we go down, stop by your place again? First I forgot my wallet, then my keys?"

"Use Felix's."

"Only *I* get the money and *I* pick up the gifts. I put in the least cash, the biggest risk is mine."

As was the money, he'd been feeling, lately. He'd never seen so much in his life. They'd left it to him like "Give it to the poor guy; he wouldn't know what to do with it anyway," and, in some ways, he believed that himself, but he felt like if it was his to protect and transport, it was his to decide how to handle.

Jesus, he *hated* working for other people. He'd paid his dues *twice* over now, but, still, if he was caught with the package he'd get a hundred years if he said he had no partners.

He put his forehead in his hand, said nothing. He had nothing more to say. He just worried about the money. "Nothing happened with Masha, Pen," he told her. Didn't know why. Thought, That was stupid—lying with so much going on.

But she didn't say anything.

"I have to go with him, Penny. He may have asked me as a test. If I let him go, I fail. Things are innocent or calculated. I got to be prepared for both."

They hung up.

He packed a small bag, checked the Glock, took a piss. Answered the phone again. Bunny said, "Good morning. This is your lucky fucking day."

"Where are you?"—no street noise behind him.

"Nothing like that."

"*What,* then."

"Fuck *you*, then; I'll keep it to myself."

"I'm having a bad day, Pasqualito. It's not even ten o'clock. Don't add to it. What's up."

"I accept your apology. So I'll tell you one of the first guys I asked got back to me quick, said a character named Vlady bragged to a dancer that he'd done a hit for somebody. That's why he disappeared for a while. Sound right? With a rifle. Like Oswald did, he fucking told her. The hardest kind to do. The dancer told my guy. You there?"

He'd stopped breathing. He opened his eyes. Didn't realize he'd closed them. "Yeah."

"My guy doesn't know where he is, though. Are you there, or no?"

"It's okay," he said. Sat down again, had to. "It doesn't matter. That's fine."

"Why not? Why don't it matter?"

"It just don't," he said. His voice like someone else's, speaking in the room.

"You know who he works for? You got beef with them?"

"I know some of his people."

"Any riff?"

Fucking his wife. "It's better you don't know."

"Hold on, Irish. Don't do nothing stupid. It's a whore's word. In addition to the fact that you can't do nothing now for a long time. Till after . . . Christmas. And all the presents are exchanged—"

"I know."

"Fucking . . . call me back. I'm going to have some Spaghetti-Os."

"I'm not calling you."

"Nobody actually does that. What you're thinking of. You understand what I'm explaining to you?"

"Never pull the trigger yourself."

"Fine. Exactly. Now I'm getting off this fucking phone. You wait till after Christmas."

They hung up. He sat there. On his new couch. The hole above his head plastered over and repainted, so many months ago. He got up and looked at the window.

Fee'd fired Vlady a few months before the shooting. Looked him up again, then, he guessed. The only thug Fee knew who wasn't connected to the old man anymore. Fee maybe promising him something. Maybe set him up somewhere. In Canada, maybe.

Either way.

No matter.

He looked the new window over. Reckoned with his reflection. Sickening. Fee using one bodyguard against another. One servant against another.

He went out. Jogged to the storage place. Had to cover his interests for a while, bury his treasure, eliminate enemies. Then start over. Once more. You want to make God laugh? he thought—tell him your plans.

He unzipped the duffel, and started figuring his share. About one fifth of what was left. Which was what? How much was *left*? He zipped it up again, moved the whole thing over to his locker. What he had to do wouldn't take long. Fuck Bunny if he didn't understand. He shouldn't come poking around anyway.

*Je*sus, though, wouldn't Bunny be happy to hear there was only one partner left to split with.

Home again. He jogged it, a bit, walked it. Went upstairs and waited. Answered the buzzer and went down. Opened the passenger door to the Pathfinder and looked in at him.

"Throw your shit in the back," Fee said. "I got scallion cream cheese. That all right?" Was smiling. Hadn't been smiling all day.

Fourteen years.

"That's fine."

He threw the bag back. Pulled the jacket around him carefully, got in.

They dropped their shit off at the house. Fee was hungry again. They got back in the truck, went back down the road, to the inn. Pancakes and sausage, Fee ate. And eggs, tomato, toast. Coffee. Juice. Asked the waitress if they served desert now; he'd like to see a menu, he said. Glad to be away, it seemed. Martin had coffee, a sandwich. Fee tossed his napkin on the table when she'd cleared. Stretched his feet into the aisle. Looked like the yuppies' don. Martin thought, A rising star about to fall. "Something on your mind, Fee?"

He looked up, surprised. "Nothing at all. I'm full, finally."

"Why'd you do this? Why'd you come up?"

"To get away. No other reason. Why?"

"Bad timing."

"It's two hours away. You said it yourself."

"Bad timing."

"It's not. You remember Puerto Rico. That was perfect."

"I lost two grand."

"I dropped a few, myself, but you had a good time. We have to en*joy* things now. Everything's going to be different after this." His eyes blurred over.

Worried again we won't be friends for life?

Or maybe scared, still, for real, to defy his old man.

Tell me what's really on your mind, Felix. I have to kill you soon. What's the point in keeping quiet?

"He won't even care about this," Fee said. "It's family. Everything's forgiven, you know?"

"I know."

"I think maybe the thing that could bother him is its being low down. I know you're going to say he's down in it, too, but his deal is for a good cause. He's finally legitimizing his oil interests. All his other money is tied up in the hotels in Canada. He's buying tankers, though. Rigs, refineries. Selling all his shares in the Russian banks and cigarette factories. He wants to disappear into the upper echelons. Let these new Red Godfathers try to run the streets. All these *mafiyatchiks* pouring into Brooklyn every day. He's going to forfeit all their tribute. He wants to change our name again, too, disappear anonymously. He says if these new guys want to be famous, get books written about them? Good, they can read them in jail."

Martin nodded.

Thought how in nine months of slaving on oil rigs, it had never occurred to him that somebody owned them. Somebody *ran* them, and he'd been grateful to that somebody for a job that most men didn't last a week in—he'd been *long;* he'd lasted nine *months*—but somebody owning them? How could you ever put a face on that guy? "What's he going to change your freaking name to?"

"Pashley."

"That's a name?"

"He saw it in a phone book in London."

"You going to change yours?"

"Depends how things go."

"If he forgives your getting rich, you mean."

"Uh-hunh."

"Well, it's family, you said—everything's forgiven."

Fee said, "Uh-hunh." Didn't seem convinced. That was fine. Better he was off-guard.

"How's your mother? They going to get divorced?"

"No, he loves her. This other bitch is just . . . something else. He was twenty the last time he knew her. That's all. It'll pass."

"How is she? Your mother."

"The same. Better. We just wait, now. She's got an excellent chance, they said the other day."

"Good."

"Yeah."

Martin said, "He'll come back. You'll see. Well . . ." shrugged.

"If she lets him," Fee said, "right?"

Martin smiled.

Shoot him outside the house and bury him, he'd been figuring, when they were first driving up. Ditch the car and take the bus back. Say he'd disappeared. *"Left me there. Did you check the money? Go to the storage place?"* But he'd have to do it and then bury him and drive down and just take the cash, he knew now. Couldn't just shoot him and go home. Had to bomb with the whole nine fucking yards. Pick up Penny and go. Murder, rob, and run. Clear the witnesses, come the time.

Which would be right away. Bunny. Monya. Monya no one would care about. And Bunny being dead wouldn't ever be solved. No cop had ever solved a gangster death he'd ever heard of.

There was a movie like that. This guy saying for every person you kill, you had to kill a couple more to stay ahead of it—

"—snuff box?" Fee said.

"What?"

"The Fabergé piece. You know the story behind it?"

"Sunnyside? That night?" The fabric above the passenger-seat window. Burning. In little snaps of flame.

"No. I told you about that. The piece itself. Where my father got it from."

"Uhn-uhn."

"It was my mother's. A wedding gift from some friend of her father's, back in Russia."

Martin nodded, said okay.

"About a year after they're married, my father's got no cash. He's spread out too thin. Like now, with the tankers. But thirty years ago, he's en*tirely* strapped. He can't get his hands on enough to do this certain deal. So he needs a retainer, to keep things open a few more days. He takes the snuff box, gives it to the guy. For collateral. Doesn't tell my mother, though. Said the three days it was gone were the longest in his life. He kept trying to keep her out of the living room because all he could see, with all the shit that they had in there anyway, was this gap on the mantel, where it had been. But he got the cash he needed, finally. Got the piece back and put it over the fireplace again, got richer with the new deal, whatever it was. But, like twenty years later—this is the thing—a new life, and a continent away—my mother picks it up off the piano and says, 'You know, Alexi, I always hated this piece. Why don't you sell it?' And he did. He told me, Sometimes you make decisions alone because you know, instinctually, that the results will benefit everyone. He never questioned his instincts again."

Martin raised an eyebrow. "You think she knew?"

"He's pretty slick; I don't know."

"So you're saying you figure it's okay going against him now."

"I'm just saying you remember how you said he'd be proud?"

"Uh-hunh."

"Well, if he's not, I figure I can throw that story in his face and run like hell while he thinks about it."

Martin said, "Get some sneakers."

Fee smiled, shook his head like it all seemed silly, no?

Martin thought, Yeah, it does.

I still have to kill you.

They didn't talk, driving back. Felix kept yawning. The sunlight bending on the windshield. They walked across the yard and the grass was long, whipped against their shoes. He thought, Get far from the house. Looked at him. Thought, Why'd you only hire Vlady once? Fee said, "I'm going to take a nap. I ate too much."

He nodded. Automatically. Hadn't thought Fee was going to talk, somehow. At all. Had almost forgotten what he sounded like.

Fee said, "You mind? A little refresher? After, we'll do something rural. We'll hike, hunt."

"Hunt?"

"Yeah, go out in the woods, walk around. If we see something, we shoot it." He went down the hall, Fee, closed the door. Martin stood there. Walked into the living room and sat on the couch. Took his jacket off and laid it beside him. Put his head back, looked at the ceiling. Time passed. Memories curved and disappeared in the flatness where he stared, got replaced with others. He closed his eyes but they still came. They whelmed, like waves.

Fee woke him. Was already brewing coffee.

He looked down at himself.

A blanket on him.

He looked next to him but it was gone. Looked around him. Saw it. Draped over the arm of the recliner.

"You must have passed out before me even" Fee calling in from the kitchen. "You've been out four hours."

He sat up. Moved the blanket off. Asked if the call had come, but knew it hadn't. He had to ask, though.

"Nope. Nothing," Fee said. "Just Penny. I was half asleep. I think she hung up on me. I have no idea what I said to her. I called Bunny before I lay down, told him we were two hours away. Said I had to check on the house for my parents, make sure the locals didn't move in."

"The coffee ready?"

"Yeah. If the phone rings, don't answer it. It'll be her."

"What if it's Bunny?"

"I gave him the voice mail for my cellular. The phone I'm keeping off. Come on, have your coffee; we're going to lose the whole day."

He got up, took the jacket off the chair, walked into the dining room. Fee had the rifle in his lap, checking it over, had gotten it from the shed. "You want the shotgun, Q?" It was lying across the table.

"No."

He couldn't even imagine it.

He poured coffee, sipped it. Wondered if he'd have to wash blood off trees. How the fuck you do that?

Fee said, "You ready?"

"Yeah. I have to piss."

"Piss in the woods."

"I have to now."

He did have to. Though nothing came out. He flushed the toilet and took out the Glock. Pulled the slide back softly and felt the rap of the bullet as it jumped into the chamber. Switched the safety off. Set the gun back in the pocket.

Fee unlocked the shed and asked him was he sure he didn't want the repeater, then put it away. Asked if he'd ever told him the time Penny fired it. Martin shook his head, his mouth too dry to talk. "We came up here for the weekend," Fee said. "We were still in school. She was meeting my parents for the first time. So my father, big charmer that he is, asks her does she want to shoot guns. She says sure. So, we go around the back of the house, set up a few cans, he explains everything to her. Demonstrates. He tells her to put on her ear protection, give it a go. 'Okay,' she says, and she takes it from him. We back up. She hefts it. Looks it over. Sights. Exhales. And *bang*, the can disappears. You know what she does?"

Martin shook his head.

"She goes, 'Woo. Direct hit. Did you see that?' and she spins around to look at us. With the gun still aimed. We hit the deck—just *dropped*. My father flops on his belly. It took him ten minutes to get his wind back. She's like 'What? What's the matter?' "

Martin nodded.

"You don't think that's funny?"

"It's funny."

"You're not laughing."

"It's funny."

"I'm glad you think so"—looking his face over, Fee. Said, "Come on, let's hunt something." They walked a few yards. Fee stopped. Said, "I have to ask you something." Turned, but didn't look up. Spoke at the ground. "I'm not sure if I even care, but."

Martin watched him. Took his hand out of his pocket, let it hang. Fee had the rifle by the stock. In his left hand. This wasn't the moment.

"I'm sorry, but . . ."

"What."

"Did you ever sleep with her? When you went out? I guess you did, right?"

The one thing he'd never fucking found out from her, if she'd ever told him.

Fee was looking at him, waiting. Apologized again.

Take a chance—say no. "Too Catholic, no. I tried, though."

Fee looked down. Nodded. "About a month ago—two now, I guess— she told me something. That guy Marco Duomo? From the prom, and the thing with her father? She slept with him. Freaking lost it to him. I can't stop thinking of it. I can't touch her. I haven't been with her since she freaking told me." He looked up.

". . . natural," Martin said. Couldn't get the "that's" out.

"I guess."

"It'll pass."

"I guess."

Still looking at him, Fee. Not mentioning that she'd asked him to kill the guy. Keeping it his own business. Taking those things as they came to him now. Becoming a workaday wiseguy more and more.

Why didn't you try it again, though? Martin thought. Why didn't you hire Vlady to do the work on me again?

Fee smiling. Something else he wanted to say. "How's Masha?"

"The hostess? Okay."

"Yeah?"

"Yeah."

"You still love her."

"*Ma*sha?"

Fee shook his head. "No, not Masha."

"What is it? What's on your mind, Felix?"

Still smiling. Now like it was all just funny to him. "It's okay, Q. I know how it is."

"You don't know; you're being stupid."

"No, my head is clear. I had a deep sleep."

"Your head's a mess. With this Marco thing."

"I'm trying to tell you it's okay. I understand. You love her from twelve years ago."

"You don't—"

"Listen to me. I'm married to her. What you have is just a feeling. Based on something that's not real. It's a crush on something that can't ever even be. I love her, but I'm married to her. Once you have that, it changes."

"You're going to fuck everything up with her, Felix. You're going to *lose* her. And she's a good . . ."—he couldn't think of a word.

She's all. She's perfect.

"I know. She's the best. But you can't understand. I envy you. It'll always be perfect in your memory. Painful, but perfect."

"Fee, I fucking told you—"

"But," he said—"now listen to me—better pain than nothing at all. Believe that. I wish it hurt. I've been thinking about other people lately? Women? You"—he shook his head, Fee—"bag all those hotties at the club. A different one every night. That's not easy to see. It gets to you."

Martin knew it had bothered him. Guessed, now, it was half the reason he'd done it so long. Was the reason he'd had to screw that Masha, definitely. He'd *seen* Fee looking at her right from the start, at the interview—Fee'd been speechless.

"And that fucking Masha Kofman, Q," saying now—"Jesus Christ. She's a piece of work."

"She's a bitch, Fee."

"I like that, though."

"So go for her."

"You just told me to hold on to my marriage."

"I'm saying anything right now."

He nodded, Fee. Said, "Yeah. I'm sorry." Looked down, jounced the rifle. Prepared to go, again. "Any more advice?"

"Uhn-uhn."

"You want to go?"

"Uh-hunh."

"Okay," and started walking.

Martin thought, What the *fuck*? and watched him. Followed him. Thought, Why, then? Why'd you do it? Because you *did* do it. And now *I* have to. *Will.* A fucking . . . mob guy *will.*

They walked, the woods snapping where they stepped.

They ducked branches, went deeper, the light from the clearing of the house disappearing, all around them green soon and a silence beyond that. Martin watched him, watched his head. The bounce of his walking. The thick hair that she loved. Thought, What, you felt bad after, Fee, because Vlady fucked it up? Shot the wrong fucking Quinn? The fates fucked with *your* brother, then they fucked with mine. That was enough? You quit tempting them?

Or did you *want* him to shoot Frito? he thought. Make me need you as much as you need me. Two best friends with dead brothers?

And why use Vlady, man? *God,* he thought—the insult. You know I *hate* that motherfucker.

Fee's head rose . . . fell . . . rose . . .

Martin took out the piece, kept it behind him, arm stretching down. Slipped his finger in the trigger guard. Fee's head up, down. On the downstep, he'd shoot him. Like a march.

Answer me. Shoot you in the stomach, I should. Let you writhe, beg me to save you or kill you. Make you tell me why. I had to hear it from someone who hears it from a whore?

"—you hear me?" Fee said. Had been speaking.

"What?"

"It wasn't the Italians."

What?

The what? "What wasn't?"

"Who shot Frito."

They stopped. Had the rifle hanging lax, Fee. Turned. Saw the Glock. "You going to shoot a moving target with a pistol, Annie Oakley?"

"What?"

His eyes falling, though, Fee. More apology in him, still. "It was Vlady," he said. Martin's heart going so hard his hands jumped, jumped. He looked up, Fee. "I'm sorry, man." Eyes steady. "I'm so sorry."

Martin shook his head. Or didn't. Maybe flinched. He didn't get this.

Shoot him. In the stomach. He'll talk. He'll beg to die.

"He bragged to one of the dancers," Fee saying. "He was screwing her, a while back. She told me, a couple of days ago. Said people were asking about it, all of a sudden, and she was scared. We never found out who it was before because *you* said we shouldn't ask. You said to wait till the cops were gone. But then you never brought it *up* again. There had to be a reason you kept it quiet, so I didn't press it. Brothers are strange with each other. They're *strange,* man. I thought maybe you *knew* who shot him, or something. I minded my business. But when people started asking, the girl came to me. She wanted protection. Vlady hated you, man. You should have given him his gun back."

Martin looked at him.

Are you serious?

Fee smiled. Tried to. "It was probably all he wanted to shoot you for. And for pimp-slapping him, of course. Calling him 'asshole.'"

Martin looked at him. Couldn't think of what . . . But did see it. The possibility. Vlady deciding to come back at him, gutter-level, then fucking up and moving on. A thug giving his best shot at something, but blowing it. A dozen guys in the neighborhood had stories like that. Nothing even out of the ordinary, really.

Fee frowned. "I don't mean that, of course. I never should have kept him around. I just . . . I'm trying to tell you I'm sorry and you don't have to worry. Because he's dead"—looked down. Looked up—"I killed him"—stared, a moment. Then blinked. "I found out where he was. I went to see him. The dancer said he told her someone had hired him for a hit, so I asked him flat out. Said I just wanted to know what gun he used. If it had been one of ours. That I didn't care about anything else. Who it was, or when, or where, or the money. I didn't want to know. That was his business. But he denied it. Flat out. Plus he was scared. I just knew."

"You . . ."

"What."

"You should have told me. You should have let me."

"I felt terri—"

"You should have *let* me"—the only strength he had left, in his throat.

But he'd have the rest back soon, he knew. Because his lungs were filling up again full, already. His heart beating hard, regular.

Fee said, "I was ashamed, man. He'd been on my payroll once. I was responsible." Like, Can't you see that? his voice saying. Where a week ago it would have cracked. And he probably would have cried.

Different now, Martin understood. Ahead. Way ahead now, his Felix was. Just like that. Broke his cherry. Made his bones.

Or, was full of shit.

Do I care? he asked himself. Do you care, Martin Quinn?

No.

I don't.

If he tried to kill me, I just tried to kill him. We're square. If he can let his beefs go, I can. Shit, I already have.

He looked at the ground, and at the Glock. Raised it, pointed it at the woods, held it there. For a second, thought to turn it on him. But it was true. Nothing else made sense. He would always be loyal, Felix. You're not going to kill him. "Jesus, Fee, that's why you fucking came up here?"

"I was freaking out, man."

"Could your timing be worse? You know what kind of money we left down there?"

"I have more. You don't—I know that—but I'll always spot you. You think Bunny would take the stake money?"

"No. The plan he's got in mind, he needs millions; he'll never settle for thousands again."

He kept the gun out there. Pointing at everything, nothing. His vision blurred. The woods were getting dark.

Fee waited.

He switched the safety on with his thumb, brought the gun down.

three

They asked what they could, he and Davis, got the answers they expected, and read over the pages again quickly, asked for a minute to talk once more. Davis telling him nothing else then that he didn't already know. "Just give me your pen, counselor"—held out a hand for it. "I wish they'd sent Ferguson himself."

Davis said, "He's the US attorney; he's busy."

"This guy's a dickhead, though."

Davis took the pen out from his jacket, gave it over.

Martin said, "It hurts my self-esteem." Walked back to the table. "Here?"

"By all the Xs," the dickhead fed prosecutor said. "All six pages."

He signed. Flipped the page and signed. Looked up at Corso and Dolan, and smiled. "So, I'm through with you two?" Flipped another page. Found the Xs. Signed.

"Soon."

"How soon?"

"Tomorrow."

"Good. Then I get moved?"

"Yup."

"Fine. Send a woman, this time."

"A what?"

"A woman. A female. You know any?"

"An agent?"

"Yeah. I'll tell it better to a woman. You guys make me want to never open my mouth again. A fed female who doesn't smoke. I'm sick of going to take a piss and finding this one's butts floating around."

Dolan smiled. Pulled a chair out from the table and sat, and lit one. Exhaled, and smiled harder. The first time Martin had seen him pleased. Even with all the time in front of the television.

The lawyer left.

Corso got on the phone.

"Well, this is it, then," Davis said. Had an awkwardness to him. In his eyes. Slight squint. We're not exactly friends, Martin thought—it's true. Davis said, "I'll keep in touch, when they let me."

"Yeah, keep an eye on the papers"—and dropped back on the couch. Davis stood there, out before him.

"You should count on—"

"You put your briefcase next to a blank pad," Martin said.

"Excuse me?"

"Your briefcase"—kept his voice level—"on your left"—Davis didn't look—"is next to that blank yellow pad. I think it's yours. So take it when you go."

He frowned a bit, Davis. Said all right.

"It's cool," Martin said. "I promise."

"Okay."

"What were you saying?"

"No, nothing. Just count on this next part taking at least a year. But you know that."

"I know that."

"Yes."

"Yup," Martin said, and stood up again, put out his hand, thanked him. "Be good, counselor."

Davis said he would. Nodded. Said, "Yes. You, too. You're going to help a lot here. You're going to get a lot of bad people off the street."

"That's right. A bunch of no-good-niks."

Opened his briefcase and put the pad in, Davis. Went to the door. Waited for Dolan to let him out. And was gone.

Corso got off the phone. Martin spoke from the couch—"So, you're done with this case?"

"For a while. Debriefed up front, then more later, when the trials start."

"They going to give you a medal? A raise? No, right?"

"This is the job. You're looking at it."

"You want to lock somebody up?"

"Who?"

"A heavy. A gorilla. Russian. Someone Ferguson won't give a shit about."

"A hitter?"

"I guess."

"That Ferguson wouldn't want? Why won't he?"

" 'Cause it's just a shooting I know about. That shook up a lot of rich people in a rich neighborhood. But if you trail him a week, guaranteed he'll be doing something wrong. The cops are clueless. They think he's MIA, or K. But he's probably in Canada. And that makes it definitely federal, right?"

"Maybe."

"But you got to do something for me."

"No shit."

"I need to see somebody. In private."

"That list on the table over there—you really know all of them?" Corso said. "Like you told that fool lawyer you did?"

"Some better than others."

"The person you want to see on that list?"

"Shouldn't be."

"But they are?"

"Not for long. Totally uninvolved."

"Penelope Pasko?"

"That's right."

Corso nodded. Said, "Okay. Maybe."

"You'll set it up?"

"When?"

"Now. You're done tomorrow, no?"

"What do you think, Kevin?"

"Love to meet her," Dolan said.

Martin stood up, walked to the phone.

"Hold on," Corso said. "The toughguy?"

"I have to know if I can set it up first."

"Just bring her here."

"What are you, serious? She lives next door to Felix's old man; she'd never do it."

"Then what, you want to meet her in a supermarket? A ladies' room in a movie theater? What?"

"You guys really work like that?"

"Where?" Corso said.

"Near her mother's house. In Westchester."

Thought about it, a second, Corso. Said, "Okay, that's fine. It's probably perfect, in fact."

Martin called her cellular. When he told her it was him she didn't talk.

He'd said it was "Martin Quinn," which was over the top, but he let it go. Had to. Said, "I'm in federal custody. Protected. Are you okay?"

Nothing.

"I didn't kill him."

Still.

"I'm sorry."

He couldn't say her name.

Corso walked away.

He forced it, spoke it mechanically—"Penelope."

"What happened," she said.

"Terry Hughes. A guy I've probably told you about, from when I was a kid. Followed us upstate. He shot me. And Fee. Then I shot him. I don't know why yet. Why he came. You still there?"

Silence.

"Hello?"

"Yes."

"I have to speak to you about some things, though. Find out if anything happened while we were away. That's all. Anything you might have noticed."

"Martin—"

"Not over the phone. Because you're innocent they're going to let me talk to you in private. Turns out they're human beings, these guys."

She was quiet.

He let her be.

"When?"

"Tomorrow, if you can? Can you go up to your mother's?"

"I'm there now."

"Even better. Meet me at that park? That little lake there? In the morning? Nine?"

"Fine."

"Are you still smoking?" he said. Tried to laugh.

"What?"

"Good. Bring your cigarettes. We'll relax and talk. Okay?"

He let her understand.

"Okay."

"How are you. You all right? You holding up?"

"Uh-hunh." Flat. Wary.

"Good. Tomorrow at nine."

H e'd heard about cons keeping razor blades in their cheeks twenty-four hours a day. Cut little pouches in the walls of wet flesh, and stored them. Between his cheek and bottom gum was the best he could do. He looked in the mirror and mouthed different phrases, practicing. Slid it back with his tongue, every ten words or so. Was glad it was only a small, padlock key.

He'd turned his wallet and the rest of the key ring over to them. Turned out his pockets. Taken off his shoes. "Let's go," Corso yelled in. "You know what the traffic's going to be like? Come on." He flushed the toilet, ran the faucet. Stepped out. Again, Dolan patted him down. Chest and pits, and down his body. In the beltline with the fingers. Then the pockets, front and back. The crotch. The crack of his ass. His thighs and calves and ankles. And once more up the socks.

He stepped into the shoes. He bent, tied them. Corso handed him the officer's sweater and the flight jacket. He put them on; then ran his fingers through his hair, above the bandage, carefully. Corso watched him. Said, "You're fucking her. No doubt in my mind, now."

"Cuffs?" Martin said.

"In front."

"Bless your Eye-talian heart." Put his hands out. Asked if they could take them off when he talked to her.

Corso shook his head.

Martin said, "It'll traumatize her."

"That's too bad"—not looking up. Closed the left one—"She shouldn't have married a gangster."

"He was a law student when he asked her."

"Whatever"—closed the right one. "Still no."

"You'll see. You'll get a look at her. You'll take them off."

He sat alone in the back. Corso pulled the LTD around the hangar, and Martin saw them, up ahead, in the distance. Clean, cold steel, tilting, a bit, in the sunlight. He said, "There they are." He leaned between the seats to see them clearly through the windshield.

"What?" Corso said.

"The Twin Towers. That's New York to me, right there. When I was a kid, real little, they were building them, and my old man used to take me down and put me on his shoulders so I could see the foundation. The holes. These two big fucking caverns, going down. A hundred feet, supposedly. You remember it, right?"

"Vaguely."

"What about you, youngster? You were still in Oklahoma, I guess. Were you even born yet?" Corso smiled. Dolan didn't answer. Didn't correct him on the state. "Yeah, we went to France for about a year, and when we got back, there was this fucking building. Like only a quarter of the way

done, but the steelwork going just up. Up, up. We came back and my parents were like, Do you remember New York? But I only did because of the
towers. Connected them with the holes. Being on the old man's shoulders."

"What were you doing in France?"

"My father was a musician. John Quinn. You never heard of him, I'm
sure. He cut an album and it did well over there. So we went and stayed a
while. My brother was conceived in Par-ie."

Married the accent, he thought. Probably heard it in the womb.

"The one that got shot?"

"Uh-hunh."

"Any more? No, right?"

"Just him. Christopher."

"And the old man?"

"Dead. Something in his heart. He was born with it."

"Passed down?"

"Congenital? No."

"Good, we wouldn't want you dropping off."

"Like your Sicilian hit man."

"You got it."

"No, I'm a horse," Martin said, and kept looking around. "What's with
this nature preserve?" He watched it pass. Grassland, some trees. It looked
soaked, still. Had looked that way when they'd driven in.

"How should I know?"

"I bet there's a dozen bodies buried in there. You should pick up a
shovel while we're out."

He thought of Vlady. Wondered where he was rotting. Somewhere
upstate, he guessed. Fee working fast but smart. A few hours out of a normal day, if you planned it right.

Fee was in the ground somewhere, now, too. And Terry Hughes. Resting in peace. Two young men in repose.

"So this is your little field trip," Corso said. "Like I promised. Enjoy the
sights."

"You ever find out who Floyd Bennett was?" he said.

"Yeah, matter of fact. He's the patron saint of stool pigeons. Ironic, no?"

"Yeah, that's funny." He sat back in the seat.

"Aw, you can dish it out, hunh?"

"I can take it."

"Sure you can."

And he could. It was going to be easier than Corso could know. "What kind of kid were you, Corso?"

"Me?"

"What were you like?"

"I was fine. Decent enough."

"You get your ass kicked around, in the schoolyard there?"

"At Holy Name School? I ran it."

"What about you, youngster? Good SATs? Captain of the football team?"

"Lacrosse," Dolan said.

"La-what?"

No answer.

"They let you smoke on the sidelines?"

"That's right."

" 'That's right'? Good one, man. Yeah, I was a good kid. They want you to be a priest, Corso? The nuns and them?"

"Of course."

"Me, too. When I was in college, for a while I thought about being a lawyer? Then I read this article that said there'd be a million of them in the country by the year two thousand."

"So you turned to crime? That's tragic."

"Did I say that? You know, you think you got all the answers, and you got like two. My whole life, once we got back to New York when I was a kid, everywhere I looked, there was Mafia. Downstairs from my house. High school. I met Felix in a fucking *high* school. On Park *Av*enue. I didn't even know there was a Russian Mafia."

He thought, Even Penny was connected.

Then they'd all stuck together.

They were the only kind of people that they knew how to know. To trust.

"I'll bet you feel like you run into cops all the time, right, Corso? Look around in a crowd, Christmas shopping, you spot one on his day off. Acting like a father, a husband. But you know he's one. It's the same thing with wiseguys."

"Except we can spot both."

"You think I can't? Please," he said, realizing how stupid it was, even while he said it. Considering the circumstances.

"How those cuffs feel?" Corso said. "Can you spot *them?*"

"You going to tell me ever, why you were following us?"

"You going to tell me why you shot two people?"

"You know"—he leaned forward again—Corso didn't look at him—"I got a problem with that. I got to say. If you really think I'm a cold-blooded killer, and you sit there—"

"We've discussed this—"

"—and you *sit* there, talk to me every day—"

"That's *business,* son. How many killers you know, you dealt with every day?"

"But you're going to cut me loose, practically. I'm saying, for the sake of argument, if I *had* killed them, I'd feel I shouldn't go free."

"Supply and demand," Corso said.

"What's that mean, how we're talking about things?"

"Everything has a price."

Martin leaned back. Looked at him, a moment—bit of profile watching the road. Fucking guy has a conscience, he thought. Inside of that rock head. "So you *do* feel wrong. Well, then, you deserve to know the truth. I didn't do it."

"Funny guy," Corso said. "I don't feel wrong. Just underinformed."

"Soon you'll get all the details? Then you'll feel wrong?"

"Then I'll have all the details. Tell me this—is the heroin still on the way?"

"What heroin?"

"Is it, or no? You going to stop doing the right thing *now*?"

Martin smiled. Said, "Finished, I got to figure. 'Deal canceled,' like."

"No package on the way?"

"Not yet. It takes months. You know that."

"Where was it from?"

"You don't know? Tough shit. Ask Ferguson, a month from now."

"How are those cuffs?" Corso said, looked in the rearview.

"Is that a deal?" Martin said.

He looked back at his driving. "Let me check out the area when we get there."

Which would be fine. It was no risk, Corso'd see. A little lake and some trees. One road going in and leading out. "It was coming from Vietnam," Martin said. "How long were you on us? A week? A month? Not too long, right?"

"You want to know where you fucked up?"

"One name on that list that that dick lawyer brought doesn't fit. That P.R., Crazyhorse. Never been to Anastasia's, no connection to me except something from back before all of this. Am I right? He's a coke dealer? Crack, probably, and other shit? I saw Terry Hughes punch all his teeth out once. That's it, no?"

Dolan looked at Corso. Corso saw it. Didn't like his tell. Dolan looked back out the window. "I got him from a guy in Treasury," Corso said. "They had a shit case for swag fives and tens, but they knew he was real dirty, so they gave him to us."

Martin shook his head. "This would have gone a lot fucking smoother if you'd just grabbed Terry Hughes," he said.

"He was the cleanest of all of you, those few weeks we tailed you."

"He was an arch criminal."

"Then you did the state a favor."

He didn't feel like talking anymore; that was it. He looked out the window.

Wanted to ask Corso if *he'd* ever killed someone. If he knew it caused a stench in your head that you could smell, but no one else could. And wouldn't ever go away, probably. He was becoming pretty sure of that.

His reflection eyed him back, in the window. He saw Felix, too. Eyes frightened, the blood pooling out around his face. "And that fucking print is Terry's, I assume, from my Glock? Right? That's the reason you haven't brought it up. Your lab guys have got it for going on a week."

Terry's Sig had had partials all over it, Davis had already told him. Terry hadn't been counting on anyone ever checking it so carefully. He'd set things up too nice.

"Yeah, it probably is Hughes's," Corso said. " 'Eighty-five percent certainty' they're saying. So, you showed him the gun one day. Big deal. You'll still lose in court, if we want you to."

"Yeah, you been saying." He closed his eyes. He'd only do two years at *most,* now, he knew. They had *noth*ing on him. "But you still don't believe me, right? That I didn't kill him?" He opened them, looked at Corso again.

"I'm going to wait till I see the wife," Corso said.

They went across on Houston Street. Martin looked out at it. They passed Thompson Street, Saint Anthony's, Sullivan Street. Went up Bedford to Hudson. He didn't bother looking back. "You think I can get some things from my apartment before they move me?"

"I doubt it. If someone's watching it, they could tail who we sent."

"Too bad."

He'd asked just out of restlessness, he knew, though. Curiosity. Everything he needed was right where he wanted it. He grazed his tongue along the edge of the key.

Davis had the letter that he'd tucked in the yellow pad and would get it to Juliet's mother at the UN. Frito would have it in a week. Should have apologized to Juliet in it, he thought, for making her interrupt her studies. But it would always be tough-going with her, he guessed. Got to get a new car, he thought. Realized his mind was hopping around like mad, he was getting so nervous. "What's going to happen to my car?"

"Auction, probably. What is it? I don't remember. Maybe I'll buy it."

"Gran Fury."

"A Plymouth? That's fucking old Bureau issue. I'm still trying to forget them."

"Good shape, though. New engine, new everything. I was going to do the interior next. *Ev*erything inside. Now some fucking sixteen-year-old from Long Island's going to drive it. All souped-up for him already. His first wheels. 'Thanks, Daddy.' "

He slid the key back down with his tongue. Had nearly spit it out on "Thanks."

They went up the Henry Hudson. He watched the boats.

Corso said, "Let me ask you something."

He listened.

"You told me upstate that you went out hunting."

"Uh-hunh."

"Pasko's prints were on the rifle and the shotgun in the shed. No GSR on him, but his prints on both. But there were none of yours on anything but the Glock."

Fee's prints on the hot-pink watering can, too, he thought. "No interest in hunting."

"But Pasko—explain this—was wearing a cashmere turtleneck and four-hundred-dollar shoes."

He smiled.

"Explain *that*."

"I can't."

Though he could.

"We go out, walk in the woods. If we see something, we shoot it."

The only way to fly.

He watched the Hudson. Choppy and thick-looking, deep.

On the Cross County, the phone buzzed. Dolan answered it. Listened a minute, said, "Tell Paul," and handed the phone over.

Corso listened. Dolan lit up a cigarette, cracked the window an inch. Corso said, "Thank you," and hung up. "You can scratch Rocco DiNabrega off the list. Two in the grape, from behind, getting in his car. The garage on Grand and Sullivan. No witnesses."

Martin looked back out the window. One word filled his mind. One face. Bunny.

It had just been a matter of time. Making the moves now, all at once, to take back the empire. What did Terry say? Nobody stays in power that long?

They pulled off at the Bronxville Road exit. He gave the directions. Wondered if Bunny had done it himself despite his warning that night on the phone about taking care of murders alone. But it didn't matter. Only one thing could have pushed Bunny to take the chance he did in the first place. Driven him over the edge just long enough. He hadn't found the money.

He sat in the car with Corso. Dolan patted her down, checked her mother's Buick. She stood away from it, didn't watch him, looked around at things. Was wearing the leather jacket. Had the sleeves rolled up. Like a high school girl in her old man's blazer. She'd worn it going up to her mother's from his apartment, one morning, when it rained; he'd forgotten.

He watched her. She didn't look over. Not once since the first time, when they'd pulled up. She stood with her hands crossed in front of her. Like her mother, he guessed.

Dolan came back, got in. Corso went out to talk to her. She paid close attention—respectful. Nodded. Nodded. Answered like, Yes, she understood—her eyes on Corso's. Close attention. The car filled with the stink of smoke. He tried his window. Child-locked. Asked Dolan to crack it. "All the way, this time, please?"

He dropped it, a bit, Dolan.

Penny nodded. Nodded.

He couldn't watch anymore. He said, "Dolan, listen, can you hear me all right?"

"I'm sitting right here."

"Seamus and Seaneen are two famous thieves, and they break out of jail and head for cover in the country, but they need some money, so they hide in the bushes. And here comes Paddy, a farmer, leading his donkey. Seaneen says to Seamus, 'Watch, now, how I steal this simpleton's ass. Follow me.' And he goes up and slips off the rope that Paddy's leading the donkey with, puts his own head in it while staying in step, waits till Seamus has the donkey out of sight and then halts. Paddy turns, says, 'Who in Heaven's name are you?' and Seaneen says, 'Sir, I am your donkey. But it wasn't always so. You see, I used to drink and come home late. And one night my mother tried to throw me out, so I beat her with a stick, and she prayed to God for vengeance, and I became the donkey you've owned all this time. I guess today she prayed for God's mercy.' Paddy says, 'Sir, there's no denying God's will, but please forgive me for any harsh treatment you've received through the years,' and Seaneen shakes his hand, and they go their separate ways. Paddy goes home and tells his wife what happened, and she cries and says, 'God's going to get us for treating a fellow soul with such brutality, Pat,' and she and Paddy pray. But, then, after a day or two, she says, 'You know, Pat, I think it's time you got another donkey, went back to work,' so Paddy goes to the market and checks the animals for sale. And all of a sudden he sees that his old donkey is one of them. He looks the thing over, up close, to be absolutely sure. And it's it. It's his donkey. He can't believe it. He says to it, 'So . . . Drinking and beating your mother again, eh? Well, if you think I'm buying you a second time, you're crazy.' "

Dolan tried not to laugh. But his head bobbed, a bit, where he was looking out his window. Martin sat back. Satisfied. Sat up again, looked out. Saw Corso pointing down the hill to the bench, asking her something. Maybe *Was it all right?* She nodded, walked down, Corso coming back. Opened Martin's door. Martin ducked out and stood up before him, was blocked from her view, if she turned around.

"She's a good girl," Martin said. Corso watching his eyes. Looking mean-fucking-serious.

"I'm going to tell you something, and I want you to listen. I'm doing all this, as they say, to make you a better witness. I will shoot both of you, though. Fill out a two-page report. Don't make me."

"You got it."

"Yes?"

Martin nodded. Brought his hands up, waist-level.

Corso eyed him for another long second, took out his keys. "You sit on that bench. At the end of it. Her on the other end. I want you sitting. I'll be standing close, by that tree there."

Martin looked past him. "That tree right next to it?"

"The other one. On your right."

Maybe twenty feet back from the bench, it was. He said, "You didn't threaten her at all, did you? Scare her at all?"

"No."

"Otherwise she'd never say a word to me."

"That's why I'm doing *this*"—he jangled the keys. "Don't fuck yourself up, Quinn. You come through this right, you and her hook up somewhere down the line."

"Still don't believe me."

"Even less, now. *I'd* kill for her." He put the cuffs away. Stepped aside. Watched him. Said, "Go."

Martin went. Kept his eyes on her back. Heard Corso coming down the hill, keeping his distance, going to stand where he said he would. She turned, looked at him. He sat. Said hi.

"Hi."

They angled their bodies toward each other, polite. "They know nothing," he said. She nodded. Like he'd asked how she was doing. "You have to do most of the talking," he said. "Just say bullshit if you want. Like I'm asking you questions. You bring your cigarettes?"

She said yes. Didn't go for them. Following his lead, and staying cool. The fear inside her reigned in, but was there in her eyes. Coming off like innocence.

Christ, he was happy to see her.

"I'll tell you when to light one," he said. "Just talk." His heart already going. Had started up coming down the hill. He'd have to do it soon.

"You look so pale—" she said.

"Not about that," he said. "Get that look off your face, please. Talk."

"Frito . . ."

"Uh-hunh, talk."

"Called me. And said you were okay. The papers said you were being held. That you'd been stabbed in court. Were in a coma."

"I know. I saw them. I'm fine."

She nodded. Was letting him play it.

It would all be clear to her in a minute, he reminded himself.

She said, "We had the funeral."

"I have the key to the locker."

She started to squint. Stopped immediately. Sniffled.

"It's in my mouth. Different number now . . . 821."

"You . . ." she stopped herself.

"Talk please, Penny . . . Please."

But she shook her head.

He'd thought he might have to explain it. Really didn't want to, but.

He said, "When we went upstate, Terry followed us. To kill us. On Bunny's order. I think that's Bunny's game. Only one that he plays, apparently—get everyone to ante up, then try to steal the pot. I think he once did it to his own cousin, Carlo. He's going to live his life pulling in short money, I guess, but I'm not mad at him. That's the truth. I'm alive; you're alive; the dough's safe. I did blame him at first. Then I blamed the whole way I grew up. But I realized the other night that the only thing making me sad, and *mad,* was Felix. His being there was Lexi's fault. Lexi pushed us, all our lives, and that's fucking evil. Felix never should have lived this way."

"But when did you—"

"With *these* guys," he said—"in the suits—I told them there's a hundred guys I could give them, and a thousand leads, so I'm immune to prosecution for now, but I only told them that so they would let me see you. I'm only giving them Lexi, though. The rest I'm sending them goosechasing. So I might be in custody a year. Maybe two. Just because I pissed them off. And Rocco's dead, by the way. So you're all filled in. Now it's your turn, for real. Tell me something. You're filled-in." He knew it was a lot to process. He smiled, tried to be encouraging.

"My mother got a new fucking satellite dish," she said, "and she's planting rhododendrons." He looked away, didn't want to even smile. She was such a trouper. "Pink, white," she said. "Everyone in Westchester has them. What happened to Rocco?"

"Bunny." He looked back at her.

"Big bushes," she said. "She's got me carrying them, and dropping them in the holes I dig."

He winked. Knew it was hard for her not to just fire her own questions back. "Never give up," he said. "Eight twenty-one." He gave her another second. Then, "Tell me more."

She thought, a moment, said, "We had the funeral. I saw people I hadn't seen in years. From college. My sorority. They'd all read the papers, I guess, but no one would ask me anything. I could hear them whispering in the back. It was so awkward." She looked down. "It was humiliating actual—"

He held up his hand, to excuse himself. Faked a good, deep cough.

And it fucking *hurt*. Jesus *Christ*. All throughout him. He hadn't counted on that.

He opened his eyes, looked over himself. He'd wrapped a forearm across his torso unconsciously. He leaned, spit the key in the grass, between them, at their feet.

"Eight twenty-one," he said. "Go ahead."

"Are you okay?"

"I'm fine. Go ahead. Do you see it?"

She nodded. Didn't look. "They . . . wouldn't ask me about him," she said. "Because the papers talked about the club. And Terry Hughes's connections to—"

"You're going to have to be careful when you go to the storage joint. Do you have a little cousin you could send in, or something?"

She looked at him. Said, "I can do it."

"*They* wouldn't be at risk; *you* would. Wait a couple of blocks away—"

"I can *do* it." Angry suddenly.

At the interruptions, maybe.

Or his weakness.

His fucking ribs were killing him, though. It was embarrassing. "You're going to have to keep an eye out for Bunny. *While* you send someone in—"

"She's also redoing the patio," she said. "Doesn't like the terra-cotta anymore." Her eyes flat.

"Take out a cigarette, and drop your lighter," he said. "Get the key. Put it in the pack."

"She's going to go with marble," she said, and took them out. Smiled weakly past his shoulder. At Corso. Held the cigarettes up. Nodded thank you. "I think he put his hand on his gun," she said.

"I'm sorry. I didn't think of it."

"Uh-hunh." She put one in her lips. Fumbled the lighter and watched it go off her thigh, land in the grass. "Imported. From Ravenna." She stretched her foot out and dragged it back, bent and grabbed them both. Brushed her hair off her face, lit the cig. Put the lighter away.

"In the pack," he said.

She turned her head, a moment, and moved her hair again. Off from her mouth. Brushed her lip.

"Don't keep it in your pocket—they're going to frisk you again."

She stared at him, a long second. Took a drag and blew it out. She didn't inhale.

It was in her mouth.

"You still have to inhale," he said.

She crossed her hands on her lap. Waited for him to say something while she adjusted the key.

He continued. "In a while—a year or two, at the most—they'll cut me loose, and I'll contact you. Give some of the money to my mother and Frito, and hold the rest. As much as you can. I got a letter to them. They'll get in touch with you. Then, in a while"—he used it again, the phrase. Didn't like how it sounded. Unsure, out of power—"we'll be all right," he said. "We'll be together. You should smoke that thing." She kept it where it was. He said, "Okay? It's clear?"

She crossed her legs and looked at the lake. Let the cigarette burn.

"Okay?"

"That's your plan."

"Yeah, why? You got one?"

"Send some little cousin in to steal Mafia money."

"Pen," he said. "That's near a million bills you got in there." He nodded, at her mouth. Which was clenched too tight. But she was disturbed over this. And sad, of course. She'd get past it with time, though, he knew. "It comes with risk," he said.

She didn't look at him.

"You *know* that," he said. "Please don't fucking sit that way. And look at me, please. This isn't the kind of talk we should be having."

"I parked across from Bunny's when you two drove upstate," she said. "I used my mother's car."

He said, "Okay." Thought, Not a bad idea. "What happened? Can you look at me? What did you see?"

"He saw me." Took another drag. Just into her mouth. Blew it out. Looked at him.

He didn't breathe.

"Keep your face straight," she said. Flicked the ash. "He got suspicious. We went to the storage place."

O God, he thought. Jesus Christ. They hurt her.

He looked for signs in her face, but it was clear.

"He threatened me."

"He did something to you?"

"No, he didn't."

He looked, careful, in her eyes. Saw there was something that she wasn't saying. "Do you swear?"

"We were standing there, and the locker was empty," she said. "Do you understand that?"

"Yes."

"Do you?"

"Yes."

"All the money was gone, Martin. *You* did that to me. You *moved* it." He closed his eyes. "Look at me," she said. "I thought you'd *stole*n it, for God's sake. God damn it, Martin, look at me."

So it was half his fault. Terry'd tailed them, and Bunny'd found the locker clean, called Terry up and told him to work. Found it empty and pressed the gun to the base of her skull. Called Terry right there, from his cellular phone. Wouldn't leave time to make another mistake.

Half my fault.

A third. She'd been sloppy, Pen.

Poor Pen.

"Look at me," she said.

He did. But couldn't say it to her eyes. "I'm sorry," he said, looking past her. Said it again—"I'm sorry, Penelope."

She just stared at him, though. Dead on. He could feel it. Maybe to say something else? Or she was done? Had made her point?

He didn't know.

But why would Terry shoot them? he thought. Without having the money? Why would Bunny say to kill them? "Penny?" He kept his eyes past her. "I have to take your word, that he didn't hurt you. But did you hear what he told Terry when he called him?"

"What?"

"When you found the locker empty."

She turned away.

These details didn't matter to her. He had to know, though. "Did you happen to hear what he said to him. I'm sorry to ask."

"No."

"No, you didn't *hear*? But he did call him, right? On the spot. I'm right about that."

"It was your idea I watch him," she said.

He looked at her. And waited. She finally turned again. "What?" he said.

"It was *your* idea. You said I should follow him everywhere. That's what *you* would do, you said."

"I did?"

"You going to say you don't remember?"

"I . . . Jesus . . . I'm sorry," he said.

He understood now. He got it. They *had* beaten her.

"Don't," she said.

"I . . ." His throat was clenching. He'd cry if he couldn't talk.

"Don't," she said.

"We'll get through this. Maybe two years. It sounds like a lot, but we've waited longer."

She took the cigarette up and drew on it. Breathed the drag in this time.

Exhaled. Had something else to say, he saw. He tried to breathe. And wasn't going to cry.

"I waited in the window," she said, "the night you came. My en*gage*-ment party. I watched you walk down the block. You hadn't changed. You were better. You were a man suddenly, coming down the street. I'd changed, and you'd changed with me. I waited in the room, because I knew you were in the house, and I couldn't breathe. I waited until I knew he would come in and get me, and I couldn't face that, so I came outside. I talked so I would make myself breathe. I pretended I didn't know you were standing there."

He had known that. Something inside him that was smarter than hope. She'd walked in the room and gone straight to her friends, and he had known it was bullshit. "It's two years, Pen."

"When you left . . . when my father died . . ."

"I'm sorry," he said.

"No, not that." She laughed. A blunt, ugly sound. Disgusted. "Not *nearly* that anymore." She took a good drag. And he knew what it was she was going to tell him, now. The secret he guessed all men wondered if their women were keeping. He didn't look away from her, though. He could give her that much. Look her right in the face . . .

"I was pregnant," she said.

He heard the words. Didn't think they'd get inside him, because he expected them—"I'm sorry," he said.

"I had to do the unthinkable—"

"I'm sorry—"

"And I loved you. And would have kept . . ." She stopped.

He repeated himself.

"No more. Don't say it again."

He looked down.

A child, he thought. Ten years ago. How would it be? Fair, like us? And happy?

Or would it be sad. Some children were sad.

"I parked across from Bunny's," she said. "And I waited. I'd driven there trembling because you'd left me. I parked the car and took out my phone and started calling you, and then, after a while, it all just exhausted me, and I was about to hang up, and then Fee answered, of course. When I really had nothing to say. Still, I nearly begged him to come back, just hearing his voice. And, then, all of a sudden, I hung up on him. Because I'd gotten an image of something. My mother, when my father didn't come home, that first night— the night you and I had been together. I walked in and she was downstairs at the kitchen table, had been there since eleven. And I realized—sitting in the car, after calling you and Felix—that she already knew he wasn't coming back. She didn't think I was him coming home, or anything like that. She wasn't sitting there worried about him at *all* anymore; she was worried about *us*. Smoking cigarettes all night and figuring how we would survive. That's when Bunny found me—when I was zoned-out completely. Thinking it was my own fault for being dependent on my husband's money, and yours, when the deal came through. I looked up, and he was at the window. Told me to roll it down. I wasn't even paying attention, anymore. He left us with nothing, my father."

"Penny, tell me if he hurt you. I don't know if I can take it, but please tell me." He looked at her. Saw she was waiting for him to.

"He didn't hurt me, Martin."

"Okay," he said. He closed his eyes, nodded. To show he was done asking her. "Okay. I'm sorry to keep—"

"I guess he threatened me, a bit. But I don't think he even had to."

He looked at her. Thought, What does that mean?

"I think I would have told him anyway how to find you."

He looked her in the face. Closely. Asked her what the hell that meant.

She said, "I told him, Martin. I wasn't going to have you just leave again. The locker was empty. I turned, I looked at him. He was already looking at me. I thought you'd stolen it. *I* told him where you were. And Terry was with us, at the locker. He didn't follow you up there; I gave him directions."

He shook his head. Tried to shake this shit into sense.

"The money was gone. That's what Bunny expected when he found me watching him. He thought I was outside keeping an eye on him while you were steal—"

"You fucking . . . killed us."

"I didn't know—"

"You killed us."

"I didn't have—"

"Felix, Terry, me, Rocco. We're all dead—"

"You killed yourself," she said. "I'm pregnant. Again. It's yours." She dragged on the cigarette. Flicked the ash. Said nothing.

He watched her. Because it was all he could do, he understood suddenly.

"Close your mouth," she said. Exhaled.

He did.

She looked past him. Looked at him. Dragged again and looked at the lake. "That agent knows exactly what I just said to you," she said. She snapped the cigarette away.

He said, "Yeah." Though he didn't know what she meant by it. Didn't know if he cared.

"The locker was empty and I looked at his face, and I knew. You and Felix, or this *sec*ond baby." She shrugged.

Which meant the choice had been simple, he guessed.

"Bunny said what he had to," she said. "Made his threat. I said I had spoken to you on the phone. That you hadn't taken off. That you were where you said. I told him maybe *you*'d taken it to be safe, because Felix was acting reckless. Cracking with the pressure. He said he would send Terry to find out where it was, or get it back. Which just made *sense*. Of course. I told him where to find you because I figured either you'd all handle yourselves like armed gentlemen and come home, or . . . well . . . everything would fall apart. And, then, baby? What would really matter anymore, anyway? If everything fell apart."

He shrugged. Nodded. Guessed he understood.

"But I swear to you, Martin. Honestly. Why would he shoot you? In front of *me,* he just told Terry to get you or it *back.* That made sense. He just wanted to know where it *was. I* wanted to know. Why would he shoot you?"

He shrugged. He shook his head. "I don't know. Tee came around the side of the house . . ." He shrugged. Tee came around the side of the house and said, "On your knees" . . . And I pulled my gun to try to shoot him.

O God.

He was coming to ask for the money, and I tried to shoot him.

He wanted us down because he knew I was armed, figured Fee was, as well. He was just making sure. He was scared. He was going to ask where the money was, but I didn't give him time. I turned Billy the Kid on him. O Jesus. "Jesus Christ. Holy shit. I fucked up so bad." He shut his eyes.

"You fuck up everything," Terry had said. After I'd started to kill him.

Penny said, "That's all you have to say? You fucked up bad?"

He didn't look up.

"Well, pray, Martin. Pray you never in your life have to make a decision like the one I did."

They didn't speak, a while.

She lit another cig. Looked at it in a way that made him know it was her last. Crossed her leg over her knee and propped her elbow on it, looked at the burning tip in front of her face. Considering it, almost. She said, "Something occurred to me the other day. A few months back, he asked me if I ever slept with you, and I told him no. I told him I lost it to Marco Duomo." She laughed again. An even uglier sound, this time. From down in her throat. "But it worked out. He didn't touch me after. It's how I know this baby is ours."

Our baby, he thought. Looked down at her belly. Could he touch it?

"But I realized he'd asked me once before. When we were dating. In college. And it occurred to me that if I'd told him then, the truth, he probably would have never invited you to the party. None of this, at all, would have happened."

"Penny, we can do this. Two years. You keep all of it. Frito can get a job."

"If I go back to you—if Lexi goes to jail, and I leave Felix's mother, meet you in the middle of nowhere, we take off together—then Frito's dead, Martin. We're dead. My mother. Yours."

"I'm your husband, Penny. When it's all cleared up, that's the real truth here. There's only us. There always only was."

"Lexi wants a grandchild."

"Lexi's going to prison."

"He wants a grandchild. And my mother's got a mortgage."

"What does *that* mean?"

"If he goes away, that's it for me. I'm history."

"And if he stays out, I do what? What about me?"

"I don't know."

"What are you telling me? I chance it alone? Call you when he's dead in twenty years? What are you—"

"My mother has a mortgage. This is our child."

"What are you telling me? You won't go with me? Bring my son?"

"My mother—"

"Fuck your mother."

"No," she said, "not again. And you don't know it's a son. Gangsters have daughters, too."

He breathed in carefully—a part of his head saying this was the last time they'd *speak* if he wasn't careful. The last time he'd see her. His ribs throbbed. "Pen—"

"The money is mine—"

"That's fine—"

"—as a widow, as a mother, as plaintiff. My insurance benefit, my child support, my wrongful death settlement. All *three* of you owe me—"

"Don't do this," he said. "I don't mean the money. I don't care about the money. Don't leave me."

"I wish I could know for just a moment," she said. "How it would have been if you hadn't left. It would be enough to sustain me."

"Don't do this . . ."

He watched the cigarette. It glowed hotter when the wind moved.

She said, "You'll look the judge in the face. You'll tell him, 'No, Your Honor, I don't know a soul.'"

He looked at her. She almost smiled. She said, "You can lie, Martin. And live with it. I've been doing it for eleven years."

"Don't . . . do this"—his voice stopped.

She tossed the cigarette. Reached and took his hand, and kissed it. She was crying now. She wiped his hand beneath her eyes and let it go. Her tears on his knuckles.

He didn't watch her walk away.

Or hurry up the hill to her car, ignoring Corso saying "Miss. Mrs. Pasko, don't . . . Fuck—" Crossing up the hill after her, Corso. Her car door opening, closing.

"She's going home," Martin said, but didn't bother to turn. The car starting and pulling away. "She's just going home."

Corso saying "Go," and Dolan pulling after her—the sound of engines falling away.

She'd be fine.

Probably swallow the God-damned key to be safe. Or throw it somewhere she could get it. But she'd be fine. Was the kind who got older and smarter. She'd be fine.

He stood up. Turned. Corso looking down the hill at him.

He stood there.

"Stay there," Corso said. Looked down the road again, then back. A good twenty feet between them, and not liking it at all. "Don't fucking move."

Martin shrugged. Raised his hands up, from the elbows, palms forward.

"Stay there." Reached in his pocket, Corso, and took out the cuffs. Took a step.

"I got nothing," Martin said.

Said, "Quinn—" and stopped. Didn't want to do this differently. Didn't want to draw his gun.

"I got nothing now, man."

"We're going back to Brooklyn. Just stay there." Took another step.

Fifteen feet.

"My father's from Brooklyn."

"Good. Stay there. We'll go back."

"He had everything. I got nothing." Shook his head and dropped his hands. Looked at the ground. Corso started again. Big, long strides.

Martin ran. The tree the first thing between them, and he saw Corso slow, a second, and rethink it and keep on.

Martin ran. Trees to the edge of the park, and he kept beside them on the lake side, then cut up the hill, crossing Corso's pursuit path, Corso too far behind to even spot.

Got speed on the road and used it, a few seconds, but heard Corso coming then, and knew he would fire. Jumped a row of hedges and crossed a yard, saw his reflection streak a garden door, and hurdled the next hedgerow. Was back on a street. A neighborhood. All fences. Long, high rows of unstained wooden posts joined together without a break to see through. He ran and checked them all. No other street for a hundred yards.

He took the gutter for the length of a few properties and heard Corso on the pavement again, then crossed the road and leapt for a fence, and tore something open inside him.

He swung his feet up and threw himself over, and dropped. But his legs failed. They crumpled beneath him.

He got up. Started again. He couldn't lift his arms. He ran with them dead and looked around him. This yard was vast. The fence in all directions. And full-grown trees. The house looking further away the more he slowed, and the fence beside it obscured with flowers. It would be lower there, he knew, beside the house. He moved to it. Tried to lift his arms as he ran. Would have to take it running again and throw himself over with the momentum.

Corso hit the fence, back behind him, other side of the yard. Both shoes at once, it sounded like. Scaling it like a kid, and vaulting over. Martin heard him drop. Call out. The pause while he aimed, and Martin knew he was giving him time to stop. That he could stop. He could stop, and go to his knees, and lie down slowly.

He took the pain and threw his hands up, and jumped—at the section of fence between the bushes. But he hung there, out of strength. Corso fired.

The pain was sudden, and he fell.

When he lay there for a moment, it spread throughout him, joined the rest. It hurt to breathe.

What had she said? She couldn't breathe? Knew he was there in the house at her engagement and she couldn't breathe?

There were flowers above him. Pink and white. On bushes. Were they hers? The ones she'd planted? Was this her house?

But it wasn't, he knew. It was someone else's. Didn't turn his head to check. Hers was too far, and these bushes were too big. They were towering. Blooming in fistfuls around him. Though it could have been how he was looking at them. Where he saw them from. How he was lying. It could have been hers.

"Call an ambulance"—Corso coming fast across the yard, behind him. His voice jarred by the running. "Yes, you in the window. Call 911, tell them an officer's been shot. Motherfucker . . ." Then was there over him. Weird face, studying frantic. "Jesus Christ, I hit you high, no? Where'd I hit you? Christ"—eyes searching. Roaming.

"Low, I think. In my back, like."

Kneeled beside him. "This *blood* on your front? This an exit wound? Can you wiggle your toes?"

He tried. He was, he felt.

"Yeah, they're moving," Corso said. "Stop it now. I think you're going to fucking make it. How you doing? You going to live?"—looked in his face, and smiled. Then kept checking him again—eyes shooting all over him.

"Yeah, I'm good," he said.

"Oh, yeah, you're good?"—smiling, his voice. Assessing. Searching.

"I'm good."